"An exhilarati... Zoë is a kick-butt heroine . . . fantastic."
—*Alternative Worlds*

Praise for
SPECTRE

"An excellent follow-up to Zoë's first outing, and the ending will leave readers hungry for more." —*Booklist*

"This follow-up to Weldon's debut urban noir paranormal mystery, *Wraith*, provides intriguing background information on Zoë's birth and sets the stage for further adventures. Fans of urban fantasy and supernatural detective stories should enjoy this foray into the borderlands between life and death."
—*Library Journal*

"Weldon takes readers on a fast-moving adventure of murder, mystery, the dark side of survival, and a romance that is ready to bloom. *Spectre* provides fans with action and danger at every turn." —*Darque Reviews*

"This novel is full of twists and turns . . . fun and intense."
—*The Witching-Hour Inquirer*

"The darkness and graphic danger that permeate the novel make it a chilling and scary read." —*Romantic Times*

Praise for
WRAITH

"*Wraith* is a highly original addition to urban fantasy. Fun and intense in turn . . . I thoroughly enjoyed this story. I look forward to reading more about Zoë Martinique and her world."
—Patricia Briggs, #1 *New York Times* bestselling author

continued . . .

Ace Books by Phaedra Weldon

WRAITH
SPECTRE
PHANTASM
REVENANT

A ZOË MARTINIQUE INVESTIGATION

PHANTASM

Phaedra Weldon

ACE BOOKS, NEW YORK

THE BERKLEY PUBLISHING GROUP
Published by the Penguin Group
Penguin Group (USA) Inc.
375 Hudson Street, New York, New York 10014, USA
Penguin Group (Canada), 90 Eglinton Avenue East, Suite 700, Toronto, Ontario M4P 2Y3, Canada
(a division of Pearson Penguin Canada Inc.)
Penguin Books Ltd., 80 Strand, London WC2R 0RL, England
Penguin Group Ireland, 25 St. Stephen's Green, Dublin 2, Ireland (a division of Penguin Books Ltd.)
Penguin Group (Australia), 250 Camberwell Road, Camberwell, Victoria 3124, Australia
(a division of Pearson Australia Group Pty. Ltd.)
Penguin Books India Pvt. Ltd., 11 Community Centre, Panchsheel Park, New Delhi—110 017, India
Penguin Group (NZ), 67 Apollo Drive, Rosedale, North Shore 0632, New Zealand
(a division of Pearson New Zealand Ltd.)
Penguin Books (South Africa) (Pty.) Ltd., 24 Sturdee Avenue, Rosebank, Johannesburg 2196,
South Africa

Penguin Books Ltd., Registered Offices: 80 Strand, London WC2R 0RL, England

This is a work of fiction. Names, characters, places, and incidents either are the product of the author's imagination or are used fictitiously, and any resemblance to actual persons, living or dead, business establishments, events, or locales is entirely coincidental. The publisher does not have any control over and does not assume any responsibility for author or third-party websites or their content.

PHANTASM

An Ace Book / published by arrangement with the author

PRINTING HISTORY
Ace trade paperback edition / June 2009
Ace mass-market edition / June 2010

Copyright © 2009 by Phaedra Weldon.
Cover art by Christian McGrath.
Cover design by Judith Lagerman.

ISBN: 978-0-441-01887-1

ACE
Ace Books are published by The Berkley Publishing Group,
a division of Penguin Group (USA) Inc.,
375 Hudson Street, New York, New York 10014.
ACE and the "A" design are trademarks of Penguin Group (USA) Inc.

PRINTED IN THE UNITED STATES OF AMERICA

10 9 8 7 6 5 4 3 2 1

1

March 21, late night

I suck at magic.

Had no idea what I was doing.

Which was probably why I found myself looking at a six-foot purple flame burning an astral hole in my mom's living room. Earlier I'd pulled the rug back to reveal the huge pentagram painted on the wood floor beneath. The big *Book of Everything* lay open on the papasan chair, turned to a page I evidently had no business reading, and I was pretty much trapped between the flame and the fireplace.

Screaming seemed the appropriate thing to do—so I did.

Only—no one could hear me.

My name's Zoë. Martinique. And in the span of two weeks, I had lost my mother's soul, banished my best friend from my life, scared the crap out of my cop boyfriend, experienced crazy erotic dreams about another cop in whom I spent some recoup time (hey—clean thoughts here!), learned I was being stalked by two secret societies, as well as possibly damned my soul for all eternity.

Oh—and the cherry—my great-uncle was responsible for it all.

Period.

All of these things combined have proven one thing to me—I am the winner in the world's most-dysfunctional-family contest.

Top that! Ha!

Oh, and I'm mute. Not deaf. Though some people tended to think those two were synonymous, so when they discovered I couldn't talk, they started shouting at me really slow.

Idiots.

Though that word pretty much applied to me at that moment, as I attempted again to get around the flame. But if I tried to move to the right and jump on the couch, the damned thing moved with me. If I tried to fake it and jump to the left, it matched me again.

And forget going *through* it. I'd already tried that and had one hell of a burn working along my right shoulder where the flame touched me. My jacket was still smoking. I had to face it—the flame was stalking *me*. Literally pushing me up against the fireplace.

Just as I was about to see if a human could climb up a chimney, I heard the bell over the front door chime, as well as felt the vibration on the hardwood floor. Seeing past the flame was getting difficult—I could make out the arch between the botanica where I was pinned, and the tea shop where the front door was.

A beaded curtain usually separated the two stores—but I'd taken the damned thing down. Got tired of seeing it move with a breeze and thinking someone was in the house. Don't ask me where that breeze was coming from—I had no idea. I'd been jumpy—and with good reason. Knowing complete strangers were watching me was worse than *not* knowing.

As I pressed myself against the mantel of the fireplace, I heard someone call my name, and I screamed out—both with my silent vocal cords as well as my thoughts.

What the hell are you doing? came the voice in my mind. It was a male voice—but it wasn't Joe's. Whoever it was could hear my thoughts. So—I must have overshadowed (slipped inside of their body—kinda like possession but not really . . . at least not to me) them at some point. Unless it was a ghost?

Speaking of ghosts—where were Tim and Steve? Wasn't there something they could do? Oh, Tim and Steve were the resident ghosts of Mom's combo of house and shop (half botanica and half tea shop)—a couple who died in the basement. Pretty gruesome. Now's not the time to elaborate.

Zoë? You there?

Well, whoever it was *knew* me, and I could *hear* them.

Hang on!

I *was* hanging on. To the mantel. Two more inches and this thing was going to roast me alive!

A light brighter than the fire nearly blinded me, and I squinted, then looked away with my hand up in front of me. I was expecting to get singed any second—and let's not even talk about how bad my shoulder was hurting where the fire had touched it before.

And then the light against my eyelids dimmed to nothing, leaving me extremely cold.

A warm hand touched my cheek, and I jumped—I would have squeaked if I could—and there was the familiar voice again. I was blinking as fast as I could, but it was like looking too long into the center of a lightbulb, then looking away—I couldn't make out what was in front of me.

Not immediately.

". . . Zoë? Hey . . . look at me. You okay? Did the Portal Fire touch you?"

I blinked again. I could make out an outline. Definitely male. Close to my height. Short, tousled hair, and warm hands.

J-Joe?

There was a soft laugh. "No. Not hardly. You didn't look *into* the flame, did you?"

I paused.

There was a sigh. "Zoë . . ." It was more of a drawn-out whine than my name. Though I'd never noticed how well my name translated *into* a whine till that moment.

I shrugged. He put his hands on my wrist, then my shoulder, and guided me away from the fireplace and into the brighter light of the tea shop. Once there, I blinked even faster as I bumped into the table closest to the arch.

"Christ—you got singed! That shoulder looks bad. Sit down over here. I'll make you a calming tea and then get to work on the damage, okay?"

I could see the table and the chair easily enough, and I sat down. I hadn't realized I was shaking. Not just from nerves—mainly because I'd just nearly barbecued my ass—but because I was actually chilled. I could see the guy moving around in the kitchen, behind the cake-and-pie display. I could even see the display case pretty well.

Why can't I see this person? Why isn't his voice registering with me? Did that flame burn out brain cells?

Hey—no comments.

My shoulder started throbbing—each heartbeat feeding the stinging pain—so I reached around with my left hand and pulled my right arm closer to my chest. Ow, ow, ow. I felt a vibration on the floor and knew someone was at the back door before the lock turned and the hinges squeaked. From the sound of the shuffle, I knew it was the neighbor and Mom's friend, Jemmy Shultz.

"Hey, Jemmy!" the stranger called out.

"Well, I'll be!" came her comforting and familiar Southern drawl. She was laughing, and I could actually see her! Ah! Why could I see Jemmy just fine and not this other guy? Was he some sort of new, freaky Symbiont, Daimon, Abysmal thingie?

Oh God . . . is it TC? No . . . he has my voice . . . not a melodic man's voice.

I could hear backslapping and laughing. "Child—where have you been keeping yourself? It's been a coon's age since I saw you around here."

"Eh . . . here and there. Been a little busy since that little mess back in December. I was here briefly in January before things got crazy for me again. Heard what happened to Nona and came to see Zoë as soon as I could."

"Yeah," Jemmy said. "I just got back from my daily visit'n. Not sure I'm so comfortable with Nona being all quiet like that. Just staring at the ceiling."

My mom was soulless, lying in a bed at a long-term facility in Alpharetta called Miller Oaks. Sounded more like a mortuary to me. I knew why she was in a coma, and so did Jemmy. The doctors? Not so much. It was getting more and more expensive to keep her there, and I'd already moved into the shop and given up my apartment in midtown. Medicare and Medicaid covered only so much before the cost bled over into my mom's estate. And I was not letting them touch her shop. They could drain my accounts before taking what she'd worked long and hard for.

But I was about to hit rock bottom with the money—and I still hadn't found Mom's soul.

"Yeah . . . but what is that smell?"

"Burned magic," mystery man said.

I noticed she was coming toward me, and I waved. Her shuffle sped up, and the next thing I knew her cold hand was on my forehead, then she was touching my neck, my wrist. *Uh . . . hello? Who's that in the kitchen?*

Too bad Jemmy couldn't hear me.

"Zoë!" Her hands were on my shoulder, and I hissed air. "What you been doing? How did you burn yourself up there? Oh my," she made a "tsk-tsk" noise. "That's gonna need some special care." She placed her cool hand on my forehead again. "You feel really warm. What's wrong with the botanica? It's all hazy and nasty."

"Coyote Flame," came the male voice. He came back to the table with something in his hand. Jemmy moved out of the way, and he pulled up a chair, the metal scraping on the wood floor. "Apparently our little Wraith here decided to do magic."

"Oh noah," Jemmy said, and moved into the botanica. "What were you trying to do, Zoë? You know magic's best left to those who can do it. Your momma's one of the best." She sighed and put her hands on her hips. I was looking at her back, then looking at the blurry guy beside me. "Well, there's bandages and rubb'n alcohol on the top shelf in the pantry."

"I won't need it."

"Oh? You got a bit more in those—"

There was a low laugh and whispering. And I could see Jemmy chuckling.

And then he answered. "You could say that."

"Well, then you get Zoë all better, and I start cleaning and cleansing. I swear . . ."

And she toddled off.

My attention focused on Blurry Dude. He put a hand on my forehead too, only his touch was still as warm as it had been before. And then he put his hand over my eyes.

Why can't I see you?

"Because of the burn. The Coyote Flame touched your skin—and you looked into its heart. Its purpose when summoned is to protect the Portal from intruders. Causes loss of sight, breath, illness, and eventually death."

Death?

He made a heavy sigh. "This would have worked if you'd been OOB, Zoë. Why in the hell aren't you out of body? If you want to build a gate, just do it—the Coyote Flame is for magicians who can't walk astrally, not Wraiths."

I suppressed the urge to reach out and pop this person in the face. *Well, nobody told me that.*

He laughed again. "It's okay. I can fix it."

I rubbed at my eyes and tried to see him. It was like one of those weird films where everything's in black-and-white except for the main focus. Only everybody else was sharp, and he was blurry. It was just damned intolerable.

Mental note: *never look into the purple flame.*

"You don't recognize me, do you?"

Uh . . . Can you give me a multiple choice?

"You and I traveled through a similar door back in December," he said as he put his hand over my eyes. This time his hand turned cold, and it was like ice against my forehead. I winced—just a bit scared this was gonna turn into brain freeze. "Remember Allard Bonville? He pulled us through the door, but he was more experienced, so the Coyote Flame didn't try to prevent us from traveling. It's sort of a guardian against amateurs—only with a bit more danger."

Bonville. Shadow door.

. . . little mess back in December . . .

. . . was here briefly in January . . .

This guy was talking about that little Shadow People incident I'd run into with Rhonda and—

He moved his hand away from my eyes. I blinked once, and his face came into sharp focus.

DAGS!

Dags winced, closing his left eye. "Yow—you need to dial down the astral yelling, lady."

I stared at him, taking in every inch. I hadn't seen Dags since he'd brought me coffee in the hospital that day when Joseph vanished, his tether to the physical world severed. Dags had disappeared not long after. I'd tried calling him in the two weeks since I somehow released Holmes in the warehouse, but his number had been disconnected.

It'd been over a month since I'd seen him—and he'd changed so much in that time. Something about him was different—physically as well as astrally.

Before Christmas, a week or so after Hirokumi was killed and Susan was saved—and, of course, I made the deal with TC to become the Wraith again—Dags, Rhonda, and I became involved with a Ceremonial Magician named Allard Bonville. Or rather—Rhonda and I became involved with him because Dags had joined the man's circle of spooky friends. We learned that Dags had received magical tattoos on his hands and could summon a weird light that blasted out shadows.

That little side adventure had nearly cost him his life when Bonville dragged him physically through the Abysmal plane. He'd died briefly in the hospital later—and been revived.

By me.

I admit the events were a bit hazy—and before now I'd been a little uncertain with him even when he'd come to the hospital with Joe to see me.

But that didn't stop me from grabbing him up and hugging him as tightly as I could despite the screaming pain in my shoulder. I also couldn't stop the embarrassing flood of tears that spilled over my cheeks and nose. It'd been so long since I'd had any real contact, especially with anyone I considered a friend—my mom was always a big hugger. And I'd gotten so used to Daniel's smile . . .

"Hey, hey, hey," Dags said as he pulled away but didn't let go. He kept his right hand in my left one and wiped at my tears with his left. "Shhh . . . take a deep breath."

I nodded and did what he asked—though it was hard. I was afraid I'd do that hiccuping crying I used to do when I was a kid—the big cry that usually put me out for a good couple of hours.

Watching him—I was amazed at how much he'd changed in just a month. No wonder I hadn't recognized him.

For starters, his ponytail was gone. He'd cut the back off pretty short though I noticed strands of hair that hugged his neck, but the top and sides looked more like he'd just rolled out of bed. And he had sideburns. His face seemed older somehow—as if he'd grown up in a short amount of time. And his eyes . . .

There was something different about his eyes. Had they been like this that day in the hospital when he coded? I couldn't remember no matter how hard I tried. There were so many other problems back then—I'd sort of dismissed him as being a sort of side character.

"Let me do something about that shoulder." He put his hands together, palms facing each other kinda like he was praying. Abruptly, a soft white light leaked out from between the two of them.

That's when I remembered the tattoos on his palms. I'd completely forgotten about them.

He reached out with his left hand, palm glowing, and I could just make out the circles—were they spinning? He held it over my shoulder. Then he held out his right hand, palm facing down, and the light shone through the hardwood of the floor.

My shoulder stung, and I winced.

"Be as still as possible," Dags said in a very deep but firm voice.

I did as he said. And within seconds the pain vanished. He sat back and rubbed his hands together. I looked at my shoulder. My jacket was still burned—but my shoulder was—

How'd you do that? I turned and looked at him. I'd seen him use the light from those tattoos to banish the oogy from dark corners—namely Shadow People.

But—I'd never seen him use it for healing.

"A lot's happened in the past month."

I'll say.

His hand was on my forehead again. "Jemmy's right, Zoë. You feel okay? You're very warm."

I nodded and closed my eyes. I knew I had a fever—felt the heat in my eyelids. But I was afraid I'd been fighting off a cold for over a week. *I'm fine. I just— Thanks for coming in when you did.*

Dags frowned at first, then nodded. Originally, for Dags, communication with me was more like images in his head. And he sometimes had to interpret what he saw to understand what I was saying.

Dags . . . you can hear my thoughts now? Not just pictures?

"Yeah . . . long story . . . for later, though."

"Hey, Jemmy?"

"What's wrong?" Jemmy came out of the botanica, a broom and a black candle in her hands.

"Do you know where a thermometer is? I think you're right—Zoë's sick."

"Well, I wouldn't be surprised. Especially with the smell in here. But I know where Nona keeps them. You stay here." She set the broom down and ambled off.

He released my arm and turned to pick up the now-cooled cup of tea. "You drink this and tell me what the hell you were doing opening a doorway."

I took the tea and sipped it. It was sweet, and I recognized hibiscus, as well as something else in there that was familiar. *You know what's happened?*

He nodded. "Most of it. I've been up to see Nona myself. Archer—you call him TC—was the one that took her soul?"

Yeah—but how could you know what's happened? I haven't seen you—or spoken to you. And your phone's been disconnected. Even Jamael didn't know where you'd gone.

He smirked. I didn't like it much. Reminded me too much of Joe. "I have my sources. And like I said—I've got most of it. TC's never contacted you?"

No. And I thought that he'd eventually contact me somehow— threaten me with a ransom or something. I mean, why else take my mom's soul, right? I sighed. *I'm doing this by myself—I've always had Mom and Rhonda to tell me what to do. You know, what something means, how I use it, what's wrong with it. But I've been alone at this—and I finally decided I needed to just open a door to the Abysmal and go get her myself.*

Dags pursed his lips and nodded slowly. "You know traveling through the Abysmal in a physical body can kill you."

No shit.

"Why magic? That's not really your forte, is it? Something wrong with just going OOB and stepping into the Abysmal?" He nodded to the botanica. "Instead of trying to burn yourself?"

And here it was—the truth. I didn't want to tell him. I didn't want to face his sympathy either.

But Dags was a smart guy, and he was watching my face. He tucked a finger under my chin and looked into my eyes. "What is it, Zoë?"

I blinked back tears again—because I knew I was going to have to admit to something I didn't want to. *It's because I can't go OOB anymore, Dags.*

I'm no longer a Wraith.

2

Still the same day—keep moving

THE look on his face was priceless. And I might have laughed—that is if I weren't so upset.

He cocked his chin down, looking at me through his dark eyelashes. His palms glowed a soft blue-white, and I felt my eyes widen as I pointed to them. *Hey . . . your bright-light thingie's coming on.*

With a smirk, he held his hands out to his sides, palms facing up. Abruptly two women in glowing white appeared on either side of him. On his left was a handsome elderly woman with soft, wavy white hair. She almost looked like Veronica Lake's mother.

On the right side was a younger woman with medium-length brown hair. Her eyes were dark and her face familiar.

In fact, *both* of them were familiar . . . like I'd talked to them before.

"That's because you have, Zoë," the older woman said. "You were there when we were originally fused to the tattoos in Dags's palms."

Ah! That old memory of mine kicked in, and I felt myself

smile from ear to ear. Alice and Maureen! Rhonda and I were investigating their deaths.

"You remember!" Maureen, the younger of the two, smiled.

Dags looked from me to Maureen and then to Alice. "So . . . you've met."

Alice, the older woman, nodded. "You were unconscious at the time, dear."

He nodded. "Oh."

And then I did remember it all—the Shadow People and the souls. Bonville and his shadow door. The sound of Dags's screaming beside me and a field of flowers as we moved through the Abysmal plane. I put my hands to my head and gave a silent groan.

Dags was beside me again and put his arms around me. "Hey . . . what's wrong?" He put his hand on my forehead again. "Zoë—you really *are* warm."

A sharp pain between my eyes came and went. I pulled my hands away and looked into Dags's gray—were they gray before?—eyes. Ouch.

"We tampered with her memory," Alice said. "Up until now she didn't remember much about Bonville or—"

Or the fact that I pissed off TC. He'd shown up then as well. I rubbed at my nose and gave a silent groan. I saw it all now in my mind's eye—TC taking Allard's soul and me . . . me betraying him and blasting him to kingdom come.

Again.

Hell, no wonder he took my mother. He'd been pissed. But I at least had a better understanding of it now. I just wished I'd remembered it earlier.

"It wouldn't have changed anything," Maureen said.

Dags pulled his hands from my shoulders and gave me that quirky smirk again. Joe had had that kind of smirk. But on him it'd looked smart-ass. On Dags it just looked—damn he looked different.

"I am different," he said, taking in my thoughts again. "In several ways. One difference is the girls here."

And they're familiars, right? I kinda remember that part.

Maureen nodded. "Yes—we protect his Abysmal—"

"—and Ethereal being," Alice said.

I didn't remember that. I looked from one to the other. *You're telling me that Dags has both parts of the planes?*

"Yes." The two women said this together.

"It happened when Bonville pulled me through the shadow door," Dags said. "A physical presence can't exist in the Abysmal, Zoë. And since I was already halfway to phreak-city"—he held up his hands to indicate the tattoos—"the touch sort of changed me—a lot like it changed you when TC touched you. But we can talk about that later."

But you never said anything about this when you saw me in the hospital!

"No—but then what happened to me wasn't the soup of the day, was it?" He made a face. "Girl—get a grip. I'm fine. I'm actually now just as freaky as you—and I'm here to help you any way I can to get Nona's soul back."

I nodded at him.

"So"—he sat back—"what do you mean you're not a Wraith anymore?"

I held out my hands. *Just that—I can't go OOB. No matter how hard I try, it just sticks.*

"Sticks?"

My soul. It's stuck to my physical body like it was before.

He reached out toward my right hand. "Let me see the mark."

I held up the arm. *That's gone. It disappeared when I helped Holmes move on.*

I got that look again. "You did what?"

And so I gave him the *Reader's Digest* version of what'd happened in the warehouse—all the way down to Daniel walking in on me at the end.

He looked very serious and pursed his lips. Then he chewed on his lower lip. "Have you seen Daniel since then?"

I shook my head. *No—not much. He called about a day after it happened—after driving me back here in silence. Said he had some thinking to do. It was nearly a week later before he wrote me an e-mail—saying he needed some time.*

I knew it was a Dear John letter. The memory of those days—that anxiety of not knowing what to do, of not wanting to take another breath if I didn't know where he was or what he was thinking. Trying to understand what it was I'd done wrong—wishing I'd told him sooner about what I was. Replaying what had happened over and over, and wishing I hadn't let him go with me.

I couldn't eat, or sleep. Tim and Steve had been incredible, reminding me how important it was to keep up my strength—otherwise, what was Nona going to come home to? I had been a real mess.

And if I was being honest with myself, nothing had really improved much.

"And Rhonda? Why haven't you asked for her help?" He paused as he looked at me. "Okay, Zoë—take it from the top. Tell me everything you can remember."

The beauty of being able to communicate like this was that I could sort of zap it in—just ball all the memories into one painful cup and throw it on him. Dags had gotten used to my delivery being a bit forced when I was upset—since getting blown out of his chair the first time back in December.

This time wasn't any different—except he didn't fall out of his chair. He did close his eyes and wince. And his nose bled. Damnit.

After sorting out the conversation and attempted kidnapping from Francisco Rodriguez, Dags's expression hardened. He looked older suddenly—mature. And then I realized it was his face that was a little different. He'd matured some. Wasn't covered in the baby fat so much.

"Baby fat?"

Oops. Gotta watch those thoughts again.

"So you kicked Rhonda out." He sat back and folded his left arm over his stomach and rested his right elbow on his arm. Then he rubbed at his lips with the index finger of his right hand. Dags looked thoughtful. "I'm not sure Rhonda's as big of a threat as you think she is."

It's not the threat part—it's that she lied to me. I pointed at him. *Even you broke off a relationship with her. Was it because you suspected something weird?*

"No, it was because I couldn't return her feelings, that's all." Dags shrugged. "I'm not going to lie to someone in a relationship—that just ends up hurting both people."

I felt a twinge of guilt at that—I'd lied to Daniel and not told him what I was. And now—

"Don't beat yourself up about Daniel, Zoë. He'll come around. And if he doesn't"—he lowered his arms—"screw him. But"—he leaned forward—"what I want to know is why you can't slip your astral body out." He looked at Maureen, who looked at Alice, who looked back at Dags. It was a ring-around-the-rosy sort of thing. "Any thoughts?"

Alice shook her head. "No—senses tell me she's still Wraith—and a very powerful one. Her abilities have doubled since we last met."

I sighed in frustration. *Then why can't I OOB?*

Dags stuck the pinky of his right hand in his ear and wiggled it. "Okay—remember—we still register volume with your inner voice." He lowered his hand. "But as to why not? I have no idea. When did it happen? As in when did you notice it?"

What happened with Holmes was Valentine's Day—and Daniel didn't call for a while. I got so wrapped up in getting the shop running, getting Mom settled, insurance bullshit—before I knew it, about four weeks or so had passed. I pursed my lips as I thought about the calendar in the kitchen on which I'd been marking the days—the days with no call from Daniel. *Just this past Monday . . . the seventeenth. I was in the kitchen looking for coffee—and I climbed a chair 'cause Mom some-times left coffee up on the top shelf. But all I got was dizzy, then I fell backward. Woke up about an hour later.*

"Zoë—you hit your head?"

I nodded. *No biggie. I'm thick-skulled. But just after that I heard something in the basement and tried to OOB to see what it was—because I'm really not that scared of spiders when I'm astral, and there are a lot of spiders down there. But nothing happened. After a few days of not being able to OOB—*

"You took the initiative to do a little bit of magic?" Dags said. "Do me a favor—don't do that anymore, okay?"

I nodded. *No problem there.*

He pointed to my head. "The white streak's still there."

Not as much as it was. It'd gotten to be about an inch and a half thick. Now it's actually fading.

"You're kidding."

I arched an eyebrow at him. *Do I look like I'm kidding?*

He laughed. God, I loved that laugh. Mainly because it was the first laugh I'd heard in weeks. Emotion welled just beneath my eyes, and I moved forward and tackled him, hugging him again as tightly as I could.

And he responded to me, taking me in his arms again and rubbing my back as my shoulders heaved, and I drowned again in one of those damned tidal waves of sorrow I was getting so prone to.

God, I was a basket case.

I also noticed offhandedly that the girls weren't there anymore. I didn't know if they hung out in Dags's hands or if they were invisible. It was kinda like they were letting me have some privacy.

"Shhhh . . ." Dags said in a soothing voice in my ear, and he kissed my hair. "It's okay—I'll help you find out what's happened, okay? And we'll fix it—I promise."

And I knew inside that he meant it. Unlike a few of my fickle friends who disappeared when the pot got too hot. Namely Joe Halloran. One kiss and poof—he was outta there.

And it wasn't even a good kiss.

. . .

Not really.

. . .

Well . . .

Jemmy came down the stairs then, a long white stick in her hand. "Sorry—but this wasn't where I thought it was. Oh . . . what's wrong? Thank the great electron—she's finally crying. Praise be you came, boy. She hasn't cried not once."

That wasn't really true. I had cried. Just not around Jemmy.

Dags deftly touched my cheek even as I buried it deeper into his neck. "Zoë—lean back. We need to take your temperature, okay? You feel really hot to me."

I did as he asked, and sniffed, trying to hide my face from him. 'Cause you know how faces get all puffy and blotchy red when the crying jag starts. But Dags wasn't having any of that and pushed my hair behind my ears. I looked at him—and again was amazed at how much he'd changed. He turned and took the electronic thermometer from Jemmy, pushed the button till it clicked, and coaxed me to let him stick it under my tongue.

"Jemmy—can you heat up the chamomile tea for me?"

She patted his shoulder. "Sure thing, hon. I'm sure glad you're here." And she moved into the kitchen.

I'm fine.

He shook his head. "No, you're not."

Yes, I am.

"I'll win."

Oh?

"I spank."

Oooh . . . wasn't sure I wanted to know this side of Darren McConnell. *You going by McConnell or McKinty?*

"McConnell. It's my mother's name. McKinty was the name I used when I bartended."

My lower jaw started to ache from jutting out so long. Geez . . . how long did these things—

Beepbeepbeep . . .

Dags took it out before I could and looked at it. His dark eyebrows arched up, and he looked at me with puckered lips. "You're going to bed."

Huh? Why? I took the thermometer and looked at it—102.6

I blinked. *This thing is broken.*

But Dags was already standing and taking the cup he'd brought out back to the kitchen. He said a few things to Jemmy—in French!—and then came back to me. I pointed at him. *You spoke French.*

"Yes," he said. "Yes, I did. Now—" He reached down and took my hand and pulled me up. "Upstairs. Get under the covers, and I'll—"

He went rigid—his hands at his sides. His palms burst into light, and Maureen and Alice were back.

Only—

They'd done a wardrobe change.

Holy shit.

Before—when they were just there—the two of them seemed kinda normal. And whatever it was they were wearing seemed sort of nondescript. So much so that I couldn't remember what it looked like. Not much detail.

Yet now they were both dressed in what I would call armor—only with a very female style. They both looked the same age—my age—and one was dressed in white, the other in black. They were the queens on a chessboard.

Wait—bad-ass queens on a chessboard.

And Dags was in the center.

What the hell—

"The Cruorem," Dags said. "They're nearby."

That name rang a bell—that was the name of Bonville's group, which of course was some wacko Ceremonial Magic cult. What is with all the groups? It's like a Yahoo! Group Who's Who list of the Weirdest Idiots of Atlanta. After remembering that night—I'd also sort of remembered that I considered them a joke. But Dags and the girls didn't look like they were joking.

"There were a few that were actually pretty powerful," Dags said, as Maureen moved in one direction, long, shimmering obsidian sword at the ready, and Alice went in the opposite direction, crystal weapon unsheathed. "And one of them got the Grimoire—the book where Allard took the spell that created the Shadow Door? Remember the pages and the contracts?"

Uh-huh. Memory was still a little fuzzy. I remember being full.

Jemmy came jogging out of the kitchen, a pretty impressive-looking cannon clutched between her hands.

I stood up. *Whoa!*

Dags turned and looked at her. "Desert Eagle?"

"It was my husband's."

"Warded?"

"Damn straight." She held it close, barrel pointed up. "Hollow silver, stuffed with belladonna and a little bit of my own special recipe. Where are they?"

"Outside," Maureen said from the side.

Dags looked at Maureen. "How many this time?"

"Just the same two that have been shadowing us since Savannah."

Two Cruorem? Shadowing them since Savannah? I waved at him. *You were in Savannah?*

"Long story. No time." He put his palms together in front of him, pressed, then pulled them apart. My jaw nearly hit the floor as a long, two-toned sword formed between the two. Once it was there, he grabbed it with his left hand and held it up.

I shook my head. *Okay. You win. You got weirder.*

He winked. "I told you. Now we just have to defend against whatever it is these creeps will do."

What are they after?

"Me."

???

"Told you—long story. I'll tell you over coffee one day. I—"

He stopped and frowned. I looked from Maureen to Dags to Alice . . . and got really dizzy. Suddenly I was not feeling too good.

Maureen said, "They left."

"Uh-huh." Dags nodded. "I don't think they even approached this house. Probably sensed Nona and Rhonda's wards."

Oooh . . . don't mention her name.

Dags turned to me, and the sword vanished as if it'd never existed. Maureen and Alice suddenly looked normal again too—er—as normal as two ghostly women could look. "Zoë, you're going to have to—"

That's when my knees buckled. I couldn't stop myself from going down, and Dags was right beside me. Every muscle in my body was shaking—and it felt like when I hadn't eaten anything in a while.

Wait . . . what was the last thing I ate?

Milk Duds?

I was on my back, and the ceiling was spinning . . . really fast.

This wannabe Wraith was swiftly losing steam. Fatigue covered my shoulders like a warm blanket on a snowy day, and I felt my eyes closing.

"Zoë? Don't! Zoë!"

Poof.

3

I got sick . . .

THREE days.

I'd lost three days!

And this time the dreams were sucky. No kisses. No love. No sex.

Though to be honest, sex wasn't really a priority with me right now. Without Daniel—I felt sexless. And what was worse—during the whole time I was sick, Daniel never called. Though Jemmy and Tim told me Dags called Detective Frasier several times.

Dags was there all the time, every time I woke up. He usually had something warm for me to drink, or a cold compress for my forehead. He kept his hand in mine, and I always squeezed it for him. It was nice seeing him there, before whatever it was he'd given me knocked me back out.

Sometimes I woke up, and he was asleep, either curled up in the chair he'd moved closer to the bed or on the foot of the bed. Once I woke and found him sleeping soundly next to me, his face turned toward mine.

I lay on my side, watching him, my head pounding. He looked so . . . different. I reached out with my hand and touched his face. He was warm. I moved stray strands of dark hair from his cheek, noticed how his nose turned up at the end. He really was a nice-looking guy, and I could see how Rhonda had fallen for him.

Tim was in the room, standing behind Dags, near the window. "He likes you."

I smiled. *I like him too, Tim. He's nice.*

I kissed Dags on the cheek and snuggled next to him as I drifted off again.

Captain Cooper actually came by—though he'd been stopping by Miller Oaks to see my mom ever since she'd been placed in their care. I found that out from the nurses. Always avoiding me though. Which was why I thought it was strange that he came by to see me at the shop.

Dags brought in a doctor—a new one since my old doctor got possessed, stole my mom's body for his old lover's soul, then got gacked by a couple of Eidolons.

This guy reminded me of Grand Moff Tarkin. Dude . . . he looked like Scorpius.

Have I overgeeked yet?

He had the bedside manner of a mortician—but Dags swore by him. And it appeared my only friends in the world were a Guardian, a—I had no idea what Jemmy was except damn scary sometimes—and two ghosts? The real mystery was what exactly was wrong with *me*. I had symptoms of a bad flu—but he insisted that wasn't what it was.

I just knew my hair hurt.

And I couldn't get comfortable. And I was sick of always waking up on my back.

Wait . . . that sounded funny.

Either way, Dr. Scorpius treated it like a flu. Bed rest, fluid, and aspirin.

And, oh, I needed the aspirin.

But what was really a hoot was what happened on the third morning . . .

I felt better—as in my teeth, hair, and bones weren't aching. Though I was still tired. And when I tried to get up—I sat right back down. I had no balance, and it felt like someone had swiped my legs and given me those of a two-month-old. Luckily, I have learned how to take things slow.

Heh . . . with my hospital record? I'm a pro.

Once I was upright and not in any danger of tipping over, I made a header for the bathroom. Hydraulic pressure was my gas—I had to seriously pee. When you drink that much fluid in a body that's not used to drinking that much fluid?

Lots of bathroom breaks.

After the dam broke, and I was able to walk without serious pain, I ambled to the mirror—and we all know how that goes.

I looked awful. My hair was a mess of burls—tangled, teased—a veritable eighties salute to big hair. And as I was combing it down—or trying to—I noticed something else.

The streak was gone.

Christ!

Fuck!

Holy—

"What the hell!" I bellowed. I leaned in close to the mirror and looked. It was my natural blend of coppery black and brown. All there. No more white.

So I've lost my OOB, my mark, and my white streak?

Well, yeah, it'd all been a scary pain, but this was like— imagine Harry Potter waking up and discovering he was a Muggle again with no scar!

I heard footsteps coming close and knew from the pattern it was Dags. I turned with the guilty side to the door.

When he appeared, we stared at each other.

I kinda figured why he was staring at me—I looked like a freak'n banshee.

I was staring because the guy was wearing a pair of loungers. That's it. Just a pair of low-slung blue-and-purple loungers.

Pajama bottoms.

My eyes traveled from his feet—skimming past clothing— directly to the man-girdle at his thin waist, to his pecs, then to his arms and shoulders. The only thing I could compare it to was the difference between Peter Parker before the spider bite and after.

When I met him, it was before the bite.

And now?
Yowsah.

And it didn't hurt that his hair was all tousled and had that JBF (just been fucked) look. Man . . . if Rhonda could have seen him—she'd be drooling. I kinda was.

Which was just . . . wrong.

"Are you okay?"

I pointed to my hair. "Look—look at this, Dags—the streak is gone! What is up with this?"

When he didn't answer, I fixed him with an intense glare. I didn't feel particularly powerful about it—since I didn't have any Wraith mojo to back it up.

His eyes were wide. And I mean WIDE. And he was pointing at me. "Do—do that again."

I held my hands out to my side. "What?" What was I wearing? I looked down.

Oh . . . a long tee shirt.

And no underwear.

"That! What you just did!"

Okay, I was confused again. I shook my head. "Dags—I'm too tired to—"

And *theeeeeen* it hit me.

SMACK.

I was talking.

I WAS TALKING!

I. WAS. FUCKING. TALKING!

EVERYONE was up now. Dags called Jemmy, then he called Dr. Scorpius, who told him to tell me to gargle with warm salty water.

Right, like that was gonna happen.

Jemmy and Dags and Steve were in the kitchen making breakfast—a portable one. Jemmy was going to open the store again while Dags and Tim and I went to Miller Oaks to see Mom. It felt like a lifetime since I'd been there. He'd talked to Cooper, who said there'd been no change. I reminded myself to get him a thank-you card.

Only I wasn't sure where to stick it (yeah my imagination went happy on that one too).

We were also going to spend the day at as many of the occult shops as possible, looking for anything that might explain
what had happened to me. The big book shrugged when we
asked it. No medical dictionary on Wraithy woes.

I took a shower, tamed my hair, braided it, and put on a pair
of jeans—that were suddenly a size too big—and a light
long-sleeved tee shirt with a Kevin Barry's logo on it. Dags
had brought it back from Savannah for me, and it was very
soft. I had to stop and sit down a few times, and I was light-
headed.

But when I smelled that bacon, buttery eggs, biscuits, sausage, and pancakes—my stomach sounded the alarm.

There was coffee made when I got down the stairs. Kona
coffee, something else Dags had picked up for me. I wasn't a
bean aficionado, but I did love a good Kona.

Dags was dressed in jeans, a white long-sleeved shirt, untucked, and white socks. He wore a stunning blue pendant
around his neck—and then I recognized it as the one Joe had
given me at the Phoenix and Dragon.

"Found it on the floor in the botanica when Jemmy and I
were cleaning up." He reached around to unfasten it. "Want it
back?"

"Nah," I said, just excited to hear my own squeaky voice
again.

Mental note: *lalalalalala.*

"You keep it."

"Sure? It's Joe's."

I glared at him. "So?"

He smirked again, and instead of a portable breakfast, we
decided to share one at the larger table in the tea shop. Jemmy
had already nibbled and was getting things ready to open. The
bakery had delivered several pies and breads, and she had teas
drying and steeping and a fire cranked in the fireplace.

She was set.

And I was famished. I ate my fill and had three cups of coffee. So now I was full and wired.

Jemmy had stepped outside to sweep the front porch, and
she came back in, a thin manila envelope in her hands.
"Dags—this is addressed to you."

The tea shop got real quiet.

He wiped his mouth and offered his hand as she came to the table. He glanced at me, and his left hand glowed from the palm as he passed it over the envelope. When he smiled, I smiled. "It's not cursed or anything."

Well, that's good, right?

He opened it and I watched his eyes track back and forth as I chewed on a piece of bacon. After a few minutes he handed it to me.

I wiped my hands on my napkin and took up the paper. It was parchment—of course—and the script was handwritten with a quill. I could tell because there were a lot of ink spatters on it.

Darren Gregory McConnell,

It's come to our attention that your abilities have transcended those of a normal Guardian and that you have the ear of the Wraith. We also know of her mother's condition, as well as the Symbiont who possesses her soul.

We know how to call her mother's soul back—a spell within the Grimoire holds the secret.

We would like to offer a swap. The spell to save the Wraith's mother's soul, in exchange for your familiars. Meet us at the Center for Puppetry Arts Thursday night at midnight. Failure to appear could lead to some very nasty consequences.

Jack Klinsky

"Jack Klinsky?" I looked at Dags. "Not very imaginative for a bad guy. I mean, couldn't he have called himself Voldemort or Darth Vader or something?"

He didn't look amused. I thought it was funny.

Mental note: *Dags lost his sense of humor—gained abs—but lost his sense of humor.*

"Klinsky was Bonville's second-in-command, Zoë," Dags said. "What I'm worried about is how they know about you—and Nona? Or even Archer?"

I wasn't as worried—though I thought I should be. "I'm

sure there's some sort of Abysmal psychic spiritual secret society blog somewhere on the Net—where all the bad guys can share evil deeds. Kinda like Dr. Horrible."

Nope. Still no smile. Not even a twitch. Maybe this was a message—that even though I had my voice back I shouldn't talk. I looked at the letter again. "Wonder why he chose the puppet place." That's when I gave an involuntary shudder.

Puppets.

I hated puppets.

"He works there."

I did a double take at Dags. Was he kidding? A nutcase Ceremonial Magician worked at a puppet theater? "You're kidding."

"Nope."

I skimmed the letter again. "Do you really think they have a ritual to call Mom's soul back?"

"I doubt they do—I also doubt they'd really know that for a fact. A lot of those spells were written in French."

Lightbulb! "And you speak French!"

That time he smirked. "Last time I was around Klinsky, he barely spoke English well." He nodded to the letter. "He didn't write that."

"So, do you have any ideas besides this ritual?"

He shrugged. "Short of somehow stealing the Summoning Eidolon back from Rodriguez—nope. Which is why I want to take a look into a few occult shops."

My ears perked up at what he said. "Why didn't I think of that? If I use the Eidolon on Mom's body, her soul has to come back, right? That's the way it was used on me."

That got Dags's attention. He held up a finger. "No."

"But that would work, right?"

"No, Zoë. He's too dangerous."

"Well, like he's any kind of threat to me now? I'm not even a Wraith anymore."

He opened his mouth to protest, then stopped. "No, you're not. So . . . he couldn't command your Wraith anymore. But he doesn't know that."

Oooh . . . he was thinking up something devious. And he noticed me looking at him. "I'm not serious yet, Zoë. I don't even know where Rodriguez lives. And even if I did, I doubt he'd keep the Eidolons in an obvious place."

I felt deflated. He was right. It was a hard bet that Rodriguez was just going to leave those Eidolons out for someone to sneak in and steal. And even though I wasn't a Wraith at the moment (I was thinking positive here), that wouldn't stop Rodriguez from kidnapping me and trying whatever experiments he had on his mind.

Uh-uh. He might separate me from my soul. Permanently.

"Unless . . ."

My head snapped up to look at Dags. "What?"

He looked at me with loud hesitation. "Rhonda would know where he—"

"No."

"But she might know how he—"

"No."

"But, Zoë—"

I stood up and slapped the letter on the table. "No. I don't want her help. I don't want to see her. She was a spy—lying to me and to my mom. How can you expect me to trust her anymore, Dags?"

I thought he was going to argue with me. But he didn't.

Joe would've. Hell, Joe would've enjoyed arguing.

Why was I thinking of Joe? Jerk.

"Zoë." He stood up and faced me. Not much shorter. Not when I was barefoot. "You're going to have to confront your anger—"

"I can do this," I said, raising my voice (and it was so nice to do that!) at him. "I don't. Need. Rhonda." And with that, I turned, grabbed my coat from the wall tree by the front door, and stomped outside.

Right into the waiting arms of the one creature in this world I'd been waiting to see.

"Hello, lover."

Archer.

4

It's him! Get him!

HOW many times have I thought of a situation and daydreamed how I'd react? Sometimes it's after the fact—like when someone's rude in a checkout line or bullies me at work or at school. And twenty minutes later I think of what I wished I'd said.

I'd thought and thought and rethought all the things I wanted to say to TC. And I'd also daydreamed all the things I'd wanted to do to him—castration at the top of the charts.

Yes, Symbionts have penises. Or at least this one did.

And no, I'm not going into how I know.

What I did next wasn't exactly what I'd planned—but it was quick, girlie, and totally made my day.

He had his hands on my upper arms, a smile on his face, his eyes hidden by dark shades. I smiled back at him—and brought my knee up as hard as I could into his groin.

Satisfaction was quick, and as he doubled over with his hands on his crotch, I pumped my hand in the air, and yelled out, "Yeah!"

Jemmy and Dags ran out to the front porch and stopped on

either side of me, looking down at the moaning man in the black trench coat.

"Is that—" Dags said.

"Archer," Jemmy finished. She patted my shoulder. "You did good."

I did?

Maureen and Alice appeared at that moment, and Archer vanished. Maureen vanished right after.

"Hey," I said, looking around, then fixed my glare on Alice. "You chased him away."

"No," Alice said. "He's inside—Maureen is holding him."

Yay!

I was the first one back in the house. He wasn't in the tea shop, so I ran into the botanica.

Maureen had him all right; she was standing to the right of the fireplace just outside of the singed pentagram—nice glow going there. And TC was positioned inside the pentagram. He was just sort of crouching there, his head bent forward. Pretty much in the position I'd sent him into with my knee.

I stood in front of him, my arms crossed over my chest as Dags and Jemmy came in and flanked me. Dags on my left, Jemmy on my right. Alice appeared on the opposite side of Maureen, outside the pentagram.

"Where's my mother?" I said this in the most commanding voice I could muster—though I caught the quiver as emotion overwhelmed me. My hands were clenched into fists, and I was aware of Dags moving closer to me. "Stand the fuck up and face me."

I watched TC's shoulders shake, and I thought for a second that he was crying. But that ridiculous thought was shattered when a deep laugh chased away the room's shadows. He might seem like just a big Vin Diesel impersonator at the moment, but I wasn't fooled. This man—this thing—was *very* dangerous.

He shifted and put his hands on his thighs as the laugh grew in volume. And strength.

Finally, he lifted his head. I felt more than saw the border of the pentagram vibrate. He was testing the boundaries, and I wondered to myself what it would look like if I were still Wraith. Would I see it?

"Is something funny?" Dags asked in a surprisingly confident voice.

TC's laughter ceased as if someone had cut the power. He was on his feet in a blink and standing at the edge of the circle in front of Dags. He tilted his head to the side. I wanted to see his eyes, but he was still wearing his shades. "What are *you* doing here?"

It was at that moment the reality of the situation hit me. TC was talking without my voice. He had a male voice. Not *my* voice.

Because I had my voice back? I looked from TC to Dags. I wasn't sure I liked the look on either of their faces.

"Do I frighten you?" Dags said. Which was just like the ballsiest statement I'd ever heard him make.

Him? Scare the Archer?

Ha.

Yet there was something in the Symbiont's movements that revealed what I thought was a slight insecurity with Dags's standing there. TC's attention was focused on the ex-bartender. Or was he still a bartender?

"I would name you Watcher—but no—" The Symbiont frowned, and he held his arms down and out from his body like a gunslinger at the ready. "You are something . . . made? You were sent to guard the Wraith?" He cocked his head to the side. "Or destroy her?"

Dags held his hands up to his sides, palms facing TC. The circles glowed a soft blue-white and were spinning quickly. But there were other shapes in there too—triangles?

I looked from Dags to TC. "Watcher? You mean like in *Highlander*?"

TC made a rude noise. "You watch too much television, lover."

"Would you stop calling me that?"

"I'm the only one you've made love to in the past two years."

Dags glanced at me. "Really?"

I glared at him. "It wasn't my idea."

"No—I mean it's been two years? Didn't you and Daniel ever—" He frowned at me, then glared. He was obviously shocked.

I gave a short sigh that was more like a grunt. "Can we get past the issue of Zoë's need or lack of sex?" I turned to TC. "I want my mom back *now*."

TC gave a deep but soft chuckle. "You betrayed me."

"Oh, like you've never heard that thrown in your face before. You lied to *me*, if I recall the events clear enough. You weren't trying to retrieve those people's contracts for the Phantasm; you were getting them for yourself."

"I'm an opportunist."

"You're a user."

"You like to be used."

"Shut up."

"Step in here and make me, lover."

I was about to do just that when Dags reached out and grabbed my arm. I could feel the heat from his glowing palm, but it was just that, warm. "Uh-uh, hothead. Stay where you are." He looked back to TC. "Give Nona back to us."

TC smirked beneath his shades and crossed his arms over his chest—both were ample, and I could hear the sound of leather against leather. "And if I say no?"

Dags nodded to Maureen.

I looked at the younger familiar and squeaked when a bow and arrow formed out of light in her hands. She aimed the weapon at TC, and he backed up as she released it. The glowing arrow pierced the pentagram's protective shell and followed TC even as he tried to evade it. It struck his upper left thigh, and he howled.

I turned to Dags. "Just what the hell are you doing?" I narrowed my eyes. "What did he mean by Watcher?"

Dags opened his mouth to answer, but it was Jemmy's voice that I heard. She'd moved closer to me and had a hand on my right shoulder. Her gaze never left TC as she spoke. "The Archer is referring to the Irin, child. The children of angels and men. The Book of Enoch speaks of them—of how God used them as Guardians to the planes." She shook her head. "But the Irin were all killed during the Bulwark, weren't they?"

TC straightened up, but he was favoring his injured leg. "Not all of them. There were a few that survived. So the Seraphim have been artificially creating them." He nodded to Dags. "Like him."

The Bull-what?

Jemmy looked at Dags. "But you're not—"

He shook his head. "No. But I can see where the Symbiont would get confused."

"I am not confused," TC insisted, and his voice was strong again. "I will find out *what* you are."

"Give me back my mom!" I finally yelled out. God, it was good to just scream like that.

Mental note: *voice—use it or lose it!*

Everyone got quiet. TC just stood his ground, and it took everything in me not to just push through the pentagram and knock his fucking shades off.

"He doesn't have her," Maureen said in a quiet voice.

Dags shook his head. "No, he doesn't."

My heart backflipped in my chest. I looked at her, then at Dags. "What—what do you mean he doesn't have her? How can you tell?"

"Because the Archer—if he had your mother's soul—would have brought a piece of it with him to taunt you," Dags said. "He's empty-handed. And he's—diminished."

Diminished?

"Archer," Alice said in a level tone. "Do you have knowledge as to why the Wraith's powers have vanished?"

"Screw that!" I said. "Where's my mom?"

TC shook his head. "I don't have the answer to where Nona is. I had her for a while—but then something happened that reverberated along the Abysmal plane, and I could no longer hold her. She was"—he held out his arms—"gone."

Gone?

I took a step back.

What does that mean—gone?

I felt a hand on my shoulder and pulled away. I knew it was Dags—but I wasn't in the mood for any sympathy. "Tell me what that means," I said in a low voice. But then it exploded. "WHAT DOES THAT MEAN?"

"It could mean several things," Alice said in a commanding voice. I took a step back. "But for some reason, though she's free from TC, Nona hasn't returned to her body."

"What exactly does that say?" Dags asked.

Alice shook her head. "Nona's spirit could be wandering—unable to find her body."

"But couldn't she just use the silver cord like I do?" I said in a rush. "Or like I used to?" When I could OOB, the silver cord that kept me attached to my physical body was always there, and at times—seriously life-threatening times—I'd just use it much like a bungee cord back to the body. Not a very pleasant experience—but sometimes a necessary one.

"Yes, unless she's trapped *between* the planes because there are so few Irin left. It could also mean—" And then she stopped.

I took a step in her direction. "Tell me, Alice."

"It could mean she's been summoned somewhere else."

Summoned. The only thing I knew about summoning was with an Eidolon.

And the only person I knew with a Summoning Eidolon was Rodriguez. Francisco Rodriguez once again had the Summoning Eidolon because Rhonda had trusted him. I felt my shoulders lower as I thought about what it could mean. *Why would he take my mom?*

"Zoë, we don't know that Rodriguez has her. I'm not sure he could actually use the Eidolon to summon a specific soul without her body—"

I whirled on Dags. "Is she still at Miller Oaks?"

"Yes, yes," Jemmy said. "I told you I just came from there. Her body is fine, and that Captain Cooper man is keeping an eye on her."

That was just weird to me. I felt a little better about it, but it was weird. The fact that Cooper was being nice to me. Or my family. I honestly thought he hated me.

Dags looked confused. He faced TC. "Why are you here?"

TC smiled and held out his hands. "Why are any of us here?"

I snorted. Great. A Symbiont had gone existential on me. "Why come here when you don't have my mother? You had to have known how I'd react."

The Symbiont's reaction was a little surprising. "I came here to see what'd happened to you."

Jemmy and Dags glanced at each other, then at me. Dags

spoke. "You can sense she's no longer Wraith because the two of you are linked together."

TC's right eyebrow arched over his shades as he inclined his head toward Dags. "The Guardian gets a cookie for being a good boy."

"Knock it off," I heard myself say. I took a step closer to the pentagram's edge. "Now that you're here—do you know what's happened to me?"

He moved close as well, coming quickly toward me, but stopped at the barrier's edge. It took all I had in me not to take a step back. With all my bravado in front of TC, the truth was I was still scared of him. He was something I didn't understand. There were odd feelings inside that always stirred when he was near—feelings I wasn't comfortable with.

We'd done things—together. And though I remembered some of them, much to my horror—I didn't want to remember anything more.

"Pull down the barrier," TC said in a soft voice. "Let me touch you."

"Not on your life," Dags said, and moved next to me. He put an arm over my shoulder. "Zoë's been ill, and the last thing she needs is you draining her energy."

TC shifted his gaze from me to Dags. "I am not here to destroy or weaken Zoë in any way. If you really understood our connection, you'd *know* that." He looked back at me. "What I've become, the power I have—had—was because of my link to Zoë. To the Wraith. That power has diminished and left me—"

He didn't finish.

But I already knew the answer. He was weakened. Just as I was. On some level, I understood that my losing my abilities as a Wraith—my being just a normal, twentysomething brat with a chip on her shoulder—was being reflected on TC.

He was still a Symbiont, and just as dangerous as he once was. But not as powerful.

"Remove the barrier, Zoë," he said. "Let me touch you. Let me find out what's happened. It could be that whatever has stolen your power, and mine, also stole your mother's soul."

Dags moved beside me, but I reached out and gently pushed

him back. I caught Alice watching me and nodded. I somehow felt that with her and Maureen there—nothing could happen. I needed to know what he knew—I needed to know where my mother was.

Alice nodded to me as well, and with a wave of her hand, the barrier vanished. It wasn't that I could actually see it, but I could feel a distinct pressure change in front of me—in the small botanica.

Maureen and Alice moved into the circle, flanking TC.

But he was quick—more so than I believed he could be. He moved in a blur outside the circle, and with a wave of his hand, the barrier was back—only now the girls were trapped inside of it.

Dags yelled out as he came closer to me. TC looked at him, reached out with his left hand. The hand became a mass of tentacles, as if he had the back end of an octopus inside his trench coat sleeve instead of an arm. The tentacles elongated, lashed out, and wrapped around Dags's body, concentrating on his face and neck. He was on the ground struggling, one hand grasping at the tentacles covering his face.

I started toward him—Dags was going to suffocate!

But TC was on me, fast.

And I mean *on* me.

His right arm encircled me and his lips were pressed hard and unmoving against my own, effectively silencing me and trapping me as well. I had no way to gain a footing to knee him in the groin again.

And again I could feel his tongue, pressing against my lips, forcing its way in. I tried to kick him, but he was already becoming a vine that wrapped itself around my entire body. I was only able to make the smallest of noises—my mouth was now firmly gagged with his tongue. I wanted to throw up but couldn't move.

I had flashbacks to that night in the house with Susan Hiro-kumi, the night he'd taken me in like this and I woke twenty-four hours later inside a morgue.

And my life had changed dramatically.

The room grew dim, and I had the distinct impression I was about to lose consciousness, whether from my own inability to breathe or the sheer horror of what was happening to me again and what was happening to Dags. Maureen and Alice were trapped behind the barrier, unable to help him.

Dags stopped struggling.

I screamed as hard as I could.

There was a crack, my ears popped, and the room filled with a bright, warm, calming light.

TC screamed in my mind. He wriggled against me, pulling his tongue from my mouth. His body unwound itself and vanished, and I was on my ass on the floor, gasping for breath before I knew what had happened.

Cold hands were on the sides of my face, and I blinked and looked up into the face of Jemmy Shultz. Her dark, kind eyes were searching my face. ". . . come back to me. Zoë, don't you pass out. He's not breathing—you got to help him breathe! I know you can do this!"

Not breathing. I took in a deep gulp of air, coughed. I was breathing. Sort of. It hurt like hell, as if TC had somehow shoved his Roto-Rooter tongue down my throat and into my lungs. I gave a visible shudder at the thought. But I could hear Maureen and Alice yelling at each other, and Jemmy let my face go.

That's when I saw the gun in her hands. The smoking gun. Jemmy had shot TC.

Attagirl!

I fell back a bit on my elbows and shook my head. To my right the girls were bent over—

DAGS!

I coughed as I scrambled on hands and knees to him. Maureen and Alice looked like two bright, human-shaped candles. They had their hands out, focusing—whatever it was they did—on Dags's very still body.

"We can't put breath back in his body," Alice said in a near cry as I waved Jemmy away. "He's not breathing."

"Can't put breath back in?" I said absently as I knelt beside him. His lips were blue, and I could see nasty, round suction-cup marks all over his neck and a few on his cheeks. That bastard. TC had literally tried to kill Dags when he had the chance.

"We can heal his body physically—" Maureen said. "But we can't put life *in*."

I leaned over him and pressed my ear to his chest. I couldn't hear a heartbeat.

No, no, no, no . . . that bastard was *not* taking the only friend I still had left.

And with that, my CPR training kicked in.

Up until Mom had ended up at Miller Oaks, I would never have attempted to do what I was doing. Yeah, I'd had basic CPR while taking karate. But as part of the long-term-care program at Miller Oaks, I'd taken a few more in-depth classes at the suggestion of the nurses. In case I ever had to bring Mom's body home. And she stopped breathing.

I had Jemmy and the girls straighten him out completely as I tilted his head back. I was on his left side, so I used my left hand under his neck, pinched his nose with my right, and blew air into his parted lips. I moved to his chest, placed my hands in the proper position, and pressed down.

One, two, three . . .

Air in . . .

One, two , three . . .

Breathe, asshole.

Air in . . .

Breathe!

One, two, thr—

Dags's body shuddered, and air rushed into his lungs in a fit of coughing. They were deep, lung-clearing coughs, and he fought to push himself over onto his right side.

The coughing increased, and Maureen and Alice let out a squeal as he turned away from me.

I leaned over him and watched as blood and something fleshy came out of his mouth. Jemmy got up and rushed into the kitchen, gun in hand. I was too horrified to move as I recognized what it was that had come out of Dags's mouth.

The top half of a bloody human finger.

5

There's a finger on my floor!

THAT was just—wrong.

Dags had a finger lodged in his throat?

He continued to cough as more blood and stuff came out. I kept a hand on his shoulder, not wanting to let go of him at all. I was too afraid he'd die on me. But my gaze remained locked on that—ew.

And even more disgusting was the look of sheer joy on Maureen's face as she reached down and picked up the finger. It sparkled a few times and looked as if it was going to dissolve. "Zoë, get a glass jar. I know Nona keeps several mason jars for preserves on the back porch."

I stared at the finger. Was that—was that TC's finger?

Maureen waved at me. "Zoë—quick!"

I got up, wobbly, and moved to the kitchen—past Jemmy, who was heading back to the botanica with a towel and ice—then out the back door. Maureen was right—there were two trays of cleaned and prepared mason jars with lids. I grabbed a jar and beat it back inside, only vaguely aware of a car pulling into the back drive.

Jemmy was on the floor with Alice and Dags. He was pale, and there was blood on a towel beside him. Jemmy had gotten two towels and had ice in one, holding it to his forehead as Alice held her hands over him.

Maureen met me at the botanica opening and held out the finger. I opened the jar, and she dropped it in. "Get Nona's Dragon's Blood Rede, St. John's Wort, and a small bit of sulfur." She looked insane. And I noticed her entire demeanor had changed. Her clothing—for what it was—had a darker hue to it now, and her eyes were kinda . . . red.

"Zoë, you switch with me," Jemmy said, getting up. "You stay with Dags. You probably don't know where any of that stuff is."

Nope. Nor did I know what it was.

Wait . . . did Mom really have Dragon's Blood? Were dragons real?

I handed the jar to Jemmy, and she handed me a cold, ice-filled hand towel. I knelt beside Dags. His eyes were closed, and he was breathing deeply. Maureen moved her hands away and sat back with a sigh. I put the cloth over his forehead. "Is he okay?"

"He'll be fine. I don't think he meant to nearly kill himself," Alice said with a smile. "Though I'm sure the Archer wanted otherwise. He's not going to like having a Guardian around you."

I watched as Jemmy came back to Maureen with several bottles in her hand, and the two of them moved to the kitchen, talking quietly. I pointed in their direction. "Is Maureen okay?"

"Okay?"

"Yeah. She seems a little"—I shrugged—"evil?"

Alice laughed. "She and I are both sides of the same coin, Zoë. Remember, she's the Abysmal half of Dags."

Yeah . . . they'd mentioned that before—still didn't understand it.

"But you have to remember, Zoë—Abysmal does not equate with evil. Evil is more of an opinion, or a state of living. You yourself are mostly influenced by the Abysmal plane, and do you consider yourself evil?"

Uh. Hrm. No. I could be bitchy sometimes, but I'd always sort of thought of myself as relatively nice.

"Oh shit . . ." the man in question said. "What the hell landed on my head?" He opened his eyes and looked up at me. A grin replaced his wince. "Okay . . . I'm feeling better now."

"You had a finger in your throat."

He nodded. "I got it, huh? Good. I didn't know what it was—I just knew he was sticking something down my throat to choke me." He looked past me to Alice. "Can Maureen use it?"

"She's busy on it now."

I looked from him to her. "What's going on?"

"A little mojo," Dags said as he pushed himself to sit up.

I put a hand on his shoulder and leaned down. "Rest. It's what you told me to do."

I watched his eyes as they looked at my face. I was surprised—but not much—when he reached up and tucked a strand of my unruly hair behind my ear. "So, I guess the roles were reversed this time? You took care of me?"

I nodded. There was something interesting being this close to him. I couldn't pinpoint it at that moment—I just knew I felt safe with him. Even after what'd just happened. I moved the compress from his forehead and smoothed back his hair. "Just promise me not to stop breathing again, okay?"

He smiled. "I promise."

My gaze locked with his for a moment, and something stirred, warm and fuzzy. Which was odd, 'cause I hadn't felt warm and fuzzy in a long damn time. He reached up again and pushed more hair back as it fell forward. "I miss your white streak."

I smiled. "We'll get it back."

That's when I realized I wasn't just leaning over him anymore—I was practically on top of him. His upturned nose was mere inches from my own, and his half-lidded eyes were focused on me. I remembered him sleeping beside me, keeping me warm when I was sick, and I worried that somehow I'd given him my cold.

The floor vibrated at that moment, telling me someone else was there. A customer maybe—which would be good for business. But I didn't think of getting up because customers usually went to get tea first.

I felt the footsteps, heard Jemmy say something in a cordial but tense voice, and then heard the step of shoes against the hardwood.

"Am I interrupting something?"

My body tensed, as did Dags's beneath me. We both turned our heads and looked up into the stern face of Detective Daniel Frasier.

6

My heart hurts . . .

IT felt like a lifetime since I'd seen Daniel.

Standing over me, his hands planted firmly on his hips, he looked as handsome as ever.

If a bit—stern.

And then I realized the position I was in—practically accosting Dags!

I scrambled back, just as Dags did, only he slapped a hand to his forehead and moaned. I knew he was sick from having ingested a piece of the Abysmal. I myself had gone through that yuck when a Daimon had hijacked my body back in January. Made me throw up. I was thinking he might throw up too, and I hoped the girls would help him.

Alice was gone. I was torn between making sure Dags was okay and jumping up and hugging Daniel.

He'd come!

To my surprise, he leaned over and offered Dags a hand before pausing. "Dags? Is that you?"

Dags took the offered hand and grinned. "Hey, Detective Frasier—it's me."

Daniel's eyes widened as he pulled Dags to his feet. "Are you okay? You have blood on your face."

Dags was still wobbly and Daniel supported him with his arm. I got to my feet as well and stood to the side, very happy the finger wasn't on the floor anymore. Though there *was* a pool of blood.

And as Daniel helped Dags to a chair in the tea shop, I realized what the scene had to have looked like. Rug pulled back, the pentagram visible, the floor a bit singed, guy on his back with blood—

Not good. I only hoped Jemmy had put away her BFK.

Daniel knelt in front of Dags and held the darker-haired man's head by his chin. He narrowed his eyes as he turned Dags's head from side to side. "What exactly was Miss Martinique trying to do to you? Was she trying to exorcise a Daimon out of you or something? You do know that's what her mother used to do—put on shows for customers. I walked in on one once. Pretty impressive."

My jaw made the loudest thunk on the floor as I gaped at him. I knew Daniel was referring to the time he'd walked in on Mom interrogating the succubus Mitsuri when Mom trapped the icky thing in the Stone Dragon. Of course Daniel had nearly been attacked by the succubus, as his entry had blown out the candles of the protective circle holding it in place—and if it hadn't been for my wailing scream, he'd have become a succubus snack.

He and I had had a talk about that instance, and I thought I'd explained to him my mom wasn't a shyster bilking the customers. But from the tone in his voice—my protests had fallen on deaf ears.

The only thing that saved Dags was the look of pure insult on his face. He grabbed Daniel's wrist and firmly pulled his hand from his chin.

"No, she was not. I was helping get the room back in order and I tripped, so she was making sure I was okay." Dags's voice was stern, and I noticed he held on to Daniel's wrist a bit longer than necessary. He also glanced down at the detective's hand, then looked up into Daniel's face. Dags's expression was unreadable. "Do you always barge into a home unannounced and make asinine assumptions?"

The two men stared at each other for a beat before Daniel pulled his wrist free and moved back, still kneeling. "Only on Tuesdays. My mistake." He tilted his head to the side. "You look different—I've been by the new Fadó's several times, but you haven't been bartending."

"No—I took a leave of absence."

"You really look different."

Dags nodded. "So do you. Contacts?"

Daniel nodded. "Yes. I got your messages about Zoë." He glanced over at me. It wasn't a good glance or a bad one, just a sort of neutral look. What I did notice was the lack of emotion to it. No surge of joy. Nothing. "She looks fine, but"—he looked back at Dags—"how do you know her?"

Dags pursed his lips. "That's a long story, and not one I want to get into right now. This is the first full day Zoë's been out of bed. Nice of you to drop by afterward."

The detective stood up. "Been busy, Dags. There are a lot of crazies out there. And I am surprised to see you here." He finally turned and faced me. "You okay? Were you sick, or another diabetic issue?"

I shook my head. "We think it was the flu—but it's okay now. I just wasn't expecting you to come in here—I mean you haven't been by or returned calls in—"

Daniel's expression stopped me. I wasn't sure why his eyes were the size of chicken eggs beneath his brown hair. I glanced behind me to make sure there wasn't some weird thing—not that I could have seen it—or that TC hadn't shown up again. I noticed Tim, Steve, and Jemmy were absent though, along with Maureen and Alice. But I didn't know if Daniel would even see the familiars.

A beat later his right hand had come up, pointing an accusing finger at me. "You—you're *talking*!"

Whups. I forgot he hadn't known that. My voice return was a pretty recent occurrence. Like . . . this morning?

I swallowed. "Yeah—my voice sort of came back. The new doctor was a big help," I lied.

Still lying to him.

His reaction calmed down a bit, but he was still visibly shocked. He narrowed his blue eyes. "You—so it just miraculously came back?"

Well, there wasn't anything miraculous to it in my opinion. There were so many factors that returned my voice, but not a one of them would work for Daniel. Because I'd never told him the truth.

Damn.

Dags piped up. "Dr. Magnus Fenrir is a leading specialist in unexplained maladies."

Magnus Fenrir? Oh—yeah—Dr. Scorpius. I just forgot what his real name was.

Daniel ran his fingers through his hair. He'd left it longish and kept his sideburns. He looked good enough to eat. "Fenrir, eh? Isn't that Halloran's doctor?"

Halloran? I looked at Dags. Joe Halloran?

Dags wouldn't look at me. "Yes—Detective Halloran introduced me to him a month ago. I was in a position where I needed his service."

I frowned at Dags. He was? When? Was it during the time I didn't see him? Was it after Joe kissed me?

Daniel gave a long, frustrated sigh and rubbed at his face. "Okay, whatever. So you're just as much of a fruitcake as Halloran. I didn't know you were into pentagrams and voodoo or any of this other witchy shit."

Dags crossed his arms over his chest as he stood up. He was shorter than Daniel—by about a good foot—but somehow he didn't look diminished. "You never asked."

"No, I didn't." He looked at me. "I obviously didn't ask at all." With a glance around, he sighed again. "Well, it looks like you're okay. The shop's back open?"

I nodded.

"Your mom still in a coma?"

I nodded again.

"Real sorry about that—but . . ." He shook his head. "Not much I can do." He checked his watch. "I've gotta go. Take care." And he walked back out the way he'd come, through the back door past the kitchen.

I glanced at Dags, who was frowning intensely in Daniel's direction, then I took off after Daniel.

"Wait!" I managed to get out as I got to the door. He was already on the back porch steps. I moved out into the subdued sunlight; to my right were stacks of old magazines and newspapers. Mom's idea of recycling that never made it to the center. A chill breeze blew over my skin, and I crossed my arms against my chest as my hair moved about my face. It was the early part of spring, when the days were warm but the mornings and evenings were still cool with the fading winter.

He stood on the step, looking up at me as I came closer. His face was unreadable. He nodded to me but still kept space between us. I could hear the traffic on Euclid—it seemed so far away at that moment. Someone passed by with their car windows open, reveling in the warmer temperatures as spring progressed. From their car I could hear the lonesome vocals of "Ain't No Sunshine When She's Gone."

I hadn't actually seen Daniel since that Thursday in the warehouse. Nor had we spoken on the phone. No contact other than stilted responses to voice mail and texting.

And now that I had his attention—I wasn't sure what to say.

"I guess Jamael got the color to stick on that streak too, huh?"

I touched my hair where the streak had been. I shook my head. "I didn't go to Jamael. Look, Daniel—"

"I've got to go."

Daniel started to walk away. I don't know what possessed me to put my hand out—desperation? Fear? The inability to lose anyone else close to me?

Daniel stopped and looked down at my hand. And then he looked up at me. "What?"

That one word seemed so cold. So—final. I could sense he didn't want to be there—so why had he come?

"I—we need to talk."

He gave a kind of snort and laugh, a noise I associated with sarcasm. "Talk? After all this time you finally want to talk?" I didn't recognize the man's expression. "It's too late, Zoë. I just can't—I can't deal with—"

"What? Please, Daniel." I tried to take a step toward him, but he took one back on the last step. My heart plummeted in my chest. I wanted to cry. I just wanted to—

"Zoë—" Daniel said, and he was looking at me, watching me. "I need time—I need to process everything that's happened. I'm sorry about Nona—I really liked her. And I know how hard it is to let go—"

"My mom is not dead!" I hissed.

But Daniel wasn't backing down. "No, she's a vegetable, Zoë. At first I didn't understand why Rhonda or Joe had stopped coming around—but now I think I do. It wasn't Rhonda or Halloran that did something terrible; it was your constant betrayals. Your lies. Your faked illnesses—"

"Faked? You think I've faked everything?"

He held out his arms. "What else is there? Your doctor said your vocal cords were just fine, that it was all in your head. Though I will admit he was proven to be unreliable—given he turned out to be a murderer. And then I get worried calls from Dags—only I get here and you're all over him on the floor and he's bleeding—"

"That wasn't—"

"That's not all," he interrupted. "You're a menace to yourself. You're a diabetic and you don't take care of yourself—"

"I am not a diabetic!" I hissed again. I'd meant it as a prelude to saying, "I'm a Wraith, and that plays havoc on my sugar levels."

But the rest never came out—I was too stunned by the look on his face.

He glared at me and lowered his arms. "That kind of denial is why I just can't stay. I can't stand by and watch you destroy yourself and everyone who loves you. You're sick. You need help. I'm sure Rhonda and Joe tried to help you, and you pushed them away."

I dropped my arms to my sides, balled my fists. He had no idea what the truth was—what I'd gone through—or what was out there. Watching me. Watching him.

Yeah . . . and whose fault was it that he didn't know? Because no one told him? Not Daniel's.

He shook his head and waved at me in a dismissive fashion. "See you around, Zoë. And please—use your witchy, voodoo playacting on someone else for a while." He glanced past me to something behind me. "Just don't fuck with him the way you fucked with me."

I was aware of someone behind me and realized Tim had

stepped *through* the door. But—had Daniel seen Tim? Or was he indicating someone in the house?

Like Dags?

Wait—did he think that Dags and I were—?

Daniel got in his car and backed down the drive.

The wind kicked up. The tattered pages of magazines and newspapers rustled around me. Tim stood to my right. "Jemmy, Dags, and Maureen are in the basement. Steve and Alice are cleaning up."

I nodded. It seemed I was stuck in time. Not moving back but seeing no way forward.

No future.

"Want to go see Nona?" Tim said. "I'll go with you."

I wiped at the tears on my cheek. I wanted to talk to Dags. I wanted to ask him why he'd needed Dr. Scorpius—Fenrir—and know when he'd last spoken to Joe. But I was too tired. I nodded. "I'll go get your rock."

IT was a nice drive—me behind the wheel of Elizabeth (Mom's Volvo) and Tim in the passenger seat. The sun eventually broke through the clouds, and the temperature was just right, if a little chilly. March. Spring—when love and life come to bear fruit.

Fuck 'em all.

Let me say right here—I want a new life. I'm done with this one. This isn't the one I ordered. I was supposed to be in love with a cute cop, and he was supposed to love me, and marry me, and we would have a nice life with lots of wild sweaty nights on the coffee table and make little Wraiths.

So what the hell? Where did this go wrong?

I'll tell you—that stupid night at the Bank of America Plaza. TC shows up drilling holes in people, sucking their souls, then poof. I'm a Wraith, and I'm shoving my hands *into* people, killing them—my former best friend, for one—and am being controlled by two creepy, body-possessing freakoids. I get away thanks to some help. I lose my mom, then in one swoop I lose my abilities (I hate saying *powers*—that is just too superhero) and my boyfriend.

My life sucks!

I was on autopilot, both physically and mentally. Whenever I was confused or upset, I'd always gone to my mom.

So call me a freak.

I don't care.

My mom had always been my best friend—even during those instances when her death by my hand seemed imminent due to her overexuberance during my fragile childhood years (the snowflake incident comes to mind)—and I had always tried to be up-front and honest with her.

And she with me.

And now she wasn't there.

Instead, she lay sleeping with her eyes open in a palatial-looking facility with pristine shrubbery and grass that looked like no human foot had ever stepped on it. The tiled floors were so clean I had to take care walking on them lest I fall and break my butt bone. Even sneakers—my Converse high-tops—had difficulty maneuvering on the polished surface.

The lady at the desk waved at me when I came in. "Been a few days."

I nodded but didn't speak, not wanting to have to explain the reappearance of my voice. I turned left to the end, then right at the nurses' station toward what they called the Terminal Ward.

Where patients, usually the dying, lingered in a state of eternal decay. I think I heard the term *noble rot* once. Fits.

I hated this place. All these places. I wanted my mommy home and not here in this building of despair. The air was so thick with it I was choking on the inside. But even as I neared her room, I noticed the absence of something.

Ghosts.

Shades.

I'd grown so used to seeing the images lingering on the astral plane that I barely paid attention to them. My subconscious could always pick out the living from the nonliving, the more vibrant colors from the monochromatic.

But there weren't any.

Yet I could see Tim beside me. He was half-visible, but still there. And I could see him. Why could I still see him and Steve? Or Maureen and Alice for that matter?

More questions—no answers. Welcome to my life.

I came to a stop in the middle of the hall and looked around. It was as if someone had gone through the place and simply removed everything. There weren't any more dark, moving shadows that whispered in the corners. No more dead loved ones waiting on their spouses or childhood friends.

It was all . . . gone.

Or was it that I couldn't see them anymore?

I put my hand to my face and moved quickly to Mom's room. Her name stared back at me from the door tag, WYNONA MARTINIQUE, and I yanked the door open.

The smell was the same. That of urine and Pine-Sol. I sniffed, wondering why I was crying, as I moved to the woman on the bed and looked down at her.

In the beginning, Nona had been a unique case, the doctors said. Though she was in a vegetative coma, there had been no deterioration of her muscles, no impairment of higher brain functions, no bone loss. Nothing. It was as if she were simply sleeping.

But lately that had changed. Whatever it was that was keeping her together had shifted, and now her body was dying like all the other coma patients in the center. Her prognosis was dire. They weren't sure what to do.

I did. I knew what was preventing her from getting up and walking out the door. Her soul. I noticed I couldn't see her cord anymore either—but was that because it was gone or because I'd lost that part of me that once saw such things?

"Mom," I said in a little voice. I pulled the chair up and took her hand in mine. It was cold, her fingers like ice, and I noticed a strange shadow over her face. I couldn't make out where it was coming from though. "If you can hear me—wow—that's sort of different, isn't it? Wondering if you could really hear me. But—things have changed, and I'm not sure why. I don't know if it was something I did, or shouldn't have done. I think." I sighed. "But I'm talking now, notice?"

Silence.

"It's nice—but it's also disappointing. I somehow had it in my head that when I got my voice back, you and Rhonda and Daniel and Tim and Steve would be there with me. And everyone would be happy."

More silence.

"Mom, I think I'm in a lot of trouble."

Silence, and then . . .

"Zoë, my love, you don't know the half of it," said my mother's voice.

7

Tuesday afternoon

MOM?

My mom opened her eyes and turned her head. She smiled—

Only there was something very creepy about it.

And her eyes . . . her eyes were wrong.

"Well, aren't you gonna give your dear old mommy a hug?"

My eyes widened as her left hand clamped down hard on my right one. I couldn't pull my hand free. She was grinning at me—but her smile looked like that of a skull.

I grabbed hold of the bed rail with my left hand and tried to use it as leverage to wrench my hand free—but her grip continued to crush my fingers, and I gasped.

"Yes, yes, that's it," she said. "A little pain . . . with a little pleasure . . . right, lover?"

In that instant I realized this wasn't Nona—there was something else inside of her empty body. But how? The Triskelion pendant should have prevented—

Her neck was bare. It was gone!

"Surprise! I thought this was the best way to talk to you, love. Without interference."

This was TC.

I started shaking as my mom sat up. I heard long-unused cartilage crack as he wiggled her eyebrows at me. He winced then and stuck out her lower lip. "Zoë, you need to tell Nona to take better care of this body—there are some serious problems in here."

"GET OUT!"

He held up Mom's free hand, the right hand, the one that wasn't crushing mine. "Uh, uh, uh—is that any way to speak to your poor old mommy?"

I stopped struggling and glared at him, looking out at me through my mom's eyes. "What are you doing in there? Where is my mother? How did you get rid of the Triskelion?"

"Tsk, tsk, tsk," he said in her voice. "I'm afraid I can only answer one of those at a time." He put Mom's free hand to her chin. "Let's see, which one first?"

I tried pulling away from him again, only I couldn't move my hand. Hell, I couldn't even really feel it anymore.

"Ah—I think I'll go from easiest to hardest." He smiled at me again with her mouth, and again it was the most garish thing I'd ever seen. "So, to start, the easiest would be what I'm doing inside your mother's body." He glanced down and made a face as if he'd smelled something disgusting. "I'm in here because of the hocus-pocus your Guardian friend's bitches are trying. You know they're trying to contain me, don't you?"

I really didn't know what they were doing. "They have your finger."

"Yes—and with that bit of myself they're working on a mojo that will either banish me or hold me. But they don't realize that as long as I'm inside a body, their spells and magic can't hurt me." He widened Mom's grin. "Unfortunately, much like a Wraith, a Symbiont leaches energy from the living shell. And I'm afraid Nona's energy is somewhat limited."

"Get out."

"Not until I've had the talk with you I originally came for—without interference."

I stopped pulling away.

"Now, let's see—number two is, where is my mother? But I told you that already. I don't know where Nona is. I no longer have the power to hold her. Like you being reduced back to a human, I too have been reduced to a simple, basic Symbiont."

I stared at him.

"What were the other questions?"

"Where did you put the Triskelion?" I said.

"Oh, I just love hearing your voice on you, and not so much on me. Though, when you're Wraith again, I'll get it back." He gave me a half smile. "As for the pendant, I don't know."

The weirdest part of this whole situation—save for TC in my mom's body—was that I only truly believed the last statement.

"Those were all good questions, Zoë, but they weren't the right question."

Knowing TC the way I'd come to know him—I asked the fateful question. The one I hadn't asked. "What do you want?"

He nodded approvingly. "I knew you were a smart girl." He frowned. "Not so great on the boyfriend front. That policeman is such a dick."

"Let go of my hand."

"Promise not to run off?"

"Look, you ass-hat, there's an insane cultist out there who wants me, body and soul. My mother is apparently trapped in some Abysmal dimension. My boyfriend thinks I'm sick and should probably be institutionalized. I'm not going anywhere. And I think you've broken my fingers."

He let go.

The blood rushed into the starved fingers, and the pain was incredible. It was worse than anything I could remember—except for slamming back into my body through my cord. Now, that fucking hurt. This . . . it was pins-and-needles agony as the nerve endings woke up.

I couldn't move my hand, and I was starting to see stars.

"You really need to eat a sammich or something," TC said. "If you don't have your health, then I've got nothing."

I ignored him and sat back in the chair, cradling my hand in my lap. It hurt . . . bad. But I wasn't going to let him see me squirm. "Get on with it."

"Ah. To the point. Well, I'm sure you've noticed a few changes about yourself lately?"

I glared at him. I did not want him in my mom's body.

"Of course you have. But you don't have clue one as to what is causing it, or why, do you? Oh, of course not—you weren't really the brains of your little Scooby Gang at all." He smiled sweetly. "That was Rhonda."

I gritted my teeth. Because I was mad, yeah, but also because the ache in my hand wasn't letting up. It was throbbing, and with every beat of my heart there was shooting pain.

"Well, I'll take that stern look on your beautiful face as a sign of interest." He pressed Mom's right hand to her chest as emphasis, just the way she always did when she was claiming innocence of something. He stopped and looked down. "My, your mother has ample mammary glands, doesn't she?" And then he looked at me—or rather at my chest. "Yours are rather . . . small by comparison."

Motherfuckerasswipe. "Stop feeling up my mom and get on with it." But of course I couldn't stop myself from glancing down. I'd always been quite proud of my breasts. I'd gotten mine before a lot of girls in my school. "And I'm average, by the way."

"Sure you are. Ah, but where was I? Oh, yes—you being normal once again. I suppose you think it's my fault?"

"I don't know whose fault it is. I just know you tried to kill me and Dags in my mom's house."

"I did not try to kill you," TC said in a serious voice. "I was trying to find the link between us—the one that connected us."

I blinked at him. "By ramming your nasty-ass tongue down my throat?"

"You used to like it."

"Screw you. You tried to kill Dags."

"Yes, I did. Until the motherfucker bit me. And, with that piece of me, they're trying to destroy me. But they can't, Zoë. I won't let them until we defeat the Phantasm."

I blinked. "Say that again?"

"It's the Phantasm, Zoë. He's found a way to block your power."

"The Phantasm?"

I'd met this creature in my dreams a few times, and only once in the flesh, if you could call it that. He was, by definition, the be-all and end-all of the Abysmal plane. I was never sure what that meant in the hierarchy, though. I didn't know if he was, like, say, the supreme evil, stroking a white cat.

Even though Nona and Rhonda had always cautioned me on what I called good and evil.

But in my brief encounter with him—with his warning not to make a deal with Trench Coat and his unhappiness at my decision—what I could tell about him was that he was powerful. It'd been like a low hum, the droning of an engine, the promise of something dark and terrifying and not something I wanted to draw attention from.

He'd also shown himself to me in the hospital—showing me chains that once bound him. He'd told me I could be much more. And I hadn't understood that.

When compared to the Phantasm, the Archer lost a lot of his spooky factor. I also didn't understand the reasoning behind TC's thinking the Phantasm was out to get me.

So it brought up the question: "Why would the Phantasm do that?"

"Like I've tried to tell you before—you're a threat to him. To his rule. To his kingdom. And so am I." He lay back on the bed, and I realized that Mom looked paler than ever.

I sat forward. "What did you do to my mom's body? She looks worse than before—are you draining her?"

Mom was staring straight ahead, and I got the impression he was no longer looking out through her eyes. "It's not your mom . . . I lack power to keep control over her body. Her soul's not here, but her attachment to it is quite—strong. I don't have much time, so you have to listen carefully. The Phantasm is trying to get to me, through you. I've tried his patience long enough, and that last idea I had—because of you with Bonville and the soul contracts—backfired badly. Two of the souls he hoped to possess ended up as Guardian familiars."

Uh-huh, this jibed with what those two had warned me about. "I thought Alice said it was the Phantasm that helped them—made them what they are?"

"You living souls really are stupid. The Phantasm lies, Zoë. Yes, he helped Alice, and he did give her shelter, but only to gain both her soul and that of the younger bitch. About the only thing good that happened was you cleaning up the Shadow People mess.

"But he blames me for the creation of a new Guardian, though force-made. Irin are hard to come by, Zoë. Their survival rate in the past decade has been zero. And even you were derailed from your destiny"—he grinned—"by me."

Irin. "Jemmy said that Irin were the offspring of man and angel."

"To primitive man that's exactly what they were," TC said. "When an Ethereal being conceived a child with a living mortal woman—if the child survived—it would be an Irin. A Watcher for the Ethereal Seraphim. They guarded the borders between the planes."

"Like border guards?"

TC made Mom's face smirk. It was a stiff expression. "You could say that. But after the Bulwark, very few of them survived."

Bulwark. Jemmy had mentioned that too.

"You really need to learn your own history, Zoë. Seems your mom's been falling down on the job. Do you even know who your father is?"

I frowned. "My dad was Adiran Martinique. I know he was part of the Dioscuri Experiments that my great-uncle carried out. I know Great-Uncle was betrayed by Francisco Rodriguez, and the place where they had their experiments was burned."

"Ah, but you know the truth of your dad, and you're ignoring it."

God, I hated it when he was right. Yes—I'd figured it out. With no real help from Rhonda or from Rodriguez. It was hinted at over and over again during the conversation with Rodriguez in the botanica, before he tried to kidnap me. After Cooper left, after Rhonda was banished, I'd become frightened, understanding why I was so important to Rodriguez and his group of crazies.

I knew that the unidentified body found burned to death in Domas's lab was my dad. And that he'd died—physically—years before I was born. I'd been a freak since the day I was conceived, and my father and mother had fought to make sure I'd have a normal life.

I realized after Cooper had arrested Rodriguez why my mom had always been so secretive about my dad. Why she was surprised with what I could do, but not really.

I understood why she was afraid for me, and why she tried to tell me so many times that there were things out there that normal people couldn't see, and that it was better they not know about.

There had been a lot to put together after that day—and I'd had to do it on my own.

"What's your point?" I said finally. "What was the Bulwark?"

He came out of Mom's body at that point, and though he wasn't solid, he sat on the edge of the bed. We faced each other. "Your father was the Ethereal Champion, Zoë. Being a Symbiont, I was created originally to man the front lines in the war between those that wanted the borders open and those that believed they should be shut. I didn't care either way—I was a soldier and did what I was told to do.

"The Irin fought the armies of the Phantasm."

"And the Irin lost?"

He shrugged. "Not exactly. It was a stalemate. Mainly because the Phantasm cannot breach the border to the physical plane even if he wins. He can manifest and touch it in dreams through creatures there—those that have a bit of the Abysmal in them. Like you had. But in the end, the Irin were diminished, your father was gone, and the borders were sealed. The Bulwark is what they call the last stand."

I stared at him. I didn't *not* believe him, but I didn't really believe him either. "Are you like . . . talking about a war between Heaven and Hell?"

"Those terms are human terms, Zoë. It'd be better if you didn't limit yourself to such beliefs. The worlds as they exist are much broader, and the borders between what is perceived as good and evil aren't as clear-cut."

"You sound like my mom."

"Those were her words. She's a very . . . verbose woman." He straightened. "Sometimes Irin can be changed, as you were changed. Our encounter was an accident." He smiled, and it was a pearly white smile. I hated the fact that he was handsome. Damnit. "And sometimes Fate—the bitch—can smile, and something out of nature can be born. Like you." He shrugged. "I changed you. And you changed your boyfriend."

Boyfriend?

I shook my head. "Daniel?"

He scowled. "No—the Guardian. He wasn't born from an Ethereal, but he was touched by an Ethereal power. Madness and death would have been his future—having been touched by the Abysmal physically. But it was your touch that changed him. Just as I changed you."

"I . . . changed Dags?"

I felt my heart skip on the memory of that night—in that basement—after accompanying Dags through the Abysmal in physical form. I could remember it all then—even Alice warning that my memory would be altered. Awakening in the hospital after the altercation in Bonville's basement, I'd been unsure what was wrong with Dags. The doctors couldn't diagnose what he was suffering from. He would shift from lucid moments to a day or two unconscious. When he slept, he'd cry out and be afraid of everything.

And then came the night he'd coded—and I'd gone to him.

I had vague memories of power, of needing to help someone. I thought . . . somehow I'd dreamed that I'd saved Daniel.

Was that only a dream?

When released, Dags'd kept his distance from me for a while, even through what had happened with Bertram and Charolette, the two Rogue walkers—casualties of Rodriguez's betrayal—who had taken my mother's body, and that of Dr. Melvin Maddox.

I'd seen him only once during that time, when I'd been in the hospital—again.

Dags had been approached by Randall Kemp, head of SPRITE, and inadvertently given the man my name. I'd been a little irritated with Dags then. But after learning about Rhonda's duplicity in everything, that March Knowles had been her uncle and she was a member of the Society of Ishmael, then the incident in the warehouse and Daniel's refusing my calls—I'd have forgiven him anything. Having him come through that purple flame in the botanica assured me that I wasn't alone.

". . . inevitably going to happen."

I blinked, angry that'd I'd allowed my mind to wander and missed what TC had been saying. "What?"

"Pay attention!" TC looked more irritated than menacing as he sat back on the edge of the bed. "I have a limited amount of time. I haven't eaten in a while, and I'm starved. The little spell your Guardian's familiars are casting is chipping away at my capacity to maintain any sort of physical form."

All I caught in that was the word *eaten*. I remembered the way TC had tried to consume the soul of the Cruorem's leader, like he'd tried to consume mine, like he'd tried to take William Tanaka's soul that first night. "Don't look at me—I'm not up for grabs right now."

"No, you're not. I already had a peek in there," and he reached down between his leather-entrenched legs to touch the rather large package there. "Though you are a bit frustrated. Haven't had anything good since me, have you? Nothing will compare, doll. I'm the shit."

I felt my face flush red with heat. It was a mixture of rage and embarrassment. It'd taken a while to remember that long night out of my body, the one that cinched my transformation into a Wraith. The night he'd stolen my voice.

TC's smile was the pure definition of the verb "leer." "Ah, you do remember, don't you? Nothing will ever compare to me."

"Shut the fuck up. I'm not fucking worried about you, or what's happening to you. My only goal right now is to find my mother's soul and bring it back." I pushed myself up and stood in front of him. He didn't rise from his seated position, so I was face-to-face with him. "And since it's your fault she's missing—you're going to help me."

"Oh? What makes you think I give a fuck about that talk-ative bitch?"

"Because you need me." And I knew it was true the moment I saw the corner of his mouth twitch. My hunch was right. "It's why you came back to me at the shop and risked being raked over the coals. You thought that by touching me again the way you had before, you'd regain your power as the Archer. But it didn't work, did it? Instead, Dags took a piece of you, and now the familiars have a bit of power over your physical form."

I thought he was going to explode for a second there. His jaw clamped shut, and I could see the muscles working back and forth. He finally did stand, and again I was taken aback at how tall and menacing he *could* be.

A dark eyebrow arched above his shades. "Who's Dags?"

"The Guardian?"

"Oh." He nodded. "But you're right. I came to you to see for myself. I knew that if you were still capable of Irin power, then touching you could ignite our connection again."

I frowned. "Wait—Irin power?"

"The power to shift out of the physical plane and into the other planes. As an Irin, you're not limited to the physical. This is how you were when I found you."

I nodded. "So—then there's something else wrong with me. It's not that I lost my connection with you. I've lost connection period."

TC nodded. "Which caused me to fade as well. From the moment we touched, we became linked, Zoë, and from the moment we made love, and you pledged your undying love to me, we became one."

Bile rose to the top of my throat really fast. Images flashed in my mind's eye again, of bodies entwined and a physical and mental ecstasy that existed only in a woman's fantasies.

Somehow I could stomach the idea that I'd made love to a Symbiont.

But me pledging my undying love?

Oh, puh-*lease*.

"It doesn't matter if you believe it, Zoë. You were the reason I gained cognitive thoughts, the reason I became an independent thinker, the reason I could resist an order given to me by either Rollins or the Phantasm. And the more our connection grew—the more you and I changed—the stronger I became."

I watched him, amazed at how at ease I was becoming. The truth was I was standing in front of a powerful Abysmal creature. And I was little more than a retail dropout. Just Zoë.

"When you destroyed me on that rooftop, you only destroyed what essence I'd managed to make physical for this plane, but not what I'd become. I was still there, a small voice in your conscience. So when you made the deal with me and brought me back so that you could rescue that silly little girl, I emerged again—though not as strong. That proved to me that my power came through my connection to you.

"You were the stronger one, and have continued to be. You leach Abysmal essence through me, Zoë. I'm that conduit, and I couldn't stop you from doing it. When the two rogues released your inhibitions with those Eidolons, you grew even stronger, and so did I."

It wasn't that I didn't believe him—I could almost swallow his explanations—but . . .

"So, which is it? Is the Phantasm after you or me? Is it you *because* you're my crazy straw to the Abysmal plane? Well, as it stands right now, neither one of us is a threat to anyone. Especially you, because—if I'm to believe you—you're stuck in a fiftysomething-year-old woman. What exactly are you going to ruin for him?"

"You don't get it, do you?" he said. "I'm not the problem here—*you* are. You're what he's most afraid of. What you can eventually become if you lose your soul."

I blinked. "Me? What could happen if I lose my soul?"

He sighed. "As an Irin, you would stand in his way between the borders, and he would never be able to cross over. That position is irritating enough to him. But it's also the will of the Seraphim, not that he has much respect for those nutcases. But you as a Wraith? You would be the only creature of the Abysmal plane that could defeat him, replace him, hurt him. And he knows this. But he can't touch you directly, so he's found a way to isolate you, cause you to mentally silence yourself from me—ME—the only key to our survival. The link to the Abysmal."

This was going nowhere, and I wasn't understanding any of it. I put my hands to my head. "Are you trying to tell me that the Phantasm has somehow created a block for me—made me simply a human again so the link between you and me is severed?"

"Not severed, Zoë. Blocked. If the connection were severed, then this little talk couldn't happen. You can still see some ghosts, like the one that's lingering around the rock in your pocket. But others are now invisible to you because that piece of the mental plane is blocked. I think—I think the connection can only be severed if I'm destroyed. And if that happens—"

"Then what are you talking about? What happens if you're destroyed first?"

The room grew physically cold, and I could see my breath. I looked around with wide eyes and watched as the shadows grew as if night were coming faster than the day could retreat.

"The end, Zoë . . . and nothing more."

8

The agreement

I laughed.

It was a nervous laugh, yeah. And it totally blew TC's dramatic pause.

But it was just so hokey.

He crossed his arms over his chest again, and I put my hand to my mouth to stifle my near hysterics. "You care to tell me what's so funny about Oblivion?"

I coughed a little and waved at him before moving away to the foot of Mom's bed. "Sorry . . . really. I spoiled your tagline, didn't I?"

"You think this is funny?" He turned to face me. "The Phantasm has somehow found a way to bounce you back to mere human, Zoë. That's denying you your birthright."

"Birthright? You mean this Irin thing because my dad happened to be dead when he conceived me with Mom?"

TC's expression changed, and he smiled. "Yes. That in itself is a gift. The Irin are powerful, Zoë."

"Geez, Trenchie, don't drool," I quipped. "Look—Irin or

not, my mom's lost somewhere. And that's because you took her." I pointed at him.

He opened his arms wide. "I'm sorry—I was pissed at you because you betrayed me before and ate all those Shadow People. I mean, I was starved, and you—no, wait." He lowered his arms. "It was one of those bitches that burned the contracts."

I remembered the scene from Bonville's basement. Of feeling powerful. And very full. "I've got to find my mom."

"You're not going to unless you either summon her back to her body or get your power back." TC shrugged. "That's the heart of it. And unless we work together, we're both screwed."

He doubled over abruptly, clutching his middle.

I narrowed my eyes at him. I didn't really trust him. "What?"

"Those meddling bitches—they're trying to summon me back to them—"

I smirked. "Sucks, doesn't it? Being a bit powerless."

"If they destroy me, Zoë, they destroy the only link you have to become a Wraith again."

True dat.

Maybe.

I crossed my arms over my chest. "But you said my birthright is to be Irin, which means I'm still an Irin. So even if I figure out what the Phantasm's done to block the power, I'd still be able to shift between planes again. Which means I'd be able to find my mom. Without you."

He snarled at me. "You'd never survive without the Abysmal side, Zoë. It's already touched your soul. And the Seraphim would never allow you to survive as an Irin."

Yadda, yadda, yadda. I kinda liked having this asswipe beg me for a change.

And abruptly he was on his knees beside the bed, doubled over. And I was feeling a bit torn—Yeah, I hated this asshole for everything he'd caused in my life. But truth be told, he'd also been the cause of my power. I'd been able to save a child because of the power he gave me. And he was right—about protecting myself better as a Wraith than as just an astral walker.

I didn't have Rhonda. Dags would do what he could to

help me—that much I knew. But with TC's knowledge of the Abysmal—

"Okay—what did you have in mind? Working together?"

He looked up at me and I could see myself in the reflection of his shades. "Do you trust me?"

"Hell no."

"That's good enough."

And before I could stop him, he was rushing up at me. I thought he was going to go all tentacles and octopus again, the veritable Abysmal squid.

But he didn't.

There was a push against my chest.

And then nothing.

I was sitting at my desk, in Mom's old house. The one we lived in before I graduated high school. I had a term paper due and of course I'd waited till the last minute to write it. I was always late—never on time—even in puberty.

A ghost sat beside me, the old image of a little boy with a cap on his head. I'd seen it often when I was little, only I hadn't remembered it. His name had been Bobby, and he'd been in the house before we moved in. He wasn't happy that we were there, but he wasn't lonely anymore.

And with Daddy gone—and Mom working all the time—I wasn't lonely when he was there either.

"Whatcha doing?" he asked me in that little echoey voice he'd always had.

I glanced at him. "It's a paper on the effect of the American Revolution on the country's future economics."

"Sounds boring."

"It is." I sighed and put my pen down. I wanted to use the typewriter, but Mom said not until I had it written on paper first. My thoughts down. 'Cause I had scattered thoughts. A lot. "What I want to write about is a love story."

Bobby made a face. "Bleck. Why a love story? That's all soupy stuff."

I nodded but felt the nice warmth that thinking about some of the romance stories I'd been sneaking out of Mom's bedroom gave me. I had memories of my mom and dad, being happy.

Laughing and giggling. I could never figure out why he left, and knew it couldn't be because of Mom, but because of me.

He'd left because I'd done something wrong, and Mom would never tell me what it was. So I studied hard, and one day I wanted to go find my dad. And bring him home.

"You shouldn't think that stuff," Bobby said. "About you and your dad. I mean, your daddy loved you."

I looked at Bobby with the best serious face I could make. "How could you know that, Bobby? You never met my dad."

"No, but I've seen the pictures. And I've seen the gifts." He crossed his arms over his chest. "I'd say he loved you lots—especially to make you such a nice necklace."

I was confused at what Bobby was saying. Pictures? What picture? Gifts? What necklace? "What—what are you talking about?"

"It's all down there." He pointed to the floor. "All in a box. I go through things at night when everyone's sleeping. I learned how to move things—wanna see?" He jumped out of the chair, and his eyes twinkled.

I shook my head. "No, no—well, yes, that's great that you can do that. But—where down there? You mean in the—" I gulped. "The basement?"

"Yeah. Wanna come see? Your mom's not supposed to be home for a while. I can show you where they are."

Gifts? A necklace. From my dad? I wanted to—but I was deathly afraid of the basement. I hated going down there, even just to grab the laundry. There were voices down there, and bugs, and above all—spiders.

I really hated spiders.

And apparently Bobby was getting better at reading my mind. "Aw, come on. There's lots of light before dark. And you can turn the light on. I'll be with you."

I wanted to—I really did. But I was just so—

"You're a scaredy-cat!" Bobby jumped up and down as he pointed up at me. I was taller than him now. I'd continued to grow while he stayed small. Little. Frozen in time.

And I wasn't going to let some punk ghost tell me I was afraid—I already knew that. Maybe I could find some bug spray somewhere and spray all of the corners before I started moving things.

"Come on!" Bobby said, and vanished. *"I'll race you there!"* his disembodied voice called out to me.

Oh, damnit! I needed to get this paper written. But I also wanted to see what was down there and see if Bobby was lying. 'Cause if he was lying, I swore I was going to figure out how to do an exorcism and banish his little butt.

I went downstairs, very aware of the stairs' creaking. I had memorized where each creak was and knew how hard I could step on those spots. Once in the kitchen, I saw the note from Mom, reminding me to turn the oven on. I was over an hour late doing that—so dinner wouldn't quite be done when she got home.

After flipping it on, and checking to make sure the timer was set, I pulled out the cookie jar—a replica of R2-D2 someone had done in a ceramics class and Mom had bought at a garage sale—and grabbed a couple of cookies. I took a Fanta Orange out of the refrigerator, then grabbed the flashlight from the standard kitchen I-don't-know-where-it-goes-so-I'll-put-it-in-here drawer.

After downing the cookies, getting a burp out of a few swigs of orange, I faced the basement door.

"Chicken!" came Bobby's voice.

Little shit. I stood in front of the door, took a deep breath, and wrenched it open. Darkness came out at me, along with the smell of mildew and old books. I reached to the left and fumbled for the light switch. The light came on beneath, illuminating the steps.

If I stood at the top, I could see the bottom, but nothing else beyond that. And as I stared, Bobby appeared down there and stuck his tongue out at me. *"Chicken!"*

Jerk. I huffed and puffed and barreled down those steps, my fear temporarily replaced by inherent stubbornness. And once at the foot of those steps, I stopped and looked around. The basement room really wasn't so scary if I just took it all in.

To the right were the washer and dryer, and this was the "friendly" area, the part I was used to. Mom had laid down a few scraps of old carpet on the concrete floor, kept the area free of cobwebs, and made a nice flat area with a folding table, shelves for detergent, and even a small radio. The antenna had

*long since broken off, and she'd attached a bent coat hanger
to the back of it.*

*But to the left . . . there was the spooky. It wasn't as well lit
as the washing area, and I hated it. I could see my old toys
stacked in various corners, all of them staring at me, neglected,
cursing me for growing older and forgetting them.*

"It's all right up there!" Bobby appeared again, and down
here in the dark he tended to glow, lighting up the room.

He stood in front of the wall of rusted metal shelves full of
old cardboard boxes, labels declaring the contents were Mag-
navox, Sony, and Mattel, when in truth they had been reduced
to storage containers. He was jumping up and down and pointing to the unmarked white box on the very top shelf. It sat by
itself, and I remembered the box. It'd gone with us through all
of our moves. And I wasn't supposed to touch it.

"Mom'll get really mad if I mess with that box," I said. I
heard the nervous twitch in my voice. I wanted to go back upstairs and finish my paper. The dullness of schoolwork didn't
seem quite so boring anymore—a lot safer than my mom's
anger if she caught me down here.

It was the size of any average box—maybe a bit smaller. I
guessed my old Easy-Bake oven would fit inside of it.

"Ever wonder why she doesn't want you messing with it?"
Bobby was staring at me with a cross look. *"There's something
in there she doesn't want you to see."*

"But what would that be?"

"Your dad."

My dad? I gave Bobby a look like he had a third eyeball.
"My dad isn't in that box. My dad ran off a long time ago."

*"But ran off to where? And why would he just leave and
never say good-bye to his only child?"*

The little shit was pressing all the right buttons, and I knew
this. But my own curiosity wanted to see the box now, and
maybe it was just filled with spiders, and maybe it did have
clues to my daddy inside. I was eleven, and all I wanted was to
know more of who he was, and why he left.

A folding stepladder lay propped against the wall, and I
pulled it away, mindful of bugs that skittered out of my path.
Roaches mostly, and I shivered inwardly. I hated bugs.

Once the steps were unfolded, I cautiously climbed up on them. The shelf was still higher than my head, and when I tried to move it, pulling it out, I felt something tickle my right arm. I looked up in time to see a large black spider headed down my arm to my shoulder.

I screamed and pushed back and Bobby yelled. All I could think about was the spider going up my shirt as I hit the floor and the back of my head hit the hard, cold concrete—

I gasped awake—very much aware of a gang of little gnomes taking a sledgehammer to the inside of my brain. And I was cold—shivering. And there was an all-too-familiar beeping noise.

Mental note: *aw, fuck . . .*

"Good morning, sunshine."

That voice. I *knew* that voice.

Joe Halloran.

"You're kinda loud," came another voice. That was Dags's tone, more dulcet than Joe's swaggering, nasal, sarcastic one. "Zoë? Are you back?"

"Back?" my voice croaked. And again I was immediately excited to hear my voice.

"Whoa . . . you weren't kidding," Joe said in the dark. "Though I've never actually heard her talk before."

Why was it dark? Oh, yeah. I had to open my eyes.

I blinked a few times and looked to my right. Dags's smiling face with his gray eyes looked down at me with worry. His hair fell over his eyes, giving him an even more boyish look. Why had I thought he looked older before?

He reached out, and I could feel his hand in mine. "Hey—don't scare me like that."

"You haven't been around Zoë much, have you? This is nothing—this time she wasn't even admitted."

Not admitted, huh? Then where was that infernal beeping coming from?

I looked to my left to see Joe.

He hadn't changed much in the past month. Stiff, spiky hair, lopsided, shit-eating grin, dressed in a flannel shirt and roguish attitude.

Mental note: *wow.*

He also had my left arm in his hands, turning it from side to side, twisting it around. I cleared my throat. "Can I help you with something?"

He grinned at me. "You know, you sound a lot like Stevie Nicks used to."

I nodded. "Mom says I sound like Nick Nolte."

He shook his head. "Nah, not as good-looking." Joe was still examining my arm.

"Hello? Is there something you need?"

"It's really gone, huh? That mark?"

I took my arm away and realized I wasn't in a hospital like I feared, but still at the facility where my mom was. I was in a room at Miller Oaks. And the beeping was coming from a different room. "Oh . . . no. What happened?"

Dags answered, "Well, you passed out. Captain Cooper found you. He'd come by for a visit, and there you were. The nurses here and the doctor were good. You didn't seem to be in any immediate danger."

"Cooper called me," Joe said. "Apparently Shit-for-Brains wasn't answering his phone again."

I frowned at him. Shit-for—

And then I realized he meant Daniel.

I put my left hand to my face to hopefully hide any crying I might do. "How long?"

"Two hours," Joe said. "I called Dags to let him know—"

"I just got here," Dags chimed in.

I looked from Dags to Joe. "Why did you call Dags? Why did you *know* to call him?"

The look on both of their faces was priceless. Especially when they glanced at each other to indicate the oh-shit reaction.

But I wasn't stupid. Not like everyone seemed to think. "You knew because you knew Dags was with me." I looked at Dags. "So were you there at the shop because Joe asked you to be? And not because you wanted to be?"

I was starting to get that old betrayal feeling again. It was becoming so commonplace I was thinking of actually letting it take up residence.

"No." Dags's expression was hard, and I noticed the changes

in his features again. He did look different. "I came to you when Joe told me what happened with your mom."

"He's right," Joe held up a finger. "I warned him to stay away from you. I told him not to go near you. I also told him to be in fear for his life—that you were a creature from the darkest dimensions."

"You told him I killed March Knowles and Rhonda."

He shrugged. "That might have slipped out."

"But I came to see you anyway, Zoë," Dags said. "And I stayed because I wanted to."

I looked into his eyes and knew he wasn't lying to me. I wasn't sure Dags was capable of lying. Evading—yeah. But lying?

No.

I saw a box in my mind, a white box. "I had a dream . . . or was it a memory?"

"What was it about?" Dags asked.

"Something to do with my dad . . ."

And a little boy.

And then it was gone. Poof. Just like that. Eh . . . so much for that supermemory of mine. Seems it was a Wraith thing too.

I looked at Joe. "So—Daniel never answered your call?"

"He's an ass, Zoë. Plain and simple. He won't talk to me either. But you know what? I don't care. I've gotten along without Mr. Daniel Frasier for a very long time, and I put my life back together. But then again, I wasn't sleeping with him."

His words seemed odd to me, and I pushed back from him. And that's when I saw his smile and the twinkle in his eyes. He was being a twit, and I was glad of it. Neither was I. Sleeping with him. I sniffed. "I'm sorry."

"What for? Because you saved his ass more times than I can count? Because you gave him your heart and then, when things got tough, he bailed?"

"But I never told him the truth about me . . ."

"And what makes you think he could have handled that?" Joe arched his eyebrows and glanced over me at Dags. "Me and Tiny here are your best support when it comes to all things—what was your word?—ah . . . oogy."

I smiled. I didn't want to, but it happened. And my nose was clogged. Dags handed me a tissue, and I used it as best I could without being too snotty. After a few minutes I looked from Dags to Joe. "I can't OOB anymore—did Dags tell you?"

Joe nodded. "Well, he told me what you said happened in the warehouse. I'm glad you were able to do that for Charlie. But I'm having a little trouble believing your ability is totally gone. I mean, whether or not Trench Coat is involved, you could still OOB before he showed up. But to not even be able to do that? Uh-uh. Something else is going on."

"I wondered that," Dags said. "But with the mark gone, and then her voice came back. TC showing up also cinched it with me—whatever is happening doesn't involve him. And Maureen and Alice have put a binding spell on him just to keep him out of the way for now."

Binding spell on TC.

Wait . . . I pushed up on my elbows and frowned. I'd been talking to TC in Mom's room. *Where is he?*

Right here, lover, came a voice inside of my head. *Right next to your heart.*

9

I murdered who?

THERE was a knock at the door before I could scream. I was still puzzling about TC's voice in my head when Captain Cooper strolled into the room.

He looked tired and worn-out. I hadn't spoken with him since he'd prevented Rodriguez from kidnapping me out of my mom's shop. Though we'd left the conversation at a standstill—with him noting that my fingerprints were on the bloody business card found in the bathroom at the Plaza next to the blue lady's dead body. I was never sure if he thought I was the one responsible for that death, or he wanted me to be.

It was sort of a love-hate relationship.

What? You love him, and he hates you?

Ah! Where are you?

I'm in here, babe. Safe and warm.

Oh God, no. No, no, no, no, no . . . I never wanted a Symbiont inside of my body—I'd already had a Daimon run amuck in it—and I sure as hell didn't want a Symbiont messing around in there, particularly not *this* one.

"Get out!"

Not on your life, babe—we need each other. And as long as your Guardian friend and his familiars think it's fun to use mojo on me—I'm protected inside of you.

"Get out?" Joe said. "Zoë, that's harsh. Cooper could have just left you on that floor."

Captain Kenneth Cooper was Daniel's boss, as well as a friend. Cooper was a man in his midthirties, with salt-and-pepper hair, a baby face that was losing a lot of the baby innocence. Six foot something, with broad shoulders and straight back. He was a fairly attractive man if you liked men who looked like soccer dads. Which was just wrong because I could never imagine Cooper being a dad.

I wasn't sure that he wasn't a dad, come to think of it. I had a vague memory of him being married.

You like him? He's old.

I started to react aloud to TC's comment again—but stopped when I saw Cooper.

His eyes had widened, and he took a step back. I wouldn't have been surprised if he'd reached for his gun, which was conspicuously holstered at his hip.

But I could see his reaction coming—his shock that I had actually used my voice.

One—two—three—"You *talked*!"

Joe nodded. "Yeah—we got that. What was that call about?"

But Cooper was having a bit of trouble pulling his gaping glare from me. "Wha—?"

"The call?" Joe held out his hands. "The one you got, then excused yourself from the room?"

"Oh." He pulled his gaze from me and focused on Joe. "That was Whittacker over in zone two." He turned and looked at me. "I need to know where you were between the hours of ten and eleven last night."

I started to open my mouth to answer—basically because I could.

But it was Dags who answered for me. "She was with me, at Nona's shop. She's been sick with the flu."

Cooper turned and looked at Dags. "And you are?"

The brunet stood and offered his hand to Cooper. "Darren McConnell. I'm a friend of the family."

Cooper shook his hand. "You look familiar."

"He's good—I can vouch for him. He's also a friend of Frasier's."

The captain snapped his fingers. "Wait a minute—you worked at Fadó's, didn't you?"

I watched the conversation like I would watch a tennis match. Back and forth and back and forth over the bed.

"Yes. I was bartending there. I remember you coming in a few times with Detective Frasier."

"You haven't seen him lately, have you?" .

I butted in—sorry, but I knew the answer to this one, and I wanted to use my voice. "He was with us this morning," I interrupted. Dags smirked at me, and I smirked back. "He stopped by to check up on me." Whether he wanted to admit it or not.

"Really?" There was a dangerous edge to Captain Cooper's tone. I'd had that edge directed at me, and it was sharp. "That's interesting. He'll show up at your mom's shop, and I can't get the fucker to answer the phone. The asshole's about a hair-breadth from suspension."

I narrowed my eyes at him. "Suspension? What's he been doing?"

Cooper answered me. "Let's just say he's been taking un-necessary risks in dangerous situations. It's almost like he's testing his own mortality."

Yikes. That didn't sound like Daniel at all. And I sure as hell hadn't gotten that impression from seeing him that morning.

So—what did you guys fight about? Did he finally realize he couldn't satisfy your needs the way I can?

"Shut the fuck up," I hissed.

I felt everyone's eyes on me—Dags's the most. He was still on my right and tilting his head to his left shoulder. "Zoë?"

"Sorry. I was just—I'm just very—" I was really wanting Cooper to get the hell out of there so I could tell these two I had a Symbiont hijacking my body. Luckily the fucker hadn't tried to control it. If he did that, I'd—

You'd what?

Joe spoke up. "We're all a little worried about Frasier. He's not been himself lately. But why are you worried about Zoë? Does her whereabouts have something to do with that call?"

Cooper cleared his throat as he looked at each of us. And I noticed his gaze lingering a bit on Dags. "I'm not sure—the details of the case have been left out of the news."

Joe held out his hands. "Captain—after everything Zoë's been through—I think she needs to know why you asked that. I'd like to know myself—and if Shit-for-Brains isn't going to work on it, I'd love the chance."

Since the start of this, something had seemed a little bit off—like I was missing a piece of the picture. Joe, talking with Captain Cooper so casually—I pointed at him. "You're working for him?" I pointed at Cooper.

Joe nodded. "Transferred back into Homicide a month ago. Figured Frasier was going to need some backup. Only the boy abruptly backed out. I figured it had something to do with you, but I'd decided after February just to keep out of things."

"So you were working with Daniel? As his partner—again?" I asked.

"Yep. But the word *partner* implies there are two people working together. Daniel's been mostly bye-bye."

"And if I get my hands on him," Cooper said, "then I'll be putting him on the spot for not following protocol. But"—he looked at me—"what I'm about to say I'm saying because there is a chance you might help us understand the case."

I nodded. Make all the excuses you need—just get on with it.

This isn't getting your mother back.

I wasn't going to survive this. Oh my God—with TC *inside* of me. I felt flushed, and I put my hand to my cheek. It was hot.

"Since the fifteenth, there have been three bodies found in the north Atlanta area, close to Roswell and Alpharetta, with no apparent cause of death. And when I say that, I mean it. The coroner can't find a single reason why these people died. They were all different ages, different social as well as ethnic backgrounds, and all just dropped dead."

I pursed my lips. Okay. What it had to do with me—no idea. "You've kept this out of the news, haven't you?"

"Yes. So far. The phone call was about a fourth body—only this one was found in our jurisdiction."

Dags and I glanced at each other.

"Where at?" Joe asked.

"In Little Five Points, in the parking lot of Front Page News."

Wow . . . that was one street over from where Mom's shop sat. Front Page News was a restaurant specializing in New Orleans cuisine. Now, having never been to New Orleans before or after the flood, I had no idea if it was authentic. I just knew their muffalata was good stuff. Though it had been a while since I'd visited there. In fact, I'd been more inclined to go to Zesto's on the corner than a few doors down to the restaurant.

Dags narrowed his eyes. "So—because you found the body close to Zoë's home, you think she's involved?"

"No." Captain Cooper looked at me. "I'm looking at Zoë because the victim was identified as someone who recently invaded her home and attacked her. And the victim's fiancé is accusing Zoë of murdering her."

My eyes widened. "Huh?"

"Say what?" Joe said.

"Who is accusing me of murder?"

Cooper looked directly at me. "Randall Kemp—the victim was his girlfriend, Boo Baskins."

10

The return of SPRITE

WHO the hell is that?

"*Just—be—quiet—*" I hissed, only I did it without actually making a noise. I figured I was pretty good at that. Especially after not having a voice for three months.

But to fill in the unread—Randall Kemp was the owner and pioneer of the paranormal group SPRITE, which stood for Southeastern Paranormal Research Institute for Termination and Extermination. Or I think that was it. I always got it confused. Big name, small group, with a fairy choking a ghost as their logo.

Funded early on from a trust left to Randall Kemp by his grandmother, Randall was the consummate ghost hunter—and a genius to boot. About a month before my meeting up with Trench Coat, I'd investigated a home on Web Ginn House for my largest client, Maharba (yes, we know it's Abraham spelled backward—but that apparently doesn't mean anything). In that house was a poltergeist (nasty, big squid-looking thing) and a group of ghost hunters.

SPRITE.

Randall had been able to get me on film—on an infrared camera and on audio. Boo was a part of the four-man team that witnessed me visually, as well as audibly. I was able to find the root of the poltergeist and snap its fetter. And oddly enough, SPRITE's so-called footage of me had vanished, as did their credibility. I'd always assumed that Maharba had something to do with that—pretty much making SPRITE vanish into history.

Months later Randall and company popped up again, funded by a group called the League of Six. Randall had created what I called a Ghost Zapper gun. And it fucking *hurt*. I know because I was zapped with it several times. It practically rendered me useless for a bit. Randall and company had used it on me with the intent of rescuing me—Zoë—from the ghost that haunted me. Unfortunately, the League of Six had shown up, grabbed my body (I'd hidden inside of Joe's), and taken off, leaving the SPRITE team to take the rap for the break-in. Boo had also been in on that adventure.

I hadn't seen much of Randall and company since then. There were a few times I'd seen the van around—nearby—but they'd never stepped into the shop again.

Now to hear that Boo was . . . dead?

Joe was beside Cooper. "Boo Baskins? Are you sure?"

"Mr. Kemp made a positive identification. Her parents are on their way from Florida. Mr. Kemp accused Miss Martinique of murdering Boo in order to get even for her mother's illness."

I was shocked—stunned into silence. Yeah, I know. Weird. But how in the hell did Randall Kemp come up with *that* crazy idea when I'd never even formally met Boo, or even Randall for that matter? Yeah, I'd overshadowed him in order to take hold of the situation, but ultimately I was the one that got kidnapped.

And the thought that someone would believe I—me—could kill?

Didn't you kill that—

SHUT *UP*!

Dags rubbed at his chin. "You can't possibly believe that Zoë killed anyone."

Cooper glared at Dags. "At this point in my career—I can believe a lot of things. Incidentally, may I ask you where *you* were?"

I piped up. "He was with me, like he said." The last thing I wanted was for Cooper to set his attack sights on Dags. The bartender turned Guardian had enough weirdness in his life not to have to deal with a cop with a vendetta.

"You were sick—did you see him all the time?"

"Captain," Joe said. "I can vouch for Dags. So could Frasier— if he were here. I'd also like to know you really don't think Zoë had anything to do with these murders."

"No, I don't. Honestly. I do believe Miss Martinique excels at getting into trouble—but I don't believe she has any special supernatural powers that could make her stop someone's heart from beating."

Insert crickets chirping.

After that very awkward pause, Joe huffed, "So, do you have any other suspects you'd like me to question?"

With his glare still lingering on Dags, Cooper nodded and pulled his iPhone from his belt. He touched the screen a few times and dragged his index finger upward along the surface. "There are his friends—who are also members of this ghost group he managed. Herb Maupin and Ronald Beaumont."

Joe took out his own iPhone and tapped the screen. "E-mail me that info, and I'll start the interviews."

Two more taps, and Cooper put the phone away. "You got any ideas where Frasier is? I don't want you working this alone."

"Oh, I'm not really alone. And no, I have no idea what the cheese-head is doing." He grinned. "But I'll find him."

"Good," Cooper nodded at me. "Miss Martinique—I do wish you and your mother the best. But I would caution you about Mr. Kemp—he strikes me as being a hothead." Then he glared at Dags and left the room.

"He doesn't like me," Dags muttered.

"Ya think?" Joe said. He was looking at his iPhone. I wanted one of those things. Oh! And now that I had a voice— why not! "I hate to say this—and don't take it the wrong way— but I'm kind of glad we got one of the murders in our jurisdiction. I know Cooper's been chomping to get ahold of the case."

I ran my fingers through my hair. It was a bit tangled, and I needed a comb. Wasn't sure I trusted a mirror though. I also felt bad for Randall—I mean, I'd never really wanted the guy to get hurt, or his girlfriend. And I had spent a few minutes inside of him when they'd broken into the shop.

Just dropped dead, huh?

My back tensed. I'd almost forgotten he was in there.

Well, not for long. "Dags, there's something I have to—"

You do that, and I'll kill both of them.

I stopped.

Dags frowned at me. "Something you have to what?" He was looking through the pockets of his peacoat and pulled out his phone.

You wouldn't dare.

I would have killed the Guardian earlier—but he was able to take a piece of me because I was in my natural state. All I have to do is get close to either of them, slip out of your body, and take his soul. No mark. No weapon. Just a quiet, insignificant death.

I felt my heart miss a beat.

The thought of TC killing Joe or Dags—

And then I reconsidered what TC had just said.

No mark. No weapon. Just take the soul from the body. He drops dead.

"Zoë?" Joe said.

I pursed my lips before slipping off the bed. He moved to sit on the bed and face me as Dags stood by my side. "Joe— you said the bodies have no apparent cause of death. You mean there's not a mark on them?"

He shrugged. "Pretty much—and the coroner's reports all say the same—no internal injuries as well. Now, for Boo Baskins I can't say—I heard what you guys heard. Why?"

I looked at him, then looked at Dags. "That's the way a Symbiont can kill."

Both men's eyes widened to the size of golf balls.

"Holy shit," Dags said. "You think TC murdered those people? Ate their souls? Maureen and Alice said his spiritual essence seemed pretty weak for a Symbiont with the reputation of Archer."

I waited for the internal dialogue to start. I wasn't disappointed.

I really hate that guy. And for your information, I didn't snack on those people. And you can tell if I'm lying.

"I can?"

"You can what?" Joe said.

Damnit. This situation was intolerable—for the first time in a while I could talk, and I was going to have to learn *not* to. I waved at Joe to drop it. "Thinking out loud."

"Not used to that with you."

"Me talking?"

"No, you thinking."

I shot him the bird.

If you were Wraith, you could zap his ass.

Shut. Up.

Then a thought popped into my head. *Hey, why can't Dags or Maureen or Alice sense you inside of me? I'm like . . . just human again, right? Shouldn't they pick up your Abysmal essence or something like that?*

There was a pause, then, *I don't know.*

Wow. That was a first. TC didn't know?

"I think this is a good theory," Dags said. "Is there a way to see one of the bodies?"

Joe and I looked at him. "Why?" we said in unison.

"Because even with death, there is an imprint of a person's soul on the body itself. I mean—you're in that body for a long period of time, so there is going to be a link between it and the soul. But if a Symbiont takes a soul, then there should be no imprint left because the Symbiont *consumes* the soul. There would be an echo of the Symbiont."

I had nothing to say to that. It was just too horrible to consider. To have your soul consumed like a pizza? Dags made it sound as if there was nothing left. And how did this relate back to my mom? Technically, TC took my mom's soul—

I didn't eat Nona. I simply plucked her out of a very nasty situation.

If I find out that you hurt her in any way—

"Could you tell this? You and the girls?" Joe said.

Dags nodded. "Yes. And I might be able to tell *who* killed them."

"How?" I asked.

He smiled. "You'll see."

Cue ominous music.

"Wait." I'd shoved my hands into my pockets and found a rock. "Where's Tim?"

Dags's eyebrows arched. "Tim's here? I haven't seen him."

"Me neither," Joe said. "You sure?"

I pulled the rock out of my pocket. But Tim didn't reappear. He'd been with me in the car—but when I thought about it, I realized I hadn't seen him in Mom's room either. Not while TC was there—

What did you do with him?

There was a deep chuckle inside. *Nothing. He's around. He's just choosing to remain invisible and silent.*

Choosing? Or because you threatened?

I could feel TC's shoulders shrug. *All a matter of opinion.*

"Maybe he doesn't have enough juice to go corporeal," Joe offered.

But Dags wasn't as forgiving of the question. "Hold the rock up, Zoë. In your palm."

I did as he asked and watched as he held out his right hand. The circles illuminated to a white-blue light that enshrouded the rock as well as my hand. I couldn't sense anything other than a warm feeling against my skin. What I did see was a strange pattern on the rock itself as small, thin swirls of blue-white light appeared like a crazy tattoo.

"What is that?"

Dags answered. "Those are the fetter lines for Tim. Each fetter presents a different pattern. Alice's Ethereal light makes them visible. His is still here, and strong, but I can't tell why he hasn't manifested." He lowered his hand, and the light vanished. "Maybe it has something to do with your missing abilities?"

I shrugged and shoved the rock back in my pocket. A part of me missed Rhonda and her ability to find the answers for things. Dags had once been a lot like that, and he'd been great so far at answering questions, but I was thinking we were getting into waters even he didn't understand. Much less the girls.

I snapped my fingers. "Guys—the Triskelion pendant is missing—the one I'd put around Mom's neck. I think someone stole it."

Joe nodded. "I'll look into that. Though"—he frowned—"I

was a little surprised you had that thing there, seeing as how it would prevent the wearer from being possessed."

I shrugged at him. "Yeah? I wanted to stop anything oogy from getting inside of my mom's body."

"But didn't it stop you from getting back into your own body?"

I—uh—hrm. Yes, it had. And Joe had seen that, being in disguise with the League of Six guys that had come to kidnap me that day. I'd been ordered back in my body after being zapped with Randall's Ghost Zapper and couldn't. At the time I didn't know why—so I'd instead overshadowed Joe, jumping inside of him for safety.

He nodded. "Uh-huh. So—while it was on Nona—who's to say she didn't try to get back in her body and couldn't because of that thing?"

Oh fuck.

Christ, I am such a ditz sometimes. Why didn't I think about that? And if it's true—was I the idiot who prevented Mom from getting back into her body when she escaped TC?

You really are stupid, aren't you?

"That is enough," I hissed.

And of course Dags and Joe gave me strange looks. I smiled. "Sorry . . . I'm just frustrated that I probably prolonged my mom being missing."

"Well, my call is TC," Joe put in. "Dags said he showed up at the shop—and then tried to kill the both of you?"

I was only trying to kill the Guardian—

I interrupted his internal dialogue. "He tried to kill Dags. I think he and the girls are one of the few things he's afraid of, so let's keep that in mind."

I am not afraid of—

But then he stopped as I thought up an image of Maureen and Alice letting loose on his Symbiont ass.

Remember, they actually have a piece of you now.

"Maureen was able to isolate a piece of the Symbiont's Abysmal essence," Dags said. "So we'll have a weapon in case he tries to attack again."

Joe nodded, though I could see he was trying to suss out in his mind how all that was going to work. "And the girls are sure he doesn't have Nona somewhere?"

Dags and I nodded.

"And you both believe that?"

"Of course I do," Dags said. "Why wouldn't I believe Maureen?"

"Well, because she's Abysmal essence?" Joe said with his hands spread out. "She's living inside of you—so in my book that makes her a Symbiont by default. And in my experience"—he shook his head—"Symbionts, Daimons, fetches—they're all little pieces of nasty."

"Symbionts aren't Abysmal by default," I said, remembering something Rhonda had said once when we first looked up what the hell a Symbiont was. "I think Symbionts are pretty much neutral depending on who uses them."

"Right on target," Dags said. "Good and evil are human concepts—and not something that translates well through the other planes, Joe. It's not so much a question of good overrules evil. The barriers between the planes are there to prevent the forming of chaos. The universe loves order—like attracts like. The Ethereal and the Abysmal became two halves of a whole. I trust both of them, Joe. And you should too."

"Doesn't matter how many ways you say it, Dags—I don't trust Maureen." Joe smirked. He pulled his iPhone back out, touched the screen, and moved to the door. "Just hang on," he said with a glance back, then left the room.

I looked at Dags. After listening to the two of them, I sort of figured something out. "Joe doesn't trust Maureen—why? It's like he already knows her and maybe she's messed with that trust before." I arched an eyebrow at Dags. "You care to tell me how long you and Joe have been fighting the oogies together without me?"

He shrugged. "Maybe a few weeks. He didn't tell you?"

I shook my head. "No. I wasn't kidding when I said I hadn't seen Joe since that night in Stephens's basement. When exactly did you meet up with him? I know you saw him at the hospital with me—he called you to bring coffee."

Dags nodded and sat back on the edge of the bed. "I was working at the hospital—part-time. But just after that I had a few . . . issues come up. I told you a lot's happened since then. A lot happened after I left the hospital—after the incident with the Cruorem."

"Yeah—two days after you coded, you disappeared. Just got up and left."

"I didn't have a choice." He looked at the floor. Dags looked . . . young. And incredibly vulnerable. Like he had when I'd first met him. "I'll tell you about it someday. When I can. Just know that a lot happened."

I piped up. "You keep saying a lot happened." And he had. In fact, that was all he'd told me since he rescued me from the purple-flame thingie. "Dags, you died in that hospital. I'd forgotten that for some reason—and now I'm remembering it."

"Yeah," he said, and looked at me. "And you changed that—did you know that?" He stood up and took a step closer. Our gazes locked together. "My heart stopped—and you restarted it." He smiled. "You saved me."

I was stunned. I had no idea what he was talking about. My memories were returning, yeah, but not all at once. I could remember being with Daniel, feeling powerful, omniscient, and there was movement.

Motion.

Tenderness.

Orgasm.

"Okay, we're in," Joe said as he stepped back through the door. He stopped when he saw Dags and me inches from each other. "Hey—you two okay?"

I shook away the memories and took a step back. "Yeah, yeah. We're fine. I just—" I turned and looked at Joe. "We're in what?"

Joe grinned. And it was that wonderful shit-eating grin that usually got on my nerves. "Dekalb County Coroner's Office. We're going to check out a body."

11

To the morgue we go . . . ew

I don't like morgues.

I'd woken up in one before. In the drawer.

Box.

Not the highlight of my life.

But a definite turning point.

It was late by the time we got there, the night shift well into its work. There were few cars in the parking lot and only a single guard at the front window.

The Dekalb County Coroner's Office was old—age-wise. Dingy in places, with new tile decorating the front offices, spit-polished to a high gloss nice enough to eat off of. The front receptionist was packing up for the day—it being close to five before the three of us got there. The boys rode with me in the Volvo, opting to leave their trucks at Miller Oaks. Dags had whipped out some card to the head nurse, and she'd assured them their trucks wouldn't be towed.

The wind picked up when we walked in, and the receptionist took a quick glance at Joe's badge and waved us through.

We hit the double doors and the environment changed. The polished tiles gave way to faded, cracked, and broken tiles, circa 1971. The walls had been washed until the paint no longer had any gloss. The ceiling tiles were brown with water damage, and some were only half there. A few lights in the hall flickered, giving me an instant headache.

And the smell?

Oh God.

Mr. Clean meets Mrs. Ammonia in the arena of germ-killing battles.

I think it was a draw.

Dags and I followed Joe around the winding hallways until we ended at a battered set of dingy silver double doors. With a glance and a grin, Joe pushed forward against the doors, and we followed.

It was like stepping into the future.

Literally.

Gone was the bad floor, replaced by a freshly painted one, complete with silver drains set up periodically around the room. Sparkling, shining examination tables with silver hoses lined the center of the room—and, to my dismay, every one of them had an occupant.

Luckily, they were all covered from the shoulders down.

The smell was crisper, cleaner, and there was a hint of lemon. I could also hear music—something instrumental—playing in the background.

A tall, handsome guy in a white lab coat and what looked like a welder's plastic mask was bent over one of the bodies. He straightened when we walked in and held up what appeared to be a saw. I thought of the saw the doctor used to cut off my cast when I was eight. I'd thought he was going to remove my whole arm and was quite surprised when it didn't cut flesh.

But I didn't think this one was that friendly.

He lifted up the front of his plastic faceplate and a grin lit up his dark face. "Halloran!"

Joe moved forward as the man set the saw down and removed his gloves. The two shook hands, then did that strange hug thing with the backslaps. "Hey, Ben—how's it going?"

"Just fine. Busy. So, you back again? I heard you transferred to Vice."

"For a while. Back in Homicide. Any strange deaths like before?"

Ben shook his head. "Yeah—Lex's got you one in the back. She's waiting on you." He looked from Joe to me and Dags standing by the door. "Ah—you bring friends to see me?"

"Yes and no." Joe turned and gestured for us to come closer.

I followed Dags—I wasn't trusting the saw.

"Ben, this is Darren McConnell and Zoë Martinique. Guys, this is Ben Caillou."

Ben offered his hand, and we shook it. It was soft and warm but strong. He was a handsome man, with a prominent chin, angled nose, and almond-shaped eyes. His eyelashes were what caught my attention first—they were long and curled. And his skin was a dark, rich mocha. His hair was cornrowed and pulled back into a ponytail at his neck.

"Zoë, this is the guy that makes my special soup."

I raised my eyebrows at him. "Soup?"

"The stuff I shot you full of that brought you back to your body—that night in the morgue?"

Oh. Yeah. I'd nearly forgotten about his shooting me up with something.

Wait. I touched his sleeve. "So if his soup can pull someone back to their body—"

He shook his head, following exactly where my thoughts were going. "It can't bring Nona's soul back to hers, Zoë. Ben's soup only works for astral walking. I'm afraid Nona's condition is a bit more . . . serious." And then he told me the truth. "And I already tried it."

I socked him on the arm with my fist. Jerk.

"Oh, so which drug knocked you into the astral?" Ben focused his attention on me. His eyes were dark brown and very intense.

"No drugs," Joe said. "Long story. You said Lex's in the back?"

"Yep. In the"—he held up his hands and made quotes with the index and second finger of each hand—"special room."

Joe nodded and motioned for us to follow him. We moved past bodies and went through another door. This new room was much smaller, but still new. What differentiated it from the other room wasn't so much the polished chrome or the clean floor, but the huge-ass pentagram painted on the back wall.

It also smelled different in here—much more woody. Like damp dirt.

In the middle of the room sat one of those tables with the drain and the water hose. And on that table was a body shrouded in a white sheet. On the opposite side of the table was a black-topped workbench and enough medical equipment to make the props crew on *ER* very happy.

Seated at that table, bent over a laptop, was a slim woman in a white coat. Her hair gleamed blue-black beneath the lights, and it was pulled up into a twist at the back of her head. She turned at our approach and revealed a slim, angular Asian face.

My God . . . she's beautiful.

Then she stood up.

And fucking tall!

Joe moved past the table with the body and headed straight for the giant woman in the back. "Lex."

She smiled, showing a dazzling smile, and held her hands out to embrace Joe. "Ah—Halloran. I was very happy to hear from you. We don't get to spend as much time together anymore."

They hugged.

Dags leaned over to me. "Geez . . . that woman is a good head taller than Joe."

I glanced at him sideways. "Make you feel kinda small there, Dags?"

I was a bit thrilled when he gave me a smirk back. "No. I like tall women."

And then I was a little uncomfortable. More so at how I was feeling at his retort than what he might be thinking.

Joe did introductions. Lex Takashi, one of the city's leading criminal biologists. Pathology was simply her hobby. The afterlife was her passion.

"What is that smell?" I finally blurted.

"Patchouli," Lex said as she pursed her lips at me. She was sizing me up, and I didn't particularly like it. I felt like a slab of beef. "So, you're a Wraith?"

I glared at Joe. Exactly how many people had he told? Was

I some freaky sideshow for him? A conversation piece for Cop Shop Talk? Jerk.

He jumped in. "She was—is— We're not sure. That's another problem we're dealing with at the moment."

Lex nodded. "And she has tremendous afterlife abilities?"

I crossed my hands over my chest and glared right back at her. I called her tall, but in truth the closer she came to me, I realized she wasn't that much taller than me. Maybe an inch? She just seemed tall. *Yeah—and if I had my Wraith self, I'd suck your bitchiness out like spinal fluid.*

Unfortunately, that bit of thought didn't go unnoticed by Dags. He cleared his throat as he gave me a rather terrified look. "Like Joe said, it's another issue right now."

When she focused on Dags, I saw the claws come out. She was past me—practically pushing me out of the way—and had her hands on his shoulders, looking into his eyes. Dags looked scared.

"You . . . I can feel you. The moment you walked in. I thought it was Joe at first . . . but you . . ."

Joe was on Lex fast, putting his own hands on her shoulders and yanking her away from Dags. When she'd released her hold, Dags moved to stand behind me.

My hero.

"Lex, I didn't bring them here for your enjoyment. What I need is to see Boo Baskins's body."

Lex looked from Joe to Dags to me. It appeared as if she was coming to a decision. "Beatrice Nell Baskins is here."

Dags spoke up. "Can we see her alone?"

Joe held up a hand and stopped Lex before she could protest. "Please, Lex. Just ten minutes. Okay? I owe you on this one."

There was an odd, tense moment before the tall coroner nodded and moved toward the door. But I noticed her gaze lingered on Dags before she glanced back at Joe. "Yes . . . you do. And I will collect."

Once she was out the door, it felt like the room's temperature rose a good five degrees. I expelled a breath of air I hadn't realized I'd been holding. Joe moved to the table and reached out for the sheet. I grabbed his arm and nodded to the door. "What the hell was that?"

"That," he said as he looked at me, "was Lex. Don't mess with her, Zoë."

"What the hell *is* she?" Dags said in a low voice, as he moved to stand on the opposite side of the body. "Is she human?"

Joe shrugged and pursed his lips. "That is still up in the air. Just don't cross her."

"What do you owe her?" I asked.

"We'll figure that out later." Joe looked at us. "Ready?"

We nodded, and he pulled the sheet back from the head.

It was Boo all right—but her face was frozen into a scream. I took a step back and gasped. So did Dags. He didn't gasp though. "What the hell?"

"Whatever it was she saw before she died," Joe said, "it wasn't pleasant."

Dags shook his head. "It's completely empty."

Joe said, "Are you sure?"

"Yeah, I can call the girls, but they'll say the same thing." And as if on cue, Maureen and Alice appeared on either side of him. They looked down at the body and shook their heads.

"Her soul is gone," Alice said. "Not even a trace of her is left."

"Is this a Symbiont death?" Dags asked as a formality. Though we all assumed the answer was yes.

"No."

???

All three of us looked at Alice. Dags spoke. "What do you mean, no?"

Maureen took a step back.

Alice answered. "There's no Symbiont signature. There's not even a hint of the portal where the Symbiont takes a soul. It's just a shell. As if there'd never been a soul in the body at all."

Joe and I glanced at each other. "So what the hell causes that?" he asked.

I glanced over at Maureen. She was now a good couple of steps back and away from the body, her eyes wide. And her color was a little gray.

"I'm not sure I can say—"

Holy shit, TC said abruptly.

I nearly yelled out. TC had been quiet for so long I'd forgotten he was in there, so his voice startled me. "Geez, don't do that."

"Do what?" Joe said.

I waved him quiet and waited for TC to continue.

Then, *It can't be . . .*

Be what?

"What is it?" Joe asked Alice.

I was watching Maureen as I listened to TC's words.

He sent a—

"Horror—" Maureen yelled out as she pointed to the body.

A Horror, TC echoed.

"A what?" I said out loud. "What does that mean?"

It means, TC said from inside of me, *that we're all dead.*

12

THE three of us—with TC in silent tow—left the coroner's office and drove in silence back to the shop. Alice had pretty much echoed what TC had said in my head—that we were all going to die.

And Maureen had freaked out so badly, she'd disappeared and refused to come back out—and as a physical reaction, Dags's left hand and arm had gone numb.

But what I hadn't gotten yet was what a Horror was or how it connected to anything that was happening.

Though—of course TC hadn't stopped talking in my head, and the internal dialogue was incredibly annoying.

—so much. Yes, I'd always sort of gone around the edges, skirted the actual rules to sample more of the physical plane. He'd tell me to reclaim a contract, and I'd lure them into a false sense of security—you know—yank their souls and have a little fun with the body. No, he wasn't always happy. And then you came along, and I thought I was just going to enjoy

the spoils—how was I supposed to know what would happen? And then there was the Cruorem—

Will. You. Shut. Up!

I put a hand to my head as I watched the traffic on I-20. The constant droning of that asshole's voice had drilled a hole in my brain.

"You okay?" Dags said from the passenger's seat.

I nodded. "Yeah—I'm just—" I'm just what? Possessed by the Symbiont that made me a Wraith and stole my mother's soul—and I'm scared he'll kill an innocent bystander if I—

"Zoë," Joe said from the back. "I know you don't want to hear this—but we need to call—"

I didn't have to hear the rest. "No."

"Look, we don't know what the hell a Horror is—"

"No."

"She would know about this—"

"NO."

You can't win against a Horror, lover.

"Would you both just shut up!" Oh God, that made my head hurt even worse. I whipped the Volvo to the right on the Moreland Avenue exit. Just a few more miles, and I'd be home. And normally I'd go straight to Mom and put my head on her shoulder, and she'd fix me some tea.

You really are a mama's girl, aren't you?

I hated that Symbiont.

"Both?" Dags said. "I didn't say anything."

Damnit—I was going to need to stop referring to TC out loud.

Both men were quiet—well, TC too—as I slowed down and followed the traffic signs to Little Five Points. Two turns and I was pulling into the driveway of Mom's shop. The lights were on, and a white candle burned in the window—Jemmy's sign that all was clear. No oogies in the house.

The three of us entered through the back door behind the kitchen. I stopped in the kitchen and checked the electric kettle I'd bought a month ago. It still had water in it, and I turned it on. I loved those things. Instant hot water without having to heat up the kitchen.

Jemmy shuffled in and pulled me toward her. I faced my mom's neighbor and best friend. Her eyes were sort of yellow on the edges, and I'd noticed she'd had a wheezing cough lately. I wondered—just briefly—if I could still see the death mask, would I see one on her?

"You go get changed and get comfortable. I'll finish the tea. Headache?"

I nodded and gave her a hug. I really did like this woman—even though she'd threatened to shoot me once. And I knew she really cared about my mom.

After changing into loungers and a long-sleeved thermal shirt, I slipped on my killer bunny slippers (complete with pointy teeth), scooped up the tea, and headed to the botanica, not caring if Joe or Dags had stayed. But they had—and they were waiting on me.

"I'm going to call her," Joe said. He was on the sofa. Dags stood by the fireplace where the Soul Catcher had once sat. Before it was broken. Jemmy was seated in the straight-backed chair to Dags's left—one of the ones Jemmy had brought over after rescuing them from a garage sale.

I moved past Joe and curled up on the papasan. "No."

"We don't know what a Horror is," Joe said. "I even asked Jemmy, and she's not sure."

Sipping my tea, I saw the big *Book of Everything* on the coffee table next to a copy of *Pagan Weekly*. "You look in the book?"

Dags nodded. "I did. The only thing it says on a Horror is see Abysmal, Phantasm."

"That's more than we knew before," I said. "Maybe we can just work from there."

"No, we can't, child," Jemmy said. "We need more information on this—we go to Rhonda. Souls are precious, wondrous things, and if there is a creature out there that doesn't just absorb them but consumes them so thoroughly as to leave the body uncorrupted"—she shook her head—"we have to stop that sort of thing, Zoë."

"Stop it?" I leaned forward and set my tea on the coffee table. "And how exactly can we stop it? We? Me? I can't do anything. I can't even see Tim and Steve, and I know they're in here, right?" I looked around the room. No one spoke, but I didn't need to hear them. "What good am I?"

"You're the Wraith," Joe said. "It's not just the Horror we

have to ask her about—we need to talk to her about you too. Why have you lost all your abilities? Why are you suddenly bounced back to mediocre."

"Mediocre?"

Joe smirked. "Did that bother you?"

"Yes."

"Enough to force you to call Rhonda?"

"No."

"Nuts."

"Just as fucking pigheaded as your mama," Jemmy said. "Rhonda wasn't no spy the whole time, and she sure as hell didn't stay one if she was. That girl cared about you, and about Nona."

"That girl betrayed me," I said to her. And then I looked at Joe. "And where the hell were you? I called and called, but you never came. You never fucking came to check on me, or on Nona. You—" I wanted to scream at him: *You kissed me like that and just ran away?*

But I didn't.

I knew TC heard it, but he was unnaturally quiet.

I could sense he was afraid. And he was thinking.

Joe leaned forward, his elbows on his knees. "Zoë, I never got a call from you. Nothing. If I'd known you'd called, I would have answered. What number did you try to reach me at?"

"How the hell should I know what number? It was in that damned phone that psycho bitch gave me."

Well, that brought the new character of Dead Silence into the room. Joe sat back and looked wildly uncomfortable. I sighed and slumped my shoulders. "Sorry."

"No, no." Joe held up his right hand. "That's quite all right. I mean—I knew you were mad at her; I just didn't know you'd sunk to name-calling."

Oh please.

"And if it's any consolation, if it's the number I programmed into that phone myself, I got rid of that number a week after the whole event at Knowles's house. It was an L6 pager number anyway."

I stared at him. "So you never got any of my calls?"

"None. Which I thought meant you were mad at me too. I mean, we knew you were mad at Rhonda, so she's made a point of leaving you—I think she put it 'the hell alone'—to be safe."

I stared at him, not believing what I was hearing. Either Joe didn't know what had happened with Rhonda—ergo why he was still fraternizing with the enemy—or Rhonda had fed him a bunch of lies. Didn't he understand she had betrayed me?

"What?" Joe said.

"Careful," Dags said. "Your head is gonna explode if she keeps staring at you like that."

Joe put his fingers to his lips as if biting his nails and shot a fake-pleading look at Dags. "Can she really do that? Save me, Dags!"

"Fuck you" was about all I could muster, with the bird for emphasis.

"You know, it's kinda sexy when you say it with that voice of yours." Joe looked so damned smug I could have kicked his ass. I considered my situation. *Later. I'll kick his ass later.*

"You know what Rhonda did, right?" I asked.

"Yes. She was assigned by her uncle, the head of the Society of Ishmael, to infiltrate the life of one Zoë Martinique for the purposes of determining if the daughter of Adiran Martinique could possibly pose a threat to mankind once it was known her powers of OOB had developed." He smiled. "Did I get it right?"

I blinked at him. "And you're okay with that? Joe—she lied to me. She pretended to be my friend. I told her everything, shared every fear and booyah moment I've had since I learned I could do this shit."

He gave me a sideways grin. "Booyah moment?"

"She betrayed me, and you're defending her?"

He shrugged and managed to look apologetic. "Look—I won't say what she did was right. But I'm not going to judge her solely on what her attitude was five years ago compared to how she feels now. She discovered that what you were, or what you were becoming, was much more than her uncle or anyone involved in the original experiments could have dreamed of. And she also defended you on many occasions—claimed that your strongest asset wasn't your power, but the moral conscience that guided it."

Dags and I both were staring at him after that speech.

"Whoa," Dags said. "That was deep, dude."

What irked me about what he said—well, besides the fact he said it—was that it made me feel a little bit bad about the way I'd treated Rhonda.

A little bit. I think a part of me knew that—but the smaller part of me—that was the part that wanted to be angry at someone. Anyone. And Rhonda was it.

I cleared my throat. "You spoke to her—to learn this?"

"Yeah—I tried reaching her about two days after her uncle's funeral, and she spilled it all to me—terrified you would never trust her again. I just told her to man-up, strap on her big-girl panties, and move on."

I couldn't help the smile on my face when I digested that comment. "You really said that aloud to her?"

"Yep." And he reached up and pulled his bangs from his forehead to reveal a small scar. "Got the mark to prove it."

I gaped at the wound. "Did she really—"

He grinned.

I stuck my tongue out at him.

"So, will you call her?" Joe said.

"No."

"Well, that's just being stupid, Zoë."

"Joe," Dags said, "once Rhonda was certain she'd made up her mind that Zoë wasn't a threat, and she felt close to her, she should have confided in both Nona and in Zoë as to who she was and why she was there. I can't say I blame Zoë for being angry."

Joe pointed at him. "You stay out of this."

I took offense at that and sat forward. "No, you leave Dags alone. He was with us longer than you were. And he's been through a lot because of it."

"Well, la-di-fucking-da," Joe said as he put his hands on his knees. "Zoë, I don't pretend to approve of what Rhonda did— in the beginning. And yeah, she should have been up-front with you once her loyalties turned from what the Society wanted to what she wanted. She and her uncle. But whether you like it or not, she's the only one, beside your mother, who knows you best and might be able to find out what's happened to your power. It might be some astral flu or something." He paused. "There are real threats out there—this Horror thing is just the tip of the iceberg. Because whether you realize this or not—Rodriguez isn't gone, nor is he that easy to derail on something. He seriously thinks you belong in a lab and under his care. We can protect you—"

Dags was looking at me as he said, "Joe—"

"Just shut up, Dags. Zoë has got to realize she's in real danger here. And her being just a regular girl again is dangerous for all of us. She needs to be Wraith. We need to find out what a Horror is because it's killing people. And there's nothing she can do if she can't even OOB. It's stupid pride that she's holding this grudge against Rhonda. Rhonda's been nothing but supportive of Zoë through everything, and this irresponsible, childish—"

I was on my feet. "Get. Out."

He blinked. "Hello?"

"I said get out. Run, go tell Rhonda—" It was when he'd said, "*We* can protect you." It was all I'd needed to hear, then I'd known it. I wasn't the smartest person—good grief, I was outright stupid most of the time—but there were moments of clarity. And I had one just then. I should have seen it earlier. The way he rarely spoke about Rhonda—how he already knew everything that had happened to me. I thought it was Dags who had filled him in.

No. It was much more sinister for me. Joe was still working alongside Rhonda. They were still in contact. Even now she was still meddling in my life. "How do I know what's happened to me isn't your fault somehow? Or hers? How do I know she didn't slip something in one of those hot chocolates? That she isn't still working for Rodriguez and this is her way of making me easier to overpower?"

Joe looked . . . hurt. Really hurt. And for the first time since I'd met him in that morgue a lifetime ago, there weren't any smug or sardonic lines on his face. There was only a wide-eyed disbelief there.

He stood and retrieved his coat from the edge of the couch. After slipping it on, he looked at Dags. "Good luck. You're gonna need it with this one." And then he looked at me. "Closing yourself off isn't going to bring Nona back, nor is it going to discover what's wrong with you." He left the room without a look back.

"Zoë—"

I was trembling. "Maybe you should leave, Dags," I heard myself saying. I felt—burned. Scorched. All the way to the middle of my body. I knew on some level I was in the middle of them all. Dags and Daniel were friends who met at Fadó's, and I knew Joe and Dags's friendship had grown because of me.

But right now I didn't want anybody around.

Why?

Because I wanted a good old-fashioned cry. I wanted to boohoo big-time into my pillow and not care who heard me. I was scared out of my fucking mind. There was a nutcase out there who wanted to experiment on me, a ghost-hunter dude who was blaming me for his girlfriend's death, something was killing people, and I didn't even know who the other victims were or if they were related to me in some weird way like Boo was, and my mom wasn't here.

I couldn't even see or speak to Tim or Steve.

Dags nodded. He reached into his jacket pocket and pulled out an iPhone and set it on the coffee table. "Here—I added it to my plan, so don't call Tokyo—okay?"

He waited a few seconds before moving to the arch between the two shops, then stopped. "I put Daniel's new number in it as well. He gave it to me the other day. It might not hurt to call him."

I cleared my throat, but my eyes were already burning, and a tear escaped the lower lid of my left eye. "He wouldn't come."

"I would." Dags moved to the front door, opened it, and did exactly what I'd asked him to do.

13

The white box

JEMMY was still in the botanica when I broke down. She took me in her arms and guided me to the stairs as I bawled, then pushed me to go up and wash my face. I needed sleep. I wasn't a creature from a different plane anymore. I was just plain old me, and I needed rest.

She brought up tea after I'd climbed into bed, and the cry felt good—really—though I fell asleep after a few sips of the chamomile. Jemmy had even pulled out my kit and checked my sugar—which was low—and I realized I hadn't eaten anything since lunch. A small part of me wondered about that— my sugar—since we'd always believed it was a physical side effect of my going OOB.

Or Wraith.

TC was unnaturally quiet when I finally put my head on the pillow. I thought about asking him what he thought, then decided I really didn't want to know. I was supposed to hate him. Despise him. Fight him. Destroy him.

Yeah. Right.

* * *

I was looking at that box again. It had several things scribbled on the side, but I couldn't make them out, not in the light of the basement. Bobby was so insistent that I just go take a look. But I was more scared of what Mom would do to me if I did.

"I don't believe you," I finally said, and faced him. "I need to get back upstairs and do that paper."

But when I turned away, Bobby showed up in front of me again, his hands on his hips. "Have I ever lied to you?"

I smirked at him and crossed my hands over my chest. I wondered idly if I'd ever really get breasts. Carlene and JoAnne had them, and they were three whole months younger than me! "Yes."

"Well, never mind that. I'm not lying about this. You've got to look in that box."

"Why?"

He opened his mouth, then closed it before he lifted his small shoulders. "Just so's you know I'm not lying. I really saw stuff in there from your dad."

I knew it was wrong—most of what I did was wrong these days, always making Mom mad. But Bobby was a friend, and he kept me company on those long nights while Mom worked. "Okay—I'll look."

The stepladder was still there where I thought Mom had used it before. I went up and looked at the box. The side facing me had a hole in it—a handle created out of a punched-through side. What if I reached out and something came out of that hole?

"Chicken," Bobby said.

"Shut—up!" I hissed. With a deep breath, I reached up to the box—

Something did come out of that hole—it was a human hand, only the skin was peeled back and it was all bloody and I screamed and felt myself falling and Bobby was calling my name—

OH *God*, I hate nightmares.

Tiny creatures, like little evil yard gnomes, carved out a

home in my brain as I sat up. Crying before sleep—not always a good thing for me. In the shower, I let the water run over my face and just stood there for a long time. The radio reported slightly cloudy skies and a good chance for showers. I dried off, donned my fuzzy robe, and shuffled to the mirror.

After staring at my remarkably unspecial face I cleared my throat. "Are you still there?"

I felt a stirring inside of my chest. It was like a flutter of nervousness.

Yeah, I'm still here.

"Please come out so I can see you."

I'm afraid I can't do that anymore. If I leave your body, you won't see me or hear me unless I overshadow someone else.

I blinked. "What?"

You've digressed back to life in the physical plane in its simplest form. I can't explain it, but I know if I leave you—

I put my hands on the sink's edge and took a deep breath. "What exactly does that mean? What am I going to do?"

You cannot defeat a Horror like this.

I splashed water on my face. I wanted to throw up. "So the Phantasm has won?"

No one else can command a Horror, Zoë.

"Does he make them—like he made you?"

There was a pause. *No. They're mistakes—but the kind of mistakes he takes advantage of. Horrors usually form with the right conditions—though I'm not sure what those are. I think he hoped when he created me I'd become one. When I didn't, I was sure he was very disappointed.*

I grabbed a brush. I didn't know what to do. I was completely clueless.

"You need to get Nona back here," Jemmy said from the doorway to the bathroom. I'd forgotten I'd opened it to let the hot steam out when I wiped the mirror.

"I don't know how to get Nona back." I couldn't OOB; there was no way I could step into the Abysmal like this. Not even Dags knew what to do.

I thought of my dream . . . of the box in the basement in our old house. Was it really a dream? "Jemmy . . . you ever seen a white box in the basement?"

"White box?" She nodded slowly. "Yeah. There are several

white boxes. But your mom went through them when she moved into this house—did a bit of cleaning. You looking for something in particular?"

Yes . . . and no. Maybe. From all of this I'd learned I was born Irin—a Watcher. I realized my dad had technically died before I was conceived. And yet he'd continued a life with my mom after the lab fire and had raised me. And as an Irin—what did that mean for me? Now that I couldn't Wraith—had I lost that part of myself as well?

Oh, damnit! I threw the brush across the bathroom. It bounced on the floor and skirted to a stop by the shower. "I don't know what to do!"

"Well, I'm no expert here," Jemmy said. "But it's Wednesday morning. Bakery's delivering in about ten minutes, and I need some help getting the shop ready to open. I suggest you get dressed and come help me. Maybe the answer will present itself."

It was busywork, and I knew it. But I helped like she asked. After throwing my hair into a braid and putting on a long-sleeved tee shirt, jeans, and my SpongeBob slippers, I unpacked cakes and cookies, pies and teas. I boiled water for the carafe for Tea of the Day, and cleaned up in the botanica and rearranged two of the shelves where the books had been messed up.

I snacked on tea and lemon spice cake, a poppy-seed muffin, and a tall glass of water. The customers were regulars—a few of them I knew as Rhonda's friends. They were friendly, polite, and sat out on the porch in the warmer weather or bought stuff from the botanica. A part of me wasn't sure they weren't there to spy on me.

But at the moment, I didn't care. I wanted a normal day. And then I was going to see my mom again.

And it was normal—until Captain Kenneth Cooper walked in.

He nodded at me as he sauntered up, putting his hands palms down on the refrigerator case. "Morning, Zoë."

I nodded to him. "Hi."

"You seen Daniel?"

I shook my head. "I saw Joe last night. He left here about ten or so. I haven't seen Daniel since yesterday morning."

He nodded and ordered a piece of the spice cake, then a chai tea to go. "Zoë, we've put out an APB on Randall Kemp.

Apparently one of his SPRITE friends told Halloran he was making threats against you—so I'd like for you to be careful. I'll get Mastiff over here as soon as possible to keep an eye on you."

Mastiff had been the officer to "keep an eye on" me before, when I snuck off in November and got kidnapped by Reverend Rollins. I wasn't sure he was the bomb that Cooper thought he was. I'd heard he recently made detective, so babysitting me seemed sort of a shit job. "I'll be going to Miller Oaks this afternoon."

"Is Dags going with you?"

I shook my head. "No, he left last night too."

"Zoë"—he leaned in close after a quick conspiratorial look around—"I looked him up—yesterday. You know he's like Halloran, right?"

"Like Halloran in that he believes in ghosts and alien abduction?"

Cooper's expression softened into a smirk. "So you already knew?"

"Yeah."

"Did you know that he also goes by the name McKinty?"

"That's his bartending name," I said. "It's his mother's name."

"Okay." He straightened up. "As long as you trust him. I don't."

I packed up the cake, poured the steaming water from the kettle into an insulated cup, and dropped a chai tea bag in it before putting on the lid. "Is that because you can't find anything else on him?"

Cooper took the cup and nodded. "Yes. If you see Daniel, tell him he's fired."

He started to leave, but I reached across the counter and grabbed his coat. He turned with raised eyebrows. "Captain— has he not reported in or something?"

"Nope. Not since Monday. This mystery case needs manpower. Joe's already on the case. And as much as I dislike Halloran—he's been a good cop. Well"—he nodded to me— "watch out. Mastiff will be here after lunch."

And true to his word, Detective Mastiff stepped inside the shop just after the lunch crowd started. He nodded to me and took up a chair in the corner of the tea shop. It wasn't a big shop, and Mastiff was a pretty large man—large as in broad. I figured he worked out because I doubted that shoulders were actually born that big.

He was a handsome man, with amber eyes, close-cut hair, and smooth dark skin. If I didn't know who he was, at a glance, I'd say he resembled Denzel Washington, only without the Day-Glo teeth. His suit was impeccable, and Jemmy served him tea and cake on the house.

It was close to two before I felt comfortable leaving Jemmy alone in the shop. Mastiff followed me out, and I gave him the directions to Miller Oaks. He offered to drive me, but I figured that wasn't necessary. He decided just to meet me there and was already out the door (probably to get away from the emo crowd that tended to hang out and surf the Net) when Jemmy called out for me.

"You got a phone call."

I did? I hadn't even heard it ring. "Can you take a message?"

"I already tried." She came out of the kitchen with the store portable in her hand. "But he insists he has to talk to you now."

Ah geez. I hoped it wasn't the doctor at Miller Oaks, wanting to shift my mom's body around again. I liked the private room. I wanted the private room. And as long as I could work to keep affording it, I would. Until I got her back.

Though I knew on some level that time for that was running out.

With a nod I took the phone and moved out the front door to the porch. No one was out there at the moment. The breeze was still chilly, and the sun didn't reach beneath the roof. I moved down the steps to the sun. "Hello?"

"Please walk to the sidewalk, and no one will get hurt."

I frowned at the phone—was this some sort of fucking joke? I put it back to my ear. "Joe? Is that you? That's not a funny thing to say."

There was a very pregnant pause.

"You can talk?"

Wait . . . that wasn't Joe's voice. And it wasn't Dags's either. It was sort of familiar—but not very.

"Yeah, I can talk. Who is this?"

"J-just do as I say, and no one gets hurt."

Yeah. Right. I pulled the phone away, looked at it, and pressed the disconnect button. Jerk.

Shaking my head, I turned to walk back in—

Get down!

TC's voice was a bellow inside of my head, and I don't know if I actually bent forward because he'd deafened me, or I did what he commanded. But when I did go forward, something whizzed over me and struck the wood railing on the porch to my right. I lifted my head and saw a red pompom sticking out of the back of a silver bullet.

Ack! I'd seen one of those before! A tranq! Who?

You better move!

And I did—I tried to run up the steps of the porch into the shop—

But something knocked into my ass—and fuck if that didn't sting! I landed to the right, just beside a white rocking chair on the porch. I managed to reach behind and put my hand on the tranquilizer where it protruded out of my left butt cheek—

14

I often wondered what a normal life would be like. I think I had one once. Simple days. Dealing with irate and rude customers, coming home, drinking a glass of cheap wine and just relaxing for the evening. A phone call from Mom or a girlfriend.

I think I even had a real boyfriend once. One who would bring me flowers, take me to dinner and a movie. Snuggle. Make love.

But those days just seemed soooo long ago. Especially now as I woke up with a mind-cracking headache, a sore ass cheek, and a parched mouth. It didn't take long to realize why my mouth was parched. There was something shoved in it.

Tasted like shit.

I opened my eyes and looked around. I was in a bedroom—that was obvious because I was on my side on a bed. It wasn't a very decorative bedroom. Blank white walls—not even a poster. An open closet with a few things hung up inside. I could see shoes on the floor. There was a nightstand with a clock blinking 1:19 over and over, so that was unreliable. And there was a Dollar Store lamp.

As for my condition—I discovered I was trussed up like a turkey. My hands were painfully tied behind my back and somehow attached to my ankles, which were drawn up to my ass. Whoever it was that shot me wanted to make damn sure I didn't get out of this.

You finally awake?

Well, I could "mmfff" at him, the bastard.

I can hear your thoughts, luv. Though I will admit being inside of you all tied up is a turn-on.

Phreak. Okay, so where are we?

As to where—I'd say north of the city. Near Alpharetta or Roswell.

Do you know who yet? Or why?

Not really. I know it was two young men—both of them so scared that I was intoxicated by their fear.

So why didn't you, like, jump out and suck their souls or something?

Now, I'm not really one to condone the intentional killing of human beings, but if it saves my bacon—then booyah.

Because when you're unconscious, it's nearly impossible for me to step out. And right now, being inside of you is safer than being outside of you. Remember, the Guardian's bitches have a piece of me still—and they could seriously jeopardize my plan if they knew I was here.

I frowned—as best as possible with something foul shoved into my mouth and taped in place. *You have a plan?*

Before he answered me, the door opened and two people came in. I thought I might pretend to still be unconscious, but then I figured, what the hey?

I did manage to make some really loud muffled protests when I recognized the two guys.

Randall Kemp and Ron Beaumont. Members of SPRITE. I hadn't seen Ron since that night at the house on Web Ginn House Road when the poltergeist shoved the camera into his head. Randall came to the bed first and, before I could gather my wits, slapped me hard across the face. "You bitch."

Ow, ow, ow.

"Hey, that wasn't necessary. You said it was that ghost that killed Boo." Ron took a step closer to Randall, but I did notice he kept his distance, like he was unsure about the entire situation.

"According to Mr. F, she's the one that controls that spirit.

Not the other way around, like I thought." He refocused his very-balled-up anger at me. "And I'd been worried about you, that you were being haunted by that entity, and I risked my reputation to try and save you—and got arrested! And all this time you're nothing more than a Ceremonial Magician— binding spirits to you and controlling them!"

I blinked.

And then I blinked again. Hello? What channel were you watching? Ceremonial Magician? That wasn't *my* gig—that was old Allard Bonville's gig. I'd never ceremonially done anything in my life. So, yeah, I started to protest but didn't get very far. Just a lot of "mfff" and "mwwwf."

Very annoying.

"Yeah, and Mr. F said she couldn't talk either, and she'd be really easy to kidnap."

Who the hell was this Mr. F? Who did I know whose name had an F in it and wanted me kidnapped—

Oh no.

Oh fucking no.

Rodriguez. *Francisco* Rodriguez.

That bastard had conned these two—he'd brainwashed them into thinking I was evil and needed to be kidnapped. He had someone else doing his dirty work for him. And Randall could be so gullible! I tried breaking free again, but that was useless. These two had been good Boy Scouts in their youth— the knots weren't slipping.

And my entire right side was getting numb.

They've cut off the circulation. You might want to get out of here . . .

How can I do that? I can't even OOB to sneak up behind them!

Oh. Yeah.

Ack! Symbionts were useless.

But then Randall moved to the other side of the bed and pulled at the hog-tie. Another pull, and my legs snapped forward from the strain. Then he moved to the foot of the bed and pulled me by my feet until my knees were on the mattress's edge. Ron helped me sit up—being a lot more gentle—as Randall pulled out a pocketknife and cut the ropes off my ankles.

"Stand up."

That was easier said than done—left foot asleep. So I nearly fell back down. *Christ. How long had I been in that position?*

"Randall—maybe we should just use the handcuffs in front? I think her legs went to sleep—"

But Randall was up and had the knife pointed at Ron. "What is wrong with you? Do you have feelings for this bitch? She killed Boo, Ron."

Randall's voice had cracked, and I really felt bad for him. I needed to tell him I didn't touch Boo but that something called a Horror had. And, you know, I figured he was a Ghost Hunter—he'd believe me, right?

In my dreams.

The two of them supported my shuffling feet out of the bedroom, down a hall, and down the stairs to a kitchen. The rest of the house was just as undecorated as the bedroom—like it was a brand-new home, and the owners hadn't moved in yet.

We stopped at a door by the refrigerator (nice stainless steel!). It led to a basement.

Oh great, another basement.

But this basement was finished, with berber carpet, a bathroom, and—

Wow. It was a mad scientist's wet dream down here. Worktables full of electronic gizmos, shelves of machine-looking things with Peg-Board along the walls. And there were tools everywhere. I even saw a cot to the side and a stack of *Playboy* magazines. I got the impression that this was where Randall lived. They led me to the farthest corner to what looked like a glass shower.

Then Randall stopped me and cut the rope off of my hands. I started to reach up and pull the tape off, but he shoved me forward before I could. I stumbled into the shower and nearly plastered my forehead into the opposite side. I heard the door closing and turned in time to see them shut me inside.

Not wasting any more time, I pulled the tape—duct tape!—off my mouth, spit out the wad of whatever the fuck that was, swallowed, and yelled, "What the hell are you doing?"

Uh-oh. Zoë, this is bad.

Yah think?

Randall moved away to a table on my right. On that table

was a box with switches, a dial, and lots of blinking lights. "Mr. F said the evil resided inside of you. That if I applied my ray to your soul, it would split you in half and I would see the monster that attacked us at Web Ginn House and see the Symbiont that possesses you."

Monster? Symbiont?

Hey, are you sure they don't know you're in here? I mean, he did say monster.

I think he's referring to you—when you walked astrally.

Oh. Shit. But I didn't do that anymore. I cleared my throat again. I was parched. And light-headed. I had no idea what time it was, or if it was the same day. "Randall, listen to me, what you saw back then was me out of body, understand? I used to be able to slip outside of my body at will and do things. It's called a Wraith, and—"

A bright light filled the shower and every muscle in my body seized up. I screamed and screamed until my voice ran dry. There was a wrenching feeling from the middle of my chest—I was slipping—

And then I was on the floor of the shower. I could see but not control my vision. I could hear and I knew I was still alive and in my body—but I couldn't move. I was propped up against the side like a rag doll.

ARCHER! Help me!

But he didn't answer.

And then I heard Randall and Ron screaming. I couldn't move my head or my eyes to see—but I could hear them running. And shouting.

"That's not what we saw before, Randall!"

"What the fuck is that?"

There was a scream, then a crash, then a door slamming.

And nothing.

I tried to scream for help. Something. Anything. I couldn't move a muscle. What the fuck had that bastard done to me? It was obvious TC had been forced out—especially if Randall had used a shower version of his Ghost Zapper. *But what's happening to me?*

Help.

Please! Somebody!

* * *

I heard a voice, soft and gentle, and hadn't realized I was asleep with my eyes open.

". . . happened? Oh shit, she's not responding."

I knew that voice. It was Dags.

Dags was here. He'd found me!

"They haven't caught Kemp yet, but Beaumont turned himself in." That was Captain Cooper's voice!

And then I could see him, kneeling in front of me, waving his hand in front of my eyes. "What the hell did they do to her? Drugs?"

"I don't know," Dags said. "I don't fucking know." His voice sounded strained. Upset.

"I'll call an ambulance. And once I know she's safe, I want a word with you on how you knew where she was."

I felt a touch on my arm, and Dags's soft voice in my ear. "I'm here, Zoë. Everything's okay."

I tried to sob but still couldn't move. Everything was not okay. I heard and felt Dags beside me, but I remembered a time when Daniel cared, when I felt his touch on my arm as he tucked me into bed, and *he* whispered, "Everything's okay, Zoë. I'm here to protect you."

No.

You're not.

Not anymore.

And it's all my fault.

15

APPARENTLY Mr. Kemp shot me with a high dose of electricity in some sort of Tesla invention he'd re-created in the basement of the home he and Boo had just bought. Just bought—as a present to get married—and then she'd been killed.

I felt really bad when I heard that. Poor guy needed someone to blame, and Mr. F, aka Francisco Rodriguez, had played on the anxiety and grief to make him blame me. Though from what I was figuring out, as I lay in a bed at North Fulton Hospital (yes, come with me and take a tour of all of Atlanta's finest money suckers) and flipped channels, bored out of my skull, I don't think Randall's sidebar to the Shocking Shower was part of Francisco's plan. Though it did have a very eerie similarity to the images I'd seen in Randall's head a month or so ago, of me in a glass tube but as a ghost.

Shudder.

As for my temporary paralysis—they were still figuring out how that happened. My assumption was that it had something to do with TC being shoved out of my body by the Shocking Shower. I didn't know for sure, and it wasn't a question I wanted to ask Jemmy or Dags, especially since they didn't know I'd had TC inside of me all that time. And I didn't think they'd be too happy about it.

Right now I was waiting on Dags to call me back. I had left him a message that I wanted out, and I wanted new clothes. I wanted to go see Mom. And I was seriously thinking of somehow sneaking into Rodriguez's house and stealing back the Summoning Eidolon. I mean—that would bring Mom back, right?

Or I thought so. I mean, someone had suggested that before, hadn't they?

The door opened, and I sat up, tossing the remote on the bed. "Finally."

But Dags wasn't who walked in. It wasn't the doctor; it was Cooper.

"Uh . . . hi, Captain. Is there something I can—"

"Just get dressed," he said, and opened the small cupboard where my clothes from earlier had been hung up. They weren't the cleanest clothes I had, and I really wanted new underwear. I could go commando, but I didn't really want to.

He threw my clothes at me before moving back to the door and cracking it, peeking through.

This was not typical Cooper behavior. Not. At. All. And it was creeping me out. I got up, happy there were no tubes or IVs this time, and tiptoed to the bathroom. I changed, minus panties, and came back out. He was still at the door.

"Look, Dags is supposed to be bringing me—"

"The Guardian ain't coming right now," Cooper said as he glanced back at me. "That bastard's already seen to that."

Then I stopped in my tracks. Guardian? Cooper would never have referred to Dags as a Guardian. Only one other person had called him that.

I pointed at him, and yelled out, "Get out of Cooper's body, you ass—"

But he was on me in seconds with his hand firmly smashing my lips against my teeth. "Damnit, you idiot. I liked it better when you were quiet."

I fought for a second before my old training kicked in. I relaxed, waited on him to relax, and when he did, I struck. TC was behind me, his left hand pinning my arms to my body while he kept his right hand over my mouth. But there was nothing stopping my legs. I took a huge breath through my nose and brought my right foot backward, slamming my heel into the soft parts between Cooper's legs.

I'd hoped that while being inside of Cooper's body, TC would have the same physical feelings. He'd talked about it once, how a Symbiont can experience the physical plane by overshadowing a body. I hoped he felt the pain down there.

The grunt and subsequent releasing of me pretty much nailed it that I was right. I moved away from him as fast as I could, then spun to face him, in ready stance. "You bastard . . . what did you do with Dags? And where is Cooper? Did you kill him too?"

But TC wasn't in any real position to talk naturally. He was hunched over on his knees, his hands clutching his crotch. *Hrm. Maybe I hit him too hard?*

No. Not hard enough.

"Where is Dags?" I demanded.

TC took several deep breaths, but his eyes were watering. "He's . . . whoo . . . that sucks . . ." His voice was pitched a little higher. I couldn't help but smile. Really. Can you blame me? Though I did feel a little bad for the captain. He shook his head as if to clear cobwebs. "He's been . . . arrested. The bastard . . . I think Rodriguez knows . . . what the Guardian is . . . and he's trying to get him . . . ouch . . ." He took another deep breath. "When I can stand again, I'm going kill you."

"Try it," I said. "Dags's been arrested? Why? Where is Cooper?"

"Cooper's fine." TC managed to stand, though a bit unsteadily. "He's still here. And he's going to remember you kicking him in the nuts. I'll make sure of it."

Oh. Great. That'll just improve my relationship with Cooper soooo much.

I took a step back.

But TC only held up Cooper's arms. "Would you back off? I'm not trying to hurt you—I'm trying to save both our asses. There's a Horror out there, Zoë. And it's well hidden. I can't sense it."

"And you're scared of it."

"Damn straight," he said. "Everything in the Abysmal, except the Phantasm, is terrified of them. Almost as much as a Wraith."

I frowned. "Okay, so I don't get that," I said.

"And I don't have time to educate you. We have got to get out of here."

"So you got away from Randall and Ron?"

He grinned. Okay. I decided right then I didn't like the way Cooper looked when he grinned. Not at all. It was damned creepy. Especially when I knew it wasn't Cooper looking out at me. "I smoked those two bastards. Sorry for leaving your body in shock like that."

"Yeah . . . exactly why—"

"Because I tried to hang on. Shock to your system."

"Don't do that again."

"Aye, aye, Captain. Now, can we leave?"

"Why?"

He pointed to the door behind me. "The nurses' station is right through there. Take a look for me. Just peek out there."

I wasn't that happy about turning my back on him, and I think he realized my hesitation.

"Look, I'm not here to hurt you, dipshit. If you get killed, then we're all in a shitload of trouble."

I didn't really understand that statement then, but later it would all make sense.

Moving to the door, I did what I'd seen him do earlier and peeked out. To my left was the nurses' station.

Lots of bustle, but I had a bird's-eye view.

"Oh! There you are," came Chapal's voice. Chapal (Cha-PAL) was the doctor who had examined me when I'd been brought in all catatonic and shit.

And then there was a movement by the nurses' station and a man in an expensive suit appeared and reached out his hand to an approaching Chapal.

I didn't recognize him at first as they shook hands. And then I heard his voice. Deep. Melodic.

He turned to say something to one of the nurses behind the station, and I saw his profile.

Francisco Rodriguez.

OH MY STARS AND GARTERS!

What is he doing here?

"You see him?" TC said.

I waved at him to shush. The last thing I wanted was for the asswipe to see me looking at him.

They were talking, then I heard the ding of an elevator nearby. Rodriguez turned and smiled.

What I didn't expect to see was Detective Daniel Frasier come into view.

"Ah—Detective. I'm so glad you could come." Rodriguez offered him his hand.

To my happiness, Daniel didn't take it. He only looked at Chapal, then Rodriguez before he spoke. "I'm not exactly sure why you would need me here," Daniel said. "I've pretty much washed my hands of her."

My heart clenched, and I leaned against the doorframe. Blood rushed into my ears, and I missed what was said next. I could feel TC behind me, listening as well.

". . . our attention—through my own sources—that you could sign the final paper."

"Paper for what exactly?"

Daniel was leaning up against the station. Chapal stood opposite Daniel, and Rodriguez was on his right. I was shaking and couldn't stop.

"You are aware of Miss Martinique's rather colorful medical history?"

Daniel sighed. "Yeah. She claims she's diabetic."

"No claim, Detective," Chapal said. "She is. But what we're worried about is that she's noncompliant when it comes to taking care of herself. She's repeatedly been back in the hospital, mostly through her own fault. And one of Dr. Maddox's notes on her clearly states that she's a danger to herself. She can't be trusted to take care of her own body. She also has a dying mother in a long-term facility, correct?"

Daniel straightened up and shoved his hands into his pockets. "Yes. So what you're wanting me to do is sign papers to have her committed? Doc, sir, I'm not a medical professional—"

"No, you are not—" Chapal interjected.

Daniel put up his right hand, and the doctor quieted. "But it seems to me there's something illegal here. Zoë might be a bit of a klutz, and she's somewhat careless, but she's not crazy. If you seriously say she's diabetic, then my suggestion is that you educate her and not condemn her." He turned to go. "And please, don't call me in for something like this again—" He focused on Rodriguez. "And if I'm not mistaken, there's a restraining order issued for you to keep your distance from Miss Martinique."

Rodriguez physically paled, and a part of me was cheering inside. Yes, he didn't care about me anymore, but at least he would champion me sometimes! *Yay!*

"I suggest you leave the premises. I'll be outside watching."

"Well, bully for the old squeeze," TC whispered in my ear. "Didn't know he had it in him."

I elbowed him in the ribs. "Shush."

We waited there as Chapal and Rodriguez spoke quietly, then went in different directions.

"Okay, I say we go now," TC said. "I don't think anyone's going to question you with me. But just in case, I'm armed." And he indicated the holster and Cooper's Glock.

I was not happy—a Symbiont had a gun. Unless he used it on Rodriguez. Then I'd be his cheerleader.

We were able to move past the nurses' station—with only a few curious glances. TC nodded just like Cooper would, then we were on the elevator to the parking level.

It was dark outside—and still cold. The days in the South at the beginning of spring were always a lot warmer than the nights. And I wasn't dressed for it. I shivered as I followed TC to Cooper's car. And I was pretty surprised to see Mastiff sitting behind the wheel.

Being very quiet and very still.

"What did you—"

TC put up his hands. "He's fine. Just a Daimon I conjured to keep Mastiff minding me. He figured out real quick something was wrong when I couldn't drive. So I needed him to drive."

"Release him. Now."

"No can do. I can't drive."

"No, but I can. Just get that thing out of him and let him go. He shouldn't be a part of this."

TC pursed Cooper's lips and held up his left hand. A red dot formed there—an all-too-familiar red dot—and Mastiff suddenly slumped forward over the wheel. It took a little bit for

TC to get him out of the car and propped up against the nearby concrete support pillar.

Once in the car, I backed it out, and we were on the road.

"Oh, here," TC said from the passenger's side. He leaned forward and opened the glove compartment and pulled out the Ghost Zapper. "I got this from Randall's house after I over-shadowed Cooper. It'll come in handy later."

I shivered again when I saw it. I'd been shot with that thing twice—once while OOB, then again when I'd been overshadowing Randall. Both times it hurt. Really hurt. "So you think we can use it on the Horror?"

But TC was looking at the road as I got on the interstate. "I don't know," he said. "But I'm willing to try anything."

16

WE went back to Nona's house, and Jemmy was there. She fixed tea and sliced cake. Joe called the shop line and said he'd managed to get Dags out of jail thanks to a phone call from Cooper. TC excused himself when he learned the Guardian was on his way.

I followed him outside—Jemmy hadn't seemed to notice anything.

"Your ghost friends know it's me, but for some reason they haven't told your maid."

"That's not my maid. God, you're such a jerk."

He smiled. Nope. Still didn't like that expression on Cooper. "Yes, I am. I'm going to grab a train back to that coroner. I recognized the Symbiont hosted inside of her—I think she can help me."

Whoa. Hold the phone. "You mean the friend of Joe's? The creepy giant? She's got a Symbiont in her?"

"Well, yeah. You don't think she's gotten to her age by staying human, do you? Zoë, there isn't just one kind of Symbiont. Myself"—and he put his hands on his chest for emphasis—"I'm not like any other one. That's thanks in part to you. But there are Symbionts for control, those for contracts—like the one that possessed Rollins. But that Symbiont didn't want to give up the body or the soul at the end of the contract. I'm not sure if Rollins's soul was in complete agreement with that." He shrugged. "But there are older Symbionts, part of the first brood, you might say. The Phantasm's first children. Those Symbionts he sent out to the physical plane to experience life—only, not understanding how the physical plane interacts with the Abysmal, those Symbionts had to find a way to sustain themselves inside of their hosts."

I blinked at him. "And?"

"They discovered that blood is a good manna, you might say." His, or rather Cooper's, eyebrows moved up and down. "They change a host's body at its genetic roots in order to accommodate their own needs. But the hosts are treated to one hell of a ride. Long life—give or take a century. Excellent health. And a unique craving."

I blinked again. "They drink blood?"

"Uh-huh. Not my style. Too messy. And those Symbionts are pretty boring, but they are powerful. Like the one inside of that coroner—I think her name is Hebe. And I think she could sense me but couldn't find me."

I was still on the drinking-blood thing . . . So there *was* such a thing as a vampire. Sort of.

Er . . . not really. But close enough for nachos.

On some level, I knew TC was defending Symbionts, and I got it that they weren't inherently evil—kinda like tofu. It didn't really taste like anything on its own, but once you cooked it with something, it took on the flavor of the food.

Okay . . . bad analogy, but you get what I'm sayin'.

I thought of Hirokumi and of his offering his daughter's soul as payment. And when it was all said and done, it wasn't the Symbiont that had been evil—it was the man.

The human.

Abruptly, he kissed me. TC actually bent down in Cooper's body and *kissed* me.

ACK!

I sure hoped Cooper didn't remember THAT!

And then he was gone, into the night, just like a spirit. And I had to wonder—I'd never asked—do Symbionts give their hosts special abilities?

Needed to figure that one out.

It was dawn by the time Joe and Dags arrived. I filled them in on what I had seen and heard, between Daniel and Rodriguez, and that Cooper had left to go track Daniel down and put out an arrest warrant on Rodriguez for breaking the restraining order.

What I learned from them was that after I was taken from the shop by Randall and Ron, Mastiff called to see if I'd ever left. He'd arrived at Miller Oaks, checked on Mom, and waited. After a half hour he started getting worried. Jemmy called Dags, who in turn put a call in to Joe. Joe called Cooper because Randall's van—complete with SPRITE logo—had been seen near the Botanica and Tea Shop.

Not finding them at Randall's apartment, they'd questioned another SPRITE member, Herb Maupin, who swore he had no idea where they were. But he did confess that Randall had asked to meet up with him at Zesto's in Little Five Points. But Herb had already had plans so he'd said no.

"Cooper was sure it was Randall, after he made those threats," Joe said as he lounged back on the couch with his socked feet (dingy-socked feet) on the coffee table, a cup of tea in his hand. "But we had no idea where he'd taken you."

I was on the papasan—my favorite place of relaxation. I had a blanket, Jemmy's incredible chai tea, and my Godzilla slippers on. I'd managed to get a brush through my hair, and Jemmy had french braided it to keep it out of my face. I was seriously thinking of shaving it off.

"So how did you know about Randall's house?"

Joe pointed at Dags. He was sitting in front of the fireplace, stoking the flames. He'd changed into a black tee shirt and jeans. "Remember how we have a piece of TC? Well, Maureen's tuned to it—being a part of the Abysmal plane herself. And when he was forced out of your body—"

Whoa! Hold the phone! I sat forward and narrowed my eyes at him. "You knew TC was in my body?"

Dags gave me an interestingly complex expression that meant "Yeah, you dumb broad" and "How could you be so stupid?" all at the same time. I didn't like that look on him. "I didn't at first. But after Maureen told me she suspected it, I started paying attention." He smiled. "Not to mention all the ridiculous talking to yourself you kept doing. So I figured he was hiding in you, and since you seemed okay, I assumed he wasn't in there to harm you." He set the poker down. "You're his meal ticket."

"That was dumb, Zoë," Joe said, and set his tea on a side table, just in front of a bottom-heavy goddess figure. He glanced at the big-butted statue, and his eyebrows perked for a second before he looked back at me. "If you don't tell us when TC decides to possess you, we're not going to trust you anymore."

"He didn't possess me." Did he think my butt was as big as the statue's?

"Anyway," Dags said, "when it forced TC's essence or spirit or what have you out of your body—"

I nodded. "Then it was like a blink'n beacon."

Dags smiled. I really liked it when he smiled. "Yeah. It was like looking at Google maps and seeing a huge YOU ARE HERE sign pointing to a particular spot. We checked it with Cooper and found it was a new subdivision in Alpharetta. And there was a house recently closed on by Randall Kemp and Boo Baskins. Apparently they were getting married."

I watched his face. "What? What else?"

Joe cleared his throat. "Boo was pregnant. Cooper got the call from Lex this morning."

Oh God. Boo was pregnant? No wonder Randall was seriously pissed off. His life had been taken from him. And Rodriguez was using him.

I explained my theories, that Randall's little trip in the Shocking Shower wasn't part of what Rodriguez wanted.

"Yeah, but what could that be?" Dags said.

"I assume it's the same thing he always wanted." I shrugged. "To prove the existence of ghosts—or just the existence of something beyond ourselves. Remember, he and his group went through publicity hell back in October of last year—and technically it's my fault." Well, it wasn't my fault all his tapes disappeared and his funding went south. "But the joke's on him." I beamed. "I ain't no Wraith no mo'."

"That's not really funny." Joe spoke up. "Not being Wraith makes you a hundred times more vulnerable. He knows you're not helpless—that you can defend yourself physically. Which is why, I'm sure, he told Randall and Ron to tranq you. But I have the suspicion that his motives are a lot more sinister than that."

I glanced at Dags. He frowned at me and turned to face Joe. "You care to elaborate on that theory? Your source tell you something you haven't told us?"

Source? Oh . . . Rhonda. And then the anger I'd felt at the two of them came back. Not as powerful. It was more like a slight thunderstorm than a full-out hurricane.

Dags picked up on it and held out his hand as he faced the wrath of my glare. "Hey, I wasn't in on this, remember? I was out of town. I found out about it when I got back in town and came over."

Okay. Excuse accepted. And he did look kinda cute sitting in front of the fire. So I turned my glare to Joe.

"Don't you get all high-and-mighty on me, little girl. You're the one running around here with a Symbiont inside of her—one she claimed was like her arch nemesis or something. Her Lex Luthor. I don't think your judgment in any of this is reliable at the moment. But your beef with Rhonda is *your* beef. You need to get your head on straight and stop acting like this is some movie. This is real shit, Zoë. You are vulnerable. Get Rhonda's insight on a few things happening in the background."

"What things?"

"Not for me to tell."

He made sense. He was right. But I just wasn't ready to let her betrayal mean nothing. I was mad. And, damnit—I deserved a good bout of mad.

Right? I thought so.

After a long silence: "I want to steal the Summoning Eidolon back."

I expected Joe or Dags to raise a stink. You know, yell at me and tell me I was crazy. Luckily, Jemmy was puttering in the kitchen and hadn't heard me.

"Back from whom?" Joe said.

"Rodriguez."

"He doesn't have it."

I raised my eyebrows. "Oh? I thought Rhonda stupidly gave both the Summoning and the Possession Eidolons to him."

Joe nodded. "She did. But he doesn't have them anymore. Someone stole them from him."

"When?"

Shrugging, Joe pulled his feet from the coffee table and sat forward. "I'm afraid I can't say. But there is someone who could help you with that."

Anger flared pretty hard—I threw the blanket off me and stood up—and then sat back down. I was still a little woozy from having a Symbiont yanked out and having the shit shocked out of me.

Dags was on his knees beside me, tenderly grabbing at my wrist. "Are you okay?"

"I'm heading out," Joe said as he stood. "And by the way— Mastiff's fine. He apparently blacked out while looking at Randall's home, then woke up on the third-floor parking deck at North Fulton Hospital. You wouldn't know anything about that, would you?"

I kept my expression blank and shook my head. "No." But I was glad to hear Mastiff was okay.

"Talk to Rhonda, damnit."

I tensed.

He shrugged again. "Just call me if you get kidnapped again. Or maybe next time it won't be Randall but Rodriguez himself. Or maybe even this Horror thing."

Joe was through the arch and to the door before I called out to him. "Wait—"

And he stuck his head back in. "Yes?"

"Okay. But only if you're there. And I want sleep first."

"Done."

"And I want a charm or a ward against evil people."

"Sure. Just use that necklace I gave you."

Oops. I glanced at Dags. I could just see the chain where the necklace hung beneath his shirt. "I didn't know that was a talisman."

He nodded. "Yep. You might want to put it on. I'll call you later and set up a time and place."

"Here."

"Nope. Neutral territory. I'll call." And then he was out the door. The sun was almost up.

"You need sleep." Dags got to his feet and offered me his hand. I took it and stood a little slower. This time I didn't get dizzy. "I'll stay in the other bedroom again—if it's okay. And then I can help Jemmy get the shop ready while you meet with Rhonda."

I nodded absently, my mind already trying to come up with the best zingers I could think of to deliver upon seeing the traitor for the first time in a month. But as we got to the steps past the kitchen, I stopped and frowned at Dags. "You think this is a good idea?"

He nodded. "I think for your sake it is. I think you need as much support as you can get. Remember—Rhonda still has the backing of the SOI. And there could be something she knows that could bring your mom back, or even return your abilities to you."

True.

I had to look at it that way—but I wasn't going to be nice to her.

And then I stopped after putting my right Godzilla slipper on the step. "You're not going with us?"

He smirked. "Why do you need me? You've got Joe to protect you from Rhonda." He winked. "And besides, I have something to take care of tomorrow."

Oh. Okay.

BOBBY was still unhappy with me. I just couldn't justify getting in trouble. The fact I was even down in the basement was enough to get me grounded for life!

"Chicken!"

"That's so childish." I crossed my arms over my chest. "Widdle Bit one block over is better at teasing than you."

"That's because he was ten when he died," Bobby said. His transparency shifted as he moved. "Just look in the box, okay? You don't have to get it down. It's right up there. Just look in it."

I raised an eyebrow at him, knowing it made me look a little more grown-up. "That's it? Then you'll leave me alone?"

He nodded so fast I thought his head was gonna topple off.

With the biggest sigh I could make, I pulled the stepladder over beneath the shelves where the box sat. With a deep breath

I carefully climbed up. I was just going to peek inside—and that's it. Just peek inside, then get my butt back upstairs to my desk.

Wait . . . Did I turn the chicken on?

It was dusty and yucky and dark, and I couldn't really see anything. I lifted the box, just sure a spider was going to climb out and crawl up my arm and I was gonna fall and bust my head—

Something moved quickly along my right arm. I yelled, then it was in front of me—a mouth and two eyes—and it was pushing itself into my mouth, making it hard to breathe—

I'M up, I'm up, I'm up.

And I was sitting in my bed, with Jemmy just coming in the door with a tray in her hand. "Ah . . . I thought I heard you up here. Talking to yourself?" She set the tray on the bed. "You're gonna wear that voice out again."

The tray was filled with a teacup, saucer, small teapot, several bags of tea, a plate of fruit, a slice of lemon-glaze cake, and a crepe filled with strawberries. I pointed at it and looked at Jemmy. "Did you—"

"Oh no, no. Dags made that before lunch. They are good too. He just fixed this plate for you and left. Said he had plans for the night."

Night?

I looked over at the clock—2:34 P.M.

"Yow—I slept all morning!"

"Yeah, you slept a long time. Joe Halloran called. Said to tell you"—she tapped her chin before reciting—"'Get your lazy ass up and meet me at PJ's in Atlantic Square at seven.'"

PJ's. What's PJ's? Time for Google.

Where's my computer?

I nodded. "Thanks, Jemmy."

But she lingered next to my bed. "You know he likes you."

I felt my cheeks grow hot, remembering the kiss from a month ago. How it felt in my toes and the various parts of my body. "Yeah—he and I are good friends."

"He'd be good for you, Zoë. Now, don't get me wrong.

Detective Frasier is a nice man—but to abandon you like this in the middle of a family crisis? That's not good people."

She had a point. But what I didn't want to get into was all the different times I'd lied to Daniel. How I'd avoided telling him the truth. About me.

"Thanks for worrying about me and Joe, Jemmy. But we're just friends."

Her eyes widened, and a laugh like I've never heard bellowed out of her. She held on to the door handle and smiled at me. "I'm not talking about Halloran, Zoë. I'm talking about Dags."

I frowned. "Dags? Likes me? Well, yeah—we sort of fell into a friendship, and I helped him with the Shadow People—"

"No, Zoë—" She took a step back into the room. "Are you blind? He loves you, girl."

Loves . . . me?

Dags?

"Jemmy—"

But she had her hand up. "The heart don't play favorites, girl—and it never chooses what's best. It chooses what it wants. I know you love Daniel, or you think you do. And I know you're attracted to Detective Halloran, and I can see he wants to throw you down on your scrawny butt as soon as possible."

Okay . . . it was MY turn to go totally red. I didn't know what to say. I was used to Mom talking to me this way—but Jemmy?

"J-Jemmy—"

"But Dags? That's a special kind of love he's got. It's unconditional. He'll love you till the day he dies, girl. No matter what. But . . ." She smiled. "You follow your heart. He'll mend." And with that, she left.

I sat there in total shock. It felt as if I'd had a whole bucketful of cow shit dumped in my lap.

I did not need that kind of responsibility right now!

17

IT looked like rain. Again. Much more of this, and they were gonna rename Atlanta New Seattle.

I found PJ's Coffee easily enough in Atlantic Station, a development of in-community shopping as well as condos and apartments on the east side of Interstate 85–75. Basically on the same side as Turner and across from IKEA. It was nicely groomed, heavily populated, and had the highest crime rate in the whole city.

Yay.

I'd been there a couple of times to eat at Doc Green's, and I'd been to the Regal there to see a movie. PJ's was just across the street. Of course, parking was underground, and that entrance was back around toward the interstate. I drove in, took the ticket, then parked near where my building would be.

It was nice parking, with a machine at each of the steps and up escalators where you could pay for your parking before you left. I took the escalator up, not bothering with looking for an umbrella, and emerged across the street at the Regal. A quick jog across and I was at PJ's door, and Joe was coming out, a tall, steaming cup of something in one hand, an umbrella in the other.

"Here," he said, shoving the warm cup at me. "It's a white mocha. You're late."

I tasted the coffee.

Heeeaven!

"Traffic."

He popped the umbrella open. Luckily, the rain was light, but the distant sky was looking darker, and that wasn't because it was getting later. "It's just over here. We'll walk."

"We're not meeting at PJ's? Neutral territory?"

"No. I'm taking you to another neutral territory. Follow me."

I did, sipping my mocha, still thinking up all the really mean things I wanted to say. We walked a block over to another three-story building. There was a store below, then a door to the side. Joe punched a code into the pad there, the door opened, and we walked up two flights of well-lit stairs.

The apartment was near the stairwell door. Joe produced a set of keys and opened the door. "Lucy, I'm home," he cried out.

The first thing that hit was the incredible smell—garlic and herbs and lemon. It reminded me of Mom.

The front door opened up to a small hall with a line of hooks for coats along the wall behind the door and a mat to brush off feet on a polished, clean hardwood floor. Joe removed his coat, slipped out of his sneakers to his dingy socks, and stood back. I brushed off my feet and hung up my soaked coat on one of the hooks. There were several jackets on the hooks, including a black hoodie and a camouflage-patterned coat.

The short hall led into an open room that doubled as a kitchen, dining area, and living room. The long wall was made up of windows that overlooked the square, where a large Christmas tree would be displayed in December. To the right was the kitchen, a nook really, with wooden cabinets, black countertops, and clear-door shelves. The refrigerator was stainless steel, as was the sink. And it was clean.

The dining area was in the middle of the room. Wood table with black chairs, all IKEA by style (and why not?—it was just down the road and affordable). Cone-shaped lights hung suspended from a high ceiling just above the table. In the center was a bowl with water and long-dead flower petals.

On the far left was a living area, with sectional couches in black, colorful pillows, a plasma TV, bookshelves, and a coffee table. The remote lay on the coffee table next to a stack of magazines. Atlanta's skyline was punctuated by dark clouds, and I could see lightning every now and then, crooked streaks of light cutting the gray.

Joe moved on ahead of me through the dining area and into the kitchen. I moved a bit slowly, a little shy (what, me shy?) as I saw her from behind. She looked shorter than I remembered. Her hair was brown and cut into layers in the back, and she was wearing a soft-looking mauve sweater.

Mauve? Since when did Rhonda wear anything other than dark colors?

Joe leaned in close and spoke to her—she was at the stove, and I could see the table was set for four. Four? But even as I neared it, saw the roasted chicken, the garlic mashed potatoes and yams, the Le Sueur peas, the meal that was oh-so-familiar to me, I knew a truth deep down.

I kept my expression calm as she turned around and I came face-to-face with Rhonda Orly.

For months, ever since waking up with no voice, all I'd dreamed about—except for sex with Daniel—was to get my voice back. There had been so many times in the past months I'd wanted to chew a few choice people out. Mostly in traffic. Or that really rude woman with the phone stuck to her ear who always bosses the poor clerk down at the QT next to Mom's shop.

But now that I had it back—standing on the other side of the kitchen island, staring at the friend who'd betrayed me—I couldn't think of a damned thing to say. All that mental practice, and I botched it.

Epic botch.

Well, I *could* think of a million things to say—but not one of them left my lips.

She looked—different. I was amazed at what a month could do to someone. She looked—older. A bit more mature than before. Her hair wasn't matte black anymore, and her makeup was oddly . . . normal. The only thing that still looked like Rhonda were her black fingernails and the spiderweb tattoo that snaked from her shoulder and climbed her neck. All I could see was the part of it on her neck. I'd always known it was there, but she'd kept her hair to her shoulders and mostly down.

But with it short, the tattoo was very visible.

She was staring at me, her expression unreadable. Her eyes looked . . . huge.

Joe stood to the left of us, between us, looking from me to Rhonda, to me to Rhonda.

And then it dawned on me—what he said earlier—about neutral territory. How he had a code and a key. And Rhonda was already here cooking dinner. The way he'd greeted her when he got in.

I turned and glared at him. "You and Rhonda are living together? You're *dating*?"

"You got your voice back!" Rhonda shouted out, her hands to her face.

I kept my laser beams trained on Joe. He looked a little . . . frightened. "You didn't tell her?"

"Not all of it. There were some things I thought she needed to see—or rather hear—for herself."

I couldn't believe it. These two were— Joe and Rhonda were— They were— After he kissed me like that!

Oh-*kay*, this was not the life I ordered, and I did not have to stay here. I checked my jeans to make sure my keys were still there and marched to the door.

"Zoë," Rhonda called out, "Rodriguez is looking for the Grimoire."

I stopped.

"And Randall Kemp's sister was a member of the Cruorem."

I stayed where I was, realizing that by stomping out I was running away. And Rhonda, being Rhonda, had given me an out. A way not to be a child anymore. I hung my head and took in some deep breaths and tried not to be a girl. I tried not to think of the two of them together, living day by day in each other's company, while I watched Daniel and my mom drift farther and farther away and became increasingly alone.

Yeah . . . slip on that pity-party dress, Zoë. You've gotten good at it.

"How do you know this?" I didn't turn around. I didn't want to look at her. At them.

I could hear her coming near me, her sneakers on the hardwood floor. I can't do this. *I can't do this.* I was so angry with her. So damned angry, and I still missed her so much. "I've got to go."

I was almost there, at the door, when someone grabbed my left upper arm and turned me around. I knew it was Joe from the smell of his cologne. His expression was serious, almost . . . frightened. And he put his hands on my shoulders, his grip firm.

"Go? Go where? You don't have many options left, Zoë. Your powers as a Wraith are gone. We have to find out why—because that makes you vulnerable to men like Rodriguez and Kemp. We have to get your mother back, but we can't do that until we fix what's wrong with you."

I tried to pull free, but I just didn't have the strength. In fact, I was amazed at how tired I was even after that long nap. And it didn't feel like a normal tired either—like run, exercise, play hard, good old-fashioned exhausted. This felt like a really intense flu tired.

"Zoë." Rhonda was suddenly by Joe, looking at me with wide eyes. And I was again taken by how different she looked. "Have you taken a look at yourself? You look like you're wasting away. You've dropped too much weight too fast; you're still dehydrated. Your face is gaunt, and you have dark circles under your eyes. You look sick. How are you going to help Nona if you're sick?"

I glared at her. "Don't you dare act like you give a fuck."

"I do give a fuck, you asshole!"

"Bitch!"

"Selfish prick."

"Ass-hat!"

"Cop-sucker!"

I blinked, mouth open, but I didn't say anything. That wasn't quite what I thought she was going to say, though *cock*-sucker and *cop*-sucker sounded similar. I glanced at Joe, then back at her. "You've got room to talk. At least you're really sleeping with one."

Joe turned a bright red and looked down—though I noticed he wasn't letting go of me. Rhonda just looked mad.

"Zoë—"

"Oh . . . it didn't work out with Dags, so you turned to Joe . . . maybe thought that because he was like you, some paranormal geek, that you two could settle down and make little geeks?" I heard what was coming out of my mouth, and I was shocked (a long-unused voice sometimes has a mind of its own), but what was even more confusing was the rage I was directing at Rhonda—but not because she betrayed me and Mom by pretending to be a friend so she could spy on me—

But because she had Joe. All this time—while I was alone and slowly losing my power—she'd had Joe! How was that fair? Why was I suffering? Why was my mom trapped in some other plane while the one that betrayed all of us was happy, off making nice with the cop that—

—the cop that—

Who made my knees so weak with a single kiss I couldn't stand up.

"Zoë—I've waited just as long as you have to hear that voice again, but, so help me by the Lord and Lady, if you don't shut up—"

"Look," Joe interrupted. "You girls can stand here in the doorway and throw names later. I'm hungry, and from the looks of Zoë, she needs to eat a few sammiches herself. I—"

My knees buckled. I couldn't stop them. It was as if something were standing behind me, placed its knees behind mine, and pushed me forward. Joe caught me as I flailed toward him, then I was in his arms.

Whoa. What just happened?

"Zoë?" Rhonda's hand was on my forehead. "You okay? You're really pale."

"Yeah . . ." I found my feet again and pulled away from Joe. "I just—I got really dizzy."

"You need to eat." He kept hold of my arm and pulled me back to the table. He pointed to a chair, and I sat. He sat on the end, and Rhonda sat down facing me. He ladled out heaps of food onto my plate, and my stomach growled. Even after eating what Dags had fixed, I was still hungry.

Amazing.

"Who's the chair for?" I pointed to the empty one beside me.

"That was supposed to be for Dags," Joe said before shoveling a large helping of yams into his mouth.

I looked at Rhonda. She said, "I thought maybe he'd come." And watching her—I saw her gaze lingering at the plate.

Ah! She's still in lust with Dags!

I nodded and tasted the yams. Mm. They were just like Mom's.

"You look awful," Rhonda said. "Are you getting any sleep?"

I stared at her across the table. "You sound like Nona."

She smiled. "Well, I miss her."

"I wanted to steal the Eidolon back from Rodriguez—see if I could command her back to her body."

Joe nodded. "I told you he doesn't have it."

"No, he doesn't," Rhonda said. "In fact, most of what was stolen or appropriated from your great-uncle has been liberated from Francisco Rodriguez. And Joe also told me what happened to you at the hospital. He was there—trying to elicit Daniel's help?"

I nodded and gave her a brief recap of what had happened, avoiding any mention of TC in Cooper's body. And I silently wondered what that idiot was *doing* with the captain's body. The thought that there was a powerful Symbiont running amuck with a gun was not comforting.

But I sure as shit wasn't going to tell Rhonda.

I was still a little sick to my stomach about Rhonda and Joe together. Living together. Sharing a bed.

And me alone in my bed.

"I've been to see Nona every day," Rhonda said. "I sometimes bump into Cooper there. Apparently we were both avoiding you."

"Someone took the Triskelion."

"I did that," Rhonda said. "I don't know who put that thing on her—but it would have prevented her from coming back into her body if she escaped from TC." She paused. "And that's what the Archer told you? That she left him?"

I recapped again and finished with, "He also said I was an Irin."

Rhonda didn't blink.

"You knew that."

She nodded. "As you know, I was sent by the Society to

keep an eye on you. They knew you'd been born to an Ethereal but lost track of you when you were twelve."

Twelve. That's when Mom and I lived in Oregon. "Could they not find me?"

"They couldn't sense you." She sipped her wine.

When had Rhonda started drinking wine? I noticed Joe was drinking a beer, right out of the can. Was she trying to be elegant to impress me, or him? "Sense me?"

"Irin are very rare, ever since the Bulwark—"

"Even you knew about that?" I interrupted.

She nodded. "Not until recently. The Society documented it. My uncle was very good at keeping records. But when Irin are born, they burn bright—like fireflies against a dark matte background. Psychics can see them. And you burned brightest. It was reported your father moved you around a lot to try and keep you away from prying eyes. He and Nona wanted to protect you."

I set my fork on the table. "Mom knew?"

"She is Domas's niece, Zoë. She knew—not in the beginning. And then about eight years later, your light went out."

I kept quiet. I could only listen. I was hearing about my past from someone else.

"What do you mean her light went out?" Joe asked for me.

Rhonda leaned forward, her arms on the table. "I don't know. The member doing the surveillance didn't know either. You moved not long afterward to Atlanta, and the Society couldn't track you. And then, about six years ago"—she held her hand up to imitate a surprise—"ping. You popped back on the map. Stronger than ever. And that's when I was dispatched."

Six years ago was when I was raped.

"You okay?" Joe had a hand on my arm.

I shrugged it off. "I'm fine. Just bad memories." I looked at Rhonda and grabbed up my sweet tea. "But I had a light before that time?"

"According to the sensitives employed by the Society. I've also discovered something else."

I took a couple of quick swallows. *Och. Brain freeze.*

"Recently, Francisco Rodriguez had a few spies dispatched around the South, all infiltrating groups, looking for psychic, gifted people. He's done this before. Once he found them, they disappeared."

I stared dumbfounded at her. "What for?"

"Even after the fire, and your great-uncle's death, my uncle took control of the Society, and he put a halt to all experiments on humans and their abilities to cross the planes. Rodriguez continued outwardly to support my uncle, but he secretly continued the experiments. Only on unwilling patients."

"What a shithead," Joe said as he sat back in his chair.

"How do *you* know this?" I asked.

"Because I'm now the head of the Society of Ishmael, and I have access to the records and journals kept by the members through the years. My uncle had spies watching him as well. He made Rodriguez believe they were friends."

I opened my mouth to speak, but she put up a finger. "But, Zoë, what I'm getting at is that Rodriguez also had a spy in the Cruorem. Remember them?"

"Yeah."

Joe moved forward suddenly and reached behind him to pull out his phone. He looked at the screen, got up, and moved out of the room before answering it.

I looked back at Rhonda. *Quick—scratch her eyes out!* "So—what connection would he have in the Cruorem? As far as I could tell, none of those wackos really had any power."

"They had a powerful Grimoire. Rodriguez wants that book."

I pointed to her. "You still have it?"

She shook her head. "I have a copy of it, locked away in a Veil."

"A what?"

An expression much like one of Mom's crossed her face, the one Mom had when she'd learned something and was excited to tell me. "Remember how we discovered that the book had some serious spells grandfathered into it? One of them involved the creation of a Veil. It's like creating a hole in the space around you so you can store stuff in it—and you call it out when you need it."

I sat back. "You've done it. You've finally cracked up."

"Oh?" And with that, she lifted her left arm and reached up

into the air—and her hand and wrist disappeared! It was as if she'd stuck them into an invisibility coat or something.

My mouth fell open.

She then promptly pulled her hand back out, and in it she had a small black book. Rhonda handed it to me.

I took it. The binding was leather, and it was cold. Like meat-freezer cold. I dropped it on the table and looked at her. "That book taught you how to do that?"

Her expression went from excited to worried. "Now you know why he can't ever have the book, even a copy of it."

"Where's the original?" I looked down at the book she'd handed me. I'd seen the original Grimoire—having been with Rhonda and Dags when they'd appropriated it from Maureen's apartment.

She hesitated before putting her elbows on the table. "It's safe."

Joe came back into the room. "I've got to go—there are gunshots reported at the Center for Puppetry Arts."

. . .

My heart clenched. I looked around the room. "What time is it? What day is it?"

"It's Thursday," Rhonda said. "I can't wear a watch—"

"It's just after midnight." He frowned. "Why?"

I suddenly remembered that wacky member of the Cruorem challenging Dags. Setting up a meeting at the Center for Puppetry Arts. For Thursday night!

That boob had gone there alone!

I stood. "Rhonda—what was the name of the spy that Rodriguez had in the Cruorem?"

"Oh, uh, Jack Klinsky. Why?"

I couldn't breathe. *Oh God, no. It's a trap!*

"Zoë—what is it?" Joe demanded.

"It's Dags. He's there, at the Center. And Jack Klinsky is doing the shooting. At Dags."

18

RAIN continued drizzling as we piled into the Volvo—Elizabeth being the only car big enough to hold all three of us. Joe insisted on driving—in case we got stopped for speeding, and he could show them his badge.

The Center for Puppetry Arts sits on a prime piece of property off Spring, nestled next to the Breman Jewish Heritage Museum. A cultural landmark, the Center is home to a number of famous puppets—namely Salem, the cat from the long-running TV show *Sabrina, the Teenage Witch*, and more recently, Jim Henson's Kermit, Miss Piggy, Dr. Teeth, Bert, and Ernie. The Center was already home to legendary puppets such as the Chamberlain from *The Dark Crystal* (that thing is huge!). The Jim Henson exhibit had opened up about a month before, and though I hadn't gotten to the Center to see it (I loved the Salem exhibit), it was definitely among my Things to Do Before I Die.

The Center also has three stages and produces puppet shows all year long, with either their own talented puppeteers or other troupes invited from around the nation and even internationally.

But let me get one thing straight here—I don't like puppets.

I don't like clowns. I think they're both cousins to the evil ventriloquist doll.

When Mom and I first moved here, she thought it would be nice to take her daughter to see a show. I think it was a production of *Beauty and the Beast*. The Center itself is a work of art in its construction. A zigzag walkway brings the patrons up to the second-story entrance under a large awning. The glass doors open into the lobby. To the left is ticketing, and to the right is the puppet store, where patrons can buy all sorts of puppets and accoutrements.

Just past this is another counter—usually where they serve drinks for adult shows (now those are cool puppet shows). To the left you'll see the bottom of Pinocchio's legs—not kidding. They're huge, sticking through the roof to the floor. Just past the legs is the entrance to one of two museums in the Center.

This museum is interactive. And my mom had thought—*Oh, this could be fun.*

Uh-uh.

Back then, the first exhibit in the museum was a trip-activated transforming trash can. It's still there now, but they've changed the lighting somewhat, and it's no longer tripped by opening and closing the door. When Mom and I walked in, the room was painted to resemble an alley in a city, and I had noticed the beat-up trash can to the left side.

But once the door closed behind us, the lights went out and the trash can glowed. Some huge Borodin-like piece of music right out of *Night on Bald Mountain* started to play, and the thing mutated into a huge, honking, red-and-yellow fiery bird. Later I discovered it was a phoenix.

Scared the pants off of me.

Dazed and a little upset, I charged through the door to my right and stopped in the middle of the room. It was floor-to-ceiling puppets—all types of puppets. What I didn't know was that some of them were triggered to move by pressure plates on the floor. So walking through there, I set them off.

I did not, and do not, like things moving that are not supposed to move. So the moment the closest one to me—some furry marionette that looked like a rotted ostrich—started moving and talking, I started screaming. I couldn't find my way out, and I kept stepping on the plates. Puppets waved their hands, laughed, cried out—and I just kept screaming until Mom got into the room and grabbed hold of me.

Needless to say, I didn't get to see the performance that day.

As we pulled into the parking lot, there were no police cars yet—which was just so typical of Atlanta. Shots heard right in their backyard. Where were they?

Mental note: *can you pass the creamer?*

Joe killed the Volvo's lights and the engine, and with the gears in neutral, coasted down into the drive to the right and stopped the car under one of the trees. I could see Dags's truck—and a black van parked up front. Joe pulled his gun out and held it up, making sure his clip was ready, then pulled back that top part in order to load a bullet into the chamber.

"Rhonda?" He glanced back at her.

I turned and to my surprise Rhonda also had a gun. It was much smaller. But that left me without a weapon.

Wait!

I reached forward and opened the glove compartment and pulled out the Ghost Zapper. Joe's eyes widened as he recognized the weapon, just visible in the parking lot lights. "Where the hell did you get that?" he hissed.

"It's complicated." I turned it right and left.

Joe held up his left hand—the one not holding a weapon. "Why don't you just stay in the car?"

"No way," I hissed. "That's Dags in there getting all shot up—"

Gunshots rang out again, and we all stopped and stared at the darkened Center.

"Joe—" Rhonda said from the back.

"Zoë, you're worthless right now. If you go in there, I won't be able to do my job."

"What about Rhonda?" I nodded to the back. "What makes Rhonda more qualified than me?"

"Because I can take care of myself, Zoë," she said quietly. "I can use magic. And with Klinsky—magic will be our best defense."

Joe took the zapper from me and stuffed it back inside the glove compartment. "Just stay—here."

"But—"

"I'll handcuff you to the steering wheel."

I sat back. I believed he would do that too.

So I sat in a huff with my arms crossed as he and Rhonda got out of the car and did this classic crouch-walk toward the front, but then disappeared down to the right where the bottom entrance was. I saw a flash of sparkly light like Tinker Bell and knew Rhonda had used magic to get in.

Great. Rhonda not only had Joe, but she was using magic like some movie mage. So when did that happen?

Either way, I did not want to stay in the car, but I also didn't want to sneak in, then somehow botch what was happening. But if I was out here when the police finally did decide to show up, then what? Would they arrest me for just sitting in the car?

Probably. And if Cooper showed up with TC still taking a joyride?

That did it.

I grabbed the Ghost Zapper back out of the glove compartment and eased out of the car the way I'd seen those two do. But I didn't head down to the basement entrance, or the main entrance. Instead, I went around the side and tried the back entrance—the one that faced the street. I figured maybe Dags would get in that way.

I got to it, looked around, and yanked.

And nearly pulled my arm off. Locked.

Damnit.

I yanked again though not so hard. Still didn't budge.

Another gunshot came from inside, and I yelped. Yeah, having a voice isn't always a great thing. I crouched and moved back around the building in time to see three Fulton County cars come in, blue lights flashing. Shit. Now I was stuck. And if they spotted me outside, I really would get arrested.

So I did the only thing I could think of—I ran back the other way to get to the basement door. I touched the handle just as the cop cars moved into position. The handle felt warm, and I pulled at it and went in. It was dark—really dark. But I thought I could hear voices ahead of me. I knew there was a performance stage through the double doors to my right—could they be in there?

I moved up closer to the double doors and pressed my ear to one of them. Yeah . . . I could hear the voices. And from what I could remember about the stages (yes, I did eventually see a show here), this door would open up at the front walkway. Stage immediately on the right, and the tiers of chairs on the left.

The voices grew louder.

". . . supposed to be mine, Dags! You can't dodge these forever. Does it hurt? You know . . . I made sure these bullets were full of demon bane. You know what that is?"

I had no idea what that was. But it sounded terrible.

I figured the guy talking with the nasal voice was this Klinsky guy. But where was Dags? And what did the jerk mean by "Does it hurt?" Had he already hit Dags, and this demon stuff was doing something to him? Where were Maureen and Alice?

Hell . . . where were Rhonda and Joe?

I had reached out to grab the door and push it forward—quietly—when someone seized me from behind and slapped a hand over my mouth. I stepped back, bent forward, and hoisted him over my back and then over my head. Stepping back, I aimed the Ghost Zapper at the shadow and was about to yell out at him when Dags's voice said, "Zoë—it's me."

It was barely a whisper, but I recognized it, and realized I'd just tossed Dags over my head.

Oh geez. I knelt forward to him, just visible in the light from the EXIT sign. "I am so, so sorry—"

"It's . . . okay." He moved forward on his hands and knees, then stood up slowly. I rose as well and caught sight of his face. His expression was one of pain. That was when I saw the blood on his shoulder, staining his shirt.

I put my hand out to him. "Darren . . . what happened? Did he shoot you?"

"No, he missed," Dags said. "Barely."

That's when I noticed the rip in the fabric. I put my hand out to him, but he pulled away. "Dags—Joe and Rhonda are here. And the police were called. You've got to—"

"This guy's working for Rodriguez, Zoë," Dags said in a low voice. "He's trying to—"

"Get you so he can use you as a bargaining chip to get the Grimoire from Rhonda."

Dags stopped, closed his mouth, frowned, and then narrowed his eyes. "You just put that together . . . like just now?"

Actually . . . I had. I'd been thinking about everything Rhonda and Joe had told me at the apartment, trying to work out how Rodriguez figured into all of this. He had to have known Mom didn't have the Grimoire at her shop—and it was only logical to assume that, since Rhonda had taken over as head of the Society, she would take possession of it.

And I figured that wherever that Grimoire was, it was well protected. And being well protected meant that Rodriguez couldn't get to it easily. So he would need a bargaining chip. And it was possible that he knew about Rhonda's affection for Darren McConnell through his spies—but if he'd kept up with her movements recently, he'd know she was dating a cop.

Unless Rhonda and Joe were keeping the romance a secret; therefore, they had the love nest in Atlantic Station to protect Joe?

That left Dags vulnerable.

But why have Klinsky lure Dags to this location—a public location—and shoot at him? What could killing Dags accomplish?

"Zoë?"

I blinked and looked at him. "Hrm?"

"You spaced on me."

"Sorry. I was trying to figure this out. Rodriguez—"

The door to my left suddenly opened, shoving me into Dags. The two of us went down, me on him. Dags reacted instantly and moved me to the side, putting his body between me and Klinsky as the nutcase with the really big fucking gun bore down on us. He had the barrel pointed directly at Dags's chest.

"Oh, Dags . . . you got a girlfriend? Why don't I just make this bullet for both of you?"

"Use the girls!" I screamed out.

"I can't," Dags hissed. "He used demon bane."

"That's right," Klinsky said. "Once you're dead, the Grimoire will be mine—asshole."

I thought he'd pulled the trigger when a loud noise made me jump.

The noise wasn't the hammer hitting the pin—it was the door behind us slamming open and a figure jumping through, firing away.

Klinsky jerked three times, staggered backward, then toppled, his own gun skittering on the tiled floor. Dags and I both turned to see the shooter.

Daniel Frasier.

He moved to the body, pushed it with his foot, then disappeared through the stage door.

More uniforms came in, guns drawn, and Dags and I held up our hands just as footsteps on the tiled floor revealed Joe coming down the hall out of the darkness, his gun down, his shield up. "Police—Detective Sergeant Jeremiah Halloran."

The officers lowered their guns . . . a little.

Jeremiah? His name was Jeremiah*? Why in the hell did he go by Joe and not Jeremy?* That was a question to pose—just not right then.

Hrm . . . though Jeremy really didn't suit him. He was more of a Joe kinda guy. Hey, *Joe.* How's it hanging, *Joe*? Wazzup, *Joe*? Jeremy sounded more like . . . well . . . the boy next door.

And Joe Halloran was *not* the boy next door.

"They're with me," Joe said, as he knelt beside the body. He checked the pulse and shook his head. "Who did the shooting?"

I pointed to the stage. "Daniel."

Joe was up and dashing through those same doors in seconds.

"Zoë?"

I turned back to the now-open door to see Mastiff step in. He held his hand out, and I grabbed it and used it as support to stand. "I'm glad to see you."

"I'm glad you're all right." He smiled. Mastiff really was a handsome man in a suit. Those old uniforms never did him justice. "Did Frasier come blast'n in here?"

Dags stood a tad slowly, favoring his shoulder, and nodded. "Yeah—through those doors. Joe went after him."

"Good. But I'm gonna need the two of you to follow me and give me statements, okay?"

We both nodded and followed him out through the door. As we walked through the hurriedly moving police and watched as an ambulance arrived, red lights flashing, I leaned in close to Dags. "Where's Rhonda?"

"I think she beat it out of there so the police wouldn't see her."

I nodded. Then, "Why?"

"Because she's the head of the Society. If her name goes in the paper, it could reflect badly on them." He was silent as we reached Mastiff's car. "I know you have your problems with Rhonda—and I can't blame you. I'd be pissed too. I was pissed off at her for a while—for a whole different reason. And if it hadn't been for Joe—I doubt I'd ever have forgiven her. But Rhonda Orly does what she feels she has to—to create order. At least in her way of thinking."

Huh? I held up both hands as Mastiff opened his car door and reached in to get his MP3 recorder. Police, paramedics, newspeople, all bustled around us. "I don't understand. Why were you pissed off at her? Because she had a crush on you?"

He shook his head. "No." Dags looked away. I could see his breath in the parking-lot lights. "God, I wish it were just that. There's so much you don't know."

"What?" I searched his gray eyes, and I saw hurt there. "Darren . . . why did Klinsky say if he kills you, the Grimoire will be his? Rhonda has that Grimoire, doesn't she? It's hidden in a safe place."

Dags chewed on his lower lip before looking at me, before answering me, and when he did, he closed his eyes as if what he was about to say was painful. "She has a photocopy, but not the original." He opened his eyes. "Zoë, *I'm* the Grimoire."

19

So . . . he's a book

I didn't say much after that. I mean—how do you react to your
friend telling you he's a book?

Could my life get any weirder?

Wait . . . scratch that. Pretend I never said it.

We gave our statements to Mastiff. Some muckety-muck
named Hessenflow (I kid you not because I asked him to spell
it for me) took charge and started stomping about. Since Cooper wasn't there, I assumed that TC was still walking about in
his body. I only hoped he was taking care of that body.

Dags offered to give me a ride in his truck. I agreed, and sat
in stunned silence.

"You okay?"

I nodded.

"You want to ask me any questions?"

I looked over at him. Oncoming headlights illuminated the
front of his face but cast the sides in shadows. "You going to
tell me what happened?"

"Not right now. I say we head on back to the shop, roast
marshmallows, and drink hot chocolate."

I didn't say anything. I just stared ahead. Dags . . . was a Grimoire?

Dags's phone rang. He slipped it out of his coat pocket and looked at it. "Hey—where are you?"

I assumed it was Rhonda.

"Uh-uh . . . no . . . but I did get hit with demon bane . . . Hell yes, it hurts . . . No, but it's enough to keep the girls in place . . . You sure? I never saw anything like that there . . . Basement? Okay . . . we're on our way there now." He punched the front of the iPhone and slipped it back into his pocket. "That was Rhonda. She and Joe are gonna meet us back at the shop. She's going to call ahead and see if Jemmy can find some Dragon's Blood."

"Some what?"

"Something that can counteract the demon bane." He pointed to the bandage on his shoulder that the EMT technician had put on. "It's not a lethal exposure but it's enough to smart and continue to smart. The antiseptic isn't going to cut it."

"So . . . what *is* Dragon's Blood?"

He smiled. "Dragon's Blood resin, extracted from the dragon tree, which is pretty much the oldest tree on the planet and damned hard to find. It's expensive, but the natural, positive properties and healing aspects are incredible."

I pursed my lips at him. "I think you and Maureen used it before."

"On TC—but that magic's long fizzled out."

Uh-huh. A dragon tree. Riiiight.

Jemmy wasn't there when we arrived, and everything was locked up tight. I opened the back door, shut off the alarm (my idea—getting the alarm installed), and poured water into the electric kettle and plugged it back in. "You want tea?"

"Chai."

"Sure," I said, making myself busy in the kitchen. I could hear him in the botanica. He'd turned on some lights and was making book noises, as if looking through the cases. "You need something?"

He came back in, with a preoccupied expression. "Yeah . . . but you need me?"

I looked up at the cabinet. They were nice cabinets, installed when Mom redid the room. White, tall with gold knobs. I had the one closest to the sink open and was looking up at the top shelf. Just above it was a fake ivy vine and an Animal Cracker tin. "I see the chai tea up there, but I don't think I'm tall enough to reach it."

"And you think I am?" He grinned.

I returned the grin and pointed to the stool. "Just grab that, then stand there as I get on the counter—"

"No, no, no," he said, waving me away. "You grab that, and I'll stand on the counter. If I fall, it's less weight."

Uh . . . not sure I appreciate that statement. But he's cute. He can have one freebie.

I did as he said, and he used my shoulders for support, then climbed on top of the counter. Once there, he grabbed the tea and handed it down to me. Then he looked back up. "Is that like a real box of Animal Crackers?"

I glanced up. "No. I think it's one of those, like—collector's things? Just a box."

He reached up for it. "I don't think I've ever seen—"

BOBBY was looking at me from above that box again. That box in the basement. The one that had always traveled with us. The white, unmarked box. I'd never opened it. Mom had always told me it was just a box of old stuff—full of spiders and lizards.

But there it was—and Mom wasn't home.

"Come on, Zoë," Bobby said, and his voice echoed in my head. "Don't you want to know?"

"Know what?"

I turned—was that Mom?

But it wasn't Mom standing there. It was a man. No, a boy, really. A man that looked like a boy. He wore a long dark coat and a dark blue shirt, untucked, and had brown hair. His face was kind but concerned.

"How'd you get in here?" I asked him.

He held his hands out to his sides, his palms down. "I just wanted to see how you were doing, that's all."

"Who are you?" I asked, my attention half-focused between the box and the cute guy to my right. Mom was gonna be

doubly pissed off at me if she caught me down here—and with a boy!

"You don't belong here," Bobby said. I looked at him. His usually cherubic face had an odd, lined, shadowy look.

He looked downright spooky. I mean, I knew he was a ghost and all—but ghosts didn't usually look like ghosts. Or Hollywood ghosts.

"No, I don't," the man said. "But I'm here—and who are you?"

"You can see him?" I looked at Bobby, then back at him. "Really?"

"Yes, I can see him. But what is it you want to know?"

I pursed my lips and checked my watch. It was a nice watch—one my mom saved up and bought me. It had a small diamond where the twelve was, and my name engraved on the back.

It was getting too close to when she was supposed to be home—and I needed to check on the chicken upstairs. "Look— Mom's gonna be home soon, and this is a bad idea."

But Bobby wasn't letting it go. He jumped/floated down from where he'd been perched on the box and got between me and the shelf with the box on it. There were about a billion other boxes there too—but that box on top seemed to shine. "You said you wanted to see what's in the box!"

"Well, yeah." I took a step back. Bobby had never yelled at me before. "But I'm more worried about Mom skinning my hide if she catches me down here."

"Do you know what's in the box?" the stranger asked.

Bobby whirled around, and a strange voice came out of his mouth. Something deep and unfamiliar. "You stay out of this, or I'll chase you back to your dreams."

I stared down at him, though all I could see was the back of his head. "Bobby? That was rude."

What turned and looked at me wasn't Bobby. It was short, and it looked like him on the outside, but his face—it wasn't right. His pale skin had turned gray, and his eyes—they were gone. Only sunken, empty sockets.

His teeth—

"Zoë! Get out of the way!"

That made me crouch with fear as the stranger pulled his

*hands out of his pockets and held them out in front of him,
palms facing the Bobby thing. Circles pulsed on his palms, and
there was a blue-white light.*

Bobby screamed as the light enveloped him.

*I could see him burning—his dead flesh igniting. And as the
light touched me, it was warm—and soothing.*

*And then the skin on my left wrist started to bubble and
pucker, and my screams began. I scrambled back on the floor
to get away from the light—*

" . . . **911?** Did you test her blood?"

"Yes, I did. It's normal. She's always insisted that whole
sugar thing was nothing more than a weird side effect of being
a Wraith. And now she's not one. But that doesn't explain
Dags being out."

"There aren't any signs of struggle or that they were
attacked?"

"Look, woman, I already told you. They both look fine—
other than they're not moving."

My cue. "Not moving . . . where?" I managed to ask, though
listening to the fuss in the dark had been kinda entertaining.

"Zoë?" That was Rhonda's voice. "You okay?"

"No." My head was killing me. Little evil gnomes were
inside, whacking up the interior to make a nest. "What the
hell . . . ?" And then I opened my eyes.

Three faces stared down at me. I stared back up at them.
Rhonda was directly over my head, so she was upside down.
"Can you stand?"

"Uh . . . maybe." And then I realized I was on the kitchen
floor. And it's not a big kitchen. It was crowded, and as I turned
my head to the left I saw Dags's profile. His eyes were closed,
and he wasn't moving. "What—what the hell— Is he okay?"

Rhonda had her hand on my wrist, preventing me from
reaching out to him. "We don't know. We were hoping you
could tell us why you were both out cold on the kitchen
floor."

We were?

I pulled my hand from Rhonda and pushed myself up with
my elbows behind me. "We were . . . we were getting chai

tea . . . I . . . we were talking and then I heard . . . no . . ." I saw
that box in my mind's eye again. Why was I dreaming about
that box? "I don't know . . ."

"Dags is coming around," Joe said. I finished pushing myself into a sitting position and nudged Rhonda out of the
way—basically into the tiny hall in front of the stairs and the
basement steps.

I leaned over Dags as his eyes opened. He blinked a few
times, then focused on me. "Who's Bobby?"

AFTER finding the Dragon's Blood and a few other things in the
botanica, Rhonda made up a poultice thing and had Dags press
it against his shoulder. Joe finished up the tea as Dags and I
curled up on the couch. We'd both changed into more comfortable clothes—me in my blue plaid loungers and long-sleeved
gray thermal top and Dags in his . . . wow . . . blue plaid
loungers and a thermal tee shirt. What . . . he buys at the same
Kohl's I do?

After bringing us tea—man, I like chai—Joe sat on the floor
on the other side of the coffee table, talking on his phone, and
Rhonda joined us in the papasan, with my laptop in tow. *Hrm.*
I couldn't remember the last time I'd checked my e-mail.

Joe ended the conversation. "Well, Detective Frasier—after
his oddly heroic move at the Center for Puppetry Arts—has
once again disappeared. And so has Cooper. I hope they're
having fun together."

My heart fluttered. Cooper not answering. I reeeeally hoped
that bastard kept a good eye on that body. If not, I swore that
when I went Wraith again, I'd kick his ass.

"I guess Daniel's behavior is really bad?" Dags asked. "I
mean, this isn't like him, is it? He's always been a good cop?"

"Well, yes and no," Joe said. "I've known Frasier awhile.
And he definitely has a dark side. We all do, Dags."

"Yeah . . ." Dags said softly. "It's that dark side that's starting to worry me."

"Daniel's had a pretty rough time lately. I mean, realizing
you were married to a real bitch. And then finding someone
like Zoë, and getting the shit beat out of you on top of a building and enduring a coma for a couple of weeks. Then having

your ex-wife murdered in your house. Having to go through the trauma of being a suspect and finally, when you think it's all good—you can hear your girlfriend who said she couldn't speak in your head, but you don't know it's your head and you think it's your ears, and then you see—"

I closed my eyes and remembered the argument. That night—in the botanica. Jemmy had left and it was just us.

"But I heard you!" he'd shouted at me.

I'd shaken my head and tried to make him hear my thoughts—because that's what he had to have heard, right? My talking to Charlie, Lt. Charlie Holmes, Daniel's *deceased* mentor.

And when I'd thought about it—the situation made sense. We'd discovered that only a near-death or actual-death experience and a possession by me would allow someone to hear me in his mind.

And since he'd met with that near death by TC's hand—when I'd placed myself inside of him after my own body had been taken—didn't that qualify him?

But then—why hadn't he heard me more than that once?

But I'd known there was something else that night—I'd seen it in his eyes. He wasn't the same man that night as he'd been earlier in the afternoon when he'd put roses on the back porch and insisted he should come with me to the warehouse.

Something in that instant had changed him.

Something he'd seen.

He'd walked out of Mom's shop, insisting he needed time to think.

He'd had a month. No word. Nothing. Not a smile, or a card, not even a phone call to see how my mom was doing.

And here I was—still pining over the loss of something I feared I'd never really had.

And what was that, exactly?

Ah. Yes. A normal life.

"Okay, Zoë," Rhonda said. "What is this dream you keep having?"

I told everyone about the dreams, then Dags gave an account of the dream he'd just had, which was an exact match to what *I* had just dreamed.

Joe sighed. "So let me get this straight." He pointed to me. "You've been having these dreams about a ghost named Bobby and a white box. But each dream's been a little different."

I nodded.

He pointed at Dags. "And you just had the dream, or rather were a part of the dream she just had when you two were snoozing on the kitchen floor."

"Apparently."

He shook his head. "I don't get it. There's no weird connection between you two, is there?"

Dags and I looked at each other. He winked. That made me snicker.

"What?" Rhonda asked. She hadn't cracked the laptop open yet.

"Nothing, really," I said. "For me, sometimes the dreams are just so damned real. Like they really happened."

"Well, is there a white box in the basement?" Joe asked.

"Yeah, I think there is," I said. "I mean, I always remember there being a box that looked like that, but Mom always told me not to touch it."

Wind picked up outside and made the windows behind us crack. I shivered and was glad Joe had lit another fire.

Rhonda had her arms crossed over her chest. She was looking at me and Dags really hard. "Did you see and talk to ghosts when you were younger?"

I shrugged. "I don't remember if I did. I mean . . . a lot of my childhood is a blur. Except for those memories that Mom's real strong in." Like the snowflake incident.

"Remember how I said you used to glow to those that watched you? And then you disappeared? How old are you in that dream?"

"Uhm . . . I think I'm like twelve."

She shot a look at Joe. He wasn't watching her. Instead, he got up and ambled into the kitchen. I heard a drawer in the kitchen open, rattling, then he came to the arch with a flashlight. "You talk among yourselves. I'm going to have a look downstairs for this box."

I nodded as he opened the basement door and disappeared.

"Zoë, you vanished off the radar at about that age, calculating your date of birth with the correspondence of additional stars in the heavens. Your parents kept your birth pretty much a secret as best they could."

"Why?"

"Because your father insisted. I believe he wanted his daughter to lead a very normal life. With no strange things happening."

I thought of Bobby, and I knew on some level the dream was more of a memory. But the memory always got to a certain point and ended. "So what happened?"

"I don't know. It's kind of like you are now. It was like you were Irin, then you vanished for eight years. Then bam! You're back and stronger than ever."

Dags set his mug down on the coffee table. "So you're thinking that the same thing that happened then might be what's happened now? That's all great—but what exactly *did* happen?"

Rhonda looked at me. "Zoë, do you remember anything odd that's happened lately? Some weird occurrence? Maybe even a blackout like you just had?"

I set the way-back machine to scour, and looked for something that was odd. But then—everything up until the whole blue-fire-trying-to-eat-me moment. And before that—

Wait. No. I wasn't able to OOB before that. Which was why I had resorted to magic. When exactly was it that I noticed I couldn't—

"I blacked out before."

Rhonda sat forward. "When?"

"I was helping Jemmy put a delivery away. This was maybe . . . a week ago or so. I thought it was low blood sugar. I tried going OOB the next day, and that's when it all started. And then it all just faded away."

Dags said, "But you didn't come into contact with anything? A stone or an amulet? A new ghost? Or maybe even a book?"

I shook my head. "Nothing I can remember." His mention of a book made me think about what he'd said earlier. "Why did you say *you* were a book?"

That got a rise out of Rhonda. She almost slammed my

computer (hey!) on the coffee table and stood up. "You *told* her?"

"I didn't tell her what happened. Not yet."

"I forbid you to tell her, Darren. That is not something she needs to know."

Her tone and her clutched hands brought him to his feet. He threw the cloth with the poultice on the table. "I think she does. She's my friend, and at least I"—he pointed to his chest—"do not plan on lying to her or hiding the truth."

Oops.

Man, you could hear Whoville go poo in the silence that comment brought. I could almost see the static electricity surrounding Rhonda's entire body. In fact, I was expecting Dags to erupt in flames at any minute.

The basement door came open. "No. No white box down there. Though I did find quite an assortment of spiders, roaches, and a lot of boxes with jars of things I just don't want to know the names of—" He rounded the corner and stopped and stared at Rhonda and Dags. He looked at me and I shrugged. *Hey, I'm not special anymore. You dah man. You handle it.*

"Okay, kiddies," Joe said as he took a step forward and held out his hands. "It's time for us all to get together."

"No," Rhonda said. "He's going to tell Zoë about what happened."

Joe looked confused. "Okay—lots been hap'n, dearie. Which hap'n?"

She pointed back to Dags.

Joe appeared to get it. "Oh. Yeah. So. Why are you getting all scary hoodoo on him? I think Zoë should know too."

Rhonda rounded that look on Joe, and he smartly took a step back with an inaudible *whoa.* "Why?"

Dags cleared his throat, and she looked back at him. "You're not in control of things this time, Rhonda."

Okay. That was it. And though I would have loved to have stuck around and seen the battle of the stares, I went up to Joe, and whispered, "Let's talk upstairs in Mom's room," and moved out of the room.

20

MY mom's room isn't like what many people expect. Rhonda said it best once, that when she finally got to see Nona's room, she was shocked at how normal it was. Most people think it would be more like some room full of velvet, peacock feathers, beads, and crystal balls on the dresser. The walls would be draped in fabric and the floor covered in Indian rugs.

Nope. Not Mom.

Mom had the most normal room in the house—I say most normal because I still thought the headless lamp in my room was a Halloween decoration. Mom had always been careful at what she spent her sparse money on over the years. And her bedroom was indeed her pride and joy.

But it wasn't full of gitchie goomies or velvet, and not even a crystal ball. Her bed was an antique sleigh-style bed she'd found in McDonough, Georgia, at the antiques market. She'd fixed it up herself and restained it. And her sheets and duvet were a matching set with a high thread count, all handpicked in a burgundy print.

The dresser was another period piece—and don't ask me what period 'cause I don't know. I buy Rooms-to-Go, prefabricated and easy to just set up from a big square box. Doll furniture.

The dresser was always clean, with a single jewelry box on top of it that my dad made when they first got married. She said he was good with wood like that, and she loved the box. Kept it with her all the time. Pictures in carefully chosen frames—from cheap to expensive—flanked that box. Images of me at different stages of my life, from toddler to tweener.

Happy times with my mom. Always happy pictures of Mom and me.

In the corner of the room stood an armoire, another piece she'd taken a long time to pick out. My memories centered on being dragged from antiques store to antiques store, being bored, as Mom looked at countless pieces. This one was made of sassafras wood with a pearl grain finish. It was big and boxy, and *so* Nona.

The walls were painted a soft, warm olive, and the floors were covered in rugs, but they were Oriental ones, not Indian.

That's how I remembered the room, but that wasn't what we walked into.

The floor was completely covered in stuff. I could make out papers, handwritten, as well as all her jewelry strewn from one end of the room to the other. The armoire was open and the clothes piled on the floor. One of the doors was leaning from one hinge, the others ripped out at the nails.

The bed was a disheveled mess, with pillows torn apart and stuffing—polyester, not feathers, since Mom was allergic to feathers—decorating everything like beige snow. The mattress was askew, as if someone had looked between it and the box spring.

The drawers were all pulled out and her things piled here and there.

And in the center of the mess was the shell, cracked and broken, of the jewelry box. It lay in a stomped-on wreck amid glass from the now-destroyed picture frames on the floor. My mind reeled when I saw it.

They'd done a serious killing job on the jewelry box. All my dad's handiwork was now just a busted mess of thin wood. And Mom's jewelry was hidden amid the glass and papers.

I wouldn't really call myself a crybaby, but for the past month I'd found myself oozing tears at the sound of a sneeze. And seeing my mom's things destroyed like this—her life ransacked—all because of me—

I didn't realize I was on the floor with the broken box in my hand until I sensed someone warm beside me, his arms around me from behind. I thought for a fleeting minute it was Daniel—that Joe had gotten hold of him about the break-in and that he'd come to comfort me.

Common sense is a cruel being, and I realized it was Joe trying to get me to stop touching things. Evidently the house had been broken into and the room ransacked. I needed to stop contaminating the scene while he called it in.

But I pulled away from him and held up the jewelry box as he shifted from behind me to my right. "My dad made this, and someone broke it."

He took it from me—and in that instant light flared from his hands. Both of them. I blinked at the intense glow, then refocused on Joe holding the box in both hands, the wood between the glow. "What the hell?"

"There's something in the box," he said, just as Dags and Rhonda entered the room.

"Are Tim and Steve in here too?"

"Yeah, Tim's right beside us."

Oh, this just sucks, me not being able to hear or see them.

"Joe," I said. "What do you mean, there's something in the box?"

He turned the box in his hands (what was left of the box), his eyes intense. "There's something inside of it."

"Inside?" I said. "There isn't any inside. There's nothing left of it but a frame."

"To the physical plane, yeah." Dags smiled as he knelt down beside us. "But not so much in the astral."

Huh? I didn't get it at first—but then Rhonda was on the floor next to us, her knees crunching into glass as well. "You mean the box is multidimensional?"

"Exactly."

"I didn't know Dad could make a multidimensional box," I said, and stared at it. "I guess I need to be Wraith to see the other side?"

"Actually you'd need to be OOB to see it, and access it. Though I can sense it, I can't stick my hand in there and retrieve it." He looked to my left and focused on something. I glanced over but saw nothing.

Then Dags looked back to me. "Steve said neither he nor Tim can access it either, but they can see it."

"What is it?" Joe asked. "An Eidolon?"

"Shhh . . . What, Steve?" Rhonda said, and I guessed that Tim had been talking over him.

Everyone was silent as they listened to Steve. And suddenly I realized how awkward Rhonda must have felt when I was having all those conversations with other people who could hear me and she couldn't. I felt bad suddenly, and a little bit impatient. "What?" I said.

Rhonda looked at me. I was amazed again at how different she looked, how much older she seemed. "Steve said it's a key. A physical, metal key lodged in the astral plane."

"A key?" I looked at Rhonda. "Why would Mom stick a key in the astral plane?"

Rhonda ran a hand through her choppy hair, a sure sign of frustration for Miss Orly. "To be honest—that key might not have been put there by Nona."

"Who else?" Joe said.

Rhonda took in a deep breath and released it quickly before speaking—and she looked right at me. "Adiran Martinique."

DAGS and I were in the botanica as before while Joe called in a few favors. He didn't want to officially report a burglary—because we had no idea when the room had been touched. I hadn't gone in there since Mom disappeared. Jemmy had—but she wasn't answering her phone.

It was getting late, and I wanted to sleep. But I wasn't sure I could, so I was pacing. I was no closer to getting my mom's soul back into her body. The only solutions I could come up with seemed impossible now—with no Eidolons and me just simply a normal person.

There was also an unbelievable core dump rattling around in my head. So Rhonda and everyone says I'm an Irin, or used to be. I'm that way because my dad died before I was conceived. I could evidently talk to ghosts as a child—those memories were coming back now. And then I couldn't and completely forgot about it—or blocked it out, as Dags suggested. For some reason Dags and I shared a dream. TC was overshadowing Cooper and probably having the joyride of his life.

And Dags was a book. I still needed that story.

I rubbed my face with my hand. I was going to need some serious help getting to sleep that night. I looked at the fire, which was little more than embers. I had no idea where Rhonda had gone. I'd put the piece of the jewelry box in my room, into the attic crawl space for safekeeping.

"Zoë," Dags began as he stood in the middle of the room and I paced in front of the fireplace. "Why was Bobby wanting you to look into the box?"

I sighed. "Because he said there was something in there my dad made for me."

"Did he say what?"

"Not that I remember. He just said it was important and I needed to see it." At that moment, all the memories of Bobby abruptly dropped on my head like a house, as if I'd somehow opened a locked door. The afternoons spent in my room, in the backyard, Mom wanting me to go out and play with other kids, take up sports, get out of the house, and my not wanting to go too far away from the children on the street who couldn't leave their houses.

Ghost children.

"Dags . . . I used to play with ghost kids. All the time. It was nothing to me." I looked at him. "Why did I forget that? I used to go OOB all the time . . . and we'd play on the roof. They were all over the neighborhood where we lived in Seattle, and then in Portland. Bobby was in the house in Portland . . . and he hated it when I had to do homework."

"Zoë, what is the last memory you have?"

I stopped and looked at Dags, and suddenly he didn't seem so small anymore. In fact, he seemed larger-than-life. His eyes were an intense gray, but his expression was kind. I didn't see many kind expressions these days. "Last memory?"

"What is the last memory you have of the ghosts?"

"Bobby and me—going into the basement. He said something about that box."

"Like in your dream?"

"Yeah, but I always thought it was a dream. Just a recurring nightmare. But I don't ever remember Bobby going all evil and ugly like he did in that last dream."

Dags said, "That's because your subconscious didn't want me in there and fought to get me out."

"Neat trick there, Pancho. You gonna tell me how you did that? Like is it part of the new you?"

"I have no idea. But for now, I want you to try and remember that last memory in as much detail as you can. First off, why did you go looking for the box?"

I shut my eyes and felt Dags take my hands in his own. His were warm, and I offhandedly wondered if that was because he'd summoned his familiars or if he just naturally had really warm hands.

I did concentrate on the memory—a dream really—and I told Dags what I saw as it popped up. "I was in my room, doing homework . . . and Bobby wanted me to go downstairs to look in the box."

"Why?"

"I wanted to—" The memory came back a bit at a time. It was like dumping a puzzle out on the floor and all the pieces were turned backward, showing just the cardboard, and I had to flip them over and start finding like images to put wholes together. "I had homework, and I wanted to write a romance. And Bobby seemed to always know what I was thinking. He told me—"

Something caught in my throat, and I squeezed my eyes tight. They burned with tears, and I didn't want Dags to see—though he'd been through quite a lot with me since the debacle with the Society and L6.

"Keep going."

"It's just that—he said he'd seen pictures of my dad. And that he knew my dad loved me. He said—" I opened my eyes and looked at Dags. "He said my dad had made me a necklace."

Dags's eyes widened as well. "A necklace? He made you one?"

"That's what Bobby said. And that it was in that box." I shifted my weight where I knelt on the concrete floor and looked up at the metal shelves. "But it's not here. The box isn't in the basement."

"Zoë, did you open the box back then? In the dream or in reality?"

"I—" But that's where the memory ended, and in the dream I always woke up. "I saw a spider and hit my head. And then I always woke up."

"So you don't know if you ever really looked in the box?"

"No, but I do remember the box after that. It was always there, in the basement. And I remember seeing it here as well. I helped Mom move into this house. In fact, it was while I was moving stuff down here—including that box—that I first saw Tim and Steve. Though Mom insisted she'd seen them before she even bought it." I smiled. "She would listen to them bicker about what color things should be, then she'd do just that and make them happy."

"But you'd already started traveling out of your body by then?"

I nodded. My eyes burned again, and I thought of my mom. "I want my mom so bad, Darren."

He looked very serious as he reached out and took me into his arms. We weren't a perfect fit—I was still a little taller, but not by much when we were both barefoot. And it was good to have warm, human contact. "It's all right, Zoë. We'll get Nona back. I'm not letting this one go."

He pulled away first but kept his hands on my arms, rubbing them up and down. I smiled at him and sniffed, very glad I wasn't wearing makeup. "You okay?" he asked.

I nodded.

"Good. Now—when it comes to stones and your father's previous line of work as a jeweler, it makes me think it might have been an Eidolon in the box—but the only Eidolon I know of that was never found was the blue one."

I reached up and tucked a few stray hairs behind his ear. "You mean—you think my dad made me a necklace out of an Eidolon?"

He nodded. "Maybe. But how could such a stone benefit you?"

I searched his face. "What does the blue stone do? If it's like the others, maybe it amplifies power or something."

"That sounds right. Objects of foci can be used in both a forward and backward position; it can be used for the positive and the reverse." He smiled. "I never really use the word *negative* because it's not that the effect is evil but just the opposite."

"You sound like Rhonda."

"I know." Dags nodded. "But what's the opposite of *amplify*?"

I knew this one! *"Quiet?"*

"I don't mean to break up your little party in here—"

Joe stood at the foot of the stairs and put his hands on his hips. His expression was odd as he looked at us, then I realized Dags and I were still touching, standing face-to-face.

Dags and I immediately backed away from each other. "No, no, it's okay—" he said, just as I said, "Don't you ever knock?"

Joe smiled, but I noticed it did not meet his eyes. "I just got some disturbing news. Cooper's been doing a bit of investigating on his own—which is why he says he's been absent. And apparently, after backtracking phone records, ATM, and miscellaneous surveillance as well as questioning neighbors"—he looked at me, then Dags, then back to me—"the last person to see all three of the victims, including Boo Baskins, was Detective Daniel Frasier."

I was still stuck at "disturbing news"—Cooper had been doing investigating? Or was it TC? And if it was TC, what was he doing? Honestly reporting or filling in the blanks for his own ends?

And if it wasn't TC—then where was he?

Then I registered exactly what Joe had said—it bounced around a little before completely settling. "Wait . . . you mean someone saw him with each person?"

"Yeah. Phone records also confirmed he's been in contact with Randall Kemp and Francisco Rodriguez lately. And neighbors confirm seeing his car at Boo's house—one of them took down the license plate. ATM footage has him with Randall before he kidnapped you, withdrawing money. And the bouncer over at Opera—"

I stared at Joe—waiting for him to continue. All these records—evidence. Again, was it really Cooper or TC?

Hell—do I tell these guys?

Yeah . . . and get my ass reamed?

NO.

But I somehow already knew what he was going to say. Opera was one of the more popular dance clubs in downtown Atlanta. Situated a block from the Four Seasons, it was a combination events hall and club.

"The bouncer there identified Daniel as being the man with Boo Baskins before her body was found."

Daniel was with Boo. I didn't have a very vivid recollection of the girl alive. Emo lite. Gothlike. And dainty. And she could talk and didn't have any dark secrets.

At least nothing as dark as mine.

Dags said, "So does this mean that Daniel is a suspect in all three murders?"

"Suspect maybe," Joe said. "But in all three instances no one can come up with motive." He pointed to me as he moved into the room and scratched his spiky head. "And there's still the fact that the coroner can't quite explain how each of them died. Does that sound like Daniel?"

"Maybe he was doing his own investigation?" I volunteered. I know it sounded lame, and I was grasping at any explanation as to why Daniel would have anything to do with those three individuals.

"I'd like to think so," Joe said. "But the man's been a total asswipe for the past month. There are things going on back at the station that have pretty much put him on everyone's shit list."

"Like what?" Dags said.

"Bad behavior," Joe said. "Picking fights with people he usually gets along with. Irritable. And no one's seen him eat or drink a thing."

Dags and I glanced at each other. But it was Dags who said, "That's an odd thing to notice."

"Not so much if you suspect someone is drinking on the job. We watch our own—to see if they're heavy on the sauce. But no one could catch Daniel drinking—anything. Not even a cup of water from the dispenser. I've been to his house several times, and he never answers—and you know how much Daniel loves to stay in at night and watch old movies."

This last comment he directed at me, and I nodded. It was one of his favorite things—not that he and I had ever had the opportunity to really enjoy that type of evening. And if we had, maybe we'd have had more time to develop a more romantic relationship.

Maybe.

But right now all bets were off on the Daniel factor.

"So what are you going to do?" Dags asked.

Joe put his hands on his hips, and I was suddenly very aware of his shoulder holster and the big gun nestled inside of it. He'd never really worn a gun before—or at least none that I'd noticed. He wasn't wearing his usual jacket but a tee shirt. His flannel shirt usually covered the weapon, I guess.

He looked like a real cop, a real law-enforcement officer.

"Right now Cooper wants me to locate Daniel—and then I need to watch him for twenty-four hours. See what he's up to. But the problem right now is that no one can find him. Cooper's had a unit on his apartment, and he hasn't been home in forty-eight hours."

My eyes widened. That was very much unlike Daniel—and if he hadn't been coming home, then where was he staying to shower and sleep?

Dags cleared his throat. "Does he have a new girlfriend? Perhaps someone he's staying with?"

My heart lodged in my throat, but I didn't say anything.

"That's our initial thought—but we can't find him even to tail him to anyone. Cooper thought maybe he'd eventually turn up with Zoë." He looked at me directly. "But I have my doubts."

I did too. I'd lost him. I'd completely lost Daniel. I didn't believe he had anything to do with the deaths—he wasn't some Abysmal monster sucking out souls. And I refused to believe there was a Symbiont inside of him—Daniel's presence with each of the victims was his own way of detection.

And he was being distant and untraceable because he was working the case.

Or something.

Yeah . . . and I believe in the tooth fairy too.

I pursed my lips. Unless there *was* such a thing as a tooth fairy, I thought, and with my luck it would be a short, round, hairy man with big rabbit teeth that ate children.

Joe pulled out his phone and pressed a key. After a few seconds he hung up and shook his head. "I've tried Daniel three times now—and usually by now he's picked up and been real irritated with me. He's not even answering." He gave me a sympathetic look. "I'm sorry, Zoë. I know how much he means to you."

I shrugged. "I evidently don't mean that much to him though, do I? I blew it with him, Joe. I wasn't honest, and he finally just got fed up with me."

"Maybe," Joe said. "I have to go find him. Talk about a needle in a haystack." He ran his hand through his hair. "Rhonda's on the horn asking some of her Society buddies what they know about setting physical objects into spatial, astral boxes." He shrugged. "Makes no sense to me. So, what exactly were you two talking about?"

I gave Joe a quick recap of what I'd told Dags.

"But the last thing I remember was seeing a spider and falling."

"Yes, and you bumped your head. Did you lose consciousness?"

Memory of that event was still mostly like a dream, and it was hard to see it as anything but a dream. "I always thought I hit my head because I didn't remember anything else. Or I just woke up 'cause I hated spiders. But if you're thinking something else happened . . ."

"Did Nona find you?"

I opened my mouth, then shut it. "I—I don't know. I can't remember anything else. Joe, I always thought it was just one of those weird dreams."

"And when did you start having those dreams?"

Now I could answer that question. "Just recently—about the time I couldn't go OOB anymore."

Joe and Dags stared at me. It was Dags who said, "You think it might be your mom trying to tell you something?"

!!!

I'd never thought of that. "But what?"

"That maybe there was something in that box that could

help," Dags said, rubbing his arm. "And if it's *like* a Summoning Eidolon—"

Joe shook his head. "Zoë—"

I held up my hand, knowing exactly what it was he was going to say. "Look—when the evil Maddox summoned me back into my body, when he had me all pinned on the table in the Stephenses' basement, didn't he *just* use the Summoning Eidolon?"

Dags shrugged. "Uhm . . . I wasn't there."

Joe continued to shake his head. "Zoë—forget the Eidolons, okay? You keep bringing this up—nobody's using any Eidolons to pull anyone back into their body—got it? Let it go."

I was not going to let it go—but before I could give any kind of argument, Rhonda stepped back in from the front porch. When she came into the tea shop, where Dags and Joe and I had moved to, I noticed she looked a lot paler than usual—and that was pretty pale. Her face looked—weird.

"Zoë," she said in a very quiet voice, then looked at me and Dags, "Miller Oaks just called—"

Miller Oaks.

That's where my mom's body was.

At that minute Joe's phone went off.

Rhonda glanced at him, then looked at me. "Nona's body's gone."

21

THE sky was a velvet backdrop to a vast ocean of stunning jewels when we arrived at Miller Oaks. This was the kind of view of the sky that I couldn't see from in town. The weather had been pretty clear all day, and the temperature was starting its spring climb into the heat of doom. Azaleas were in bloom along most of the scenery and outside the long-term-care facility. By the beginning of April, everything would be covered in yellow fuzz.

I called it the Tennis Ball Season.

When everyone's car had the sheen of a yellow tennis ball.

The dazzle of the blooming flowers was overwhelmed by the flashing lights of five Fulton County police cars parked along the front and side entrances. Joe threw Nona's car into park just outside and had his badge up and faced out for presentation to the uniformed officers guarding the doors.

"They're with me," Joe said as he pointed at me, Rhonda, and Dags.

"This isn't your jurisdiction," the cop said as he put a hand on Joe's chest.

"Chester," a deep voice said. "Let them through."

I looked past the officer and saw a tall, broad-shouldered African-American dressed in a nice, tailored suit and shiny shoes. He had a very handsome face and a stern expression. Captain Cooper stood beside him down the hall and looked relatively small beside him.

And Cooper wasn't a small man.

But he was winking at me.

Oh, geez . . . TC was still inside of him.

The four of us approached the two men, and I was vaguely aware of the lack of nurses and orderlies in the hallways. Or even residents. It was like someone had put all the Wheelchair Wandas and Willies in their rooms.

Cooper did the introductions. "Joe, this is Captain Morgan Haskins, in charge of the situation here. Captain, this is Sergeant Joe Halloran."

The two shook hands, and again I was amazed at how short everyone looked next to the captain. "Detective Halloran—" The man's voice was like a mixture of James Earl Jones and Laurence Fishburne. "I've heard a lot about you."

The look on Joe's face was priceless as he glanced at Captain Cooper. "Well . . . I'm not sure if that's good or bad. But I have heard some very impressive things about you, sir." Joe looked around and found me and pulled me up closer. "This is Zoë Martinique, the victim's daughter."

I looked up with wide-eyed wonder as my own hand disappeared inside of the captain's. I was relieved to find his skin warm to the touch and his grip gentle.

"Miss Martinique," he said, and smiled. "I promise you we'll get to the bottom of things shortly. But I do have to ask you a few questions."

I nodded. I was staring at his face . . . and there was something about it that wasn't . . .

"Where's Dags?" Joe said.

I blinked several times to look away from the captain and turned my attention to our position. Looking around, I said, "I don't know. He was right here." I had the sneaking suspicion he'd done his little "I'm not really here" shtick and was around doing his own investigative work.

Fine by me. Dags I trusted.

"And who is this young lady? I haven't—"

When he stopped talking abruptly, I turned and looked at Rhonda, then I looked up at him. His eyes were wide, and his expression completely unguarded.

Joe started the introduction, but Haskins was already stepping forward and reaching for Rhonda's hand. "Miss Orly—it is an honor to meet you. Your uncle's pictures and description did not do you justice."

Joe, Cooper, and I looked at Rhonda, then looked at Haskins as he kissed the back of her right hand, then we looked back at Rhonda again. Excuse me?

"Sir—you know Miss Orly?"

"I knew her uncle. My father was a supporter, and we were often invited to their house in the country."

Red sirens went off in my head. Ah! This was a Dioscuri thing! This smelled of that Ishmael Society—especially with the way he reacted to her. Like she was some sort of princess or something.

"May we talk for a moment?" Haskins said to Rhonda.

"Whoa," I said, and held up my hands. "My mom? What about my mom? Who the fuck is trying to find my mom's body? Didn't anyone see who took her?"

I had my mouth open to say more but someone grabbed my shoulders and turned me just as Haskins and Rhonda stepped away from us as well as the entrance we'd come through. Cooper/TC had both his hands on my shoulders and was looking at me, searching my face.

"What?"

But he looked at Joe. "Both of you follow me."

And we did. Down the hall, away from the uniformed officers, and directly into Mom's room. It was empty—her nightgown neatly folded on the bed as well as the booties they'd had on her feet. The side pantry that doubled as a closet was also open, and the spare change of clothes I'd always kept there was gone from the hangers.

I looked at Cooper. "What—what happened?"

Cooper had his hands on his hips. "According to the nurse—your mother got up, got dressed, said good-bye and thanks, and walked out."

"Walked out?" Joe and I said in unison. And in harmony.

Sighing, Cooper nodded. "Are you two dense? I'd have the

nurse tested for drugs or alcohol, but I'm almost sure she'd test okay. But the doctors I spoke with said there was no way your mother could do that. Not after the month of atrophy to her muscles, the lack of use—" He shook his head. "I don't buy it."

Joe spoke up. "What did Haskins say?"

Cooper looked at him. "He hasn't heard that story yet. As far as he knows, somebody came in and took Miss Martinique's body." Then he looked at me. "Guy gives me the creeps. He's more than what he seems, Zoë. But like this, I can't really see what it is."

His familiarity with me put Joe on alert. He was looking from me to Cooper. "What do you mean 'see'?"

I decided to divert that question, in case TC thought it would be fun to expose himself. Literally. "How was she taken?"

"Someone picked her up. There was a car waiting outside."

"Make? Model?"

"The nurse didn't notice—she was too busy standing at the front door with her mouth open." Cooper pursed his lips. "But she did mention several times that Miss Martinique was very gracious." He snapped his fingers. "Oh, and she asked about a necklace. A green one."

Joe and I glanced at each other. "A necklace?" Joe said.

"What—you know about a necklace?" Cooper looked at me.

I nodded. I was feeling a little dizzy. When was the last time I'd eaten? "Oh . . . uhm . . . yeah. It was a family heirloom." Mom actually owned an Eidolon pendant, a green one. It was the Creation Eidolon. I'd kept it when they'd put Mom's body in the hospital, and I'd hung it over the door to Mom's shop.

To be honest—I wasn't sure where it was. I'd forgotten about it. That might be a problem.

Cooper's phone rang. He took it off his belt, checked the number, then held up the index finger of his right hand. "You two stay right there." Then he moved away toward the window. It was looking to me like TC was enjoying being a cop for a day.

Something brushed against my cheek, then traveled down

my back. I shivered visibly and wrapped my arms around my chest.

"Zoë?" Joe said as he stepped closer. He reached out and touched my shoulder. "You okay? You know . . . your voice is getting worse, and you're awfully pale." He leaned in closer. "You know where Dags is?"

I shook my head at him, but I wasn't really paying attention. There was something here . . . in this room . . . and it wasn't anything I could see.

Damn it all for not being Wraith! If I could just be what I was, I knew I could find my mom!

And what the hell made off with her body? It didn't take Rhonda or Dags to tell me something had invaded my mom's body, possessed it, and driven it right out of here. Which was, of course, easier than trying to carry it out.

Unfortunately I knew who it wasn't—and I knew who was going to say it was.

"That Archer creep did this, didn't he? He's got her soul; now he just possessed her body and walked right out with it."

I looked up at him, at his face. And for a strange second I wanted to reach up and touch his cheek. He looked so distraught—like Daniel used to when he—

Like Daniel used to.

Where is Daniel? Damn . . . I'd nearly forgotten what Joe had learned about him and his connection to the three deaths.

Cooper closed his phone. He didn't look happy.

"Things just keep getting weirder and weirder. Joe—we've got to head back into Decatur. They've found another victim near Little Five Points."

I felt my heart drop. Back to Decatur?

"You said victim, not body." Joe asked, "Someone alive?"

"According to what that dog-named guy just said on the phone."

I knew he meant Mastiff. Joe's expression turned from a frown, to a smirk, then back to a frown. Cooper was acting just a tad more off than usual, and Joe noticed.

I stepped to Cooper to divert attention again. "What about my mom's body?" And I gave him an extra-glary look.

He looked down at me, and I could see just a hint of red flare in his eyes, a reminder that he was there. But I didn't back

down. "Miss Martinique—I understand your frustration. But
the best I can do is put a missing person bulletin on the body.
She's not dead—she was alive while she was in here. So it's a
kidnapping. We'll do what we can. But Haskins is in charge of
this case, not me."

He was reminding me he wasn't really Cooper, then he left
the room.

My God—where was my life going? And where was my
mom going? Where did whatever it was possessing her take
her body? The gravity of the situation wasn't lost on me. Hours
before, when Joe had been telling me to forget about using any
Eidolons to bring Mom's soul back, I knew where her body
was. Even without knowing how I was going to get her soul
back—having her physically there was almost like having her
back. Almost.

But now—I had no Mommy soul, no Mommy body, and no
Summoning rock.

I suddenly had an awful thought.

Okay, I'd been having a lot of awful thoughts lately—but
this one made me stand straight up, shoulders back, breasts
out. "What if—" I said in my outside voice.

Joe was beside me. "What if what?"

I looked at him. "What if what possessed my mom's body
was the Horror?"

He made a face. I wasn't expecting that face either. It was
a pinched look, kinda like you give a child who just pooped in
her pants. "Come on, Zoë. You don't believe TC on that, do
you? I'd bet real cash it was TC piloting your mom's body.
And aren't Symbionts supposed to heal their hosts?"

"Only if there's a contract between the Phantasm and the
host," said a new voice.

Both of us turned and saw Dags at the door.

"Where the hell have you been?" Joe asked.

"Looking around." He was watching me. "Do you feel it?"

My eyes widened. "Yes—it's touched my cheek twice.
What is it? Does Maureen or Alice know?"

Dags shook his head. "No, but whatever it is—it's powerful."

I put a hand to my lips. "The Phantasm?"

He looked worried. "Could be." Dags held out his right

hand, and the circular patterns tattooed there glowed softly. Alice appeared beside Dags, a soft, transparent ghost.

"Whatever this is, Zoë, it's residual. Its main body isn't here anymore."

I didn't like the sound of that. "You mean—whatever's touching me—is just like an afterthought?"

She nodded. "I'm not sure I know what it is we're dealing with."

"A Horror?"

Alice shook her head slowly, but she wasn't really looking at me anymore. Her gaze was more focused on the room. "I don't know. The Phantasm has this kind of power, Zoë. It's strongest here."

I turned and looked at the room as well. Joe was uncharacteristically quiet as he stood off to the side and watched our conversation. But Alice was right—I'd sensed something when I'd stepped inside the facility—something oogy.

And the oogy was almost overwhelming here. "Where did it take my mom?"

"Too bad I didn't LoJack her ass," Joe muttered. "Which reminds me—I plan on doing that to you."

I looked at him. "Me?"

"Your body's been hijacked twice and kidnapped once, and just the other day Rodriguez tried to have it taken away as well. Your family's one big missing persons case."

We heard footsteps approaching at a dead run. Alice vanished, and Dags lowered his hand as Rhonda came to the door. Her face looked pinched—and she was flushed. "I have to go. Something's happened."

Joe shook his head—so did Dags and I. "What is it?"

Rhonda said, "Tyrone Miller—he was one of the last recruited members of the Society before the split. He had an affinity for clairvoyance." She looked sad as she spoke. "I'd hoped he'd see reason. Maybe open his eyes to Rodriguez's hidden agendas. But it appears whatever is killing people got to him."

We all looked at one another. Joe spoke. "Wait . . . I thought Cooper said the victim was still alive."

Rhonda frowned. "What victim? I just got the call from my

aide—that Tyrone's body was found outside of Rodriguez's house."

Well. Okay. That was news.

"Did you report it?"

"No—Haskins was with me. He'll handle this."

I pointed to the floor. "No, he needs to handle this—he needs to find Mom's body!"

Joe held out a hand. "Rhonda, you need to report that body to the police—"

"No." It was a simple answer. And it was final.

I looked from one to the other. *Lovers' spat?*

Neither of them spoke.

Then Rhonda said, "Cooper's waiting outside for you."

That was his cue. He looked at me. "You going to be okay?"

I nodded. "I have to be. Hiding in my closet and clutching my stuffed bear isn't going to help matters right now." No, but it sure sounded like a plan to me. Only . . . what ever happened to my stuffed bear? The one I used to keep in the closet in the old house?

And then he did something he hadn't done in a long time— not since that night at the Stephenses' home. In the basement.

He hugged me.

Joe felt warm, and so very nice as I wrapped my arms around him.

Being held like this—something I missed from Daniel—I almost started bawling like a little girl. But that wasn't going to help him leave. I knew if I did start to cry, he wouldn't leave, then Cooper would get mad.

I didn't want Cooper mad.

When he let go, I was amazed at the emotion in his expression. I was so used to seeing Joe with a permanent smirk on his face—I wasn't used to him being all . . . well . . . human. "If you hear from Daniel, call me."

I nodded. "I will, only don't hold your breath."

He turned to Rhonda and hesitated.

I looked at her too, and was a bit taken aback by the expression on her face. It wasn't a mad look—after all, her boyfriend had just squeezed the stuffing out of me. It was more of a disappointed look. She held out a hand as he stepped toward her. "I'm fine. I have to go with Haskins. His men will clean up here and get back to you."

Dags held out his hand to Joe. "I'll take Zoë with me."

Joe handed him the keys to Mom's Volvo. "Watch your back."

"You watch yours."

Dags's expression mirrored Rhonda's. Jemmy's warning that Dags was in love with me rang in my head. Och. I really liked Dags. He was cute and fun, and he had powers—but he also had two women permanently hanging about. Besides, Dags knew how I felt about Daniel.

But not Joe.

Though I had told Dags about Joe's kiss. His opinion had been that Joe acted on pure adrenaline, and that it probably meant nothing.

Me? Every time I thought of Joe's kiss my toes curled.

I didn't think it meant nothing—which made me just nervous enough to be uncomfortable around him.

Er . . . when we were alone.

I felt my face heat up as Joe reached out and touched my cheek, then moved out the door.

Rhonda spoke to Dags. "Be careful. I'm afraid Rodriguez's followers will be after Zoë worse than ever. They'll blame her for Tyrone's death, which I'm sure Rodriguez will help along."

Both of us looked at her slack-jawed. "Excuse me?" I said. "Blame me for a guy I don't even know? What about pointing at Rodriguez?"

"Yeah, well, we all know followers aren't exactly the brightest." Rhonda smiled. "That's why they call them followers."

I smiled. Damnit—I missed her. But I was still pissed.

"Rhonda." Dags spoke up. "Exactly how large is the Society of Ishmael, as opposed to the splinter group?"

"Originally we had close to fifty members, either original participants in the Dioscuri Experiments or related somehow. When Rodriguez's group split off, the original formation was cut nearly in half."

"So we're talking roughly twenty-five members for each?"

She nodded. "But of those, maybe ten to fifteen in each are active. But they are dangerous, Dags. My people won't move against Zoë. I've never lied to them about the reality of what Domas was doing and about what effect it had on the subjects." Rhonda looked at me. "I know you want to find Nona—but your first priority is to get your powers back, Zoë. You have to become the Wraith, or there's no way to even begin looking. You've wasted enough time."

I held out my hands. "I know that," I said in a less-than-friendly voice. That comment was uncalled for. But true. I had wasted a lot of time—but it wasn't my fault I had lost my abilities. "But exactly how do I do it? I don't even understand how I lost the Wraith to begin with."

Haskins appeared in the hallway behind Rhonda. "We have to go." He looked at me and nodded. "Be assured, Miss Martinique, Miss Orly has informed us—me—of what's happened, and we will do everything in our power to find your mother."

He nodded to Dags and disappeared.

I looked at Rhonda. "Society?"

She nodded as well. "Haskins has an excellent reputation. We'll do what we can." And then she was gone. All business. And so little of the Magical MacGyver I missed.

I turned and looked at the room. At the neat way everything was arranged, including the bed. Everything was neat. "My mom's not this neat. She never folds dirty clothes."

"Maybe a clue as to who's in her body?"

"Maybe." I moved across the room to the window and looked out. I saw Cooper and Joe drive off, then watched as Rhonda got into a limousine with Haskins, and I thought—*I really don't know her at all, do I?*

"There is one person we haven't asked advice from," Dags said. "Someone who seems to know as much about your abilities as you."

I pulled my gaze from the window and looked at him. I knew what he was going to say, because the same thought crossed my mind as well. "Maharba."

He smiled. "At maharba dot com."

22

I'LL admit—trying to get in touch with Maharba wasn't the first thing on my list of good ideas. But since that list consisted of hiding in my closet and chewing on my shoes—I didn't have an argument. The first thing out of the gate was figuring out how to contact them.

Yeah—I had the e-mail address. The one I used to send reports back. But I hadn't heard a peep out of them since the whole SOI Adventure. I'd sat and stared at the computer screen many times while alone in the shop—trying to understand how Maharba figured in the Society of Ishmael or League of Six.

All Maharba had requested was information on what Francisco and Knowles talked about in that room—and then they gave me advice on the Eidolons, albeit after we'd already heard about them. They had helped.

And then there'd been nothing.

Not a word. I'd e-mailed Maharba several times—offering my services. I'd needed the money to keep paying for Mom's health care. But they'd never answered.

It was close to dawn by the time we made it back to the shop—me with reassurances from several of the officers under Haskins that they would follow up on all leads to find my mother's body. What I feared was that the nurse's story of her getting up and walking out would snowball into something reaching the proportions of an urban legend.

And to be honest—I really didn't want Mom's ego to get any bigger than it already was.

The air was chilly again—winter not wanting to let go. It'd been the weirdest weather pattern I'd seen in Georgia. But then, as my mom always said, "Don't like the weather? Wait a minute."

I flipped on the light in the tea shop and moved into the botanica. I half expected Tim or Steve to show up—asking questions—offering to make tea.

Steve loved tea.

But there was nobody there.

Not even the Stone Dragon faced me. As far as I knew, it was still in pieces in Stephens's basement. With a sigh, I opened the fireplace curtain and grabbed a few pieces of old newspaper and wadded them up into loose balls for kindling. I had a small fire nearly started by the time Dags came into the room, a steaming mug of what smelled like hot chocolate in each hand.

He'd snagged Rhonda's recipe, and I was damned grateful. That wench made the best hot chocolate around.

He handed me a steaming mug topped with melting whipped cream. I gestured to the closed iBook on the coffee table. "Rhonda left the computer down here."

Dags set his mug on the coffee table and took off his long coat. After tossing it on the sofa, he settled down in front of the computer and lifted the lid, his back to the slowly warming fire. His face was immediately illuminated in the light from the screen. "You still have Maharba's e-mails?"

"Yeah." I turned away from the fire, feeling a bit blah, and plopped down beside him to lean up against the papasan. "Just open MAIL."

He did and to my surprise a red 1 popped up on my dock icon. Dags clicked on it and a single piece of mail was bolded in my in-box.

We both leaned in close to the screen, me setting my mug on the table, and read the sender.

Maharba.

I looked at the mail date. This had arrived less than an hour ago.

Dear Miss Martinique,

First let us express our utmost distress at the catastrophe that has befallen your family. We have unlimited resources at your disposal—you have only to ask. We would also like to congratulate you in your recent evolution. Your increased growth should prove to be even more exciting as the year progresses.

The reason we write to you now—we have learned of a larger threat. Apparently there is a Horror let loose within the physical plane. This creature has already misused its power and killed four souls, not to mention the soul of the body it is inhabiting. We must warn you—without your power, you will be helpless to stop it. And it MUST be stopped. We had cheered at your recent evolution because such a power would be necessary to defeat such a creature.

We are aware of your present condition and have taken steps as before to rectify the situation.

Maharba

I sat back, blinking. *Son of—*
Son of a bitch.
Sonofafuckingbitch!
"What do they mean 'rectify the situation'?" Dags shook his head. " 'Steps as before'?"

Dags pulled out his phone and dialed a number. After several seconds he said, "Hey, it's Darren. I'm going to forward you an e-mail from Maharba. Give me a call when you get it." He disconnected, put his phone on the table, and gently took the laptop from me. A few quick clicks—forwarding the mail to Joe Halloran and Rhonda—and he pushed it aside.

Then he moved behind me and started rubbing my hunched shoulders. It was a tentative touch at first, then he grew bolder and applied more pressure.

It was wonderful.

Human contact, no matter who you are, is essential to the

human condition. We all need physical contact, the tactile certainty that we're not alone. It'd been so long since I'd had any kind of reassurance like that. My mom had been quick with a hug, or a kiss. Always touching me. Even Rhonda and I were good at hugging.

Daniel had been very affectionate.

Once.

And even Joe—

Yes . . . even his touch, both with his hands and his lips . . . had made me feel warm.

But there hadn't been any of that in over a month. Nothing. Jemmy had been a good friend, but I'd always sensed she was still slightly afraid of me.

And Dags—I still remembered Jemmy's words.

"He's in love with you."

That was just . . . ridiculous. Wasn't it? I'd always seen Dags as a sidekick. Like Rhonda. During the whole investigation with him and Rhonda and the Shadow People, he'd always seemed so standoffish. Like he was a little intimidated by me.

I had to wonder—now that I wasn't Wraith—was he no longer afraid of me?

I was never afraid of you.

The voice in my head surprised me, and I twisted where I sat, looking back at him, looking at me. The computer screen had shut off, and the fire was the only illumination on the left side of his face. His dark hair fell in chopped elegance along his forehead and in front of his ears, like one of those animes Rhonda was forever watching.

"I hear you—"

He nodded. "We never lost our communication."

I shook my head. "No." And I shifted where I sat and faced him. He settled in with crossed legs, and I crossed my own. "So, I wonder what they mean by 'rectify'?"

He shrugged. "Dunno."

"Who are they?" There was a clump of hair over his eyelashes. I reached up and moved it to the side.

"I don't know." He reached up as well and touched several strands of my hair on the left side. "I miss the streak."

I nodded. I did too. And the mark on my arm. Somehow they made me different. Special.

"Zoë." His expression looked pained in the shadows of the fire. "You are special. There isn't a badge or a button that will make you that way. You just are."

"Look at me, Dags." I pointed to my chest with both index fingers. "I can't do anything anymore. At least for a while I could OOB and gather information for people. And, okay, yeah—so I went all scary recently and killed my ex–best friend." I winced at that memory. "But I brought her back. Twice, really. But now—I'm nothing more than some mall girl, fit only for selling clothing. Or shoes."

Dags reached out and put his right hand on his right knee and his left hand on his left knee. Then he turned them over, palms up. The circles weren't visible. "You think these make me special? I don't, Zoë. I think what they are—what I did to myself, what happened after . . . I see them as reminders that I stepped into an existence with greater responsibility to the world and the people in it. I can't lead a normal life anymore."

I looked down at his palms and put my hands on top of his. I traced the circles with my fingers, and he flinched. He smiled. I smiled as well. And I was amazed at how smooth his palms were. With tattoos I thought there would be scars.

And they were warm. I pulled his right hand up to my cheek and brushed it against my skin, again amazed at how warm his skin was to the touch. I hadn't realized I'd closed my eyes, and opened them. He held up his left hand and hesitantly brushed my hair back from my face.

"Zoë, I—"

"Ssshhhh . . ."

Looking back, I don't really know why I did what I did next. I tried to justify it over and over in my mind—maybe thinking it was just a weak moment, or my overactive libido.

But when pushed against the wall, the only reason I could come up with was . . . because I wanted to. And I knew on deeper levels that he wanted to as well. It wasn't in the way I used to pretend Daniel wanted me, or the way I sensed Joe's desire in his kiss, but in the way I felt when I was with Dags.

It was how I used to feel with Rhonda—before truth reared its ugly head.

Safe. Protected.

Loved?

I reached out with my right hand and touched his dark hair, like silk against my cold fingers, and pushed it back behind his ear. His jaw was set and his eyes wide as he looked at my face. I moved my hand to his neck, and felt the smoothness of his skin there, dazzled by the shadows the flickering light of the fireplace cast on him.

His right hand moved from mine where I clutched it. He touched my face, his fingers warm against my cool cheek, as if his body held a fever. His fingers traced my ear, my neck, then he threaded them into my hair, pulling me close.

But I was already easing him to me as I flattened my hand against the back of his shoulder. His head inclined to my left and I tilted mine to the right as our lips touched. Just a hint of hesitation for both of us. His were soft and supple against mine, warm and shy. Small, sharp kisses grew longer as our confidence matured, and we pressed ourselves in deeper, his tongue soft and gentle before his lips moved from mine and kissed my cheek, my neck—

Heat flared swift and almost painful inside of my chest. I knew desire—had been acquainted with it for years—but there was just enough of the hint of innocence that fed the beast inside of me, the passionate me that wanted, craved, and demanded the touch of wanton desire.

Darren's heat mirrored my own as I pulled him to me, unfolded my legs, and lay back on the floor, on the rug that hid the pentagram beneath it. I pulled at my sweater, yanking it over my head. To my surprise he took it from me, quickly folded it, and placed it beneath my head.

I couldn't see half of his face as it was shrouded in shadow, but somehow the darkness didn't take away from his pleasure as he leaned over me and showered me with small, tender kisses, his left hand bracing himself, his right hand tracing the line from my right shoulder to my right breast. He cupped it softly, so gently in his hand, and I wanted to feel both his hands on my skin.

It was a front clasp and I irritably snapped it free. He sighed with delight as I arched upward, demanding he take me. Darren's kisses moved from my lips to my neck, then trailed so softly and slowly to my right nipple. I gasped as he teased it with his tongue, and I reached up to grab at his back.

He bit, and teased, and I couldn't stop the low moan that escaped between my lips.

Oh God, oh God, oh God . . .

Even as he moved to my left side I found my fingers fumbling at the buttons of his shirt. I felt like a schoolgirl, accepting a man for the very first time. An experienced man.

And I wanted him inside of me, IMMEDIATELY.

Darren sat up, straddling me, and unbuttoned the remaining buttons. He pulled the shirt off, revealing what I already knew to be a soft, smooth, well-defined chest. I reached up to him, and he leaned forward, placing his hands on either side of me. I wanted him against me, needed to press myself into him.

But he was moving down again, licking the sensitive skin between my breasts, making a trail to my belly button as he moved himself farther away. I growled with pleasure and frustration, but he was determined.

With no hesitation, he moved his tongue along the line of my jeans as his fingers unfastened them. I tried to wiggle out of them, but he was quick to ease my tension, pulling at the sides until they were below my knees. I was able to kick them off as he toyed with the pink thong I wore. I caught a smile in the shadows as he knelt even farther and pulled at the thong's sides, making a game of touching me along my legs until goose bumps decorated my arms, my stomach, and my thighs.

And then he was there—and I gasped loudly as his tongue probed and found the most intimate parts of me. He used his fingers to massage and to hold as my pelvis arched, and I bit the index finger of my right hand.

The orgasm was fast—too fast—and I cried out. I'd never cried out before—not like that. But the intensity made me weak as he trailed his tongue up along my stomach, pausing long enough to tease each nipple.

And then he was unbuckling his own jeans, and I was a maddened, frenzied beast trying to pull him toward me. I barely gave him enough time to pull them from his feet before I pulled him to me, my right hand reaching down to find—

He was hard, and hot, and so very—

Wow.

I wanted to see; I wanted to touch and tease and lick and make him writhe the way he'd made me. But he was stronger than I realized. He reached up with his right hand and pinned my wrist beside my head as he covered my right hand with his left over his penis. I guided him inside, and once he'd entered, I pulled my hands from his and grabbed the curve of his so-firm ass.

He arched upward, bracing himself against the floor with his hands to either side of me as I wrapped my legs around him and pulled him deeper and deeper; then there was a rhythm between us. No guessing, no floundering. He was moving, and I was bracing myself to receive him.

But I wanted more—I wanted to see him.

We were between the coffee table and the hearth, but I have very long legs. I lashed out with my left leg and shoved the coffee table away. By doing so my kegel muscles tensed, and he moaned again.

Oh, no you don't, I thought to myself. *Not yet. Not yet.*

But I was also containing a fire within myself. My passion was insatiable as I wrapped my body around him and turned him to my left, coming up on top of him. His eyes widened, and their gray was almost blue. This time I positioned myself on him, took his wrists in my hands, and pinned him down. I kissed him as I moved my pelvis back and forth, up and down, in an endless wave of pleasure. Both of my own, and in time to what I saw and felt from his body.

"Zoë . . ." It was a tight word, his neck muscles tense. He was looking at me, and I already knew what he was fearing.

I smiled at him. "I know . . ."

I somehow knew his timing—how wasn't important—and I easily moved off him, our juices and warmth lingering enough that I was able to use my hand for the last few steps—

His back arched up as I felt the rush in my hand. He was hot and powerful and I wanted so much to feel that pulse inside of me. But unprotected sex—

Even in the throes of passion, Darren had cared. He had worried. And I felt my eyes grow hot with emotion. Sex with emotion.

It wasn't sex with Darren—it was making love.

He was panting and looking at me, his eyes dark slits. I turned and grabbed one of the towels he'd brought in with our mugs and cleaned him and myself up. After tossing the rag at the couch, I pulled off one of the afghans my mom had made, the orange-and-black one, and leaned in close to him, nestling myself into the crook of his arm.

He held me, and kissed my head. And we lay like that for a long time, in front of the fire, basking in the afterglow, and I felt—

I felt—sated.

I heard him say, "This—this changes everything, doesn't it?"

I was going to answer him—wanted to answer him—but another voice spoke out of the dark before I could.

"You're damn straight it does."

23

DANIEL'S voice was the last thing I expected to hear at that moment. I scrambled from where I was, so warm and comfortable against Dags. But what sucked was the shame that darkened everything—just blanketed it in something that felt dirty. I was naked, with another man.

And the man I always dreamed of being naked with was now standing in the middle of the botanica, over me and Dags—holding a gun—

WTF?

"D-Daniel?" I managed to say and the two of us eased back from the gun's barrel and tried to pull the afghan up over my breasts. Dags moved me back and wedged himself between me and the gun.

"What the fuck is wrong with you?" Dags demanded. "A cop pulling a gun on friends?"

"Friends?" Daniel's voice was thick, his cadence slow. He sounded nothing like himself. He wore a white long-sleeved business shirt, the sleeves rolled up, and a pair of black suit pants. But it was his face that frightened me the most, and the expression just visible in the flickering firelight. "What sort of friend fucks my girlfriend?"

Oh? Well—excuse me for not realizing treating another human being like she had the plague was being a boyfriend.

I pulled the afghan up with me as I stood, my own anger and ego puffed up like a hairstyle from the south side.

Dags got up as well, and I noticed he was pulling his jeans on and wincing as I reached out to push the gun's barrel aside and point a finger at Daniel. "Girlfriend? Oh, fuck you, Mr. Detective Man. You're the creep who disappeared on me—wasn't there when they put my mother into Miller Oaks. What—you suddenly gone all player on me? Thinking I'm your sometime ho?"

His eyebrow rose, and he brought the gun up to my face, between my eyes. I could feel Dags moving forward behind me. "Don't even try it, Romeo. You get closer, and I'll blow her fucking head off." His gaze shifted back to me. "I think I liked it better when you couldn't talk. In fact, I think all women should be seen and not heard."

"Daniel—"

"You fucking shut up!" he bellowed at Dags, and moved the gun to my right. I knew it was pointing directly in Dags's face. "Zoë, get your clothes on. Fast. Or I introduce you to your next ghost friend."

Ghost friend. Damnit! Were Tim and Steve still in the house? Gads—and had they seen me and Dags in the living room? Well, of course, you idiot—any spirit within the house walls had noticed our romping. I was careful as I knelt and grabbed up my jeans, thong, bra, and sweater.

"Just the jeans and the sweater, Zoë." He grinned but kept his gaze and his gun aimed directly at Dags, though he did lower the weapon and point the barrel at Dags's chest and not his head. "I want you naked underneath. You're coming with me—and this way I don't have to take too much off when I'm feeling a bit horny."

I dropped the thong and the bra and started putting on the jeans. But I felt as well as saw the soft glow starting in Dags's palms. No, no, no . . . what good would the Guardian Light do in this situation?

But just as I moved to the side, away from the fireplace, Dags moved, his palms open and his stance wide. He was quick, but Daniel was quicker, and I heard the sickening crack of metal against bone. I turned in time to see Dags hit the floor, his palms dimming.

His eyes closed.

And there was blood, lots of blood.

"Why did you do that—"

The blow was unexpected. I wasn't prepared, and I wasn't balanced. I lost my footing and fell back against the shelves of books behind me, knocking several of Mom's gitchie goomies onto the floor. I dropped the clothes and went down on my butt, still not sure what had happened.

And then, abruptly, Daniel was kneeling in front of me, and his face filled my world. His blue eyes held an odd, eerie light, and I knew then that it wasn't Daniel, *my* Daniel, looking out at me. This was something else entirely.

The gun in one hand, he grabbed my jaw with the other and pushed my head into the books behind me. "You—will do as I say if you want your little boy toy to live. First, get dressed."

He backed away then and watched as I pulled my jeans on. I tried really hard not to cry, but from the pain on my cheek from the slap, to the brusque manner in which Daniel treated me, compounded with the fact I'd just made love to a friend and now he lay bleeding on the floor—I was crying buckets.

Once I had my top on, he grabbed my upper right arm and pulled me up. He slapped a pair of handcuffs in my hands. "Put these on your lover—behind his back. Don't want him summoning those two bitches or his sword when he comes to." He glanced back at Dags. "*If* he comes to."

I took the cold metal handcuffs and stumbled to where Dags lay still. I'd hoped he wasn't really unconscious—that maybe by some miracle he was faking it. But when I saw the side of his face I knew this wasn't a game—it looked as if Daniel had pistol-whipped him in the temple. There was blood on the side of his face, and a nasty bruise was forming. He was unconscious—perhaps even a concussion.

I moved him gently, remembering his hands on me, his lips against my skin, and the tears came again. I fastened one wrist, then the other. Daniel stepped over, shoved me away, and pinched the cuffs as tight as he could. Dags's wrists were going to lose circulation if someone didn't find him soon.

I hoped Tim and Steve could do something for him.

Then Daniel was grabbing my hair and hoisting me to my feet. Still holding my hair, he looked at the floor and moved to a spot in the center, but closer to the door. "This is about the center of the pentagram. I can feel it beneath me. Very glad your mom's not here to activate it though—would have some trouble getting you out of here."

"Where—" I swallowed. "Where are we going?"

"The Abysmal." He smiled. "Though the Archer was my original prey, I figure if I have you, he'll come to me."

I knew then that most of what TC had told me was true. This was something horrible conjured by the Phantasm to destroy the Archer. And I was stuck in the middle of it.

And I was also powerless to do anything about it.

Well, I guess I could kick him—but what if he shot Dags?

There was a loud noise, the breaking of glass, then shouts all around us. I tried to move out of the way, but Daniel still had my hair and pulled me back with him to the other side of the botanica. The lights came on and I could see Joe, Mastiff, Cooper, and several other uniformed officers, all with their guns pointed at—

Ah! Don't shoot!

"Let her go, Frasier," Cooper said, and his voice was like steel. But was that Cooper—yes—somehow I knew it was. I knew that TC wasn't there anymore. "We followed you from Rodriguez's home. This house is surrounded. Let her go."

I looked at Joe, caught his eye, then glanced over at Dags. Joe looked where I looked and his face nearly broke, but he kept his hands up, his gun aimed at me and Daniel. I knew he wanted to check on Dags, but he remained fixed and centered. Even as Daniel pressed the gun's barrel into the side of my head, he didn't flinch.

But I did.

"Let her go, Daniel," Joe said in a quiet voice. "Or whatever is passing itself off as Daniel. She's not a threat to you—I'm sure you can sense that."

"Oh . . . Halloran, right?" Daniel's voice said from behind me. Daniel had his hand wrapped in my hair and his arm in front of my neck. "Yes, yes—his memories of you are not friendly—" He paused. "Oh . . . what's this? He believed you were a threat—a threat to his relationship with this." And he pulled at my hair. I hissed. Daniel made a "tsk" noise. "Poor Detective Frasier—he was so wrong, wasn't he? You weren't the threat at all."

"What the fuck is he talking about?" Mastiff said. "Danny's gone all wacko on us, hasn't he?"

Joe cleared his throat. "Detective, what you're looking at isn't Daniel Frasier. It's more dangerous than you realize. Trust me."

"Isn't Daniel?" Mastiff said. "You're outta your mind. I'm look'n at him. That's Daniel Frasier."

"Shut up, Mastiff," Cooper said, and took a step forward. "Take Halloran's warning."

I stared at Cooper, amazed. *Is it possible he believed Joe? This once? Or has he seen enough weird shit in the past nine hours that he's willing to believe anything? Or does he remember being overshadowed by TC?*

I was betting on the latter.

Dags made a noise. I tried to go to him. Daniel pulled my hair.

"Dags, stay still," Joe called out.

But the Guardian wasn't going to. I could tell he was trying to move his arms, to bring his hands to the front, and couldn't. Blood covered the side of his face, and I had to look down out the corner of my eye to see him. "Not . . . not Daniel . . ."

"Yeah, got that. Need a bit more. Symbiont? Daimon? Fetch? Little Shadow dude?"

"Horror."

Joe smirked. "Fuck."

"Y'all are crazy," Mastiff said. "Detective, let Miss Martinique go, or I swear I'll shoot out your kneecap."

"Oh?" Daniel said. He twisted suddenly, wrenching me with him. I heard the gun fire, and the others yell. I didn't know who he was shooting at, but this had gone too far. I'd been waiting for a break—some instant where his guard was down just a little. And firing the gun was it.

I raised both my arms in the confusion and rammed both of my elbows back into his gut and chest. He made an "oof" noise and let go of my hair. I dropped straight down to get out of the way 'cause I knew what was next.

Gunfire—it was all above me. I moved on hands and knees

to the door, beside a downed Detective Mastiff. He'd been shot in the arm and was bleeding. That's when I saw Rhonda standing just outside the doorway of the shop. Her eyes were closed, her hands were out, and she looked serene.

"Get out of the way!" I called out.

But she wasn't moving.

I turned in time to see Daniel go down, his body filled with bullets. He crumpled over, and I heard myself scream before I realized I'd done it. I scrambled up from where I was and ran to him, but he was down, his eyes closed. I was nearly to him before someone caught me from behind and held me.

"Let me go! Daniel! Let me go!"

"Shhhh!" Cooper said in my ear behind me, his grip strong as he held me around my middle. I'm sure it was like holding a wildcat—I wanted to be near Daniel. I had to be.

It wasn't his fault.

"It's not . . . his fault . . ."

"He's gone, Zoë," Cooper said.

Joe was kneeling beside Dags, removing the handcuffs. He also checked on his friend's head, then helped him stand up. They moved past the still form of Daniel and into the botanica just as Rhonda stepped through the door.

"I told you to stay in the car," Joe said.

But Rhonda was ignoring him, moving to the kitchen and going through the cabinets. She abruptly returned with a first-aid kit and motioned for him to sit Dags down in one of the chairs at the table in the tea shop. More officers piled in and out—and I finally pulled myself free of Cooper.

I turned to where Dags sat, and Rhonda worked on cleaning his head wound. I was again taken by the care in her face when she looked at him and the gingerly way she cleaned the blood. She really did care for him—and if she knew we'd just—

There was a slight tinking noise from somewhere. Almost like a marble dropping. I looked around the botanica, but there were only officers, and flashing lights. One of them came up, and told Cooper, "The bus is here."

The bus?

That was for Daniel. I was aware of Dags looking up at me. I smiled at him as he winced when Rhonda applied some astringent. "Ow, woman."

"Well, it'll get infected. But I know you—you won't go to the hospital."

"I'm fine . . ."

I saw Joe in the botanica side, kneeling beside Daniel's body. His silhouette was moving in front of the fireplace. He looked so sad.

I heard the tink noise again.

With a glance at Cooper, I walked into the botanica side and stood beside the body, beside Joe.

"He's gone, Zoë," he said in a soft voice. "It used him, then bailed. Whatever a Horror is." He sighed. "The witness identified the person who attacked him as Detective Frasier. And then Rhonda called me—the surveillance tapes showed the person that openly attacked their man was Daniel as well. One of our uniforms spotted him, and we followed him here."

"He—" I started, then blinked several times to keep the tears back. "He wanted me to come with him. He said Archer was his first goal, and I was his second."

"Yeah, I can believe that." He stood and looked at me, then he looked past me to Dags, then he looked behind him at the floor, at the underwear.

Mine, and Dags's.

And then Joe looked sadder than I ever thought possible. The smirk was gone, and his shoulders slumped. "You made love."

It was in a small voice—only for my ears. I didn't have to answer. I didn't want to. I wasn't ashamed of what we'd done—well—was I?

The tinking noise happened several more times, only louder.

Joe wasn't anyone to me romantically—so why would I care what he thought? And why would he care as well?

"So . . . he finally did it, eh?"

I nodded. Again surprised that he seemed to know Dags's feelings when I hadn't.

"Was it good?"

Ah—how rude! "That's none of your business."

"You've been waiting how long for Daniel to bone you?" Joe looked hateful. "Was it worth it? Was it your touch that made him go all evil like that? Was it something inside of you, Zoë? That thing I saw kill Rhonda?"

I took a step back—what was he saying? He thought Daniel and I had made love—and Dags had walked in on us?

"Wait—you've got it all wrong. I didn't—"

"Spare me the details. Conquest made. Daniel's dead. I guess I'm pretty lucky I'm not one of those on your list." He turned to go as Dags came to stand next to us.

"Tim says"—he looked at Joe—"something's not right."

Joe glared at the floor. "Daniel's dead, Dags. There's nothing right here."

"No." Dags was shaking his head, and I noticed that his palms were in tight fists. But the glow was still visible between his fingers. "There's something else. Something . . . building."

Joe sighed and moved around us, into the other room. Dags turned and looked at me. "Are you okay?"

I stared at him. I wasn't angry—I was just—

Numb.

That's when I heard it again, but it was a plink this time. Of something metal hitting wood? "Did you hear that?"

"I've been hearing a lot of things." He reached out to touch my arm, but I pulled away. I don't know why—but I just didn't want to be touched at that moment. Not with Daniel dead at my feet.

Dags took a step back, and he looked away. "I understand."

Oh hell. I couldn't deal with all the drama just then—we'd made love. But that didn't make us lovers. The lover I'd convinced myself I wanted was dead, and Joe—

Joe was—

"Captain—the ME's here!"

"Good—everyone clear out. Let him have some space."

I moved away, back to the tea shop. I could feel Dags behind me—

And something else.

Rhonda yelled out first before I heard the scuffling. I turned at the same time Joe did and saw Daniel wrestling with Dags. He managed to kick his foot into Dags's leg, and the Guardian went down on his back. Joe surged forward and grabbed at Daniel. Daniel reached out with a strength I'd never seen and shoved Joe back by his face—but not before reaching into Joe's shoulder holster and removing his gun.

I ran back toward the botanica as Daniel brought the gun up and aimed it at Rhonda. I was jumping in front of Rhonda, knocking her back—

There was a crack—

"Zoë!"

24

I'D never been shot before.

So I didn't know I had been. I remembered going after Rhonda—with my heroic and yet stupid attempt to push her out of the way. And then I was knocked away from her and into something immovable. I think it was the doorframe—that opening between the botanica and the tea shop. Things happened in a weird time frame—like everything had been slowed down. I was looking up, but I was also on my side—kind of like in stereo.

And nothing was moving—or wanted to move. It was like I was just inside of myself but had no control, even if I tried.

I could see Daniel standing to my right—still standing in the doorway between the two shops. He had someone next to him—a woman—or was it a girl? The images were blurring really fast. But I know he was looking at me.

The girl screamed, and I recognized Rhonda. Daniel—his shirt riddled with holes and blood, his hair disheveled—had his right hand around Rhonda's throat, clutching her neck. I could hear Cooper too—and he was yelling at Daniel to let Rhonda go.

But Daniel was talking—and none of it made sense.

". . . not good, not good. Damnit . . . you stupid bitch, you weren't supposed to get shot . . ."

I was amazed at his words—had he really called me a bitch? And who was it that got shot?

There was more screaming, and the pressure in the room changed. I recognized the sound in my ears, like the roar of a tornado—and the smell. The scent of burned air, of something electrical on fire. And then I watched as Daniel and Rhonda disappeared, much the way Dags and I had disappeared months ago when summoned by Allard Bonville.

Into the Abysmal.

A dam burst at that moment, and pressure built up from somewhere in my chest. There was pain, but it was like an echo of what it should have been. I was cold, and it was hard to breathe. I tried to breathe faster, but it wasn't working—

And then I was choking. There was something in my throat, and I was coughing it up.

". . . nicked a lung. Someone get that damned ME in here—"

"But he's a dead-body doctor—"

"He's still a doctor—do what I said! And get on the horn—we're gonna need an ambulance."

I heard all of this from a distance. I saw Joe holding someone who was trying to get to me—someone with dark hair and eyes—someone whose body seemed to glow with a golden light.

It was hard to breathe—and I didn't really want to anymore.

Zoetrope . . .

Oh, I hated that name. Hated it more when Mom used it.

Come here, honey. There's something I need to show you . . .

I looked around but couldn't find the voice.

"Mom . . ." I heard myself say out loud.

Mommy's not here—but she's safe. I need you here—please, Zoetrope. Be a good girl.

But I was always a good girl.

Joe and the man with the golden halo blurred away, and I could hear him call my name.

* * *

I'D been here before—in that place that wasn't a place. I remembered sitting here, as I was sitting now, on the back porch of Mom's house. Jemmy's house wasn't there anymore across the way. But Jemmy was. She was walking over the field with the darkening sky, the smell of rain in the air, and there was someone by her side. But he was all transparent, like a ghost in a movie.

I wasn't alone on the porch either. Tim was sitting on the steps, his back against the railing as he read a book. I could see the cover—it was *Siddhartha*. Mom had read it once. And Steve was sitting beside me in one of the rocking chairs.

"Good to see you again," Steve said. "It's been rough this past month."

I nodded. "So—am I dead?"

"Not yet."

That was reassuring. I pursed my lips. After nearly a month of not speaking—I wasn't sure what to say to him. Even though I had my voice.

Tim looked up at me, a smile on his face. "You finally got boned."

I sneered at him. "I guess you were watching?"

He shivered. "Breeder sex? Oh God, no."

Jemmy was nearly to the house now—her straw hat flopping in the wind. The person with her wasn't as clear as before, as if the closer he got to the house, the dimmer he became. I leaned forward, aware suddenly that I was in my jeans and sweater. My hair was down and flying all over the place. I wasn't wearing my black pants, turtleneck, and bunny slippers.

Where were my slippers? I missed my bunnies.

The doorbell rang, and Steve stood. "I'll get it. That'll be A."

"A?" I turned in my chair as Steve moved into the house. The back door was gone, and I could see through to the front door. A man stood there, dressed in a flannel shirt and jeans. I thought at first it was Joe—until he followed Steve through the house, and I realized he was someone I'd never seen before.

He was tall, and wiry, Hispanic, with a beautiful face and a ponytail of blue-black hair. His eyes weren't as dark as I thought they'd be, and his nose was more Roman than Spanish. He moved to my right and nodded to me. "It's nice to see you, Zoetrope." His English was spiked with just a slight accent.

"Do I know you?"

"You can call me A."

I nodded. That was good.

"You mind if I sit?" He pointed to the chair that Steve was in. But Steve was now on the steps with Tim, and they were playing a game of backgammon.

"No, sure. Cop a squat."

Jemmy was nearly to the steps. It was really taking her a long time. The man was no longer with her—in fact, there was no sign he'd ever been there.

"You see the crossroads?"

He was pointing past Jemmy. I stood up and looked, hooding my eyes with my right hand. It was bright, but there wasn't a sun. I hadn't noticed it before—but yeah, there was a crossroads. Just to the right of the house. "Was that always there?"

"Nona bought this house because it used to be," A said. "This was farmland, and that was where the roads crossed." He started to rock, and I turned and looked at him, the wind at my back. "You'll have to walk out there soon."

I nodded. I kinda knew that. "Have to? What happened to free will?"

"That's my fault, Zoetrope. Most of what's happened is my fault. I wanted you to have a normal life—and I planned on it. I sacrificed a part of myself to ensure you wouldn't be an Irin—but in the end I failed both you and your mother."

"Failed?"

He didn't answer me at first, and then, "All your young life I tried to shield you from the planes and their existence. But your light drew them to you. Until you were twelve and finally you were made invisible. But then you were pushed into your destined existence again by your death in Piedmont Park—and because you were touched by the Abysmal before you could attain your full destiny, now you are a Wraith." He sighed. "I failed in protecting you—in giving you a safe, normal life."

I wasn't sure what this man was talking about. I already

kinda knew my being a Wraith was bad, and at the same time good. Which was just a little freaky from my point of view.

I had my hands up. "Wait, wait, wait—I died in Piedmont Park?"

"When you were raped, Zoetrope. He stabbed and killed you. But because you were Irin, your body survived. Even when you were away from it."

"But—" I shook my head. "I—when I touched Holmes at the warehouse, I was in my body—"

"Ah." He nodded slowly. "*Sí.* That was the beginning of all of this. I wish I had the time to explain everything to you—"

Tim checked his watch. "You got about two minutes, A."

"I know," the stranger said. "Zoetrope—there is a key—in your mother's house. You have to find that key and use it. It's the only way to save the world."

"Save the world?" I laughed at him. "Aren't you being a bit melodramatic?" I frowned at him. "You're not gay, are you?"

"Hey," Tim said.

But A only smiled. "No. I'm not. But you need to listen to me, and to your friends. They'll guide you. Both the living"—he looked at the fields visible from the porch—"and the dead."

"But I can't see the dead anymore. Or even touch them. I'm not a Wraith anymore."

"True—that part of you was hidden, and you'll have to get it back. And right now, the only way you can do that is to be the Irin."

Irin.

There's that word again.

He stood. "I don't have enough time, Zoetrope. You're dying, and there at the crossroads you'll have to exchange places." He moved inside the house, and I followed him. "She's not strong enough to do what needs to be done."

A stepped into the kitchen and scooted a step stool I didn't recognize over to the cabinets beside the refrigerator. There he stood on the stool and reached over the top, to a place I couldn't see. His hand came back clutching what looked like a tin box. And when he stepped down and set the box on the counter, I recognized Mom's old Animal Cracker box, the one with the cages with animals on it.

It was made of tin and had a lock on the front. It looked vintage.

"Find the key, Zoë. And you can use my mistake to make it right."

I looked at him, and it was like looking in a mirror. "What mistake did you make?"

He reached out and put his hand on my cheek. My body tingled, and my physical body involuntarily jumped.

A voice from somewhere in the room yelled out, "Clear!"

A looked up. "Not much time. You have to go."

"Go? Go where?"

And then as I looked at him, I recognized him. I'd only seen one picture before—one my mom had missed when she cut them all up.

"D-Daddy?"

"You have to go, Zoë," he said to me in Spanish, and even though I couldn't speak the language, I understood him perfectly. "I love you."

And then he was gone.

DADDY!

I ran to the back porch. Tim and Steve were gone, but Jemmy was there, standing on the top step, holding on to the railing where Tim had been. She waved at me with her free hand. "You'd think on the other side I'd be healthier. Well, come on, girl. Time to go."

"Go where?"

"Back."

But what was back? The crossroads were visible from the porch, as was somebody standing in the middle of them. "Who's that?"

"You ask a lot of questions—I don't envy Nona her job with you."

I frowned down at Jemmy. In all the years she'd been palling around with my mom, I'd never heard her talk like that. Especially to me. "Excuse me?"

"You're not done yet," Jemmy said. "You have to make it right—you have to stop the Horror."

"How?"

"Listen to Adiran, child. Always listen to your parents."

Abruptly we were at the crossroads. Jemmy, me, and

someone—only I couldn't make out who. It was more of an image than a person, with no real definition. I started to address the image, but Jemmy put her hand on my arm.

"You have to let go of Archer, honey. He's not part of things right now. But he'll be there—when it's time."

I gave her a quizzical look. "I didn't know he was still with me."

"He's always with you. He's a part of you." She grinned. "Whether you like it or not." She checked the dainty silver watch on her wrist. "You got to get back now, child. And remember—you won't be the Wraith, not until you reclaim yourself from him."

I blinked at her. "I won't what? Reclaim myself?"

She shook her head. The breeze was kicking up, and the sky darkened. I wasn't sure if the storm was coming, or if it was already there. "I wish we had more time. But it seems we're always cutting it too close." She looked past me to the image. "Okay—take her back. Good luck, you old fart."

Jemmy shoved me into the other person—

. . . Mama?

25

"WE got a pulse!"

"We need to intubate—tilt her head this way—"

"It's not possible he got up and walked out of here . . . He was full of bullets . . ."

"There are bullets all over the floor—maybe they fell out?"

"Bullets don't fall out of a body, Mohan."

All these voices greeted me just as a miasma of incredible, burning pain in my chest heralded my arrival back to the land of the living. The physical plane. Breathing was damned difficult and I was choking as something was shoved down my throat. I couldn't move—and there was something coppery in my mouth.

"Get her still—get that IV in—we need to calm her down. She's fighting us."

"She's not gonna make it, is she?"

I knew that voice—that was Dags's voice. So solemn. I couldn't open my eyes, but I needed to see him. I needed to talk to him. He could help me—I had to find the box. The tin box.

The key.

And then I was there, above everything, looking down at

the EMTs working quickly on my body. I was sprawled in the middle of the botanica's floor. And there was blood—

Oh fuck. Look at all that blood. All over my chest.

There were frantic movements—from all sides. And I was watching it all—with an almost detached mind.

And then it hit me—I mean it broadsided me. I was free.

I was free! I was out of body and floating in the air.

I threw my head back and screamed with delight. I twisted and whirled about, flinging my hands out to my sides. I was free, and I was powerful. It was different this time—unlike it had ever been before. I could *feel* the planes coursing through my soul, feeding me again. It was as if I'd been starved of life and finally been given an ocean of the purest water to drink from. And here . . . in this house . . . there was so much to take in . . .

There were things that didn't belong here—beings that had crossed the borders. They disobeyed. All manner of Abysmal things.

Dags was the brightest of those souls—his own essence being mostly of Ethereal matter. He would taste the most powerful, but he was also guarded by the two familiars. And I could see in the center of his soul—a book with pages of pressed gold. Beside him was Joe—

And his essence gleamed a soft blue. I knew that essence— I'd seen it before with Rhonda. And I'd tasted it. There was something just a little bit different about him. Maybe it was because he'd died once, and touched the Ethereal plane with his own living soul . . .

Maybe.

It was wrong for souls to return to the physical plane once they departed, right? Wasn't that the rule? Or was that the exception? My mind was still a bit hazy on things—on what I knew and what I'd been told.

He wasn't supposed to be here.

And I was there—in front of Joe—with only a single thought.

Joe yelled and put his hands out—but my own arms passed through him. And I noticed—

Wow . . . my fingers looked normal at first—but then grew into long, spindly spears that pierced his physical shell in his chest and touched his soul encased beneath. But I caught his gaze in mine and saw—

A skull.

The death mask.

I pulled back even as a larger part of me screamed out in protest, wanting to touch his soul, to devour his essence. The death mask—on Joe? But—how? Seeing the mask always spoke of death for that individual. No! Joe couldn't die! I wouldn't let that happen!

And then Dags was between us. In his hands was a gleaming sword, pulsing with the blue-white light of the Witch Fire.

Witch Fire . . . how did I know that?

"Get back—Zoë! Please!" Dags was saying, and I thought I saw tears in his eyes. "Don't make me use the sword—you won't survive it."

Won't survive the sword? Why would he think that? I'm not some damned creature of darkness.

"Dags—" Joe said in a slow tone, his hands still up but his expression more one of curiosity. He looked fine now—no mask. And he didn't seem to be perturbed that I'd just shoved my fingers into his torso. Or had he not even seen me do that? "She's not much different. Look closely at her—"

And then Dags was lowering his hands, the sword gone— and Alice and Maureen were there, flanking him. To my surprise, as well as Joe's and Dags's, the two women bowed at their waists to me. Everything around us stopped—the EMTs, the police, even the air, froze in place.

Except for me, Joe, Dags, and the familiars.

"Zoë," Dags said, "you look just like you normally do. Nothing really wigged out or fancy. Are you"—he blinked—"a ghost?"

"No, she's not a ghost, but an Irin," Alice said from her bowed position.

"Now, wait a minute—" I said. "What's going on?"

But Alice was already straightening up. "I see now what your father had in mind—the only way to defeat the Horror, to become the Wraith again, is to fulfill your destiny."

Joe's eyebrows knitted together, and he looked at Dags. "You get that?"

Dags shook his head and glanced at each of the familiars. Maureen straightened up as well. "Uh—no. Not so much."

Alice spoke, "Zoë is—by birth—an Irin. A Watcher. A being that watches the borders between the planes. There is an Irin for every border—" She paused. "Or there used to be. But since the Bulwark War—they were all destroyed, and the ability to father more was lost."

I blinked at her. Joe's eyebrows rose. And Dags—he looked at me, then looked at Alice. "Bulwark?"

Joe said, "Doesn't that like mean fortress, or protection?"

We looked at Joe with stunned expressions. Even Maureen. He shrugged. "What? I read."

Alice nodded. "Partially. The Irin maintained a battlement that protected the planes from one another—to prevent meddling from entities such as the Phantasm, Daimons, fetches, and even the Seraphim and Nephillium. Your father was part of that defense, choosing to work with Domas to strengthen the Irin's powers. Domas was afraid of everything, and the thought that such creatures, things he couldn't see, would have free rein over his world pushed him to make the Dioscuri Experiments."

"Dioscuri," Joe said. "Wait a minute—isn't that a Greek reference?"

Dags ran a hand through his dark, wild hair. "Yeah—the Dioscuri were brothers. Twins, right?"

Alice nodded.

"I don't remember the particulars, but they share immortality? As in they enter into Olympus and Hades?"

Joe grunted. "So—they could go anywhere?"

"Yes." Alice nodded. "Domas wanted to not only bring back the Irin—but to fortify them. So he carefully chose his candidates—unfortunately he was betrayed in the end. Even when he had nearly achieved what he set out to do."

Listening to Alice brought back the conversation I'd had with Rodriguez in the botanica. "You mean people like Bertram and Charolette?"

"Wackos," Joe said.

"Yes," Maureen said. "Too bad they couldn't get psych reports back then. But they weren't the real betrayers."

And then I knew. "Rodriguez was."

Alice nodded. "He was the one who set the fire that destroyed the laboratory that day. He thought he'd killed the Dioscuri trainees. And he believed he'd also taken all the Dioscuri materials."

"But March Knowles had them, didn't he?" Joe said. "Rhonda's uncle?"

"Yes. He was Domas's partner, and he kept the originals with him. Rodriguez was more than a little pissed that he didn't get everything—and so he continued to try and create an Irin himself."

"But—" I looked at Alice and Maureen, then back to Alice. "But what happened?"

"In its simplest form? Rodriguez created a monster," Alice said. "He had no help—didn't want any. Because he was so afraid he wouldn't get the power himself. He believed if he had the power of an Irin—if he could jump from plane to plane—he could control the universe."

I smirked. "You mean he believed he could control God?"

Alice nodded.

I rolled my eyes. Yeah . . . I believed Rodriguez's ego could think that.

Stupid git.

"What did he do?" Dags asked. "What do you mean, he created a monster?"

I glanced around. Everyone was still frozen in place—and I was worried how long things could stay like this.

"Don't fret, Zoë," Alice said. "They're not frozen. *We* are. And we can hold this for a while—but what we say is important for the next steps."

"Okay . . . if you say so."

"Why is it she can talk like this but not as Wraith?" Joe asked.

"Because her voice is linked to the Archer," Alice said with a bit of scorn in her voice. "It was he that derailed what could have been the most powerful of Irin. Without his link to the Abysmal, she can no longer be Wraith. But neither is she Irin again. Yet."

Joe rubbed at his face. "Okay . . . I'm getting thoroughly

confused on this. But"—he nodded to her—"please, keep going. Rhonda's life is in danger wherever it is Mr. Possessed took her."

I looked at Dags. "Rhonda!"

"Daniel took her—" he said. "Or whatever is possessing Daniel did."

"When you say took—you mean like through the planes?"

Dags raised his eyebrows. "They vanished right in front of us. Maureen is sure he took them into the Abysmal."

I blinked. "Your trip through the Abysmal—it was agony, and it only took a few seconds." Oh God. I could only imagine what sort of pain Rhonda might be feeling if the thing in Daniel took her through the Abysmal in physical form.

"Don't worry," Alice said. "Rhonda Orly is protected. But only for a while. Please listen carefully."

I nodded, but there was a part of me drawn to getting her back. *And how do they know Rhonda is protected? Because she's a witch?*

Joe rubbed his finger over his lip. "So, what exactly can an Irin do—but Zoë's still not able to do?"

Alice said, "In reality—we're not sure why Rodriguez would want to be an Irin. They're not terribly powerful. The Irin only have the ability to banish creatures back to their places of origin—keeping things where they should be. Banishing ghosts and spirits wandering aimlessly. A Wraith has the ability to release that spirit's fetter—when it can't move on. But at the same time—the Wraith has the ability to devour that spirit and gain more power. And like an Irin, a Wraith can cross borders and planes easily."

I'd experienced that tug of the human soul with Rhonda. And when I overshadowed someone—I tended to slowly suck away their power.

"The monster?" Dags prompted.

Alice nodded. "Rodriguez tried to make himself into an Irin—but because he'd already gone through the Dioscuri training, he was tainted with the Abysmal—which is the easiest of the major planes to touch. What he did was split his soul into two parts. He had the basics, but he wasn't strong enough."

"Basics?" Joe said. "You mean there's like a recipe to make an Irin?" He grinned.

No one else did.

"Sorry," he muttered. "Just a bit jumpy."

"What he did was create what you've heard called a Horror."

I pursed my lips. "His split soul became a Horror?"

"His Abysmal half did. And this Horror possessed him, becoming the dominant side of him until it became too powerful and started killing people. It killed anyone that survived the experiments, looking for the documents—"

"Documents?" Joe said.

Alice sighed. "The list Domas kept about suspected Irinborn. The Society had been tracking them for years—not as the Society of Ishmael, but under many other names. Your father was called to battle one last time."

"The Bull thing," Dags said.

"Yes. He and the others were successful—they destroyed the Horror. They destroyed a part of Rodriguez, his Abysmal half. But there wasn't enough of a sane man left. There were so many casualties." She looked at me. "And Adiran was no longer able to come home to you."

I put my hands to my face.

Finally. A reason for why he never came home.

Dags was beside me—his hand out to me. But Maureen reacted first and grabbed his wrist. "Do not touch her."

He turned a very angry face on her. I don't think I've ever seen him angry. "Why not? I'm not afraid of an Irin. That's Ethereal light—"

"Darren," Alice said. "I will explain it later. We're running out of time."

"Yeah," I said. "I need to get to the Abysmal and get Mom and Rhonda back."

But the expression Alice gave me made me step back a minute. "No, Zoë—it's not them that's running out of time. It's *you.*"

I held up my hands, palms facing them. I also noticed they weren't all talony anymore. Just me in black and bunny slippers. *Oh, I missed you guys!* "Whoa—back up. I'm running out of time?"

She pointed past me to the frozen scene in the botanica. "Your life is at the crossroads. If your body dies now, then you become nothing more than—" She hesitated, and I could see she was having trouble putting whatever it was into words.

"Sea foam?" Joe said.

I stuck my tongue out at him. "I'm not the Little Mermaid."

Alice and Maureen looked at each other. Dags's eyes widened as if he could hear their unspoken thoughts. He took a step back. "No . . . you can't be serious. Why didn't you tell me that before?"

I looked from Maureen to Dags to Alice. "Tell him what?"

It was Alice who stepped toward me and took my hands in hers. "We told you the story of the former Horror and Rodriguez to explain how they're created. This new Horror is also born of a split soul."

I stared at her face, always in awe of the soft glow that illuminated her Ethereal skin. Her eyes were sad. "The soul that split this time is yours."

Uh . . . say that again?

Alice moved to the other side of me. "We still don't know how it happened—but we suspected it was your soul when we saw you again."

"But"—I moved back from them—"I didn't do any wacky experiments on myself. I never wanted any kind of crazy power—"

"We know that," Alice said. "We also know your abilities grew with the use of the Eidolons last month because of Bertram and Charolette. But then something happened and your soul was rent into two pieces."

I put my hands to my chest. "I'm like Rodriguez now?"

"Oh, heavens no," Alice said. "Not even close."

Dags stepped forward. "But are you saying that whatever is possessing Daniel is like . . . Zoë's evil twin? That that is what's been killing those people? What killed Boo Baskins?"

Okay . . . I was gonna be sick. I put a hand to my mouth.

Maureen nodded. "Yes. Zoë doesn't have any control of it. And somehow it's inside Daniel Frasier. We don't know when or how—might have happened because of whatever it is that's arrested your Wraith development. We just know that it has to be stopped."

Alice said, "Zoë—the Horror inside of Daniel is you. And if you don't banish it and take it back into your soul—you'll suffer the same fate as Rodriguez."

"Yeah," Joe said, as I had a nice little quiet fit in my head. "So what does that mean? Rodriguez is still alive and causing mischief? Or is that really his evil twin, Skippy?"

"He lost half of himself—half of his soul. Without the other half, he wasn't able to transmigrate."

I shrugged. "Trans-who?"

"She means move to the next plane of existence," Joe said.

"Thank you, Rhonda-Joe," I quipped. "I guess sharing a bed sort of pushed a bit of her know-it-all powers up in you."

"Stop it," Dags said. "So Rodriguez was trying to get ahold of Zoë in order to regrow his other half?"

Alice nodded. "He was wanting her and the Grimoire that belonged to the Cruorem. Rhonda knew this—was told this by her uncle once he found out. That was when she joined her uncle in working against Rodriguez. She's been in your corner a long time, Zoë."

Meh.

I was still mad at her. "But what would having me do? How would I help him get his soul back?"

Alice shook her head. "I don't know. In the beginning, as we were studying you—we thought it was Rodriguez who separated you from TC in order to initiate the Horror's creation. But then we realized too late it was something else. Something we hadn't expected."

"What?"

"An Eidolon," Dags said. "The blue Eidolon. It's here, isn't it? That's what kicked off TC and Zoë's connection—made her lose her powers. The one her father made."

Alice nodded. "Maybe. We're not sure. But we know the Phantasm was able to harness her Abysmal half and send it after Archer—to destroy Archer is to destroy a part of Zoë."

"Where is the ole fiend?" Joe said. "Anybody seen him?"

I pursed my lips. *Not in a while.*

"What the fuck is *that*?" Cooper said to my right, no longer frozen.

Whups.

I turned and looked at him—he was with Mastiff by the front door. Mastiff was seated in one of the chairs at the table, his arm bandaged. Cooper had been kneeling, talking to him, and was now standing and staring wide-eyed at—

Me.

Joe had regained his composure and was looking from me to Cooper. "Captain—can you see Zoë?"

Cooper's expression looked like someone watching a horror film. I'd never seen that look directed at me before. And then he moved to the entrance between the two shops and looked at the body lying there. And then he looked at me.

Uh-oh. This could get sticky.

"See her? What the blue blazes is she doing there?" He pointed at me where I stood, then pointed at the floor in front of the fireplace. "And there?"

"This isn't good," Dags said.

"No shit," I said, and immediately reached out with my right hand. It once again became a blue-white fist of talons that pierced his skull. His mind unfolded in front of me like one of those new technogadget computer screens—with images of the past few days playing out in AVI windows. I saw the one of him seeing me in two places and plucked it out. Within seconds he was on the ground and there was an even bigger ruckus.

"What'd you do that for?" Joe said in a hiss as he stepped back to let the EMTs shift half of their number from my body to Cooper's, though he was moving and moaning pretty good.

"He'll be all right. I just took that single memory from him. He's fainted. Geez." I looked at Joe. He was turning white himself, then I realized that the last time he'd seen me stick my "hands" in anyone was with Rhonda, and I'd stopped her heart. And then restarted it.

Oops.

But I had to wonder—how did I know how to do that? Was it part of what I was *supposed* to be? If I believed Alice.

I looked at Alice, Maureen, and Dags. "I think we need to go somewhere else."

And then I was in Mom's bedroom. Just poof. Bewitched. I could hear everyone downstairs. I already knew what I had to do. I turned to the door to head to my room, where the remains of the jewelry box were—

"You looking for this?"

I spun then, a blur of motion as I faced the voice coming from the open closet.

I'd always been afraid of closets as a child—slept with the light on in case the monsters I saw would come to get me. Those monsters had always been hairy like big spiders, with drooly teeth and red-glowing eyes.

But nothing was as scary as the monster I saw looking out at me from the closet. It was dressed in an expensive Italian suit, leather shoes, a red rose in its lapel, and a mustache upon its oily lips.

Francisco Rodriguez.

And he was holding up the remains of my mother's jewelry box.

26

THE thundering on the stairs announced the rest of the Scooby Gang was on the approach, having figured out where I'd popped to.

Rodriguez took a step from the closet and smiled at me. Geez, I hated that smile.

"How did you get in here?" I heard myself saying in a voice full of calm that I was *not* feeling right then.

"I had a key," he said. "Nona was always a trusting idiot. Never got her locks changed."

Asswipe.

It was as he was standing there that I noticed something else about him. Something he hadn't had before. As a Wraith, even when not OOB, I could sometimes see strong auras. The energy surrounding someone—kinda like their soul, I guess. Like I'd always seen Mom's and Rhonda's. And Jemmy's sometimes.

I couldn't ever remember seeing Rodriguez's aura—which made sense considering Alice's tale that he'd lost part of his soul.

What I could make out if I tried really hard was black.

And it looked like—shadows.

I sensed anger and rage from him—but I also got the impression they weren't *his* emotions.

Dags and Joe arrived at the top of the stairs. Dags was the first one in and the first one Rodriguez took a shot at. Not with a gun—but with something else. A bolt of lightning?

What was this? Dungeons & Dragons?

Luckily, Dags's hands were loaded (hands were loaded . . . LOL!) and he held them up, deflecting whatever was aimed at him. Only whatever it was sort of physically blasted at the doorframe—even I felt the blast. The impact against Dags caused a weird blue light to bubble around him for an instant, and he staggered back.

"Dags?" I said.

"I'm fine. I think." He swallowed and moved back. "I think Alice is hurt though. He threw something pretty hard at us."

"So, where did you pick up that little power?" Joe said as he stepped through the door. He looked so nonchalant in his jeans, shirt, and shoulder holster, his gun out and held up in his right hand. "'Cause from what I heard, you didn't have any anymore. You sort of screwed the pooch a while back, didn't you?"

"I still have my natural talents."

Joe laughed. "You have talents?"

"You're the one who destroyed Mom's jewelry box." I pointed at him. "But how did you get in here?"

Dags put his hand on the cracked doorframe to my left. "Because he's used what spells he stole from Bonville and created a doorway in the closet. I didn't notice it before—but what's worse is he's made the doorways between his home and yours through the Abysmal."

Idiot! I shook my head at him. "Don't you realize what that kind of exposure does to you?"

But Rodriguez only shrugged. "It doesn't seem to have affected Mr. McConnell."

"Give me back the box." I held out my hand. "And I won't hurt you."

"You won't hurt me?" He started to laugh. "Zoë, you stupid girl. You have no idea what's *in* this box, do you?"

"A key."

His expression fell. "Okay—so you know what's in the box. But you don't know what it unlocks."

"The Eidolon."

Ha. I was two-for. *Neener nee.* I took a step closer, but he held the box up in both hands. I could now see the key that I couldn't before. It was small, and just tucked inside the astral plane. It was also giving off a really bad vibe. Like it was festering. A thorn in the skin too long? Something physical that shouldn't be in the astral?

"Give me the box, Rodriguez."

"How'd Tyrone die, Rodriguez? You sacrifice him or something? Is that how you got this power? 'Cause I know on good authority you tend to dabble in black magic," Joe said.

I sighed. *Let it go, dumb-ass. I have things to do—like save Mom and Rhonda? You know, your girlfriend?*

Joe made a face at me. *Whoops*—I guess he could hear me again. And if that was true—then was I on my way to losing my voice too?

"Ask Zoë."

I narrowed my eyes at him. There was something just not right about him. Something—almost familiar.

"Oh shit," Maureen burst out with. "It's the Archer!"

What?

We all looked at him—and I tried hard to sense TC's cocky attitude. So this was where he went after Cooper? To my enemy—Rodriguez? So I couldn't really stop myself when I blurted out, "This is where you go? To him?" And then I thought of something Dags said once. "Oh my God . . . it's a contract. That's why I couldn't tell! He's not overshadowing you."

Rodriguez sneered. "Who knew he was in the cop? The captain himself showed up at my house just after we finished with Tyrone—he was weak, and in need of sustenance." He held up his right hand and it crackled with electricity. "And now I have youth and power."

Hrm. I frowned. Evidently Mr. F here didn't read up on the exact uses of a Symbiont. I knew TC. He didn't. If anyone was gett'n used, it wasn't Trench Coat.

Dude was in for a rude awakening. Archer couldn't connect

with me anymore—couldn't gain power. But with him bonded to a former Traveler like Rodriguez . . . I was just waiting for the fireworks to start.

"So Archer killed you and took your body?" Joe said.

Rodriguez sneered at him. "You really are just all muscle and no brain, aren't you? Archer is a Symbiont. He can't possess a dead body." He looked at me, the remnants of the box still in his hands. "Now that I have the Archer, you're nothing. You'll never regain your ability to be the Wraith again, much less an Irin."

I narrowed my eyes at him again. I could almost feel Archer—the familiar glow increasing. Rodriguez thought it was power. I thought it was a countdown. "So—why are you threatening me with the box and the key? If you have the Archer—this incredible power you seem to think he signifies— then why do you want this Eidolon?"

He smiled. "Ah—but why is that, Miss Martinique? Have you wondered why all of this happened? Have you puzzled it out yet?"

I glanced at Dags and Joe. They were glaring at him. Dags had both hands spread open, palms focused, though his left palm was dark. Alice was definitely out of commission for the moment. I sort of wondered how familiars fixed that problem. Like, did Dags have to plug in to an Ethereal juice box somewhere?

"Have you?" Dags asked me.

I looked at Rodriguez. "My dad made a blue Eidolon. He made it because he wanted me to have a normal life."

Rodriguez made a scrunchy face. "Stupid Adiran. Did he really think after what happened that he could father a truly human child? And that child could ever be normal?"

"He loved me."

"He was foolish," Rodriguez said, and lowered the box. I knew this was Rodriguez talking, not TC. "He loved your mother more than common sense. Did you know it was me?" He pointed to his chest with his right hand. "Me that realized he wasn't living anymore? Yes, yes, that was me. I knew there was a fifth body in that laboratory. And it wasn't Domas's body like they all thought it was. It was Adiran's body—burned beyond identification. So when he showed up in physical form everyone assumed he'd survived. But I could see." He pointed at his eyes. "I could see."

Joe leaned in close. "Is it me—or is he sort of losing it?"

I leaned in to him. "Just keep watching. Trust me."

"Is he right? Is what he's saying the truth?"

I nodded but directed my attention to Rodriguez. "Did my father know you had discovered his secret?"

"Not at first. I was good. I watched. I guided the Society, and I studied Domas's notes. But they were incomplete. I wanted to know how he'd done it—how Adiran had bridged the worlds. How was he able to be dead and be living."

Dags swallowed, and he looked at me. So did Joe. I ignored them. "You experimented. On yourself."

"Yes, yes. I no longer had the applicants that Domas had, and his youngest niece—the only niece talented enough even to try tests on—was hopelessly in love with a dead man."

Wait—youngest niece? I had extended family somewhere?

"When Nona announced she was pregnant, I was shocked. Almost horrified. How could this be? Adiran was nothing more than a spirit. And then I knew he had to be more, and I had to achieve what he had achieved. And yes, I used the same techniques on myself. And I was able to walk between the worlds—to become solid while out of my body—and I could fly—"

Joe swore.

Dags remained quiet. Maureen stood just behind him, but I sensed she was ready to defend her Guardian at a moment's notice.

"But it failed," I said, remembering my father's words. "You missed something important. And instead of attaining the ability to walk successfully, you split yourself into two halves." I took in a deep breath. "You created a Horror."

Rodriguez's glare, if armed, could have sliced me into pieces. He took a step toward me, and I held my ground. "It was your father who destroyed half of me."

"The half the Phantasm controlled," Maureen said.

"Your father knew what would happen to you if he didn't make it back. And he'd planned all along to seal your powers with the stone. He'd only half told your mother everything—

and Nona understood so little of it. When he was locked to the Ethereal plane—that knowledge was lost. And your mother— seeing her vanished husband's power reflected in her child— used that Eidolon the only way she knew how."

My memory of that afternoon became clear now—not so shadowed. I had indeed found the Eidolon in that box, and it had knocked me back. Not a spider. And my mother had—

My mother had used it. And I'd forgotten all about Bobby. And the other ghosts.

Everything.

Until the rape. And the spell was broken.

Joe had been following my thoughts. "So why did it happen this time? Nona's been in a coma in a long-term-care facility. There's no way she could have sealed Zoë's power again."

Rodriguez laughed. He was looking a little pale now. And sweating. He breathed a bit hard too, as if he were running uphill.

Any minute, I was sure.

But we needed information first.

"Tell me," I said.

"I don't know the particulars. I just know that you some- how touched or got near the damned thing again. And that triggered Nona's spell. You were sealed once again, only it took a little longer to take hold. And when that happened— with you as a Wraith—you were separated. As I was."

"Separated?" Dags said.

"Her connection to the Abysmal had just evolved, you idi- ots." Rodriguez's color worsened. He was nearly as white as paper. And then his cheeks were tinged with red, as if he were sunburned.

"Hey, you need to sit down?" Joe said, Mr. Polite to the Bad Guy.

But Rodriguez reached inside his suit jacket and pulled out a gun. He aimed it at Joe.

Everyone stepped back but me.

"You leave me alone. Zoë's Wraith is out there, killing people, building power, and the Phantasm is using it. I don't intend on getting stuck here on the physical plane while he comes through and has his fill of souls."

I stepped forward, facing down the gun. Like it could affect my OOB form? "I don't understand—you're saying when I was locked away from my Wraith abilities—it gained its own form?"

"Just like mine did." He licked his lips. Wiped his forehead with his shirtsleeve. He was turning bright red now. And it was a little disconcerting. "And once it roamed the Abysmal plane, the Phantasm snatched it up. He sent it after the Archer—to destroy your tap into his territory. But you were already fading from view. He was laughing at you—marveling in the new skin you'd left him."

Skin?

I wasn't liking the sound of this.

I moved quickly this time and snatched the box from him. He didn't put up much of a fight—he was panting too hard. Sweat fell from his face in rivulets. And he was the color of a ripe tomato.

Stepping back, I reached my hand into the area where I could see the key. It vanished from sight as my fingers wrapped around the cool metal of the object, and I pulled it back out. I held it up to him. "This is the key to where that damned Eidolon is."

Rodriguez nodded. "The Phantasm wants it. He wants to destroy you—and Archer—"

I wanted to ask him more. To know what it meant that the Phantasm was wearing my other half. I was still missing information—there were holes that I didn't understand.

But there were also holes starting to form on Rodriguez's body. He still clutched the gun, but circles starting burning through, with dark, black smoke billowing out of them. He opened his mouth to scream, but more smoke came out. And in that black nothing I saw faces writhing and screaming. I could even hear Rodriguez's unspoken cry for help.

"Get back!" I yelled.

But Dags, Joe, and Maureen were already out the door when Francisco Rodriguez exploded from the inside out. Luckily I was incorporeal, technically, so most of the meat and blood, bone and organ went through me.

Doesn't mean I didn't notice it. I did.

I also noticed that Rodriguez's soul was no more.

Poof.

And when the oogy cleared, I saw an all-too-familiar face looking back at me with black shades.

He held out his hands. "Hey, lover. I told you I'd get the answers we needed. Now we go kick some Horror ass."

27

"ZOË——get out of the way!"

You know—you just had to love these guys.

Joe and Dags ran back into the room, Dags with his palms facing TC, blue-white Witch Fire churning just an inch from his skin. And then Joe, with his gun unholstered and aimed at the Symbiont's chest.

TC gave all of them a half smile—and put his hands out to his sides. He wasn't wearing the long trench coat anymore, but had switched up to a leather peacoat with a flared collar. Either way—it was still the Archer.

Vin Diesel, in stereo.

I can't say I was too afraid, and my libido—now fully awakened again—did give a little meeeeeooowwww . . .

I knew he wasn't fully back yet—he'd burned up Rodriguez's soul only to gain just enough juice to get the information we needed and go after the Horror.

Which meant—going after Daniel.

I stepped between the two men and TC and held out my own hands. "Relax—put your weapons away. Please."

"Zoë—that's him—isn't it? That's that Archer guy," Joe said as he kept his gaze and his aim on TC.

"Yes, that's him." I glanced back. TC looked as cocky and arrogant as ever. "And he's not here to hurt."

"Oh?" Dags said, and his voice cracked just a tad. "Then what the hell did he just do to Rodriguez?" He looked around the room with barely subdued joy. "Who else's body is splattered all over Nona's things? You know she's gonna be mad about this."

Yes, I knew that. But I'd worry about that later. *And why is he so happy?*

TC spoke up to defend himself. "I exacted a payment upon a man who had evaded his punishment for a very long time." Archer brushed his hands together. "And I must say"—he put a hand to his lips and gave a dainty burp—"it was tasty."

"Oh, for fuck's sake," Joe said. "How the hell are we gonna explain this mess? Just say that Rodriguez exploded in Nona's bedroom?"

TC shrugged. "Not my problem." He looked at me. "Got the key?"

I held it up. "It fits a tin box—looks like Animal Crackers."

Archer nodded and disappeared.

I turned back to Dags and Joe. They were lowering their weapons and not looking very happy. Especially Dags. "You're going to explain this, right?"

I smiled. *Maybe. Not now.*

Archer appeared again, his hands clasped in front of him with glee. "The box is downstairs—did you realize you've got a houseful of people down there? And they're wheeling your body out, by the way."

Joe was still looking at the bedroom. "This is . . . wow . . ."

"Okay, lover. As you are right now, you're technically sort of just an out-of-body soul. Let's get things moving and get the Wraith up and running. A little physical, and we should be back in business."

TC started to step forward, but I held up my hand. "Not so fast. Weren't you listening?"

Joe snorted. "Wow . . . all muscle and no brain."

TC looked at Joe and pointed to him like some thug on the street. "Look, man, I can rend your body into a million pieces and suck your soul through this with a straw." He held up his right hand to show the spinning red light.

"If you could really do that"—Joe crossed his hands over his chest, his gun still in his right—"you'd have already done it. Look, I don't buy this whole nice-guy routine you got going with Zoë here. You're evil, you're a pawn, and evil pawns only look out for themselves."

Cooper's voice was coming up the steps. Evidently the captain had recovered. "Halloran?"

Joe swore and reholstered his gun. "Look, I'll keep Cooper busy." He looked at Dags. "You call and tell me what's happening." He glanced at TC. "And if he makes a move, dissolve his Abysmal ass."

"Joe," I called out to him and picked my way over the bits and pieces of flesh, bone, and blood—though I didn't know why. I wasn't going to leave a mark. He waited for me just outside the door, at the top of the stairs but away from the bedroom and Dags's eyesight. His expression was less than happy. "Look, whatever they do, don't let them pull the plug. My body's going to seem hopeless for a while—like before."

He looked at me. "You slept with him. With Dags—not Daniel. I was wrong."

I blinked. What the fuck did that have to do with anything? "What fucking business is that of yours?"

"Well, in case you haven't noticed, dearie, the boy loves you. Has loved you for a while, and until now you barely gave him the time of day—except to use his little power here and there. And now you slept with him?"

I stared at Joe—really stared at him—and through him. Being Ethereal didn't make me omniscient. It didn't make me godlike. I wasn't much different than I was before, and Joe was still mostly unreadable. "What does it matter to you?"

He kept his voice low and pointed to his chest. "I happen to like Dags. A lot. And when Daniel went south, we turned to each other. He kept an eye on you, and one on me and Rhonda, protecting both of us. The boy's been through hell you can't even imagine, Zoetrope Adiran Martinique." He glanced down, then fixed his stare at me. "I also know that after what happened—Rhonda's been in love with him since the day she met him. And in the end, what she felt she had to do—she's willing to love him from afar. He won't trust her again. And I can't blame Dags. And now you're playing with his heart?"

I stared at Joe, amazed at the depth I suddenly saw there. He made me feel angry, and small, and stupid. "No—"

"Do you love him?"

I blinked. I opened my mouth to answer and saw Daniel in my mind's eye. I saw his laugh, his beautiful blue eyes, and remembered the way he touched me. He'd loved me once—and broken my heart.

Joe closed his eyes and shook his head. He sighed before looking at me again, and his eyes were dark. "That's what I thought. Well—I'm glad I didn't make the mistake of taking you to bed before helping you. 'Cause I couldn't deal with the emotional mess you'd make out of me, Zoë. At least with Rhonda I know where I stand—because she's in love with Dags."

I stood with my eyes wide, trying hard to understand what I'd just heard. What did he—what did he mean? He'd managed to make me feel like shit and a complete asshole all in one paragraph. He'd also hurt me by telling me he'd made love to Rhonda—and why should that hurt?

Why?

"Halloran?" Cooper was at the bottom of the stairs. I made sure I was invisible, no longer corporeal. It didn't look like he'd seen me.

Joe turned. "You okay?"

"Yeah, I'm fine. Not enough food, I guess. Or sleep. Look, they've taken Miss Martinique's body to Grady Memorial to the trauma unit. It doesn't look good. The bullet nicked her heart and lung—massive internal bleeding. I need to get back to the station and initiate a manhunt for Frasier. Can you make sure she's secure? I'd hate for him to sneak into the hospital and finish the job."

Joe nodded. "We need to find Rhonda Orly as well."

"Already on it." Cooper stepped away.

Joe looked back at me. "Gotta go. Look, you three do what you have to do. I'll make sure they don't pull your plug. But the clock's ticking, Zoë. If you fail, you, Rhonda, your mom, and Daniel are dead. Got it?"

I had it.

As I watched him leave, I realized I had too much on my mind. I didn't need this kind of emotional confusion. Not just then.

Someone touched my shoulder, and I turned. It was Dags. I was amazed he could do that—especially when I was incorporeal. But then, Dags was nearly as different as me.

"He cares about you," Dags said. "Did you know that?"

I nodded. "I do now."

"Blah, blah, blah," TC said from behind us as he came out of the room and stood on the other side of me. He reached down and stole a kiss before pushing me into Dags and heading down the stairs.

I shivered, remembering what his tongue was like. A snake—on steroids. And I had to wonder if maybe his genitals were actually in his mouth.

Dags made a noise, and I looked at him with apologies. "Stop seeing pictures."

"That's like saying stop breathing, Zoë. Come on," and he was bounding down the stairs as well.

We followed TC to the kitchen, where he floated up and took the tin down from where I'd seen my dad take it in my dream. Though I no longer thought of it as a dream, but more of a sidebar. He handed me the box, and I slid the key inside. One turn, and it was open.

I'm not sure what I expected to see—or had built up in my head I'd see—like maybe bright light, or something like one of those springing snakes jumping out 'cause, you know, that's so like my mom to do. I think I was a little disappointed when all I saw inside was a bundle of white cloth.

"Careful," Dags cautioned.

I glanced at him. His eyes were huge and a light shade of gray. *Is it me or are they getting grayer?*

With my tongue between my teeth and lips, I reached in—

"Wait!"

—And nearly jumped out of my Ethereal body. In my surprise at Dags's yell, I also shut the tin box.

"What the fuck?" TC said in his deep, almost scratchy voice. Hrm . . . it was kinda like my own.

"If that thing contains this Amplifying and/or Quieting Eidolon, shouldn't TC or I take it out? Wouldn't it be bad if you touched it?"

I pursed my lips and looked at TC. He actually looked thoughtful too, then nodded.

I handed the box to Dags.

Dags opened the box again and removed the wrapped cloth. Setting the box on the counter, he placed the cloth beside it. I stood to his right, TC to his left. I hated the fact that I was physically—well, as physical as the astral could be—aware of his presence.

With care, Dags pulled the cloth away to reveal a soft, powder blue stone. It was fixed inside a silver filigree backing and on a chain wrapped around a—

"Is that . . ." TC pointed at the cloth. "Is that a—"

"Voodoo doll?" I said in a higher-pitched voice than I intended. I started to reach for it, but Dags batted my hand back as he lifted it for everyone to see.

It had been a Mattel doll at one point in its career, with long brown hair, dark eyes. But this doll didn't have legs, or arms, or even clothes—just a necklace with a blue stone wrapped around its chest.

Dags pointed at it with his other hand. "That is more than mildly disturbing."

"She used a fucking voodoo doll," I said.

"Not really," Dags said as he looked at it. "It's more like sympathetic magic. Same principle as voodoo—and they do share a few commonalities. Not many. There's a single long, dark hair wrapped around the Eidolon itself." And he plucked at it and unwound it.

There was a slight pressure between my eyes, then a pop. TC made a slight noise as well, and I looked at him. "You feel that?"

"Yeah—didn't like it."

"My guess is I just released what little remained of Nona's spell." He started unwrapping the Eidolon from the doll, then set the doll back in the box and closed it. "I'll let Nona dispose of that however she needs to, without harming Zoë."

!!!

"It's still disturbing." Dags held the necklace out. "My guess is we need to use this on the Horror."

TC spoke up. "It'll need to be summoned with it. Because once in the Abysmal, the playing field will be even."

I looked at him. "What does that mean?"

"Okay, haven't you been listening?" He made a wiseass

face. "The Horror, the thing inside of Daniel, is technically you. The Abysmal piece of you that this thing separated. You'll have equal strengths, and equal failings. So you'll need this to gain the advantage. There's only one catch."

Dags looked at me, and we both looked at TC.

"You can't take that thing into the Abysmal plane." He nodded to the blue stone glowing softly in its cradle. "You're going to have to lure Danny-boy back into the physical plane."

28

IT wasn't long after the police left that we had a houseful again. Of ghosts.

Tim and Steve were the first to show up—and I gave the two of them the biggest hugs I could muster as an Ethereal being. Apparently like this we were technically on the same plane, so they were as physical to me as a brick wall.

We were all seated once again in the tea shop—the rug in the botanica still had my blood on it, and I did find it mildly oogy. I was on the counter, my legs folded up, looking as normal as could be. TC stood to my right, looking for all the world like a bodyguard. The only thing missing was the earpiece and wire.

Boo Baskins's ghost showed up as a black-and-white shade that remained in the corner, and I couldn't figure out where her tether was since I assumed it was Randall. I had no idea where he was.

Tim and Steve were in the kitchen making a light snack for Dags. Maureen insisted her Guardian needed to eat—he really needed sleep as well, but there wasn't any time. Jemmy had pointed out that since the Horror had Rhonda's body in the Abysmal, now was the perfect time to act.

And it was a dark moon.

Imagine that.

"Why here?" Boo asked.

"Well, relative space," Dags said.

I looked at Boo and felt terrible, knowing she'd been pregnant. And then I had to wonder—where was the spirit of the child?

"Not there yet," Dags said, again hearing my thoughts. "She wasn't pregnant long enough for the soul to enter."

But I still stared at Boo and remembered that my first encounter with her had been at a haunting on Web Ginn House Road, where Maharba had sent me to check out a poltergeist.

Wait . . . Maharba. I looked at Dags—and apparently he'd caught my thought as well. He stood and walked quickly into the botanica, returning with the computer, which had a little of my blood on it.

I started thinking out loud to Dags as he booted up the computer. "So I'm thinking we should just enter the Abysmal from here."

Dags nodded. "If you head into the Abysmal from here, then they stand a good chance of appearing about the same place as Daniel took Rhonda."

I nodded. "Then I should be able to detect Rhonda's spirit easily and just zero in on it. Then lure them back to this plane."

"In fact," TC said, his voice even more gravelly than before, "I'm counting on it. He wants you in there on his territory."

I looked down at him from my perch. "The Horror?"

TC shook his head. "The Phantasm." He looked at all of them. "You do all understand he's really the one pulling the strings here. The Horror isn't anything but a toy, an extension, a tool he's using to manipulate the physical plane." He looked up at me. "The one place he can't go as long as you're alive."

"Because I was born an Irin?"

TC nodded. "And when I came along and touched you"— he held out his hand—"I strengthened your hold on the Abysmal—which made you a little more than an Irin."

"You wouldn't happen to know how to use e-mail, would you?" Dags asked, looking up from the computer. "Because that's exactly what Maharba said."

"Really?" I jumped down and went to stand behind Dags, who was sitting at the table. Tim came out with a platterful of goodies and a glass of milk.

I looked at Tim. *Milk?*

"To keep up his stamina. Sorry, but I was all out of Viagra." He gave me a wink and walked away.

Oh damn.

How embarrassing.

"Looks like you got a response from Maharba about an hour ago."

I looked down to read.

Miss Martinique,

We are sure by now that many secrets as to your origin and birth have been revealed to you. Please understand that we were only peripherally aware of what occurred on the night Professor Domas's lab exploded, and did not have any knowledge of Mr. Adiran Martinique's unique—condition.

We have been and will continue to be a source of support—and though we have on occasion tendered our requests with stern words and suggestions, we are here to guide you as much as possible.

On the current situation, it is vital that you lure the Horror into the physical plane in order to defeat it. If it remains in the Abysmal plane and you engage in combat, the Phantasm will know of your presence, and your diminished abilities (from Wraith to Irin) will be a disadvantage. The Phantasm controls the Abysmal plane and cannot enter the physical plane as long as you are alive.

We are aware of Miss Orly's plight, but as things stand, it is better that the Horror be brought into this plane to be dealt with. In this plane, the Phantasm does not have power and cannot do more damage.

Please stand by. We will be contacting you shortly.

Maharba

I looked at Dags. "Contacting me?"

"That's what it says."

"I don't vote on listening to this." TC shrugged. "Whatever

the fuck they are. Getting the Phantasm's attention is what you *want*. If you can stir it up, make it push the Horror after you so you can lure it back here, then that's what we need to do."

I nodded. "So—when I get its attention, do I bring it back here?"

TC lowered his head. "No. Bad idea."

Dags said, "Why?"

"Because the initial boom that'll happen the moment Zoë reconnects with her Horror will pretty much level everything for a hundred-mile radius, Guardian Boy. You're going to need to set up your reentry point somewhere else. A place that's not easy to get to, not easy to get away from, and which, if it goes, won't destroy so many people as to make an Infernal."

All eyes turned to TC.

I was the one that finally spoke. "A what?"

"It's a hole—through the planes. There are lots of them, really. Places where lots of souls died at one time or on a continual basis. Auschwitz is one of them. So are the areas around Hiroshima and where the Trade Center was. Think of them as dead zones."

Dags looked at his hands. "Are these zones dangerous?"

"What I just told you about were Soaks, smaller areas like those her father"—he pointed to me—"sealed up. But if you make one by killing a lot of souls, then what you get is an Infernal, a doorway for the Phantasm to come through. Once he figures out what you're doing, he'll try for that, Zoë. Which is why the smack-down has to be above."

"You mean like on a building?" I asked.

He nodded. "What's the tallest building in Atlanta?"

I knew the answer to that—it was ingrained in my memory. Because it was the same building I'd been snooping in when all this started. The same building I'd seen TC in for the very first time. The same building where my life, and his existence, began an almost symbiotic relationship.

"The Bank of America Plaza."

He gave me a slow smile through his shades. "Fate, lover. It's all about Fate."

* * *

IT was decided that TC and I would enter the Abysmal from different points. He was going to slide in and move to the point closest to where the top of the BOA Plaza would be in the Abysmal. Since compasses don't work in the Abysmal plane—much less a GPS—TC would act as my beacon to lure Daniel to him, then TC could, along with my help, open the border between the worlds and bring him through.

And then it would be up to me to guard that border and not allow him a way to get back in.

The next step after that would be to use the Eidolon. I had no idea how to use it—all I could do was hope that when the time came I'd figure it out.

Yep. Once again, I was living life through trapdoors.

Yippee. Go me.

What I didn't know was how I was going to get the Horror—Daniel—to the other opening without him opening a door on his own.

Yep. Thinking on the run again. Otherwise—the big question was whether I was going to get this all done before my body died.

And I gave up retail sales for this?

Joe arrived right on time, having made sure that my body was securely hooked up to life-support machines. Again. He left Mastiff on guard, making sure nothing went crazy. Like, no wacky Society flunky coming in and unplugging the machines. Mastiff I trusted. He could kick ass. Even with a bandaged arm.

Joe and Dags's job was to somehow get permission to get to the top of the Bank of America Plaza. Now, it was my understanding the only thing up there besides the birdcage-looking doohickey—which was said to be coated in real gold leaf—was a building that housed the orange lights that gave the cage its nighttime glow.

I didn't really know. I'd never been up there. And I had no idea how to get to the top of the building—I'd leave that up to the cop and the Guardian.

Dags had pulled back the blood-soaked carpet—which I was going to need to replace—to show the pentagram underneath it. It wasn't necessary for me to be in the pentagram to open the door into the Abysmal. It was more like a target.

I'd discovered the pentagram back in November, when my mom and Rhonda decided to interrogate a succubus named Mitsuri. Let me go on record again as having nothing to do with this whole Wicca Magic Voodoo stuff. I'm a Wraith. That's my story, and I'm sticking to it.

Though no matter how much fun I tried to make of things, I was getting increasingly worried about my mom, her body, and Rhonda. What was I going to find when I got to the Abysmal plane? A walking corpse? Was Rhonda one of the Shadow People by now? 'Cause you know I was still mad at her, but I really didn't want anything too bad to happen to her.

Unless I did it.

Everyone went over what they were to do. Tim, Jemmy, Steve, Randall, and Boo were to guard the gate in the botanica. Joe and Dags were to get the Eidolon onto the roof of the Bank of America Plaza. TC was to wait at the corresponding point in the Abysmal plane.

And I was to corral the Horror to where TC would wait.

Okay . . . it all sounded so neat. Then why was I worried?

Could it have been that usually plans that involve me went horribly wrong?

TC grabbed my hair and pulled me toward him—and kissed me—before disappearing. I staggered back, my thighs tingling, and looked over at Joe and Dags waiting by the door. Joe's expression was one of complete smirkiness.

Dags looked—confused.

Shit.

I straightened up and smiled. "It's his way."

With that, Joe grabbed Dags and, with an arm around the shorter man's neck, tried to kiss him. Dags put his hand up in time for Joe's lips to meet Dags's palm. Joe released him and looked at the hand. "Is that Maureen's or Alice's?"

"Does it matter?"

"Well, the goth chick is hot."

Dags reached up and whacked the back of Joe's head. Joe gave a laugh, and the two left in Joe's truck.

"You know both of those guys are in love with you," Jemmy said in a quiet voice. She was in the botanica side, standing by the fireplace. She was east. The communicator. The mediator. Even her dress was a sunflower yellow.

I didn't answer her and simply moved to stand in the center of the pentagram. I didn't need any of that just then. And I appreciated everything that Dags had done for me. Really. How he'd stuck by me. And Joe—he was someone I could count on when I needed him. When he didn't disappear.

But if I had to follow my own heart, it was with Daniel.

I looked at Jemmy. "I love Daniel."

She smiled at me. "Love is hell, Zoetrope."

I nodded. Yeah, it was.

And then I spread my arms wide and allowed the shadows creeping along the corners of the room to lengthen and swallow me whole.

29

I'M not sure what divine being thought that this was the life I had ordered. It was not. And like any good consumer, I really wanted to find the customer-service window and make a complaint. Only—life didn't have a complaint person. Oh, there were prayers, like at Mass when my mom used to pray about better things because she hated the life she had.

And I used to sit there, kneeling on the tattered bench beneath the pew in front of us, my head down, listening to her. Mom never prayed quietly. It was like she wanted everyone around her to know how miserable she was. How she was stuck with a child and a job that gave her no respect.

Talk about guilt. But that was what religion was all about to me back then. Feeling guilty. Guilty because of sin. Guilty because I cost my mom so much money. Guilty because I talked to things and people that weren't there. Guilty because babysitters and kindergarten teachers alike called me weird and smart-mouthed. Guilty because they all told me I was the devil's child. I was full of sin.

Guilty because I was born in sin.

But the truth was—I wasn't born in sin. My birth itself was an accident. Had to be. My dad was technically dead—a Traveler without a body—and yet he'd made himself corporeal for my mom and fathered a child. The child of a human and a—

What exactly *was* my daddy? An Irin?

That was what was in my head as I stepped through the veil—border, whatever—and into the Abysmal plane.

I thought for a minute I'd made a wrong turn. This did not look like the same plane I'd bebopped through before with Dags. That plane had had fields of flowers, farmland, nice cottages, and even a blue sky.

The place I stepped into looked like the back alley in any industrial city in the world. The sky was soot black, no stars visible at all. Not even the usual electric glow that was present in most metropolises. The alley's walls were high, but I could just see what looked like TV antennas strung over the buildings' roofs. The sides were brick—but not like any brick I'd ever seen. As I neared the wall to my right, I thought I saw—

"What the fuck are you look'n at?"

I screamed like a girl with pigtails as I jumped back. The damned brick had talked to me! My hands to my mouth, I looked again in the dim light—and that's when I realized the light was coming from me.

I looked down and realized my entire appearance had changed.

Significantly.

I had my bunny slippers on again, and they looked happy. I was all in my usual black, but there was an eerie glow to every inch of me. And I was somehow not quite on the ground.

"Hey . . . what the fuck are you?"

I looked back at the brick. There was a face there, with two beady eyes, a pointy nose, and puckered lips. "Me? Who or what the fuck are you?"

"I'm asking the questions here," the little face said.

"Shut up, Bane. No one's listening to you. Can't you just let us get some sleep?" said another brick, about six bricks up and to the right of Bane.

"No one's asking you, dickhead," Bane said back. "We got another one of those damned traveling muckety-mucks in here again. Damned things keep coming and going, waking us up."

"Another one?" I narrowed my eyes at the one called Bane. If I put my imagination to use, it almost looked like my old fifth-grade social studies teacher, Mr. Haverty. He looked all scrunchy and ill-tempered too. It was easier to think that I was talking to him rather than some possessed brick on the side of a building in the Abysmal plane.

Know what I mean?

"Yeah, you're the second one that's showed up here—and that last guy was ill-tempered."

"He wasn't as much of an ass as you, Bane," Dickhead quipped.

"Shaddup," Bane said. "It was the girl's screams that really made me mad."

Girl's screams. Shit. That was Rhonda. "Did you see which way they went?"

"Out. That's all I know. I yelled at them to get out. The guy ignored me, and I was kinda glad. He seemed not right in the head."

Uh-huh. A brick called someone not right in the head. Hrm.

Dickhead started making sniffing noises. "Hey, you've had sex."

I moved back. "What?"

"Yeah—you smell like sex. Wasn't with that guy with the girl, though. He smelled like sex too. Lots of sex, but it wasn't what's on you. You got something else smelling on you."

"She's got some o' that Ethereal smell. All funky and weird," Bane said.

"I remember sex," said another brick to my left, whose face looked more like a young woman's. "I loved sex."

"Sex is magic," said a fourth brick down below, near my knees. This one looked Asian. "Sex Magic. You know you can bind people to you with sex."

I sighed. "Just drop the sex, okay? If that guy left here, which way did he go after that?"

The Asian said, "You smell like Symbiont. You've had sex with a Symbiont? Can they do that?"

"I don't think it's in the rules," Bane said. "But then, I've been here a long time. I think the Phanty has forgotten about me."

Phanty? "You mean the Phantasm—"

"SSHHHHHH!" all of them said. Sounded like a tire on a

tractor trailer losing air, it was so loud. Bane spoke in a whisper. "You want him to hear?"

"Hear?" I leaned in close. "He can hear if I say his name?"

The brick nodded, which was kinda weird to see. It sniffed. "You do smell like Symbiont. But there's something else about you—something familiar. It's just been so long."

I moved back and looked at the wall, and if I looked carefully, I could just make out lots of faces on the bricks. Not on all of them, but on most. "Why are all of you bricks on a wall? Were you ever alive or living?"

"Alive?" Dickhead said.

"It means had a soul," the Asian said. "Some of us. Some have never transmigrated because of the border breakdowns."

Border breakdowns. "You mean the Watchers?"

"No Watchers, no movement."

Oh. Great. Something else to feel guilty about. Because there were no Irin these—brickheads—were just hanging out, slowly becoming bricks?

Alice, meet Wonderland.

"I'm sorry about that, but is there someone else or some-*thing* else I can talk to about finding this guy who came in with the screaming girl?"

All of them went quiet—and the silence was deafening. "Hello?"

Nothing. Not a peep.

Oh bother. I looked around a bit more and saw an opening several feet to my right. With a sigh I moved toward that opening. At first I thought it might really go Alice in Wonderland, and the opening to the alley would keep growing farther away.

But I reached it and found myself on a dirty street. There were streetlights—sort of—though more like really big glass jars hanging from metal poles. I nearly yelled out loud when I found myself floating easily up to take a closer look at one of the jars.

And wished I hadn't.

I thought at first it was a jar of fireflies. Er . . . nope. Not bugs. Inside—flitting about—were bits and pieces of what looked like people. And each piece would actually morph into another body part as it moved and floated in some sort of viscous, greenish liquid. They bounced against the glass, and when that happened, they flared a bit brighter in green, so the lamp itself was always flickering.

Kinda like really spooky firelight.

I floated back to the ground—well, sort of above the ground. I wasn't exactly touching it with my bunny slippers. I looked down again at my slippers—*Did they have fangs before?*

I noticed the ground beneath them. Looked like wet asphalt. Wet, dirty asphalt. Wet, dirty asphalt that sort of moved and rippled as I floated over it. I was thinking I was floating because if I actually stepped on the ground, it would eat me.

Looking forward seemed the better thing to do so I did—though the view wasn't much better. There were darkened storefronts with boarded-up windows. Aging signs in just about every language there was. Torn, dirty, aged awnings whose colors had faded were still draped over some of the windows. But even as I continued down this road, I started thinking this was the back end of the Abysmal. That the Daniel Horror had used a lesser-known back alley to get in.

Why is that? Or is it just where Mom's shop is in relation to the Abysmal?

Not exactly a nice thing to imagine. And why was everything so different than what it'd been before? Was it that perception thing? That before I was more Abysmal than Ethereal, so I saw things through Abysmal eyes? And if that's so, then by looking at things through Ethereal eyes was I seeing the truth? Or just truth from what an Ethereal being believed the Abysmal to be?

Okay—that kind of thinking hurt my head worse than brain freeze. I decided concentrating on finding Daniel, Rhonda, Mom, and TC was what I should do.

So—where? I paused at an intersection. There were traffic lights. They were all red. And as I watched, they remained red. Never green. Or even a little bit of yellow. Just red.

And then—just there on the edges of my hearing, I thought there was a scream. A familiar scream. Something fluttered inside my chest, and I was drawn to the left. But why? *Is it me being drawn to TC? Or to Rhonda? Mom?*

AAHHHHH.

Mental note: *Need Abysmal guidebook. Could sell to Plane—*

Wow . . . I just had a mental note.

When was the last time I had any kind of note, much less a mental one?

I took that as a sign that I was getting back to my old self. Whatever that might be. So, let's see—Jemmy had said that things that shouldn't be here would fester, like a thorn in the skin. So Rhonda and Mom were like thorns.

Okay, I had to laugh at that one 'cause you know I'd always thought of both of them as thorns in MY side.

But enough kidding around. I looked to the left and figured that way was TC. That had to be the tug. So I'd need to tune in to the Abysmal plane and imagine what a sore would feel like—

Ouch! And there it was. In front of me—something was just wrong. Kind of like chewing tinfoil with metal fillings.

I shivered.

If I concentrated on it, the feeling grew stronger. I also found myself rising above the buildings, higher, to where there were antennas strung together everywhere. I could see windows glowing with green light but nobody inside. Were they all bricks?

And then I was still, a figure floating above a comic-book city at night. I heard the beat of wings, and with a last-minute realization, I knew those wings were mine. And they were behind me. And I was going to freak out.

I had wings.

I HAD WINGS!

But hadn't someone else said I had wings?

No time for mirrors and vanity right now. I moved forward toward the bad area. The closer I got, the more dense the buildings became, the more intense the light. It moved from being a dark green to a light mint, to a burning white as I neared what looked like the capital city of Abysmal.

And whaddya know. It looked just like downtown anywhere, USA.

Why was I not surprised? All generic.

From my vantage point there was a central square—or

rather a gathering where several streets came together. There was traffic—a lot of it. And there were cars and buses and trains running on aboveground tracks. To any eye this looked like a major city at night.

But for me—there was something wrong with it. From up there I couldn't decide what that was. I looked out past the city and its sprawl, searching for the fields I'd seen before. But all I could make out in the gloom were miles and miles of dark forests. And from those lands I could see things moving and writhing.

The feeling of wrong came again, and this time it was to the right of the city's center. I dove toward it, easily slipping between the buildings, gliding as if I'd always had wings. Which wasn't true as far as I knew.

But this sure beat taking the bus!

And speaking of buses, there was one now. Only as I passed by, I couldn't see any people on it. The interior was well lit, but nothing. In fact . . .

I moved down closer to the ground, to the train, and kept up with it. Looking through the windows there was no one there. Nothing. Not even a drunk asleep in a chair.

Where are all the people? The souls or creatures that make up the Abysmal? There can't just be talking bricks.

Can there?

A scream pierced the relative quiet of the night and I dove in its direction. I had my hands to my sides like a bullet. The sound and feeling led me to a small intersection—not as dimly lit as the first one I'd seen—and nowhere near as well lit as the middle of town. There were no cars. Nothing. And the storefronts were all closed but not boarded-up.

I eased down feetfirst, still not coming to a complete stop on the ground but just above it. I was on one corner, a closed, darkened shop behind me with CHINESE KANJI across the top. To my left was a trash can and to my right a U.S. postal box.

Huh?

"So like the Ethereal," came an all-too-familiar voice. "A cut above those of us who dwell here in the darker regions of life. Always thinking yourselves better than us."

I turned and faced the opposing corner.

Daniel stood facing me, his hands at his sides. I didn't see

Rhonda, nor could I sense her. Though I was beginning to suspect there was a lot here that I *wasn't* seeing.

I could see Daniel clear enough, as well as something else superimposed on him. It was like a ghost image—and moved like an overlay of some sort. Was that the Horror? My heart lurched a bit when I saw his clothes—the holes torn through the shirt and pants. I knew the bullets had been pushed out by unworldly means—but what about the damage inside of him?

What about that? Or mentally? Is Daniel himself still there, or is it only the Horror possessing him?

I cleared my throat. "Better than you?"

He pointed at me. "Never let your feet touch the ground here, do you?"

I ignored that. "Daniel—please—you have to tell me where Rhonda is. She can't survive here—neither can you for very long. I don't know if it's the Horror protecting you physically or what—"

"It's you that can't survive here, Irin." Daniel sneered at me. "You're not supposed to be here. And in a few minutes it won't matter." He gave me a wide, devilish smile. "Once your body dies, and your ties to your soul are cut, you'll vanish. You'll be nothing but a lousy Irin Ethereal failure—just like your father was."

On one level I knew this wasn't really Daniel talking. But on a superficial level I was letting him get under my skin. I had to believe that the nasty Daniel was the Horror. Had been the Horror all along. And that once I got it out of him, he'd go back to being nice Daniel, and we could finally do some serious talking together.

'Cause I had no doubt this experience wasn't something he was going to dismiss that easily.

I had opened my mouth to yell back at him when something pulsed inside of my chest. I felt a yank—a painful one—as if something had ahold of my heart and had squeezed it. I lowered a bit, and bent forward, my right hand going to my chest. *What—what the hell was that?*

"You feel that, Irin? That was my influence in the physical world. You're put together with life support—your body breathing from tubes, pumping blood by artificial means. Your living body can't survive without you in it for very long. And like this." He held up his hands. "Ethereal—it's almost as good as killing you while in your body."

This was what Jemmy had warned Joe about. Was it possible the Horror—no, the Phantasm—was manipulating Society idiots to disconnect my body from life support? *Is Mastiff there? Defending me? Is he getting overwhelmed?*

What the hell is happening? I didn't dare go near my body or take a peek—if I had gone in, I doubted I'd have been able to get back out for a while.

Again the tug on my heart, and I hissed.

Within seconds, Daniel was no longer across the street but standing right in front of me. I was still half–bent forward and looked up at him through my eyebrows. "Daniel, please . . . don't do this."

He gave me an almost Halloran-like smirk and leaned down to be even with my face. "You don't get it, do you? Daniel's dead, Zo-E-TrO-pah! He's been dead since the minute the Phantasm snatched your Abysmal ability away from you." He took in a deep breath and let it out slowly. "And then I was born. Such a better creature than his first Horror—don't you think?"

The pain continued inside my chest. *What the hell is happening back in the physcial plane?* Oh, how I hated this—with no communication. And the pull and tug of TC was even greater than it had been. As if he sensed something was wrong and wanted to unite now.

"Oh, and by the way." Daniel straightened up, and all I could see were his shoes. They were bloodstained and muddied. He was standing on the Abysmal asphalt, and it hardened and remained solid for him. "I already know about your little plan to get me back into the physical world and slap that Eidolon on me. There is no way in hell I'm going back there—this body can just dissolve until the soul still in its DNA turns to shadow, and all that's left is me."

At that moment I had two things come to me—doubled over in pain. One was that he'd just blown a small wad by telling me in an indirect way that Daniel's soul was still alive because it resided in his DNA. And secondly—

Somebody was whispering something to me.

Hit him!

I hissed again, covering up my own whispered "What?"

"Zoë, you're just stupid. You've always been stupid. I mean—how could the universe grant such gifts to a moron? You get clues all the time, and you're not paying attention. You get into trouble every time you turn around."

Hit him!

I was listening to both voices now—Daniel's annoying droning on about how stupid I was and the whisper.

"You'll never be anything but an underwear salesgirl. Or maybe you should work in food service—wait, no. You burn water." He snapped his fingers. "I know!"

Abruptly the pain in my chest vanished.

Hit him, you idiot!

The whisper sounded a lot like—

If you don't fucking kick him in the balls, I swear I will disown you!

MOM!

30

ONCE I realized who was whispering, my initial thought was to find out where she was. But then I thought about what she said, and she was right.

". . . moronic view on things. You're just a stupid, dumb bitch . . ."

I took in a deep breath—surprised that Ethereal beings actually breathed in the Abysmal—straightened up, opened my chi, aimed, and kicked the ever-loving shit out of his balls.

In fact, I kicked so hard I lost my footing and actually landed on my ass in midair. Nice trick. Need to see that one work in the physical plane. Daniel might be possessed by a Horror, but he was still a man, and the Horror was in a man's body, subject to all the aches and pains that physical body had. I wasn't surprised at all when he doubled over and went down on his knees.

I also suspected the sensation wouldn't keep a Horror down as long as it would a normal man. So once I had my balance, I struck a right cross across his jaw. He fell backward, sprawled on the corner.

After a few seconds I let out a whoop of pain and shook my right hand a couple of times. *Good God, that hurts!*

That was great—but you're gonna have to get him to Archer.

Mom? I looked around the empty corner, but all I could see was the shop, the postal box, and the trash can. "Where are you?"

Go get Rhonda and get out of here—

Daniel was moving again, if a bit slow.

"Where's Rhonda?" I shouted out.

That's when I heard the weirdest noise—sort of like stretching or tearing metal. I turned to look at the postal box. Was it moving? No—that wasn't making the noise. I turned and looked at the trash can.

It *was* moving, and writhing and bending and twisting. I moved back from it as it actually formed into something that looked like a human. Within a few seconds it was Rhonda— standing in front of me. And she didn't look so good. Her skin was ashen—like gray smoke—and her eyes were white.

I wanted to ask a thousand questions as to why she wasn't screaming in pain like Dags had that time; but she was limping toward me, her hands out. When she fell into my arms, I didn't bother to ask. She was light against me, like lifting a feather, and I darted up above the buildings. "Where's Mom?" I had to ask.

"She's fine." Rhonda's voice was almost as gravelly as my own. Her expression was one of pain. "Just get me out of here. Please, Zoë. I can't take . . . I just didn't know . . ."

I nodded to myself and rose as high as I could, with her in my arms. I paused in midflight and listened for TC. I felt him pulling and dove in that direction to a tall building several miles away. I was a bullet as I approached the building, and I could see TC from where I was. He stood on the building's edge, waving his arms—the only other moving thing besides myself.

The building on this side wasn't as ornate as the one on the physical plane. It was flat, with just a few buildings for maintenance. But like everything else it looked—empty.

Until it exploded.

THE concussion of the impact literally blew me and Rhonda backward. I tumbled in midair as Rhonda screamed. I kept hold of her through the turmoil until I could orient myself and figure out which way was up. My wings beat as quickly as they could to stop my momentum—and I was amazed at how they worked much like my heart or lungs did. It was all an autonomic extension of myself—something that just worked without my thinking about it.

When I was able to steady myself and look back—there wasn't anything left of the building's roof. Not even TC. But I knew inside he wasn't gone—he was still there. Lurking.

But what I needed to know was what had caused the rooftop to explode in the first place.

"I swear I'll destroy you and your body!" came a cry from above me.

I twisted and looked up.

Daniel was coming in fast, his left arm at his side, but in his right he had thrust out a huge ice blue sword, and he was being carried through the Abysmal air by two enormous white wings. The wings glowed with an almost Ethereal light, and I had to spring to my left to avoid a collision. But he was prepared for that and lashed out at me with the ice blue sword in his hand.

It nicked my left leg, and I screamed.

Goddamnitthatmotherfuckinghurt!

And I nearly dropped Rhonda. She held on to me with a strength I hadn't realized she had as I dove away from Daniel.

But he was after me, sword blazing.

"They're black," Rhonda said in a quiet voice. I was surprised I could hear her through the rush of wind.

"What?"

"Your wings—they're black. And they're just as huge."

Oh. Okay. Black wings. That's nice. "I'm more worried about that sword."

"Can—can you use one too? You are equals, remember?"

Equals.

Maybe. But that was between me and the Horror inside of Daniel. Daniel was being punished, his body abused by the Horror, just as Rhonda's was, by being dragged into this stupid battle. And I wasn't dumb to the fact that the Phantasm was the one pulling the strings.

So—I can have a sword too, eh? That's great—but I can't

do any fighting with Rhonda in my arms. And what about the gate? Where's TC? If I bring Daniel through at a different point, Dags and Joe won't be there with the Eidolon, and there's no way I can defeat the Horror without it.

That much I'm sure of.

"Put me down," Rhonda said. "Archer will find me."

I knew that. But—"I don't want him eating you. I'm working with him, but I sure as shit don't trust him."

"That's good to know, Zoë. Maybe you are finally growing up."

As I moved back and forth through the night sky, zigging and zagging to avoid the thrusts of Daniel's sword, I glanced down at Rhonda. There was something different about her face. Something . . . older?

"Archer won't eat me." She gave me a devilish smile, and it looked really white and creepy with her gray skin. "You'll have to trust me on this."

Uh-huh. Right. So why had I just gotten a chill down my spine?

I dropped down a few feet, my ears popping at the change in pressure, and darted between buildings. The target building was still a smoldering hunk of ash, but the building next to it was just fine. And flat. In fact, there appeared to be a garden of some sort on top of it.

I came around the side of the building, then straight up, and somehow landed—er, sort of—on the roof. It was more of an actual stumble-run. I tripped and dropped Rhonda, then I crashed into a potted tree.

Hrm . . . needed to work on my landing.

Luckily I hadn't really hurt myself, but the terra-cotta urn the tree was in—that was a different story. I think I'd used my head—no sweat.

"Douse your wings!" Rhonda hissed as she sort of picked herself up as well.

Douse? Was that a word? But somehow I could feel something itchy on my back and knew the wings were gone. It was just me again, bunny slippers à la Zoë.

I kinda liked this me better.

Taking a quick glance around, I saw that I'd been right that this was one of those rooftop gardens. Though I was a bit surprised at all the green. I hadn't seen any green since arriving, so this made the garden sort of stick out like a beacon. There were trees everywhere—from apple, to plum, fig, pear, and cherry trees. There were bushes in low pots, and several large squares of actual grass, where the concrete had been covered over in dirt.

There was an arbor too, just in front of a large apple tree. It was painted white with red, white, and pink roses wrapping around it.

"This looks like a Garden of Eden," Rhonda said as she looked around.

Yeah, which was making me more nervous by the minute. "I've got a bad feeling about this."

"Yes, Zoë, and, like all your bad feelings, it's come just a little too late."

Rhonda and I turned to face the arbor.

I expected to see Daniel there, his wings up, his sword in hand. But what greeted us was something a lot less dramatic.

I'd seen the figure before—dressed like this. It'd been outside the old demolished building across from Perimeter Place. He'd stood beside me as the Symbiont in Rollins worked its way toward Hirokumi and the child Susan inside the trunk of the Reverend's car.

He wore a simple black hoodie, pulled down over his face, which was shrouded in shadows. From his waist down there was still nothing, only a hint of what could have been legs.

Or tentacles.

The hoodie was short-sleeved, and his arms stuck out with muscular precision. In fact, his whole torso looked different than it had, as if a boy had become a man. And that man did some serious weights.

Rhonda took a step back, and I could see in her eyes that she felt the power emanating from this figure.

I'd faced him recently too—and he'd turned himself into a clown. Because he knew I hated them.

He straightened, and I was again aware of his bulk, the curve of his shoulders and definition of his chest beneath the soft cotton of his shirt.

Phantasm.

"Welcome to my garden, Irin. My Garden of Eden."

"You ditched the clown suit?" I said, with a bravado I did NOT feel. But hey, what else was I gonna do?

He reached up with his hands and took the sides of the hood. I tensed—I'd never seen his face. Only the images he'd wanted me to see. The mask the first time, and the clown the second. Would he show me his face this time?

But when he lowered the hood, the face wasn't original. It was Daniel's visage. Only his eyes were solid black. "Does this face suit you better?"

"Let Daniel go," I said, and took a step forward.

"Ah." The Phantasm held up his right hand. "No, no, no. I see something else in your heart—oh, a recent victory! My, my, my! Zoë! You had sex!"

I gaped at him. *What? Is this written on a billboard somewhere?*

"Perhaps a change of scenery." And he moved his hand across his face.

It shifted and changed, and abruptly I was looking at Dags's face.

I gritted my teeth. "Stop it."

"Oh? You don't want to see the face of your lover? Come now—you do realize how hard he's fighting for you right now, don't you? He and that bumbling mortal, trying so hard to save the woman they love."

Shit. Damn. It had been pointless to keep secrets, hadn't it? Because the Phantasm always seemed to know everything!

"You . . ." Rhonda said in a small voice to my left. I looked at her, and she was looking at me. "You slept with . . . Darren?"

Oh. Shit. Not. Now.

Christ.

I glared at her with as much sarcasm as I could muster—and I got a lot of that. "Get a grip on yourself, Rhonda. I can't have you go all jealous right now."

"But you know how I feel about him!"

Sonofa—

"Rhonda—it was a moment, okay?" *Well, it was longer than a moment, but still—* "Get over it. I'm not in love with Joe."

Joe? Why'd I say Joe?

She looked as confused as I felt. "Joe? Did you sleep with Joe or with Darren?"

"I slept with Darren! And what the fuck do you care? You slept with Joe!" There! I'd said it. I don't know why that felt all good but it did.

Her eyes widened even more—if that was possible. "No . . . we never . . . I never . . ." She put her right hand to her heart. "Zoë, Joe's in love with *you*, and I'm not in love with him. I could never sleep with a man I'm not in love with."

There is a noise that happens, in my head, when I realize I've made a terrible boo-boo of ultimately epic proportions. It's kind of like the cracking of glass, lots of it. And there is a scream.

This was one of those instances.

I knew I'd fucked up. Big-time. And let my libido make a monkey out of me. I'd slept with a man I didn't really love. I liked Dags, a lot. And he was a great friend. But—

"Oh God, you don't love him," Rhonda said. "All this time I didn't see that. I didn't realize it—"

The Phantasm was laughing. And that was pissing me off. I turned to face him. "Will you knock it off already? Wipe that face off and show me what you really look like."

He did stop laughing, but not smiling. Instead he held up his right hand.

Daniel appeared then. Just *pop*. Beside the Phantasm, his sword glowing ice blue light. His wings were folded back, and his eyes were now totally black as well. And he was pointing those eerie peepers at me.

"I look like many things, Zoë. I warned you months ago not to take the deal with Archer. But you ignored me. I tried to warn you about the chains that some would put around you. By that I meant your father. And still you moved on, you evolved into something that not even I could control, or defeat.

"Until miraculously, the chains I'd tried to warn you about took hold of you and set you free. Your Wraith self—the part birthed by yours and Archer's unions—was loose and mine for the picking. I failed before in controlling a Horror—in making it totally mine. And your father defeated me with the power of the Eidolon that bound you." He smiled, and I wished like hell he didn't look like Dags. "And now I have the key to undoing what your father did. If you'd died as a Wraith—I would have been defeated because you would have ruled here in my stead. But as an Irin"—he smiled—"I can simply do to you what I did to your father."

And with those words he lifted his right hand.

The air beside the arbor warped and twisted as something materialized. It took a wirelike shape and wrapped itself around the roses and wood of the structure. Abruptly it became solid—and I gasped as I stepped back.

It was a snake—a black snake, with tiny black wings and a human face.

A's face.

"D-Daddy?"

It turned and focused black eyes on me, and a forked tongue slithered between its lips.

"I control your father's essence, Zoë. I can change his form into anything I want. This is his Abysmal self, the part of him that was trapped here when he sacrificed himself to defeat me. An eternity as my plaything—isn't that right, Adiran?"

The human snake head turned and looked at the Phantasm, then looked back at me. This was my father? But what about the man I'd seen in my dream? The man with the ponytail and the flannel shirt? The man Tim and Steve called A?

"He did it to protect you," the Phantasm said. "So now I'll use him to kill you." He waved his hand again, and a gate opened. A hole into the living world.

And to my horror, the snake thing dove inside of it. I yelled out and tried to get to the gate, but Daniel was there, waving his sword, and I staggered back.

"Now, Zoë," the Phantasm said, "it's time to finish this. It's time to fight your Horror."

Abruptly, Daniel's body erupted in flames. He screamed as his flesh melted away, vanished into bone, until there was nothing left of him.

"DANIEL!"

He was gone . . . I'd watched him melt away completely.

No . . . there was something left.

Standing where he'd stood was a magnificent female being dressed in white light. Its wings were points of crystal that reached almost the breadth of the rooftop garden. Robes of white moved in the wind and glittered with snowflakes of solid ice.

Her skin was pale and glowed with its own internal light. Her eyes were silver inside of sparkling eyelashes, and her hair was a silver-white and flowed around her robes. Yet along the left temple and down the length of its strands was one dark streak, a black river that ran through a snow-blind mountain.

And her face was my face.

"May I show you, my dear Zoë, your Horror. Your Abysmal self. And my key to your destruction."

31

LET me go on record as saying this right now—and not in a gay way. But wow . . . my Wraith self was very sexy. She looked like a Valkyrie. Not sure about the white, snow-queen look though.

She held out her right hand, and the sword appeared there again. The same one Daniel had been using.

Daniel!

"You've got to fight, Zoë," Rhonda said as she stood beside me. I still sensed animosity and frustration from her, but she was calmer. And she was still very gray.

"Fight? With that?" I looked at her. "Maybe I should open a door for you? Get you home?"

A scream brought my attention back to what was in front of me. White Zoë was rushing at me, her sword drawn and wielded over her head in both hands. I moved to stand in front of Rhonda and yelled out myself—

Something shifted inside of me. It wasn't a bad sensation—but it was definitely not a natural one. Not natural in that I didn't think this was supposed to happen in the physical world. I felt my wings unfurl in an instant, my physical shape shifted, and I was larger than before. I screamed out as I felt my teeth lengthen and every one of my senses heighten in an instant. I could see better than before, and the White Zoë's movements seemed sluggish. Almost as if she were moving through water.

As she swung the sword at me I lifted my right hand to block—and found I was clutching a sword.

Not just any sword, but a *flaming* sword.

Sweet!

I've never had a sword lesson in my life, so I was also thinking the opposite me hadn't either, so that meant she was just as unbalanced as I was. So we were evenly uneducated in how to use one. Which meant she would revert to the same techniques that I'd use.

Meaning hack and slash, baby.

White Zoë came at me, hacking from left to right, and I blocked each blow. It was like fighting a mirror reflection. If I advanced, she retreated in a predictable way. And the opposite was true. I shot up in the air. So did she. I did a roundhouse kick as I dove at her, and she performed one as well, but in the opposite direction.

Neither attack found its target.

"This is nuts." I moved away again, and she followed me. I pointed the sword at her, and it shot flame. Her sword spewed ice, and the two canceled each other out.

What good was it to fight oneself? If the opponents were evenly matched? But along this thinking I moved back to the garden, where Rhonda stood where I'd left her, and the Phantasm hadn't moved from the arbor. I landed and banished the sword.

White Zoë did the same, standing next to old Phanty.

"You see the futility," he said.

I felt my wings fold, but they didn't disappear this time. I also realized I was a little larger than Rhonda, by a good two feet in height. Was this the actual size of my Ethereal self? An Irin? Might be. I was still figuring out the rules. Hell, it could have been my ego.

Mom always did say I had one hell of an inflated one.

Yes, you do.

I jerked around, looking. There was her voice, again. Where the was hell was she?

The Phantasm was gliding forward, not really walking. Just sort of moving. He still wore Dags's face. He stopped in front of us. "The only way to win is to defeat yourself—which of course cannot be done. Sacrifice is the only way."

I closed my fists into balls. "Sacrifice. Like you did with Daniel? Was that the Horror's contribution to this stupidity?"

"I don't have that kind of power, Zoë." He frowned at me. "There is nothing I can sacrifice because I have nothing that means enough to me to give up my existence."

Something moved inside of me.

I bent forward just a bit. So did the White Zoë.

The Phantasm laughed. "Ah . . . so it's happening. In just a few minutes others will sacrifice what they have to try to prevent your father from killing you. But their lives will be in vain."

I stepped forward. "Mastiff!"

He frowned. The Phantasm reached up and tapped his chin. "Mastiff? No. That's not the name I'm seeing. No, no. I'm afraid he failed. No, there are two others there, fighting so hard to prevent the monster from killing Zoë's frail body—"

Two others.

Shit! That could only mean Joe and Dags!

"No . . ." Rhonda said. "Please . . . don't kill him."

"Oh?" The Phantasm smiled at her. "Would you like to make a sacrifice for him? Perhaps something of value to me?"

Value? I looked at Rhonda, then back to the Phantasm. "Stop it. Rhonda, don't listen to him. He can't do anything for you."

"Yes . . . I can. I've granted millions of favors, wishes, restored lives, and extended lives throughout my reign, Zoë. But it is my wish that is my fondest desire. My wish that is most important."

Wish? The Phantasm has a wish?

"Please . . ." Rhonda said.

But before the Phantasm could react, I felt a slight pulse in my chest. This wasn't the echo of distant pain, not like the other experiences. No, this was something more—something warm and fuzzy. Well, at least to me. The Phantasm didn't look so happy. In fact, what he did with Dags's face was just . . . yuck.

"That bastard! That bastard!" he screamed.

Hooboy. I hate to think who the bastard is—'cause he just made the Phantasm really mad.

My bets are on Joe.

"I'll destroy him and those bitches once and for all—"

And then he was gone. Just like that. A tear opened behind him, and he stepped backward.

But the White Zoë remained.

"Destroy him and those bitches—"

"Oh shit."

Rhonda took a step forward. "He's gone to kill Dags." She looked at me. "You've got to stop him."

I had a good idea of where Phanty had gone—to the hospital room at Grady—but I wasn't sure if I opened up a gate here, I'd end up there. And if I did step through—would I still have the ability of flight?

Can I get there in time to stop him?

"Not fucking likely," the White Zoë said.

I took a second look at her. Her expression appeared to be animated now, where before she'd looked like stone. Her movements were no longer exact imitations of mine, and she was different. Not so much like a puppet.

She stood in front of me, her sword drawn, her wings unfurled. "Now I can fight *my* way."

"What happened?" I thought of my own sword, and it was in my hand, its heat a comfort in my palm. "You're different."

"That's because that bastard was using me, as he always had. In here I'm his to command. But in your world . . ." She smiled, and I didn't particularly like it.

Mental note: *do not smile like that unless you want to frighten small children and animals.*

"In my world, he can't control you," I finished for her.

She smiled. "Exactly. So there I was free to do his bidding—but on my own time."

"So it wasn't his idea to possess Daniel. That was your idea?"

"Yes. To get to you the fastest. And it worked. I isolated your heart, broke it, and made it pliable. You lowered your defenses, but I had hoped that in the end it would be the other cop that would take you. I hadn't counted on the Guardian. And that complicated matters."

"Complicated them?" I asked. *Am I missing something else here? It wouldn't be the first time.*

"I can't believe you did that," Rhonda said.

I glanced over at her. "Will you please build a bridge? It was just sex."

"It's never 'just sex,' Zoë!" Rhonda screamed at me. "Now, damnit—you save him!"

Save him? I pointed at the Horror. "You see that? How am I supposed to get through that to save Dags?"

But to my surprise the Horror shook her head. "I don't plan on stopping you if you wish to build a gate back to your world. And I'll not stand in your way—on one condition."

I pursed my lips. "Okay—lemme hear the condition."

"Once the next stage is set, you and I fight to settle the deal on who gets the body."

"Come again?"

"Your body, Zoë. I want it all. I want the sensations, the feelings, the tastes and smells that a living body can give me. I felt them all with Daniel—but the connection was distant. Useless. I am a part of your essence, your soul. And to have control of your body—"

Okay, okay. I get it. "And if I win?"

"That's up to you. Life as an Irin, or a Wraith." She glanced to her right. "And one other thing."

I felt the hairs on the back of my neck rise. "What?"

"I want him as well." She pointed to a clump of potted trees.

A figure I hadn't noticed or sensed stepped out of the shadows. It was Archer, his hands thrust deep into his pockets. He moved to stand by the White Zoë and smiled. "Well, well. So you actually want me?"

"When I have her body and can control the Abysmal, then there is nothing stopping me from imprisoning the Phantasm." She reached out with a long, white finger and ran it across his chin.

Archer smiled.

"With you by my side, Archer?"

He pursed his lips. "Well, now how can I refuse an offer like that?"

Uh-oh. "So what does that mean?"

"Easy," he said as he tossed a small black box to Rhonda. She caught it in midair. "If you lose, that's your new home."

Rhonda looked inside of the box and gasped. "What is it?"

"It's the Eidolon," Archer said.

I stepped forward, my immediate rage directed at Archer. "How did you get that? Dags had that in his possession."

"Yes, he *did*." Archer smiled.

Rhonda said, "We have to go *now*, Zoë."

I dismissed the sword and unfurled my wings. Rhonda stepped close to me, and I took her in my arms. With a glance toward White Zoë, I could see that she too had prepared for flight and held the Archer in her arms. I flew straight up, opened a gate between the worlds, and dove inside—

And into death.

32

NOTHING had gone as we'd planned. Well, except for getting Rhonda out of the Abysmal. And once we were through the gate and into the physical world, she started screaming her fool head off.

It was night in the skies of good old Atlanta. No moon, which was good, because I'm sure my happy ass flying in the sky would have attracted attention in the daylight—especially from the Westin Peachtree, which is where we came out. I soared higher to move above the building and caught sight of the gold birdcage on top of the Bank of America Plaza.

So it was still intact in the physical world. That was good to know.

Rhonda was squeezing the shit out of me and screaming, "Put me down! Put me down! Put me the fuck down!"

WTF? "Why are you screaming so damned loud? You didn't seem to have this much trouble before."

"That's because it didn't seem so real to me—I'm afraid of heights!"

Oh. Well. Now you tell me. "You could have warned me."

"It wasn't my idea before!"

Sheesh. "Stop yelling. Are you in pain anywhere?"

"Other than the millions of pins and needles stabbing into my nerves, I'm just fine."

I looked down at her. She wasn't gray anymore, but she was about as white as the Horror had been. She also looked very tiny in my arms, still dressed in her tee shirt and jeans, and no shoes. And she was shaking.

Maneuvering around the buildings, I focused in on Grady Hospital, southeast of the Westin. With a final push, I thought of my body and felt the familiar tug of my cord and let it be my guide to find my body. Rhonda started to yell out as we picked up speed, and I aimed directly for the window where I knew my body was.

Crashing through the window hadn't been my intention—and we didn't. Somehow I'd managed to open a gate, slip through with Rhonda—and then open another one directly into the room. And what I found stopped me in my tracks as Rhonda half jumped, half collapsed out of my arms.

The room was large and looked as if it had originally been a semiprivate room, but the second bed had been removed. The only bed that remained was shoved against the farthest wall, where the sink and bathroom door were, and I didn't have time to take a look to see if that was me.

I didn't want to. Seen that movie before. I'd deal with the aftermath later.

What we stumbled into was Captain Cooper lying motionless on the floor by the door, his head bloody and his heart weak. There were two other uniformed officers lying still, one on the near side of Cooper and the other in the hallway, blocking the door.

In the center of the room, where the brightest light came from, were Dags, Joe, Mastiff, Maureen, and Alice. The serpent the Phantasm had conjured lay to the side of the room, discarded, with its head—uhm—missing. Just a carcass. I assumed that was the reason the Phantasm had abruptly left the Abysmal plane and come here.

Dags had killed its pet.

And I say *pet* because I refused to believe that thing was my dad.

Dags hung in the middle of the room, suspended by something invisible. Mastiff, Joe, Maureen, and Alice tried desperately to get close to him as he slowly turned purple, but they were getting shocked backward.

And watching it all was the Phantasm, still looking like a nightmare image of Dags and apparently the one holding the real Dags up by his neck.

I'd originally thought ole Phanty couldn't affect things directly but manipulated other things to do his bidding. As he had manipulated Hirokumi, the Archer, Rollins, Symbionts, Daimons, Horrors. But he couldn't act on anything with his own hands.

And here he is—somehow choking the life out of a living man.

The Phantasm looked at me. "He's technically not a living man, Zoë. Same as you are technically not a living woman."

Huh?

"Zoë," Rhonda screamed at me. "He's killing Darren!"

I felt the Horror in the room before I saw it. She stood by the window, Archer beside her. "It would make my life and Archer's life easier if you killed it."

She'd followed me through the gate, just as she'd said she would. Just as we'd planned. But having any form of final battle in a hospital was bad for business—period. We needed to get out of there, and the only way to do that was to stop the tug-of-war in the room's center.

"Please! Stop!" Rhonda screamed out. "I'll do anything if you don't kill him!"

I hissed. That was *not* the thing to say to a Phantasm. Even my limited brain knew that.

The Phantasm did a real neat transport from across the room to where Rhonda knelt, and smiled at her with his borrowed face. "You would do anything?"

She looked at him with wide eyes and nodded.

Oh God, Rhonda, you can't be that gullible. "Stop—" I had my sword in my hand again and pointed it at him. "Don't touch her."

"You should know the rules, Irin-Wraith. Once a request for a deal has been initiated, there isn't a damned thing you can do."

I looked at Maureen and Alice. Alice nodded at me but kept her jaw tight. "He's right—if Rhonda declares a deal, then she and he have to go through with it."

"And you asked for the Guardian's life?" The Phantasm smiled. I really hated that smile on Dags's visage. "I name a price, and you agree."

"No!" I started forward.

But to my surprise Archer was there, his hand out to me, the center of it glowing bright red. "Don't move," he said in a low voice.

Rhonda was looking from me to Dags to the Phantasm. She struggled to stand up, and I realized then that her stay in the Abysmal had taken a lot out of her. Though I was still amazed at how well she'd survived it as opposed to Dags's less-than-stellar trip through.

In her hand she had the box, clutching it as if her life depended on it.

Dags was blinking rapidly. The Phantasm was choking him even as Rhonda hesitated.

"I want the Eidolon."

Like we didn't see that coming. Of course the Phantasm wanted the Eidolon that had destroyed him. With it he could banish and summon at will. And he could possibly break down the barrier my dad had sacrificed so much to put in place—that which kept the Phantasm on his side of things.

Which made me start thinking—if he was limited to the Abysmal plane, then how was he here? If I believed the whole barrier nonsense, then he wasn't here but maybe throwing a projection of himself here. Manipulating something else that was here in the physical plane.

So—that meant it was like a radio and speakers. The radio had an antenna that caught the airwave of the music, and the tuner interpreted it and sent it out through speakers that made an echo of the music fill the room.

The only antennas that I knew of were the strange pieces of ones I'd seen all over the rooftops of the Abysmal plane. So, say he was broadcasting himself over those "radio waves," then maybe there was some sort of receiver here in the physical plane.

So . . . what was his receiver? And if I could somehow destroy that, would it like—pop him back into the Abysmal plane and cut off his power here?

Well, it was a good theory—but it wasn't doing Dags any good, as he'd now slumped forward, his arms dangling at his sides.

"Don't kill him!" Rhonda shouted.

Now—I'm not an uncaring bitch. Hardly. And it wasn't that I didn't care about Dags. I did. But I'd known Rhonda a hell of a lot longer than Dags, and watching her totally wig out like this—little Miss Tough Bitch—was very disconcerting.

And so melodramatically out of character.

Phanty had his arm out, his palm open. "Give me the Eidolon, and I will give you your heart's desire."

Heart's desire? What—has everyone taken a melodrama pill today?

I started to move toward Dags—but this time Archer reached out and grabbed my arm. The touch shocked both of us—Abysmal touching Ethereal—polar opposites in the universe. *Careful, we might explode.*

I glared at him, and he looked at me over his shades, à la *Risky Business*. Then he wiggled his eyebrows. Huh?

Rhonda threw the box at the Phantasm. He caught it easily. Abruptly, Dags collapsed in a heap. Joe rushed in and grabbed him, dragging him away from the center of the mix as Maureen and Alice pounced on him in seconds. Then Rhonda did this really bad fake-screaming thing, ran to where Dags lay on the ground, and threw herself over his body in the worst display of crying and misery I'd ever seen.

What the—

Has everyone gone loopy?

The Phantasm was laughing as he opened the box.

An eerie red light exploded from the small white square and bathed the Phantasm in a crimson bath of oil. He screamed, and the image of Dags's face melted away. I thought I caught a glimpse of a hard jawline, strong chin, and bright red hair just before his flesh melted, and any scream he could have given was cut short.

"Shit!" Joe yelled, and piled on top of Rhonda and Dags.

"You might want to disappear," Archer said, then vanished.

I stood in my spot, my mouth open, just watching as the air

around where the Phantasm was standing began to implode, sucking everything in toward itself. In layman's terms, it looked like he was becoming a black hole.

And then—

Pop.

It sounded like a kid pulling his finger out of his mouth. And everything was still.

No one moved at first—including me. I stood my ground and looked at Rhonda and Joe lying over Dags, and Mastiff sitting up with a dazed expression on his face. Maureen and Alice were gone. And everything not nailed down was on the opposite side of the room, where the Phantasm had been.

The only thing left where he'd been standing was the black box.

Even White Zoë was gone.

I held out my hands. "Okay—what the fuck just happened?"

And then I saw the hospital bed—the one that was supposed to have my body in it. It was covered in ceiling debris and several machines. "Ah!" I pointed to it.

"Relax," Joe called out as he stood. "Your body's safe elsewhere. We had a trap set for whatever it was the Phantasm was going to send."

Uh . . . oh. Wow. Glad everybody else knew what was going to happen. "I thought you were going to go to the Bank of America Plaza."

"That's what we wanted people to think," Joe said as he helped Mastiff stand on shaky legs, then knelt back down to help Rhonda right herself.

Rhonda pushed back as Dags stirred and started coughing— horrible hacking coughs. Maureen and Alice reappeared and were trying to touch his throat. He started batting at them. "I'm fine," he said in a voice that sounded more like a crow's than his own.

Mastiff stumbled to each of the two uniforms and checked them before looking at Joe and pointing. "You owe me."

Joe nodded, coughed, and nodded again. "I'll buy you a beer."

"Oh no, no, no. You're gonna tell me what the fuck it is you do on your off-hours." And then he pointed to the unconscious

Captain Cooper. "And you're gonna take the heat for this with him."

I watched Joe's face. He didn't look too terribly enthused.

I moved forward and stood in front of Mastiff, waving my hands. Joe frowned at me, then looked at Mastiff before shaking his head. No. Mastiff couldn't see me. That was a relief. I was incorporeal. Which meant he probably hadn't seen the serpent, or Archer, or even Phanty.

I wanted to be in the room when Joe explained all this to Mastiff.

With a smile at Joe, I knelt beside Dags. He saw me and gave me the silliest grin I'd seen on him. His neck was red and bruising, much like mine had been months ago when Mitsuri had tried to kill me by strangling me. Dark circles hung under his eyes, and Maureen and Alice were now behind Dags, their hands over his heart. My own heart lurched in a funny way—not like it had before.

"Who switched the Eidolons?" I said in a whisper, knowing that sometimes even though they can't see you, the physical world can still hear you. And I wasn't sure Mastiff needed to hear me just yet.

Joe asked Mastiff to go call for help down the hall, and when he'd gone he nodded to Dags. "He did. It was his idea to replace the Destruction Eidolon for the blue Eidolon."

I looked at Dags with wide eyes. He opened his mouth to say something, but his voice caught and he grabbed at his throat. I put my hand on him, noticing how it became corporeal without a second thought—it was second nature. Instead, he thought to me, *Knew Phanty would attack your body—would want e.i.d.o.l.o.n. And thought good time to whack him.*

I laughed. Yeah . . . it was a good time to whack him. "So you had already had it planned out with Rhonda that she would go all drama queen just so Phanty would take the bait?"

Joe pursed his lips. "Not exactly. It was more like we hoped you would figure it out when Archer gave it to you—we didn't know Rhonda would be the one to go melodrama."

Archer? "You mean TC was in on this?"

Dags coughed and tried to clear his throat. "Yes," he said in a hoarse voice.

Yes?

Joe explained. "The Archer wants one thing—to live and to live with power. He'll side with whoever can give him that power. We made sure he overheard a conversation between Dags and me that if Zoë touched this stone, she'd be separated from her Abysmal side forever. That's bad for him—so he'd do what would assure his future."

Dags held up a finger and coughed again. "Which is why"—his voice was still rough but getting better (*go, girls!*)—"I destroyed the Phantasm's . . . hormone-enhanced Daimon . . . and lured him here, where Archer is more . . . powerful."

I narrowed my eyes at him. "You do realize *how* powerful Archer is, don't you?"

"Yes." He smiled at me. I didn't stop him when he reached up and softly touched my chin with his fingers. "You look so . . . different . . ." He coughed. "Beautiful."

He was proud that he could help, and I knew that. I sensed it. And I sensed his elation at "whacking" the Phantasm. What I didn't say was that I was just a bit apprehensive as to what the consequences of that action would be. Yeah—everyone seemed okay for now. But could a Destruction Eidolon actually destroy something as old and powerful as the Phantasm?

I really didn't think so.

I started to stand, but Joe reached out and tried to grab my arm—he passed through me. Odd—how I could touch Dags and he could touch me but it didn't work with me and Joe. I looked at him. "Thanks for getting Rhonda out of there."

"No sweat." I started to move away, but something else in his expression caught my attention. "What?"

"Zoë—don't die on me, okay?"

Die? I had no intention of dying. "Then take care of my body. This isn't over yet."

That much I was sure of.

What had me anxious, though, was where Archer and the Horror had taken off to. The Phantasm was gone. I doubted he'd been destroyed, but—from what I'd seen—I was confident the Eidolon had done a bit of damage to his broadcasting equipment. And hopefully it'd lived up to its name and destroyed it.

For a while.

But even as the chaos around me took on an organized rhythm, I was still without Daniel.

Or my mommy. I was going to lose my mom forever, wasn't I?

Rhonda collapsed to my left, where she'd been standing with Joe. He caught her in midfall and lowered her to the floor.

"Oh, I wouldn't count me out just yet."

What?

I moved back as something dark and shimmery sieved out of Rhonda's body, and I kind of wondered if that was what my astral form looked like.

And then the image took on an all-too-familiar shape.

Mom?

MOMMY!

33

NONA was there, bathed in Ethereal light, and looking for all the world like a million dollars. Part of her was still sort of hovering over Rhonda's feet beneath the sheet. And suddenly I got it. I got why I'd heard her in the Abysmal plane. Why Rhonda had seemed and acted so much older, changed her appearance, and why she'd not suffered real serious damage in the Abysmal plane.

And why she'd acted so god-awful melodramatic.

I pointed at her. "YOU WERE IN RHONDA THE WHOLE TIME!"

Everything stopped. Joe swore. Dags coughed.

But she was there. My mommy was really there.

She was there, really there, in front of me.

Debbie Reynolds in electric white.

She put a long, red-lacquered nail to her perfect red lips. "Shhh. You want to get into more trouble?"

I didn't know whether to hug her or hit her. I was so relieved to see her—to know she was alive—

But then I remembered her body, and I slapped my face with my hands. "Your body! Oh, Mom, someone took off with your body, and I didn't—"

But she was already waving at me to be quiet. "My body's fine. Private hospital in Dahlonega. Adiran thought it might be a better idea if I got it out of the line of fire—and it needed some serious cleaning after Archer slept in it."

I—but you—and he—

Mom opened her arms wide and smiled. She'd always done that when I was a child—never letting me forget that she was there for me. That I had her love, her caring.

Her touch.

Mom . . .

Nothing could have stopped me at that moment as I lunged at her, nearly tackling her to the ground, and held on for dear life. She hugged me in return. Even though she was only a spirit, she was vibrant, and alive, and I loved every damned part of her.

"I'm so sorry, Zoë, for putting you through all this."

I sniffed, unable really to form a coherent sentence. I was blubbering like a baby as she stroked my hair and kissed my forehead. I buried myself in her ample breasts and didn't want to let go.

Ever.

"When he took you—"

"Shhh. I know, I know. It was scary for me too. But we can talk about it later, okay?" She pushed me away from her and held me at arm's length with her left hand while moving hair from my eyes with her right. "You know this isn't over yet. And what happens next will really define what the rest of your life will be."

I looked at her. "Is it really you? Are you really okay?"

"In spirit, I'm fine—and as spry as I was when I was twenty. Now, my physical body"—she wiggled her hand in the air like a wave—"that's going to take a bit of work." She looked around. "And from the looks of things, we're all gonna need a nice long vacation." Mom's gaze lingered on Dags as Maureen and Alice helped him to a standing position. He was a bit wobbly, and his throat looked awful. "You do care for him, don't you?"

I lowered my eyes. "Yes."

"But not the way he cares for you."

I didn't have an answer for her. She lifted my face with a finger beneath my chin. "I love Daniel, Mom."

"I know. And that's what you have to fight for now."

"But Daniel's—"

"Still alive. The Horror can't take any real form save what we give it." She looked at me with serious eyes. "It's a part of you—a part that, unfortunately, my early experiments with sympathetic magic rendered apart. I did exactly what your father tried to stop Rodriguez from doing." She sighed. "But no help for it now—I guess."

I think we all sort of go through that moment in life—the one when you realize that your parents are human beings, with real human lives, events that shaped them, and memories of things that have nothing to do with you. And I really understood at that moment what kind of pain my mom had had to go through—what demons she'd had to exorcise. The feeling of rejection she must have felt—being left all alone with a nutcase out there wanting her daughter.

"You know better now?"

"Yes. And whether Archer knows it or not, he gave me the opportunity to see Adiran again. I owe him that." She pursed her lips. "But that's all. Nothing else. He's a putz."

I laughed and cried at the same time.

"Now"—she wiped at my tears—"you have to win this. And you'll win it and save Daniel the same way you thought you would. With the blue Eidolon."

I looked around the room. Joe had lifted Rhonda and was taking her out of the room. He cared about her, and that was good. Even though it hurt—and I kinda knew why. "Where is the blue Eidolon?"

Dags answered as he stepped near us. "Joe has it. He and I will get it to the top of the Bank of America Plaza."

I looked at his throat. "You need to stay here and get that looked at."

But he shook his head. "No, I need to finish what I started. And then I'll—" He coughed, but his voice was better. "And then I'll take a nice vacation."

I straightened up and sniffed. I looked again at Mom to make sure she was really there. Even if it was just her spirit. "Then I'd better get this over with."

Mom moved closer. "Understand—this isn't a game, Zoë.

The Horror—your Horror—doesn't want to give up its new freedom. Your father fought Rodriguez's Horror—"

She didn't finish.

I nodded. "He won."

"And he lost. Adiran made a sacrifice that day, to ensure that such a monster didn't wreak havoc on the world his baby daughter lived in. Yeah, I think he did it for humanity too." She smiled. "But I know his heart was thinking of you."

"I got it. But I need to get to the roof—I don't want any more casualties here."

She nodded and gave me a wink before she vanished. With a glance around at the mess, I pushed myself up through the floors, taking the most direct route to the roof I could think of. I passed a few people on the way—and passed through a few as well. Though the images didn't shift much—most minds were preoccupied with worry, dread, and fear for loved ones.

Hrm . . . might need to go back and check on that one guy who's afraid he'll get caught. Caught doing what?

Once on the roof of Grady Memorial, I gazed up at the Atlanta night sky. It was cloudy—no stars visible in the darkness. And there was a lot of wind—was there a storm heading from the east? Possibly—I felt so out of touch with a normal life. The one where I used to get up by slapping the alarm, turning on the tube, listening to the news and watching the weather as I checked my e-mail and drank my coffee in my comfy pajamas and my latest creature slippers.

I miss my slippers.

I moved to stand away from the small building that housed the door to the stairs. Just as I did, it opened, and the familiar forms of Dags and Joe came through the door. Joe's gun was drawn, and Dags's palms glowed with the soft Witch Fire.

Joe was first to arrive by my side. He pulled back on the gun's slide and looked at me. "You ready?"

"Yeah—shouldn't you be on your way to the Bank of America Plaza?"

He nodded. "Yep. But we needed to coordinate—and you don't have a phone."

"Is Rhonda all right?" I said.

He nodded. "She'll be fine. If it weren't for Nona hiding out in her, she wouldn't have survived the Abysmal plane." Joe looked at me. "I didn't know either. Honest. But I sure am glad we never did the—" He made a strange face.

I wasn't getting it. "You didn't do what?"

"Come on, Zoë." He gave me a very frustrated look. "You know—"

"No, I don't."

Dags laughed, and then coughed, but he was still smiling. "He means if he'd had sex with Rhonda, he'd have been having sex with Nona as well."

I made a face and looked at Joe. "Oh yeah." And then the reality of that image came fully formed in my imagination, and I made an even worse face. "Oh good God—"

"You finally caught on, huh?" Joe shook his head and visibly shuddered. "Damn, that's enough to make me go eunuch." Joe looked down at Dags. "You good for this?"

Dags nodded and cleared his throat. "You're going to need the girls."

"That I am." He looked at me. "You promised me."

I nodded. "Don't die. Got it." I winked.

And within a second of breathing, something blew past us, shoving me out of the way with the force of a sledgehammer. I heard voices shouting; but, as I turned, I saw Dags pushing himself off the ground.

Joe was gone.

I looked up and saw him in the sky, in the arms of the Horror.

34

NOW that was just not playing fair!

Dags stumbled to his feet. He was shaky, but he was up and starting to take a few steps in the direction the Horror had taken Joe. "Whoa!"

He stopped and turned a stricken face to me. "It took Joe!"

"Yes, and I'm going to go—"

"He's got the Eidolon!"

Ah, well, shit. Looking up, I could see her there, just suspended in midair. I couldn't tell if Joe was alive, awake, or unconscious. She'd come at us hard. I fixed Dags with as serious a look as I could. "Get over to the building. I don't care how you get up there—just get there. And please be careful."

I had my hands on his shoulders—and maybe that was the wrong signal to give him. He smiled at me and put his hands on mine. "You be careful—remember, you promised Joe—"

I took my hands back with a wave. "Uh-uh. If he gets his ass killed, then all promises are off. Now get going. Maureen! Alice!"

The two women appeared then on either side of him. "We'll watch him," Alice said. "Just come back."

Oh, I had every intention of coming back—that bitch had already corrupted one man I loved. She was not about to mess up a second.

And yes. Loved. I wasn't going to admit it to anyone else, but I'd figured out how I felt about Joe during that time when he was gone. I just—well, I wasn't sure what to do with it. I still loved Daniel.

Ain't the heart just one big fuck'n nightmare.

I turned and jumped into the air—hey, I was getting the hang of this—my wings unfurling as I directed my attention to the Horror. As I got closer, I could see that Joe wasn't moving—but I could sense a pulse. He was alive. I stopped a few feet away from her—my sword drawn. Her weapon wasn't out.

What was she doing?

"Let him go," I called to her. "Joe's got nothing to do with this."

"Of course he does," she said, and gave me a half smile. "Joe. Daniel. Dags. They're all part of the same life. Your life. My life." She was holding him from behind, her arm wrapped around his chest. Joe's head was down, his arms out, his boots hanging so high above the ground. If she dropped him—

"This was the one I wanted," she said. "The passionate one. The one that was fun. But he wasn't as easy to get into as Daniel. No—" She sighed. "Daniel's heart was already tormented. You messed him up, Zoë. Letting him see you do that to poor Holmes like that."

"Stop it. Daniel didn't see anything. He couldn't see ghosts."

"Oh, but he did, Zoë. He saw it all. And you have Archer to thank for that."

Now, that wasn't a name I expected to hear right then. "What does Archer have to do with that day?"

"Did you forget what helped your physical friends hear you, Zoë? Death experiences. Joe here had actually died once, and his soul is tainted with Ethereal poison. Same with Rhonda now, though hers is a bit more gray, but that was because you killed her." She smiled. "Did you forget how Daniel actually died that day on the fire escape?"

Died?

I shook my head. "No—Daniel didn't die. Rai died."

"No, you released Rai—and when you did, it severed Daniel's spirit, and for a brief moment he was touched by the Abysmal, by Rai's retreating essence. He died. And then he was resurrected once again." She beamed. "Isn't it romantic? But the truth is that Daniel never really believed it when he saw things. He'd always seen Tim and Steve because they'd made themselves corporeal, so even when he saw them as ghosts, he didn't realize it. The boy's about as perceptive as a ball of dough. It's a wonder he ever made detective."

I chewed on my lower lip, half of my attention focusing on what she was saying and the other half on Joe. If she showed even the slightest intention of dropping him, I was going for him. Teleportation style.

And yet—what she was saying made sense when I thought of everything we'd sussed out. Why Joe could hear me and Rhonda couldn't. And then she could. Because I'd possessed her—and then she'd—

Oh no.

I finally understood. *My God, why am I so damned dense?*

I'd overshadowed Daniel—stayed inside of him and made him sick. But the truth of it was—I'd also made him able to hear me. And if he could hear me—

"He heard your conversation with Holmes. In his head while he was in the car, Zoë. It confused him, so he went inside, followed you, and he saw exactly what it was you did."

Oh damn.

Oh damn, damn, damn.

He'd seen me release Holmes's tether, but he hadn't understood it.

And so he'd left me that night—and never really come back. He thought he was going crazy—and maybe he was. If he had known beforehand—if I'd told him about me. And about Rhonda and Nona, and Steve and Tim. He'd have been prepared.

"So you see? You set him up all nice and depressed. And,

once I was free, all I had to do was seek him out and slip in-side," the Horror said. "I tried to get into your mom's body, but you had that damned triskelion around her neck." She snapped her fingers. "Speaking of which—" She reached inside of Joe's pants pocket with her left hand and pulled out the glowing blue necklace and chain and held it up. "This won't work on me, bitch. I'm not technically a spirit to summon. So you're gonna have to fight me one . . . on . . ."

And she did it.

"One."

She let him go.

But I was already beside him before he fell even a foot, scooping him up in my arms when—

BAM!

She delivered a right cross to the left side of my face. I spun backward and nearly dropped Joe. She was back again on the other side and kicked me in the right kidney. I doubled over, amazed at how real and physical this body felt when compared to how things felt as a Wraith.

"You don't get it, do you?" the Horror said as she moved past me as if to strike again, but then paused. I was of little use in defense as I still had an unconscious Joe Halloran in my arms. "Every strike I make at you affects your body, Zoë. You're still tied to a body." She held out her hands. "I'm not!"

And with that, she came at me again.

But this time I was ready for it. I threw Joe into the air, roundhoused in midair and kicked the shit out of her chin with my nice, angry bunny slipper. As she tumbled back, I moved back to Joe, grabbed him, then dove away from the hospital in the direction of the Bank of America Plaza.

I'd half expected to feel that kick I'd made—I mean, after all, she was me in a way. But I hadn't. And that worried me. I could also feel her now, powering after us as my wings beat faster and I saw the triangular birdcage on top of the Plaza.

But did she still have the Eidolon? Because no matter what she said, I didn't believe her. I knew what that thing had done to me, and, using it the right way, I was going to put her in her place.

Bitch.

I was just able to land on a corner of the flat part of the roof, beneath the orange-glowing cage, before I felt her near. I ducked under one of the beams forming the cage and was able to get Joe to the shelter of the building housing those incredible lights. He was on his side and still as I turned and felt the blow of another of the Horror's punches.

Making a conscious effort to back away from Joe, I suffered several more of her blows before I finally ducked and landed one of my own square to her face. She hissed and moved sideways, and I instinctually ducked as her booted foot nearly clubbed the top of my head. Instead, her swing went wild and I powered straight up, threading through the girders of the cage and nailing her directly in the center of her gut.

With her loud "ommph," we moved up and away from the cage, two winged harpies duking it out over Atlanta. The whole time we fought, the wind picked up, and the skies darkened the night even more. There was a building of energy—but I couldn't tell from my perspective if it had anything to do with us.

Or if this was just another one of those freaky weather patterns.

Knowing Atlanta—I was betting on the latter.

One of the Horror's blows caught me just a little to the side, and the sting from it echoed distantly. I knew my physical body had just taken a hard hit on that—and I was suddenly winded. Before I could regain my composure, the Horror was coming at me, both her hands out, and her sword appeared in one hand. I saw the Eidolon there, the chain threaded through her fingers.

I got my hands up in time to stop the blade, moving my body to one side, but then I was pushed back, and into one of the gold-leaf girders. The gold fluttered off in the impact, and I could feel an odd current building. Not electrical—but Ethereal.

And I somehow knew that Mom was nearby.

And even though my thoughts kept wandering, looking for a new place to move or figuring out what to do next, the Horror was bent on one thing—destroying me.

We slipped off the girder as one, and her speed pressed us down until we connected with the building's roof, then slid down to the ground, several feet away from a stirring Joe.

I was on my back, and she was over me. She couldn't get her sword drawn because of the way she was holding me. But then, neither could I. And then she hit me again with her right hand, then again. I wasn't able to focus—my mind was dimming, and I knew I was losing touch with my physical body.

Shit. Not yet!

But the blows stopped, and I was too dizzy to react. She was straddling me, a white avenger on top of a black advent, and she was taking the Eidolon and wrapping the chain around my neck. I tried to get it off, but the chain itself was like steel, and she pulled harder and harder.

"Die, damn you!" she said over and over. "Just be gone! I banish thee! I fucking—banish—thee!"

My vision dimmed, much like it had when Mitsuri had done the same thing to me. But there weren't any big smoky dragons looking for kibble this time. If I wanted to save my ass—and the world from this kind of menace—I had to do it myself.

Think—what else do I have to—

And then it was there, and I wasn't thinking how to use it. With a scream, I stopped trying to pull the necklace from my neck and summoned my sword and, as it materialized, I reached out with my right hand so that the blade, flaming, would drive straight into her heart.

The pressure released abruptly, and I was gasping for breath. Was my body doing the same? Gasping somewhere for air? I took in several lungfuls before I tried to move or figure out where the Horror had gone.

Or from which direction she would come at me.

But I needn't have worried.

As I pushed myself up on my elbows and looked down the length of my torso, toward my bunnies, I could see her on her back, my sword sticking up out of her chest.

Strike!

I wanted to yell out loud as I pulled the Eidolon pendant from my neck and rolled up, to the right, then to my knees. The Horror was gasping as blood poured from the wound . . . and from her mouth.

Blood?

Since when did spirits or creatures of the Abysmal have blood?

And then she changed—her entire physical being shifted, molded, and became what it had been all along.

Daniel.

"Oh my God," came a voice to my left, and I was only partially aware that Dags was there—moving from beside the small structure beneath the lights. He went down on his knees next to Daniel's body.

Daniel's clothes were tattered and filthy, and his chest heaved up and down as he gasped for breath.

Oh my God . . . what have I done?

WHAT HAVE I DONE NOW?

And I could just see the Horror, her image superimposed over his body as she lost strength as he did.

"Take her now, Zoë," came a strong, deep voice to my right. "Make the covenant with me."

Archer.

I looked over and up at him. He was solid as he stood there, his full-length coat back and flapping in the wind. His shades were in place, and he was smirking. "What . . ."

"Take her now! If you don't, she'll follow him into death, then they'll both be gone. But if you take her back, then you can be the Wraith—you can retrieve his soul."

"What . . ." I looked back to Daniel. "How can you . . ."

But Archer was on me, pulling me up to my feet by my right arm. He grabbed both of my shoulders, then held up the arm that held the Eidolon. "Put this around her neck—take her back, and we can join. *Save* him."

"Don't do as he says." Dags spoke up. "Daniel has to die."

Joe was behind him, staring wide-eyed at Daniel.

"I—" I was sobbing. Openly, and I didn't care. It was that day on the roof again—with me fighting TC and Daniel fighting for his life. "I can't lose him. I can't let him die—"

And Archer was now in front of me, ripping off his shades, and I looked into his white, dead eyes. "Then you make a deal with me now. There *is* a way to save him—but you have to take the Horror back now."

Save him?

To make another deal with the Archer?

"Don't do it," Joe said as he stumbled near us. "Don't let your heart make a stupid mistake."

I looked from Archer, to Joe, to Daniel. "I can't help it, Joe." I looked at Halloran. "I love him—I can't let him die. Not like this."

"Then do as I say," Archer said.

"My God, Zoë," Joe said. "This is a Symbiont—he just wants Daniel's body for his own."

Archer was gone from me and stood in front of Joe, who took an involuntary step back. "I do not want his body, Detective Halloran. I want what's best for me, and for the Wraith. There is a destiny here—"

"A destiny? That you and Zoë will fulfill?"

Archer paused. "You have no idea."

"Yeah, you're right," Joe said, and stepped back again. "And I want nothing to do with this."

But I was already on my knees beside Daniel. His left arm was out, and I took his hand in mine and kissed it as I bent near his face. He blinked suddenly and turned his head. He looked at me. His eyes focusing.

"Zoë?"

Tears ran over my nose and I smiled at him. "Yes, it's me. It's me."

"Oh, wow," he smiled. "Your—your voice."

"Yes, it's back. For now. But you're going to have to be still for me, okay?"

His expression darkened. "What happened to Holmes? Zoë—I saw him in that warehouse."

"I know, Daniel, I know. And I'm sorry. I'm sorry I wasn't honest with you sooner."

His eyes widened as he took in my appearance. "Oh my . . . you have wings, Zoë. Did—did you die?" And then he looked stricken. "Did I die? Oh God—the nightmares . . ."

"No," I said, and touched his face. My fingers tingled where I touched him, and he used the hand in my own and reached up to touch my face. I could *feel* his life fading.

"So beautiful, Zoë. I'm s-sorry. I was . . . in love with you."

OH GOD.

And he closed his eyes.

I dropped his hand and took the necklace in both my hands. I unclasped it and reached around his neck to fasten it.

Nothing happened at first—

And then the world exploded, and in the end, only Archer was beside me.

35

Last night, a tornado struck downtown Atlanta, Georgia. Several buildings were damaged—mostly from blown-out windows, which littered the street and Centennial Park below. The worst casualty seems to have been the Bank of America Plaza—whose illuminated birdcage construction was apparently struck by lightning, as the entire top is missing from the building.

Cleanup efforts are under way, but city planners say it will take some time before the park and many of the surrounding buildings will be open again.

THIS is getting old. Isn't it?

I know it is for me. But it's my life, and no matter how strange and impossible it seems, I have to live it.

What can I say about that night? Absolutely nothing. Basically because I can't remember anything after putting the Eidolon around Daniel's neck.

That was March 28. It was April 23 today, and Joe was at the door with a huge basket of fruit in his hand. I'd been awake and somewhat coherent for three days. Everything was working—I could hear, I could see, my chest was mending, as was my lung. The words *miraculous* and *lucky* were getting bandied about quite a bit.

I'd also just learned I was in Gwinnett Medical Center—not a place I'd been to before. But they took my insurance—surprise!—and from what I'd learned, they'd taken excellent care of me. Or rather, of my body. Apparently the Society of Ishmael, or the SOI, had donated a lot of money to the hospital and a few members were on the board of trustees.

Sweet.

And convenient. Since I knew the CEO personally.

Joe stepped in and set the basket on the wheeled table, the kind found in most hospital rooms. Then he did something I hadn't expected—he came straight to me and put his arms around me.

And he hugged me. Tight.

I hugged him back—and nothing could stop the shaking of my shoulders as the emotion that had waited for me to catch up came crashing down. Joe was the first person I'd seen when I woke. He'd been the only person, other than the doctor and a bunch of charismatic nurses.

I loved nurses. Especially the night-shift nurses. I half expected Tiara to show up.

Eventually, Joe moved away first and kissed my forehead. He was careful of the monitoring wires, but they were unnecessary. I was fine. I was healthy.

And I was Wraith.

He wiped at his face, making it look like he was running his fingers through his hair, then he reached out to the nightstand and picked up my dry-erase board. He scribbled on it, then turned it to face me.

NONA AND RHONDA SAY HI.

I smiled and nodded, and said to him, "Tell them hi. When are they coming to see me?"

He took the board back. Erased. Scribbled. TOMORROW. STILL GETTING SHOP TOGETHER.

I nodded. "Jemmy still there?"

Scribble. Erase. Scribble. YEP. SAYS SHE'S STAYING TO HELP TIM AND STEVE.

With that, I laughed. It was a hollow sound, my voice nearly gone. I shook my head as I watched him, and then said, "Will you show me now?"

He nodded and closed his eyes. I'd been waiting for this—for the moment I could peek into Joe's memory and see for myself what had happened. I lay back on the pillows and slipped from my body as easily as I ever had and moved into Joe's.

Overshadowing a willing soul was much easier than using force. And Joe's mind was a jumble. I settled myself down inside the theater behind his eyes until he came strolling out of the darkness, dressed in black, and holding a bag of popcorn.

I held up my hand. *Uh, no thanks. I don't think I'll be wanting that.*

You sure? It's really not that bad.

I shook my head. *Just show me.*

He knew what I wanted to see. I already knew the outcome but wanted to see how it had happened. *Are you sure? This might be more painful than I think you realize.*

I touched his arm. *Please.*

The theater grew dark, then light. I could see me bending over Daniel, and my heart lurched when I saw the sword sticking out of his chest. I watched myself sit back—

That was where my memory faded.

Archer appeared behind me, then disappeared inside of me at the same instant the Horror did. My entire body glowed white for a second before the glow faded to gray. I saw Daniel's soul rise, and I saw my Wraith self reach up and grab hold of it just as the Phantasm appeared behind where Dags stood.

Time seemed to stand still as I viewed things from Joe's perspective. Dags sensed something and turned just as the Phantasm waved its hand, and Dags's body was sent flying to the edge of the roof, slamming hard against the concrete railing.

He didn't move.

And then the Phantasm was yelling, his mouth wide-open, his face no longer Dags's visage but becoming something twisted, mangled, and completely unholy. I shoved Daniel's soul back into his body, not paying attention to the shudder, the physical reaction of the soul being forced back in.

Joe had his gun in his hand and moved in front of the Phantasm, who was nearing me. But the Phantasm grabbed Joe at the neck and tossed him aside—and I could see something trailing ever so lightly behind Joe. As if the Phantasm had taken something in that instant.

And then I was in the air, as was the Phantasm. Each of us growing in size, each of us glowing bright, each of us pulling a sword—

And then Maureen and Alice were there with wings of their own. Maureen shrouded Dags's body, and Alice helped Joe back to Daniel and covered them both.

And then there was a bright light.

Things went dark. I sat in stunned silence and started to ask Joe a question. He held up his hand and pointed in front of us.

Joe's next memories were of men and women in firefighter uniforms, masks, and helmets. He moved and was told to be still. Beside him was Daniel—

He's—

Joe nodded. *Not a scratch on him.*

I put my hands to my mouth as stretchers were brought in and Daniel was given an IV and wheeled away. Joe was treated as well and forced to lie on a gurney as he was taken below. Then it was dark again, and he opened his eyes to see Rhonda leaning over him.

When I came to again, I tried to talk and couldn't.

I looked at him. *And they don't know why?*

He shook his head. *I think the Phantasm took it. You still have your voice, but your Wraith power is back.*

I held up my left arm and looked at the weaving handprint there—just as it had been before. Joe had already told me the streak in my hair was back and thicker than ever. *I don't understand it. I've tried calling out to Archer several times, but he hasn't answered.*

But he has to be there—right? I mean, otherwise, how is it you're you again?

I shook my head. *I don't know. Unless this is all part of being an Irin by birth and a Wraith by accident.* I straightened up. *What is it you're not telling me? You said everyone was fine.*

As fine as they can be.

I touched his arm. *Is it Dags? Is he still in a coma?*

Yes. When Phanty threw him, he threw him hard. Knocked his head pretty good. Rhonda's keeping an eye on him. Sits with him all day.

I didn't say anything. Guilt was a good governor, ya know? *You do realize how she feels about him?*

I nodded.

And how he feels about you?

I nodded again.

He got really quiet. So I figured I'd ask. *What about Daniel?*

I felt something drop out from under me. I was yanked out from inside of Joe so quickly my Wraithy head spun. I didn't go back into my body directly but waited for Joe to open his eyes. *Now that I've overshadowed him, I should be able to hear him, right?* Since waking up, I'd discovered that the little connection I'd had with him before was gone. It was kinda like a reboot. "Tell me—what about Daniel?"

Joe's lips thinned before he said, *Daniel's— You need to forget about Daniel, Zoë. Dags tried to warn you not to bring him back.*

I blinked.

"Why? What is it? He hasn't come to see me, and I saw through your eyes that he wasn't harmed. There was no sword wound. Not a scratch. So he has to be healthy, right?"

Joe pursed his lips. I did not like his expression. *Zoë, Daniel's healthy in body—but not in mind.*

I frowned. "What?"

Girl—he remembers everything. Every life the Horror made him take. Every emotion the Horror had. Everything. Can you imagine what that kind of guilt does to a man? To a cop? Hell . . . to someone as gentle as Daniel was?

Was?

Zoë—I can see it in his eyes. He told me himself through a plate of glass. If there is one thing in this world he wants, it is the very last thing the Horror wanted.

I put my hands to my lips.

"He—he wants me . . ."

Dead.

I wanted to throw up.

Joe moved away from the bed. I sensed frustration and turmoil in him. *He's insane, Zoë. Clinically, legally, and medically insane. He's tried slitting his own wrists; he attacked a fellow patient that looked like you.* He ran his fingers through his hair. *What you did to him—it wasn't a favor. It's not the Daniel you knew. Not the one you loved.* He paused. *Or that loved you.*

Daniel's words on the roof came back to me.

"So beautiful, Zoë. I'm s-sorry. I was . . . in love with you."

Was.

Was in love with me.

Yeah.

He *was.*

36

MID-MAY, Joe Halloran was officially declared a mute by his doctors—who still had no idea why he couldn't speak. His vocal cords were fine. In fact, they were better than before. I sort of kept waiting for the day when my own voice would go.

TC showed up—had his own voice. And he had his full power back—what he'd achieved before I used my banshee wail on his ass on the roof when he'd killed Daniel. I think he was afraid I'd yell at him again. And I still didn't trust him.

Dags woke up. Rhonda was with him, and I went to see him before I was released. He looked bad, and he wanted to sleep. Maureen and Alice assured me they'd take care of him, and Rhonda promised to go by to see him every day.

Which might be why he bailed two days later. Not a whisper since. Not even a card.

Mom came home, only a little worse for wear. She was also a bit thinner—except for the boobs. Which, of course, she swore still made her look ginormous. But she's not. She's Mom. Mom's supposed to be fluffy and warm and comforting to hold.

Only—I wasn't as eager to hold her as I had been.

My insides were a jumbled mess—so much so even I didn't

want to tangle with them. I moved slowly around the shop, helping where I could. But Jemmy insisted on doing everything herself, and Rhonda was back again, and back to the emo/goth self I was used to. Which also assured me the world was sort of back to "normal."

Define normal.

Mental note: . . . *Don't have any. There's nothing left to say.*

Joe and Rhonda stopped being a pseudo-item—though I'd kind of known that wouldn't last. Rhonda was stuck on Darren McConnell. And in a way, Joe's heart was still undefined, I think. He became not only the cop fixture but the handyman, which didn't upset Mom any. I think she liked having him around in his tight jeans and tee shirts.

And as for Daniel? He was under psychiatric treatment locally—they wouldn't tell me where.

I had Mom back. I sort of knew the mystery of my dad and sort of understood that he was with me on some level. Rhonda was back, and I wasn't mad and she was rich. Joe was here.

I wished Dags would just e-mail.

You know, you figure when you sleep with someone you'd at least get . . .

I pursed my lips.

Get what, idiot? Besides complications?

I missed him. A little bit more than I wanted to admit.

IT was May 30, and Rhonda and Mom were busy making the shop smell like a florist's. Wreaths of flowers over the door, garlands along the front-porch banister. Fresh-cut flowers all over the shop and botanica.

I kept sneezing and finally succumbed to a netty-pot rinse, careful not to inhale as I poured the solution through one nostril and then the other.

Mom opened the shop later than usual, and she and Jemmy prepared the usual spread of eggs, bacon, toast, sausage, pancakes, biscuits, croissants, butter, honey—the "usual."

I settled in with a cup of chai and looked at the ads in the *Atlanta Journal-Constitution*, still dressed in my plaid loungers, an oversized tee shirt with Duran Duran on the front, and my black bunny slippers, though they were looking a little worn.

Joe came in, waved at everyone, and grabbed a cup of coffee before sitting down and taking the sports pages. Jemmy was already at the table with the crossword. Tim and Steve were busy with Mom, looking at the Style section, ooohing and aahing over the McMansions now in foreclosure.

Rhonda came in, dressed in a black Abney Park tee shirt, black capris, and black flats, with her hair pulled up into ponytails. In her hands she had even more flowers and yesterday's mail, having dropped by the post-office box. Shop mail came directly here, but personal mail we had delivered to a post-office box.

She went to the kitchen, grabbed vases, slid water and flowers in, then put one of the vases at the center of the table before handing me an envelope.

"What's this?"

"Mail, doofus," she responded before taking up a seat between me and Joe.

I looked at the front. Had my name and the right address. The postmark was for two days ago, Savannah, Georgia. Unsure, I grabbed my unused butter knife and opened it.

Inside was a card. The front bore a beautiful painting of two angels—one with dark wings and robe, the other with white wings and robe. I immediately knew who it was from and opened it. Inside were handwritten pages. Two of them.

Zoë,

Sorry I left so abruptly—but when I came to my senses, I was overwhelmed with so many emotions. Not just my own but Maureen's and Alice's as well. What I felt was too overwhelming. I also got a phone call about a problem I had to take care of in Calgary, so I went there first.

I hope this finds you well, and you still have your voice. I heard about Daniel, and I'm sorry. But I can't help but think in the end it was better he passed on. I knew from your voice and from how you looked at him—that's not a place I'll share in your heart.

Please don't think I'll hold our lovemaking as some-

thing permanent. We both needed the comforting at the time—and I won't ever fool myself into believing I'll hold a place as special in your heart as Daniel does. I'm sorry any of this had to happen to you—I've admired you since I first got to know you, when Daniel was in the hospital, and I'd always hoped I'd find someone who loved me as much as you love him.

I'm around, and if you need me, call. But for now, I think it's better for my own heart to live here, beside the water.

I love you.

Darren

I folded the pages and put them back in the card. "Zoë?"

I looked at Mom. Her expression was priceless. "I'm fine, Mom."

"Who's that from?" Jemmy asked.

It's from Dags, isn't it? Joe said in my head.

I glanced at him but didn't answer. No one could hear him but me.

"Who?" Rhonda said.

Mom said, "Zoë—maybe you should take some time off. Get out of Atlanta? I have a few contacts at the Harbor Inn down there—maybe a few days on the river?"

I shook my head. I didn't see any reason to complicate matters any more than they already were.

"Am I missing something?" Rhonda said as she buttered her biscuit.

And I felt it was time for certain things to be said. I didn't want any more surprises in my life. I set the card on the table, beneath my plate, and cleared my throat. "I need to know something," I said in a very even tone. I looked at Joe and Rhonda. "I need to know from you how Dags became a Grimoire." Then I looked at my mom. "And then I need to know from you why you felt the need to keep the truth about my father from me."

Well, that was a conversation stopper.

Rhonda turned dead white. Not bone white. *Dead* white.

Mom cleared her throat. "Would it make any difference?"

I looked at her. "For me, yeah. I spoke to Dad—in a way. In that in-between world. And I've got pieces and snatches of who he was. I want you to tell me." And I looked at Rhonda. "Both of you."

Rhonda's color didn't get any better. "How?"

I watched her. Waiting.

Finally, she leaned forward and put her elbows on the table. "A lot happened to Dags in a very short time—and it started with his involvement with the Cruorem."

That much I knew.

"You know how the familiars were put in place—because of Bonville's botched spell."

Yes.

"And you know that Dags coded one night in the hospital. You, he, and Daniel were all there, and Nona and I had been moving between rooms. But I'd already gone home when it happened."

Yep. I remembered it. Mom had told me that Dags had said he couldn't see Rhonda in a romantic way—that he wasn't ready. Though . . . had he? I remembered I was on my way out of body to see Daniel, but then I'd felt Dags—slipping away—and I'd gone to him, all full of Abysmal juice.

"But he survived—his heart stopped. He should have lost that connection with the familiars when his heart stopped. But something happened. In that single instant, he was different. And then he checked himself out and disappeared."

I nodded. I kind of knew all this. Knew he'd sort of dropped out of sight, and then I'd seen him again with Joe at the hospital, with Joseph, Dr. Maddox's long-deceased son, in the room.

She sat back and crossed her arms over her chest. "A few days after Rodriguez was arrested—I was getting things settled within the Society. I was living at the new house, getting the construction on my uncle's old house under way. I'd decided not to think about you, or about what had happened. I had things to occupy my time. And I had to decide what to do with my life."

I listened and refused to feel guilty for telling her to leave on that afternoon. She'd betrayed me. And nothing would change that.

Rhonda picked up her fork and toyed with the croissant on her plate, flaking off the top. "I got a phone call from Francisco. He was out of jail and said he was leaving the country. He said he would leave you in peace as long as I gave him the Bonville Grimoire. Naturally, I said no. And he hung up. That started worrying me, so I sent a few of our members out to do a bit of intel."

Nice power there. I felt it suited her.

"What they had to say frightened me. He'd moved away from his home, but he wasn't out of Atlanta. They also found he had a lab set up and was once again gearing up to start experiments, using the Eidolons."

Mom put her hands to her face. "He had Dags."

Rhonda nodded. "At first I didn't know about Rodriguez's connection to the Cruorem. That didn't come till later. And from what I could piece together, he learned about what had happened to Dags from Klinsky—who felt slighted that he hadn't received the power. He'd tried to become an initiate so that he could be chosen to be an initial Guardian in Bonville's plans to bring his wife and her lover back from the dead. But Bonville had refused him. And for that I couldn't fault him— Klinsky was insane.

"I didn't know he had Dags. I just started looking at missing persons cases for the appropriate age and found three. We gathered some folk—including Joe—and we were able to infiltrate his lab. That's when I found out that one of the ones kidnapped was Dags."

"You got them out?" Mom said.

"Not then," Rhonda said. "Not all of them. One of them died." She sat forward and rested her arms on the table. "We were able to get the Eidolons and a few other items that Rodriguez didn't need to have by using the red Eidolon, the Destruction stone. We weren't able to get to Dags. And that's when Rodriguez threatened to kill him unless I gave him the Grimoire."

I didn't move. I just listened.

Rhonda swallowed. "I knew he couldn't have it—that's not

a man who should ever be allowed control over anything so powerful. And I knew there were spells inside that could summon a Symbiont that might restore a bit of the man's original power."

Yikes.

"I didn't think—I just acted. I had brought the book, but I'd had it hidden away in a Veil."

I remembered her demonstration from before in that apartment. Pulling that book out of the air.

"He'd . . . he'd tortured all three of them—Dags as well as the two familiars—kept them apart. Had used some of Randall Kemp's inventions to keep their power dispersed. Dags was barely alive. Alice was little more than stone. And Maureen—"

I leaned forward.

"Maureen seemed to be his favorite. He had her contained and had somehow infused her with shadow. He was trying to create—something. We never really understood what. I was able to convince him to release Dags—"

"Wait, wait," Mom said. "How could they have done such a thing to Dags? He's so strong."

Rhonda cleared her throat. "The Darren McConnell you've gotten to know recently isn't the same man—or the same power level," she said. "Dags was dying. Because of the spell Bonville did—the familiars are *fused* with him. He can't live without them. But that bastard was ripping them out—I was surprised he hadn't actually cut off Dags's hands."

I wanted to throw up. I had no idea any of this had ever happened.

Rhonda continued. "Joe had Dags, and I made sure Alice was freed. But Maureen . . . something was wrong with her. She stood beside Rodriguez, almost like a feral bodyguard. I could feel power emanating from her and knew she was drawing it directly from Dags. But I couldn't stop her. Rodriguez ordered her to get the book from me."

"I— It all happened so fast."

I looked from Joe to Rhonda. "What happened so fast?"

"I had the book in my hand—" she said and held out her hand. "And Joe was beside me, holding Dags. I could feel Dags dying, slipping away. Alice was moving slowly—toward us. And then Maureen was there—" She swallowed. "I don't know what made me do it, or why I thought I could. But I just knew that I could not let him have the book."

She paused. "So I did something stupid. And foolish. And to my delight—Dags survived."

I was about to point at her and tell her to spill the beans when Mom said, "You used the same spell. You fused the book to them, to Dags."

!!!

A tear fell down Rhonda's cheek. "I didn't know how else to prevent him from getting it—and still save Dags's life."

"That could have killed him."

She was nodding, and I noticed that my mom was mad.

Not irritated or disappointed. But mad.

"Nona—I only had a split second. I brought the book's soul into its base form and shoved it into Dags's chest. It was a partial fusing and a partial Veil."

Now it was my turn to look and feel completely wigged out. "What the fuck?"

That's what I said, Joe commented.

"There was a flash of light, and I could hear him screaming. I could hear Maureen and Alice . . . all of them screaming. And when I could see again, the girls were gone and Dags was whole. He was . . ." She held out her hands. "He was healed. There weren't any burn marks, or bruises. And he was . . . different."

"Because you changed him. You rewrote his entire DNA. You idiot!" Nona nearly shrieked. "That's a misuse of power— you had no right to do that, Rhonda. You were taught better than that."

"What was I supposed to do—let him die? And he would have died even if we'd gotten the book away from Rodriguez. I could hear his heartbeat slipping away."

"So you bound his soul to the Grimoire's."

I stared at Rhonda, my mind flashing back to those moments on the roof. When Dags had told me not to save Daniel. That it was better to let him go. And now Daniel was insane, unable to blend back into society. Locked up in a cage like an animal.

And Dags—he was bound to a book. Different. Fused by magic. Had he given me that advice because of what Rhonda had done to him? Should he have died that day?

In the end, Rhonda and I weren't that different—selfishly saving the men we loved.

I looked at Joe. He shrugged and gestured to Nona. *Ask her. I'm still stuck back at tearing the book's soul part. Never got beyond that.*

Rhonda nodded. "I have to live with that, Nona. The Society's opinion is still out. They want to study Dags—to see what it is I created. All I could say was that he was half of each, Abysmal and Ethereal, bound together by his own soul. The Grimoire gives him power—but we don't know what kind of power. All of its spells are now a part of him. I suspect he has power he hasn't tapped."

"They want to study him?" All I could think of was a rat in a cage. No wonder Dags had left so suddenly. "You mean they want to control him."

Rhonda nodded. "I can't change that view. Same as with you. You and he and Archer represent elements that cannot be controlled—and each has the unnerving element of a human soul. Archer's soul is contingent on yours. They fear for the future of the physical plane."

I sighed. So he hadn't been kidding when he said he was a book. But I didn't know if that was good or bad. From the look on Mom's face, it could be bad. But then . . . I thought of the night by the fire. Before all hell broke loose. I had fond memories of that evening—and I couldn't stop the smile that played on my lips.

I felt something against my neck and looked at Rhonda. She was staring at me—and what bothered me most was that I couldn't read her face.

37

"**WHAT'S** done is done," Mom said, breaking the awkward silence. "And, hopefully, Dags will come back again."

I had a feeling I would see him again. I looked at Mom. "Did you consciously make a decision to not tell me about my father?"

Mom was still glaring at Rhonda. She was not a happy camper. I was just happy it wasn't me under the glare. "It was rash," Mom said as she put her elbows on the table. "I think Rhonda's decision was different than my own—because for me it was the difference in raising a daughter who would hope her father was going to come home versus the reality that he never would."

"You could have told me the truth."

She frowned. "Told a child that her father was really an angel? Not a human? That he had been a human once, then lost his physical body?" She made a rude noise. "No. That wouldn't do. I didn't lie when I said I didn't know he wasn't coming back. And even in the beginning—when he showed up after the fire—I didn't know Adiran was really dead. Because he was there—in the flesh in front of me—not a ghost. And I loved him, and I never wanted to let go."

I could feel Mom's emotion as if it were my own. The love she had for him wasn't gone. Had never left. It was something she'd forgotten. Purged so she could go on and raise a child—an Irin child.

"I didn't know till just before he disappeared. I walked in on him one night as he shifted from physical to light. I saw his wings. He realized I was there—" She looked at me, and there were tears behind her eyes. "And he didn't try to hide it. He didn't explain it either. You were about to turn four—your party was that Saturday in the backyard. All he said was that something terrible was happening—and he had to fix it. I knew it was important. And I knew it had something to do with my dad's experiments."

We were all silent, all watching her. Except for Rhonda. She was staring at the table.

Mom sniffed. "He warned me that they were watching you—our child—and that you were special. But I couldn't let you fall into their hands because they would use you. He called you an Irin—and I had no fucking idea what that meant. I just knew he was saying good-bye to me. And then he said good-bye to you as you slept, and he vanished."

I watched her. "He never came back."

"No. You waited for him to come back, but he didn't. I saw the agony in your face, in your little body. And I hated him for it. Hated him for leaving you, and leaving me. You were so different than the other children—talking to things that weren't there. Certain your imaginary friends were real. That bastard had left me alone to deal with that—with no idea how."

I was starting to see her frustration. Her pain. "The Eidolon?"

"Yes—I saw the package wrapped in the closet. And I opened it. I knew immediately it was one of those damned stones. But when I touched it—" She frowned and held out her right hand. Her nails weren't lacquered or filed, but clipped short. "Something shifted, and I started seeing them too—the ghosts and the spirits—and I realized the stone had a way of unlocking or summoning this ability. So if it could summon it—"

"It could banish it," I finished. I remembered the stone and the doll. "But—why did you wait till I was nearly twelve to use it to banish the ability?"

"I didn't know how to use it," Mom said. "I had to learn. I was Domas's niece—but that didn't mean I believed in any of this shit." She grinned and wiped at her face. "I thought I had the idea down, the desire and the concept, but I didn't have the practical application. And the more the years went by, the weirder you got."

"Did Zoë go out of body back then?" Jemmy asked.

Mom nodded, and I was shocked dumb. "I saw her a few times, wandering the hallways wherever we lived with whatever ghost was there. Her grades were slipping. I didn't know what to do."

I knew what happened next. "Then I went into the basement—because of Bobby."

She nodded. "Yes. And I'd kept those presents—the ones your dad had gotten you for your fourth birthday—I'd kept them in that box with the doll and the Eidolon. What I came home to was you sprawled on the basement floor, your head bleeding, your eyes open—the doll in your hand." Mom closed her eyes. "I thought I'd killed you."

"But it worked," Jemmy said.

"Yes, it worked. After she came out of a small coma, Zoë was as normal and ungifted as any other American teen. Completely clueless. And there seemed to be no memory that she'd ever been different. I noticed that the cars stopped following us, the odd person, the Society people. So I moved Zoë and me—to Atlanta—and they didn't seem to notice. And she was just the average girl."

Until the rape, Joe said. Then he sat forward and grabbed up his pad and pen and scribbled. NONA, DID Z DIE DURING THE RAPE?

I closed my eyes.

She nodded. "Yes, she did."

He looked at me. *And you died in the living room, technically. Does death break the hold?*

I looked at Mom. "So when I came into contact with the doll again—when I went looking for something on the top shelf—"

She nodded. "You tripped the spell again. I thought I'd done a good job just hiding the key and the doll. But the truth is I should have destroyed both." She waved at the air. "The decision to keep knowledge about your dad from you, to protect you, was a rash one, and I'm sorry. Adiran was such a loving man, and he loved you till the day he disappeared."

I smiled. "I know."

Joe got up and went to the botanica and got the laptop and brought it to the table. He scribbled again. NONA—YOU SAID THE SOCIETY DIDN'T KNOW YOU WERE IN ATLANTA.

She nodded. "Not until Zoë's power was released again."

I was staring at him. "What are you getting at?"

Just a really sickening thought. He tapped on the computer and I moved to look. He was accessing the police's database.

"What are you doing?"

He pulled up my file, saw the rape information. What he saw that I'd not seen before was the identity of the rapist. He took that name and entered it into another field. Nothing came up. Nothing. Not even a parking ticket. Pursing his lips, he typed in a few more things on a different screen and still came up with nothing.

"Joe?" Rhonda finally said something.

"What is it?" I asked again.

Instead of writing anything down he looked at me. *A guy comes out of nowhere and kills the kid you're with in Piedmont Park. He then kills you and rapes you—but this guy has no record. Nothing. His fingerprints are on file, but it's as if he was never born. There's nothing there, no history. No reason for him to do that to you.*

I nodded slowly, but I wasn't getting it. "Yeah?"

Joe ran his hand through his hair. It was growing a bit long, and he hadn't shaved in a day or two. *What if that was why he was there?*

Uhm . . . huh?

What if someone or something knew the only way to release your power was to kill you? They knew that trauma or death or the combination was what released the spell. Who's to say someone didn't just send this guy out to do just that?

I backed away from the table. That was just absurd. That was— I couldn't—

"What?" Mom was saying. "What is it? Joe? Zoë?"

Rhonda cleared her throat. "It's not an idea I hadn't already thought of."

Mom and I looked at her. "What?" Mom said.

"That someone or some group knew what would set Zoë free and sent that guy out to rape and kill her. Uncle March was the first to suggest it—during our meetings. Zoë's power is all emotion based—so strong emotion could have released it."

I wanted to scream at them. Someone was told or paid to do that to me? To another human being?

Jemmy reached out to me. "Calm yourself—it's done, child. Long ago. And that fool's soul—may it never rest in peace—is long gone."

The rape was planned? It was just some sick way to make me into an Irin? But who else would know this? Besides the Society?

There was one name that came to mind. One constant in all of this. And it seemed to know everything that I did before and after it happened.

Maharba.

EPILOGUE

THINGS settled down for a bit. But like my life—not for long.

About a week later I got a call from Captain Cooper. I'd been expecting it. We suspected he remembered being over-shadowed. And he'd been there through some pretty inexplicable situations (though the tornado did cover a lot of it up).

He asked if I had time on Friday night to meet with him at the Bridgetown Grill, across from the Fabulous Fox. I agreed, and we sat and talked for a long time.

Cooper remembered things in snatches. He remembered seeing me do some pretty far-out things—such as flying. And he knew on some level that I—and Rhonda and Nona—wasn't your average Georgia Peach. But what he needed more than anything was reassurance he wasn't crazy.

Over coffee I assured him he was sane. "It's just that there are things out there that you can't see. And they can't always see you."

He nodded. He was in a nice suit, with white shirt and blue tie. Cooper was meeting someone next door to watch *The Lion King* musical. He looked older somehow, with circles under his eyes. "I just— He isn't the same man. It's like he's tortured. I can see it in his eyes."

I kept my expression neutral.

"And when I mention you—"

I put my hand on his. "He threatens to kill me."

He sat back and sighed. "Yes. The judge ruled him insane—which caused a stink. I'm sure Boo's parents will pursue a civil suit. Right now the case is in limbo, and he's scheduled to be transferred to North Carolina today."

I sighed.

"Zoë," Cooper said after a brief pause. "We still haven't found Randall Kemp. He's completely vanished."

That bit of news bothered me. Randall was a loose end. Herb had actually joined the Society of Ishmael as a tech guy, along with Ron Beaumont. Rhonda believed it was better to have one's enemies close.

"He'll turn up, Coop."

"Yeah . . . I just don't like having him running around. And you know he'll be after you."

Probably. But I wasn't that worried. I was Wraith again, and I could catch him if I needed to.

"So," Cooper said, "you ever thought about using that little talent of yours for some police work?"

I grinned at him. "You offering me a job?"

"I'm offering you the chance to make an honest living."

With that, I laughed. "Send me the application. I'll fill it out. But what would my title be?"

He smirked. "Resident troublemaker. Eh, I'll figure something out." He checked his watch. "Thanks for talking with me—but I'm going to have to scoot."

We stood, and he paid for dinner. I left the tip. Once outside, I was amazed at how warm it still was. The sun hadn't set yet, and there were people scattered here and there, some in business suits, some in jeans, some going to the show, and some going out to eat.

We turned right, toward the crosswalk at the corner. "Take care of your mom for me," he said. "I'll be by now and then to get a good chai. Rhonda still going to work there?"

I nodded and shrugged. "Depends. Seems she and Mom have a few kinks to work out." Namely Dags—whom no one else had heard from.

I caught movement to the right—and turned in time to see

Daniel Frasier barreling down on me. He was running parallel to the building, along the sidewalk. He brought up a gun.

People screamed and ran when they saw it. I froze, trying to make a decision to either drop my body and be invisible to kick-trip him, or to touch him physically and cast his soul out.

But I never got the chance to do either. Cooper was suddenly in front of me—pulling his gun from behind him and shouting for Daniel to stop. But Daniel's face was twisted in grief, and I saw him pull the trigger—

Again—

And again—

But the bullets never hit me. They struck a passing woman, a young child, and Cooper.

Cooper went backward into me, and I crumpled beneath him. I heard shouts and screams, then the sounds of fighting and scuffling. The gun went off again.

There were people all around me as I scrambled to get out from under Cooper. I saw two uniformed officers—probably called in to direct traffic for the show. The other two victims were on the ground, with people gathered about. One of the officers was on his radio.

I knelt over Cooper. His eyes were wide and there was blood—lots of blood—all over his chest. Blood came from his mouth and spattered my face. "Zoë—"

I grabbed his hand. I could feel his soul moving at my touch. *No, no, no. Not now. It's not your time.*

"P-please . . ." he said, and I leaned. "D-Don't let them put me on machines—"

And then I saw the mask. The skull. The telltale sign that told me this person's death was imminent. *No . . . not now. You can't die!*

He was squeezing my hand. "Is there a Heaven, Zoë? Is there a God?"

I—I didn't know. I didn't know!

I looked up to scream for help—

My voice caught in my throat.

They were everywhere—on every face—staring back at me. Skulls.

Hundreds and hundreds of skulls. Driving cars, crossing the street, standing in line, gawking at the dying man beside me.

"Captain!" Daniel screamed from somewhere behind me. "Oh God . . . Cooper! Ken—oh God, Ken!"

I turned to see Daniel. Two uniformed police officers had him by his arms and were struggling to subdue him. But they couldn't. His eyes were wide, and his expression was full of surprise, shock, and horror.

Then his gaze focused on me, and those emotions coalesced into a single thought.

Kill.

He gave a guttural scream before pushing aside one officer, then the other. Two brave volunteers tried to stop him but were shoved aside and into the gathering crowd.

And he was coming at me. Though he no longer had a weapon, he had his hands. I caught enough of his thoughts to know he planned on killing me with his bare hands.

"You . . . you . . ." was all he said over and over again.

I—I didn't know what to do. I acted on instinct and reached out with my left hand.

I grabbed his wrist. Time froze. He froze. Everything around me blurred and stopped as I looked into his eyes. Eyes, I realized, that had died on that roof.

For the second time.

TC appeared, seeming to sieve from the print on my arm. He looked from me to Daniel and back to me. "We gonna waste him?"

I shook my head. "No. I want him to forget. Forget me. Forget everything that happened."

TC looked heartbroken. "That's no fun."

I shifted my gaze to him. "Where have you been?"

"Around." He pointed to his wrist. "Ticktock, lover. Time's up."

And Daniel was on top of me—but not choking me. He was still, and the officers were back and hoisting him up.

"Miss, are you okay?"

I let one of them pull me up, then I turned back to Cooper. "I'm fine. Call an ambulance . . . Call an ambulance!" I screamed as I knelt beside him.

I touched Cooper's cheek. "No . . ." I mumbled. "No, no, no . . ."

And behind the thundering in my ears, I could hear a laugh.

A cold, deep, soulless laugh.

The Phantasm.